Dear Reader,

We know you've fallen for the charismatic Stanislaski family, which is why we're bringing you two more stories in their engrossing romantic series!

Frederica Kimball has known for a long time that Nick LeBeck is the one for her, but Nick has always seen Freddie as a kid sister. Yet now Freddie has transformed from a sweet and adorable girl to a sexy, sophisticated young woman, and Nick is totally unprepared for the grown-up Freddie...

Talented Kate Stanislaski Kimball is ready for a real life—she's had enough of fame and the spotlight. She's finally coming home, and her plan is to transform a run-down building into the dance studio of her dreams. But she hasn't planned on transforming her infuriating and intriguing contractor, Brody O'Connell, into the man of her dreams...

Can't get enough of Nora Roberts? Watch for the gripping Night Tales series, coming soon!

Happy reading!

The Editors
Silhouette Books

NORA ROBERTS

CHASING DESTINY

Silhouette® Books

Published by Silhouette Books

America's Publisher of Contemporary Romance

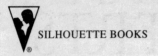 SILHOUETTE BOOKS

Recycling programs for this product may not exist in your area.

Chasing Destiny

ISBN-13: 978-0-373-28211-1

Copyright © 2016 by Harlequin Books S.A.

The publisher acknowledges the copyright holder of the individual works as follows:

Waiting for Nick
Copyright © 1997 by Nora Roberts

Considering Kate
Copyright © 2001 by Nora Roberts

Visit Silhouette Books at www.Harlequin.com

Printed in U.S.A.

CONTENTS

WAITING FOR NICK

For the family

Chapter One

She was a woman with a mission. Her move from West Virginia to New York had a series of purposes, outlined carefully in her mind. She would find the perfect place to live, become a success in her chosen field and get her man.

Preferably, but not necessarily, in that order.

Frederica Kimball was, she liked to think, a flexible woman.

As she walked down the sidewalk on the East Side in the early-spring twilight, she thought of home. The house in Shepherdstown, West Virginia, with her parents and siblings, was, to Freddie's mind, the perfect place to live. Rambling, noisy, full of music and voices.

She doubted that she could have left it if she hadn't known she would always be welcomed back with open arms.

It was true that she had been to New York many

times, and had ties there, as well, but she already missed the familiar—her own room, tucked into the second story of the old stone house, the love and companionship of her siblings, her father's music, her mother's laugh.

But she wasn't a child any longer. She was twenty-four, and long past the age to begin to make her own.

In any case, she reminded herself, she was very much at home in Manhattan. After all, she'd spent the first few years of her life there. And much of her life in the years after had included visits—but all with family, she acknowledged.

Well, this time, she thought, straightening her shoulders, she was on her own. And she had a job to do. The first order of business would be to convince a certain Nicholas LeBeck that he needed a partner.

The success and reputation he'd accumulated as a composer over the past few years would only increase with her beside him as his lyricist. Already, just by closing her eyes and projecting, she could envision the LeBeck-Kimball name in lights on the Great White Way. She had only to let her imagination bloom to have the music they would write flow like a river through her head.

Now all she had to do, she thought with a wry smile, was convince Nick to see and hear the same thing.

She could, if necessary, use family loyalty to persuade him. They were, in a roundabout way, semi-cousins.

Kissing cousins, she thought now, while her eyes lighted with a smile. That was her final and most vital mission. Before she was done, Nick would fall as desperately in love with her as she was, had always been, with him.

She'd waited ten years for him, and that, to Freddie's mind, was quite long enough.

It's past time, Nick, she decided, tugging on the hem of her royal blue blazer, *to face your fate.*

Still, nerves warred with confidence as she stood outside the door of Lower the Boom. The popular neighborhood bar belonged to Zack Muldoon, Nick's brother. Stepbrother, technically, but Freddie's family had always been more into affection than terminology. The fact that Zack had married Freddie's stepmother's sister made the Stanislaski-Muldoon-Kimball-LeBeck families one convoluted clan.

Freddie's longtime dream had been to forge another loop in that family chain, linking her and Nick.

She took a deep breath, tugged on her blazer again, ran her hands over the reddish-gold mop of curls she could never quite tame and wished once, hopelessly, that she had just a dash of the Stanislaskis' exotic good looks. Then she reached for the door.

She'd make do with what she had, and make damned sure it was enough.

The air in Lower the Boom carried the yeasty scent of beer, overlaid with the rich, spicy scent of marinara. Freddie decided that Rio, Zack's longtime cook, must have a pasta special going. On the juke, Dion was warning his fellow man about the fickle heart of Runaround Sue.

Everything was there, everything in place, the cozy paneled walls, the seafaring motif of brass bells and nautical gear, the long, scarred bar and the gleaming glassware. But no Nick. Still, she smiled as she walked to the bar and slid onto a padded stool.

"Buy me a drink, sailor?"

Distracted, Zack glanced up from drawing a draft. His easy smile widened instantly into a grin. "Freddie—hey! I didn't think you were coming in until the end of the week."

"I like surprises."

"I like this kind." Expertly Zack slid the mug of beer down the bar so that it braked between the waiting hands of his patron. Then he leaned over, caught Freddie's face in both of his big hands and gave her a loud, smacking kiss. "Pretty as ever."

"You, too."

And he was, she thought. In the ten years since she'd met him, he'd only improved, like good whiskey, with age. The dark hair was still thick and curling, and the deep blue eyes were magnetic. And his face, she thought with a sigh. Tanned, tough, with laugh lines only enhancing its character and charm.

More than once in her life, Freddie had wondered how it was that she was surrounded by physically stunning people. "How's Rachel?"

"Her Honor is terrific."

Freddie's lips curved at the use of the title, and the affection behind it. Zack's wife—her aunt—was now a criminal court judge. "We're all so proud of her. Did you see the trick gavel Mama sent her? The one that makes this crashing-glass sound when you bop something with it?"

"Seen it?" His grin was quick and crooked. "She bops me with it regularly. It's something, having a judge in the family." His eyes twinkled. "And she looks fabulous in those black robes."

"I bet. How about the kids?"

"The terrible trio? They're great. Want a soda?"

Amused, Freddie tilted her head. "What, are you going to card me, Zack? I'm twenty-four, remember?"

Rubbing his chin, he studied her. The small build and china-doll skin would probably always be deceiving. If he hadn't known her age, as well as the age of his own children, he would have asked for ID.

"I just can't take it in. Little Freddie, all grown up."

"Since I am—" she crossed her legs and settled in "—why don't you pour me a white wine?"

"Coming up." Long experience had him reaching behind him for the proper glass without looking. "How're your folks, the kids?"

"Everybody's good, and everyone sends their love." She took the glass Zack handed her and lifted it in a toast. "To family."

Zack tapped a squat bottle of mineral water against her glass. "So what are your plans, honey?"

"Oh, I've got a few of them." She smiled into her wine before she sipped. And wondered what he would think if she mentioned that the biggest plan of her life was to woo his younger brother. "The first is to find an apartment."

"You know you can stay with us as long as you want."

"I know. Or with Grandma and Papa, or Mikhail and Sydney, or Alex and Bess." She smiled again. It was a comfort to know she was surrounded by people who loved her. But… "I really want a place of my own." She propped her elbow on the bar. "It's time, I think, for a little adventure." When he started to speak, she grinned and shook her head at him. "You're not going to lecture, are you, Uncle Zack? Not you, the boy who went to sea."

She had him there, he thought. He'd been a great deal younger than twenty-four when he shipped out for the first time. "Okay, no lecture. But I'm keeping my eye on you."

"I'm counting on it." Freddie sat back and rocked a little on the stool, then asked—casually, she hoped— "So, what's Nick up to? I thought I might run into him here."

"He's around. In the kitchen, I think, shoveling in some of Rio's pasta special."

She sniffed the air for effect. "Smells great. I think I'll just wander on back and say hi."

"Go ahead. And tell Nick we're waiting for him to play for his supper."

"I'll do that."

She carried her wine with her and firmly resisted the urge to fuss with her hair or tug on her jacket again. Her attitude toward her looks was one of resignation. "Cute" was the best she'd ever been able to do with her combination of small build and slight stature. Long ago she'd given up on the fantasy that she would blossom into anything that could be termed lush or glamorous.

Added to a petite figure was madly curling hair that was caught somewhere between gold and red, a dusting of freckles over a pert nose, wide gray eyes and dimples. In her teenage years, she'd pined for sleek and sophisticated. Or wild and wanton. Curvy and cunning. Freddie liked to think that, with maturity, she'd accepted herself as she was.

But there were still moments when she mourned being a life-size Kewpie doll in a family of Renaissance sculptures.

Then again, she reminded herself, if she wanted Nick to take her seriously as a woman, she had to take herself seriously first.

With that in mind, she pushed open the kitchen door. And her heart jolted straight into her throat.

There was nothing she could do about it. It had been the same every time she saw him, from the first time she'd seen him to the last. Everything she'd ever wanted, everything she'd ever dreamed of, was sitting at the kitchen table, hunkered over a plate of fettuccine marinara.

Nicholas LeBeck, the bad boy her aunt Rachel had defended with passion and conviction in the courts. The troubled youth who had been guided away from the violence of street gangs and back alleys by love and care and the discipline of family.

He was a man now, but he still carried some of the rebellion and wildness of his youth. In his eyes, she thought, her pulse humming. Those wonderful stormy green eyes. He still wore his hair long, pulled back into a stubby ponytail of dark, bronzed blond. He had a poet's mouth, a boxer's chin and the hands of an artist.

She'd spent many nights fantasizing about those long-fingered, wide-palmed hands. Once she got beyond the face, with its fascinating hint of cheekbones and its slightly crooked nose—broken years ago by her own sharp line drive, which he'd tried unsuccessfully to field—she could, with pleasure, move on.

He was built like a runner, long, rangy, and wore old gray jeans, white at the knees. His shirtsleeves were rolled up to the elbow and missing a button.

As he ate, he carried on a running commentary with the huge cook, while Rio shook the grease out of a basket of French fries.

"I didn't say there was too much garlic. I said I like a lot of garlic." Nick forked in another bite as if to back up his statement. "Getting pretty damned temperamental in your old age, pal," Nick added, his voice slightly muffled by the generous amount of pasta he'd just swallowed.

Rio's mild, good-natured oath carried the music of the islands. "Don't tell me about old, skinny boy—I can still beat hell out of you."

"I'm shaking." Grinning, Nick broke off a hunk of garlic bread just as Freddie let the door swing shut behind her. His eyes lighted with pleasure as he dropped the bread again and pushed back from the table. "Hey, Rio, look who's here. How's it going, Fred?"

He crossed over to give her a casual, brotherly hug. Then his brows drew together as the body that pressed firmly against his reminded him, uncomfortably, that little Fred was a woman.

"Ah…" He backed off, still smiling, but his hands dipped cautiously into his pockets. "I thought you were coming in later in the week."

"I changed my mind." Her confidence lifted a full notch at his reaction. "Hi, Rio." Freddie set her wineglass aside so that she could properly return the bear hug she was enveloped in.

"Little doll. Sit down and eat."

"I think I will. I thought about your cooking, Rio, all the way up on the train." She sat, smiled and held out a hand to Nick. "Come sit down, your food's getting cold."

"Yeah." He took her hand, gave it a quick squeeze, then let it go as he settled beside her. "So, how is everybody? Brandon still kicking butt on the baseball diamond?"

"Batting .420, leading the high school league in home runs and RBIs." She let out a long sigh as Rio set a large plate in front of her. "Katie's last ballet recital was really lovely. Mama cried, of course, but then she tears up when Brand hits a four-bagger. You know, her toy store was just featured in the *Washington Post*. And Dad's just finishing a new composition." She twirled pasta onto her fork. "So, how are things with you?"

"They're fine."

"Working on anything?"

"I've got another Broadway thing coming up." He shrugged. It was still hard for him to let people know when something mattered.

"You should have won the Tony for *Last Stop*."

"Being nominated was cool."

She shook her head. It wasn't enough for him—or for her. "It was a fabulous score, Nick. *Is* a fabulous score," she corrected, since the musical was still playing to full houses. "We're all so proud of you."

"Well. It's a living."

"Don't make his head bigger than it is," Rio warned from his stove.

"Hey, I caught you humming 'This Once,'" Nick noted with a grin.

Rio moved his massive shoulders in dismissal. "So, maybe one or two of the tunes weren't bad. Eat."

"Are you working with anyone yet?" Freddie asked. "On the new score?"

"No. It's just in the preliminary stages. I've hardly gotten started myself."

That was exactly what she'd wanted to hear. "I read somewhere that Michael Lorrey was committed to another project. You'll need a new lyricist."

"Yeah." Nick frowned as he scooped up more pasta. "It's too bad. I liked working with him. There are too many people out there who don't hear the music, just their own words."

"That would be a problem," Freddie agreed, clearing a path for herself. "You need someone with a solid music background, who hears words in the melody."

"Exactly." He picked up his beer and started to drink.

"What you need, Nick, is me," Freddie said firmly.

Nick swallowed hastily, set his beer down and looked at Freddie as though she had suddenly stopped speaking English. "Huh?"

"I've been studying music all my life." It was a struggle, but she kept the eagerness out of her voice and spoke matter-of-factly. "One of my first memories is of sitting on my father's lap, with his hands over mine on the piano keys. But, to his disappointment, composing isn't my first love. Words are. I could write your words, Nick, better than anyone else." Her eyes, gray and calm and smiling, met his. "Because I not only understand your music, I understand you. So what do you think?"

He shifted in his chair, blew out a breath. "I don't know what to think, Fred. This is kind of out of left field."

"I don't know why. You know I've written lyrics for some of Dad's compositions. And a few others besides." She broke off a piece of bread, chewed it thoughtfully. "It seems to me to be a very logical, comfortable solution all around. I'm looking for work, you're looking for a lyricist."

"Yeah." But it made him nervous, the idea of working with her. To be honest, he'd have had to admit that in the past few years, *she'd* begun to make him nervous.

"So you'll think about it." She smiled again, knowing, as the member of a large family, the strategic value of an apparent retreat. "And if you start to like the idea, you can run it by the producers."

"I could do that," Nick said slowly. "Sure, I could do that."

"Great. I'll be coming around here off and on, or you can reach me at the Waldorf."

"The Waldorf? Why are you staying at a hotel?"

"Just temporarily, until I find an apartment. You don't know of anything in the area, do you? I like this neighborhood."

"No, I—I didn't realize you were making this permanent." His brows knit again. "I mean, a really permanent move."

"Well, I am. And no, before you start, I'm not going to stay with the family. I'm going to find out what it's like to live alone. You're still upstairs, right? In Zack's old place?"

"That's right."

"So, if you hear about anything in the neighborhood, you'll let me know."

It surprised him that even for a moment he would worry about what her moving to New York would change in his life. Of course, it wouldn't change anything at all.

"I picture you more Park Avenue."

"I lived on Park Avenue once," she said, finishing up the last of her fettuccine. "I'm looking for something else." And, she thought, wouldn't it be handy if she found a place close to his? She pushed her hair out of her face and tipped back in her chair. "Rio, that was sensational. If I find a place close by, I'll be in here for dinner every night."

"Maybe we'll kick Nick out and you can move upstairs." He winked at her. "I'd rather look at you than his ugly face."

"Well, in the meantime—" she rose and kissed Rio's scarred cheek "—Zack wants you to come out when you're done Nick, and play."

"I'll be out in a minute."

"I'll tell him. Maybe I'll hang around for a little while and listen. Bye, Rio."

"Bye, doll." Rio whistled a tune as he moved back to his stove. "Little Freddie's all grown up. Pretty as a picture."

"Yeah, she's okay." Nick resented the fact that whatever spicy scent she'd been wearing was tugging on his senses like a baited hook. "Still wide-eyed, though.

She doesn't have a clue what she's going to face in this town, in this business."

"So, you'll look out for her." Rio thwacked a wooden spoon against his huge palm. "Or I look out for you."

"Big talk." Nick snagged his bottle of beer and sauntered out.

One of Freddie's favorite things about New York was that she could walk two blocks in any given direction and see something new. A dress in a boutique, a face in the crowd, a hustler looking for marks. She was, she knew, naive in some ways—in the ways a woman might be when she had been raised with love and care in a small town. She could never claim to have Nick's street smarts, but she felt she had a good solid dose of common sense. She used it to plan her first full day in the city.

Nibbling on her breakfast croissant, she studied the view of the city from her hotel window. There was a great deal she wanted to accomplish. A visit to her uncle Mikhail at his art gallery would down two birds. She could catch up with him and see if his wife, Sydney, might know of any available apartments through her real estate connections.

And it wouldn't hurt to drop a bug in his ear—and the ears of other family members—that she was hoping to work with Nick on his latest score.

Not really fair, Fred, she told herself, and poured a second cup of coffee. But love didn't always take fair into account. And she would never have applied even this type of benign pressure if she wasn't confident in her own talents. As far as her skill with music and lyrics was concerned, Freddie was more than sure of her-self. It was only when it came to her ability to attract Nick that she faltered.

But surely, once they were working so closely to-gether, he would stop seeing her as his little cousin from West Virginia. She'd never be able to compete head-on with the sultry, striking women he drew to him. So, Freddie thought, nodding to herself, she'd be sneaky, and wind her way into his heart through their shared love of music.

It was all for his own good after all. She was the best thing in the world for him. All she had to do was make him realize it.

Since there was no time like the present, she pushed away from the table and hurried into the bedroom to dress.

An hour later, Freddie climbed out of a cab in front of a SoHo gallery. It was a fifty-fifty shot as to whether she'd find her uncle in. He was just as likely to be at his and Sydney's Connecticut home, sculpting or playing with their children. It was every bit as likely he might be helping his father with some carpentry job, any-where in the city.

With a shrug, Freddie pulled open the beveled-glass door. If she missed Mikhail here, she'd scoot over to Sydney's office, or try the courthouse for Rachel. Fail-ing that, she could look up Bess at the television studio, or Alexi at his precinct. She could, she thought with a smile, all but trip over family, any direction she took.

The first thing she noticed inside the small, sunny gallery was Mikhail's work. Though the piece was new to her, she recognized his touch, and the subject, immediately. He'd carved his wife in polished mahogany. Madonna-like, Sydney held a baby in her arms. Their youngest, Freddie knew, Laurel. At Sydney's feet, three children of various ages and sizes sat. Walking closer, Freddie recognized her cousins, Griff, Moira and Adam. Unable to resist, she trailed a finger over the baby's cheek.

One day, she thought, she would hold her own child just that way. Hers and Nick's.

"I don't wait for faxes!" Mikhail shouted as he entered the gallery from a back room. "You wait for faxes! I have work!"

"But, Mik," came a plaintive voice from inside the room. "Washington said—"

"Do I care what Washington says? I don't think so. Tell them they can have three pieces, no more."

"But—"

"No more," he repeated, and closed the door behind him. He muttered to himself in Ukrainian as he crossed the gallery. Words, Freddie noted with a lifted brow, that she wasn't supposed to understand.

"Very artistic language, Uncle Mik."

He broke off in the middle of a very creative oath. "Freddie." With a hoot of laughter, he hoisted her off the ground as if she weighed no more than a favored rag doll. "Still just a peanut," he said, kissing her on the way down. "How's my pretty girl?"

"Excited to be here, and to see you."

He was, like his swearing, wild and exotic, with the golden eyes and raven hair of the Stanislaskis. Freddie had often thought that if she could paint, she would paint each member of her Ukrainian family in bold strokes and colors.

"I was just admiring your work," she told him. "It's incredibly beautiful."

"It's easy to create something beautiful when you have something beautiful to work with." He glanced toward the sculpture with love in his eyes. For the wood, Freddie reflected, but more, much more for the family he'd carved in it. "So, you've come to the big city to make your splash."

"I have indeed." With a flutter of lashes, Freddie hooked an arm through his and began to stroll, stopping here and there to admire a piece of art. "I'm hoping to work with Nick on the score he's beginning."

"Oh?" Mikhail quirked a brow. A man with so many women in his life understood their ways well, and appreciated them. "To write the words for his music?"

"Exactly. We'd make a good team, don't you think?"

"Yes, but it's not what I think, is it?" He smiled when her lips moved into a pout. "Our Nick, he can be stubborn, yes? And very hard of head. I can knock him in that head, if you like."

Her lips curved again before she laughed. "I hope it won't come to that, but I'll keep the offer in reserve." Her eyes changed, sharpened, and he could see clearly that she wasn't so much the child any longer. "I'm good, Uncle Mik. Music's in my blood, the way art's in yours."

"And when you see what you want…"

"I find a way to have it." Easily accepting her own arrogance, she shrugged her shoulders. That, too, was in the blood. "I want to work with Nick. I want to help him. And I'm going to."

"And from me you want…?"

"Family support for a chance to prove myself, if it becomes necessary, though I have an idea I can convince him without it." She tossed her hair back, in a gesture, Mikhail thought, very like his sister's. "What I do want, and need, is some advice about an apartment. I was hoping Aunt Sydney might have some ideas about a place near Lower the Boom."

"Maybe she does, but there's plenty of room with us. The children, you know how they would love to have you with them, and Sydney—" He caught her expression and sighed. "I promised your mama I would try. Natasha, she worries."

"She doesn't need to. She and Dad did a pretty good job of raising the self-reliant type. Just a small place, Uncle Mik," she continued quickly. "If you'd just ask Aunt Sydney to give me a call at the Waldorf. Maybe she and I can have lunch one day soon, if she's got time."

"She always has time for you. We all do."

"I know. And I intend to make a nuisance of myself. I want a place soon. Before," she added with a gleam in her eyes, "Grandma starts conspiring to have me move in with them in Brooklyn. I've got to go." She gave him a quick parting kiss. "I have another couple of stops to make." She darted for the door, paused. "Oh, and when you talk to Mama, tell her you tried."

With a wave, she was out on the street, and hailing another cab.

Now that her next seed was planted, Freddie had the cab take her to Lower the Boom, and wait as she went to the rear entrance to ring the security bell. Moments later, Nick's very sleepy and irritated voice barked through the intercom.

"Still in bed?" she said cheerfully. "You're getting too old for the wild life, Nicholas."

"Freddie? What the hell time is it?"

"Ten, but who's counting? Just buzz me in, will you? I've got something I want you to have. I'll just leave it on the table downstairs."

He swore, and she heard the sound of something crashing to the floor. "I'll come down."

"No, don't bother." She didn't think her system could handle facing him when he was half-awake and warm from bed. "I don't have time to visit, anyway. Just buzz me in, and call me later after you've gone over what I'm leaving for you."

"What is it?" he demanded as the buzzer sounded.

Instead of answering, Freddie hurried inside, dropped her music portfolio on Rio's table and raced out again. "Sorry to wake you, Nick," she called into the intercom. "If you're free tonight, we'll have dinner. See you."

"Wait a damn—"

But she was already dashing toward the front of the building and her waiting cab. She sat back, let out a long breath and closed her eyes. If he didn't want her—her talents, she corrected—after he went through what she'd left for him, she was back to ground zero.

Think positive, she ordered herself. Straightening, she folded her arms. "Take me to Saks," she told the driver.

When a woman had a potential date with the man she intended to marry, the very least she deserved was a new dress.

Chapter Two

By the time Nick found and dragged on a pair of jeans and stumbled downstairs, Freddie was long gone. He had nothing to curse but the air as he rapped his bare toe against the thick leg of the kitchen table. Hopping, he scowled at the slim leather portfolio she'd left behind.

What the hell was the kid up to? he wondered. Waking him up at dawn, leaving mystery packages in the kitchen. Still grumbling, he snatched up the portfolio and headed back up to his apartment. He needed coffee.

To get into his own kitchen, he expertly stepped over and maneuvered around discarded newspapers, clothing, abandoned sheets of music. He tossed Freddie's portfolio on the cluttered counter and coaxed his brain to remember the basic functions of his coffeemaker.

He wasn't a morning person.

Once the pot was making a hopeful hiss, he opened

the refrigerator and eyed the contents blearily. Breakfast was not on the menu at Lower the Boom and was the only meal he couldn't con out of Rio, so his choices were limited. The minute he sniffed the remains of a carton of milk and gagged, he knew cold cereal was out. He opted for a candy bar instead.

Fortified with two sources of caffeine, he sat down, lighted a cigarette, then unzipped the portfolio.

He was set to resent whatever it was that Freddie had considered important enough to wake him up for. Even small-town rich kids should know that bars didn't close until late. And since he'd taken over the late shift from his brother, Nick rarely found his bed before three.

With a huge yawn, he dumped the contents of the portfolio out. Neatly printed sheet music spilled onto the table.

Figures, he thought. The kid had the idea stuck in her head that they were going to work together. And he knew Freddie well enough to understand that when she had something lodged in her brain, it took a major crowbar to pry it loose.

Sure, she had talent, he mused. He would hardly expect the daughter of Spencer Kimball to be tone-deaf. But he didn't much care for partnerships in the first place. True, he'd worked well enough with Lorrey on *Last Stop.* But Lorrey wasn't a relative. And he didn't smell like candy-coated sin.

Block that thought, LeBeck, he warned himself, and dragged back his disordered hair before he picked up the first sheet that came to hand. The least he could do for his little cousin was give her work a look.

And when he did, his brows drew together. The

music was his own. Something he'd half finished, fiddled with on one of the family visits to West Virginia. He could remember now sitting at the piano in the music room of the big stone house, Freddie on the bench beside him. Last summer? he wondered. The summer before? Not so long ago he couldn't recall that she'd been grown up, and that he'd had a little trouble whenever she leaned into him, or shot him one of those looks with those incredibly big gray eyes.

Nick shook his head, rubbed his face and concentrated on the music again. She'd polished it up, he noted, and frowned a bit over the idea of someone fooling with his work. And she'd added lyrics, romantic love-story words that suited the mood of the music.

"It Was Ever You," she'd titled it. As the tune began to play in his head, he gathered up all the sheets and left his half-finished breakfast for the piano in the living room.

Ten minutes later, he was on the phone to the Waldorf and leaving the first of several messages for Miss Frederica Kimball.

It was late afternoon before Freddie returned to her suite, flushed with pleasure and laden with purchases. In her opinion, she'd spent the most satisfying of days, shopping, lunching with Rachel and Bess, then shopping some more. After dumping her bags in the parlor, she headed for the phone. At this time of day, she thought, she could catch some, if not all, of her family at home. The blinking message light caught her eye, but before she could lift the receiver, the phone rang.

"Hello."

"Damn it, Fred, where have you been all day?"

Her lips curved at the sound of Nick's voice. "Hi there. Up and around, are you?"

"Real cute, Fred. I've been trying to get hold of you all day. I was about to call Alex and have him put out an APB." He'd pictured her mugged, assaulted, kidnapped.

She balanced on one foot, toeing off her shoes. "Well, if you had, he'd have told you I spent part of the day having lunch with his wife. Is there a problem?"

"Problem? No, no, why would there be a problem?" Even through the phone, sarcasm dripped. "You wake me up at the crack of dawn—"

"After ten," she corrected.

"And then you run off for hours," he continued, ignoring her. "I seem to recall you yelling something about wanting me to call you."

"Yes." She braced herself, grateful he couldn't see her, or the hope in her eyes. "Did you have a chance to look at the music I left for you?"

He opened his mouth, settled back again and played it cool. "I gave it a look." He'd spent hours reading it, poring over it, playing it. "It's not bad—especially the parts that are mine."

Even though he couldn't see her, her chin shot up. "It's a lot better than not bad—especially the parts that I polished." The gleam in her eyes was pure pride now. "How about the lyrics?"

They ranged from the poetic to the wickedly wry, and had impressed him more than he wanted to admit to either of them. "You've got a nice touch, Fred."

"Oh, be still my heart."

"They're good, okay?" He released a long breath. "I don't know what you want me to do about it, but—"

"Why don't we talk about that? Are you free tonight?"

He contemplated the date he had lined up, thought of the music, and dismissed everything else. "There's nothing I can't get out of."

Her brow lifted. Work, she wondered, or a woman? "Fine. I'll buy you dinner. Come by the hotel about seven-thirty."

"Look, why don't we just—"

"We both have to eat, don't we? Wear a suit, and we'll make it an event. Seven-thirty." With her bottom lip caught in her teeth, she hung up before he could argue.

Jittery, she lowered herself to perch on the arm of the chair. It was working, she assured herself, just as she'd planned. There was no reason to be nervous. Right, she thought, rolling her eyes, no reason at all.

She was about to begin the courtship and seduction of the man she'd loved nearly her entire life. And if it went wrong, she'd have a broken heart, suffer total humiliation and have all her hopes and dreams shattered.

No reason to panic.

To give herself a boost, she picked up the phone again and called West Virginia. The familiar voice that answered smoothed out all the rough edges and made her smile.

"Mama."

At seven-thirty, Nick was pacing the lobby of the Waldorf. He was not happy to be there. He hated wearing a suit. He hated fancy restaurants and the pretentious service they fostered. If Freddie had given him half a chance, he would have insisted she come by the bar, where they could talk in peace.

It was true that since he'd found success on Broadway, he was occasionally called upon to socialize, even attend functions that required formal wear. But he didn't have to like it. He still just wanted what he'd always wanted—to be able to write and play his music without hassles.

Nick outstared one of the uniformed bellmen, who obviously thought he was a suspicious character.

Damn right I am, Nick thought with some humor. Zack and Rachel and the rest of the Stanislaskis might have saved him from prison and the prospect of a lifetime on the shady side of the law, but there was still a core of the rebellious, lonely boy inside him.

His stepbrother, Zack, had bought him his first piano over a decade before, and Nick could still remember the total shock and wonder he'd felt that someone, anyone, had cared enough to understand and respond to his unspoken dreams. No, he'd never forgotten, and to his mind, he'd never fully paid back the debt he owed the brother who had stuck by him through the very worst of times.

And he'd changed, sure. He no longer looked for trouble. It was vital to him to do nothing to shame the family who had accepted him and welcomed him into their midst. But he was still Nick LeBeck, former petty thief, con artist and hustler, the kid who'd first met former public defender Rachel Stanislaski on the wrong side of prison bars.

Wearing a suit only put a thin layer between then and now.

He tugged on his tie, detesting it. He didn't think back very often. There was no need. Something about Freddie was making him switch back and forth between past and present.

The first time he saw her, she'd been about thirteen, a little china doll. Cute, sweet, harmless. And he loved her. Of course he did. In a purely familial way. The fact that she'd grown into a woman didn't change that. He was still six years older, her more experienced cousin.

But the woman who stepped out of the elevator didn't look like anyone's cousin.

What the hell had she done to herself? Nick jammed his hands in his pockets and scowled at her as she crossed the lobby in a short, snug little dress the color of just-ripened apricots. She'd clipped up her hair, and it showed entirely too much of slender neck and smooth shoulders. Glittery colored gems swung from her ears, and one tear-shaped sapphire nestled comfortably between the curve of her breasts.

The kind of female trick, Nick knew, that drew a man's eyes to that tempting point and made his fingers itch.

Not that his did, he assured himself, and kept them safely in his pockets.

Her dimples flashed as she spotted him, and he concentrated on them, rather than on her legs as she walked to him.

"Hi. I hope you haven't been waiting long." She rose on her toes to kiss him at the left corner of his mouth. "You look wonderful."

"I don't see why we had to get all dressed up to eat."

"So I could wear the outfit I bought today." She turned a saucy circle, laughing. "Like it?"

He was lucky his tongue wasn't hanging out. "It's fine. What there is of it. You're going to get cold."

To her credit, she didn't snarl at the brotherly opinion of her appearance. "I don't think so. The car's waiting just outside." She took his hand, linking fingers with him as they walked out of the lobby toward the sleek black limo at the curb.

"You got a limo? To go to dinner?"

"I felt like indulging myself." With the ease of long practice, she flashed a smile at the driver before sliding smoothly into the car. "You're my first date in New York."

It was said casually, as if she expected to have many more dates, with many more men. Nick only grunted as he climbed in after her.

"I'll never understand rich people."

"You're not exactly on poverty row these days, Nick," she reminded him. "A Broadway hit going into its second year, a Tony nomination, another musical to be scored."

He moved his shoulders, still uncomfortable with the idea of true monetary success. "I don't hang around in limos."

"So enjoy." She settled back, feeling a great deal like Cinderella on her way to the ball. The big difference was, she was going there with her Prince Charming. "Big Sunday dinner at Grandma's coming up," she said.

"Yeah, I got the word on it."

"I can't wait to see them, and all the kids. I dropped

by Uncle Mik's gallery this morning. Have you seen the piece he did on Aunt Sydney and the children?"

"Yeah." Nick's eyes softened. He almost forgot he was wearing a suit and riding in a limo. "It's beautiful. The baby's terrific. She's got this way of climbing up your leg and into your lap. Bess is having another one, you know."

"So she told me at lunch. There's no stopping those Ukrainians. Papa's going to have to start buying those gumdrops he likes to pass out by the gross."

"You don't worry about teeth," Nick said in Yuri's thick accent. "All my grandbabies have teeth like iron."

Freddie laughed, shifting so that her knee brushed his. "They have a wedding anniversary coming up."

"Next month, right?"

"We were kicking around ideas for a party at lunch. We thought about hiring a hall, or a hotel ballroom, but we all thought it would be more fun, and more true to them, if we kept it simpler. Would you and Zack hold it in the bar?"

"Sure, that's no problem. Hell of a lot more fun there than at some ritzy ballroom." And he wouldn't have to wear a damned suit. "Rio can handle the food."

"You and I can handle the music."

He shot her a cautious look. "Yeah, we could do that."

"And we thought we could do a group present. Did you know Grandma's always wanted to go to Paris?"

"Nadia, Paris?" He smiled at the thought. "No. How do you know?"

"It was something she said to Mama, not too long ago. She didn't say too much—you know she wouldn't. Just how she'd always wondered if it was as romantic as all the songs claimed. Oh, and a couple of other things. So we were thinking, if we could give them a trip, fly them over there for a couple of weeks, get them a suite at the Ritz or something."

"It's a great idea. Yuri and Nadia do Paris." He was still grinning over it when the limo glided to the curb.

"Where have you always wanted to go?"

"Hmm?" Nick climbed out, automatically offering a hand to assist her. "Oh, I don't know. The best place I've ever been is New Orleans. Incredible music. You can stand on any street corner and be blown away by it. The Caribbean's not bad either. Remember when Zack and Rachel and I sailed down there? God, that was before any of the kids came along."

"You sent me a postcard from Saint Martin," she murmured. She still had it.

"It was the first time I'd been anywhere. Zack decided that as a crew member my best contribution was as ballast, so I ended up doing mostly kitchen duty. I bitched all the way and loved every minute of it."

They stepped inside, out of the slight spring chill and into the warmth and muted light of the restaurant. "Kimball," Freddie told the maître d', and found herself well satisfied when they were led to a quiet corner booth.

Very close to perfect, she thought, with candles flickering in silver holders on the white linen tablecloth, the scent of good food, the gleam of fine crystal. Nick might not realize he was being courted, but she thought she was doing an excellent job of it.

"Should we have some wine?" she asked.

"Sure." He took the leather-bound list. His years of

working a bar had taught him something about choosing the right vintage. He skimmed the list and shook his head over the ridiculous price markups. Well, it was Fred's party.

"The Sancerre, '88," he told the hovering sommelier. It was a profession, Nick had always thought, that made a guy look as though he had an ashtray hanging around his neck.

"Yes, sir. Excellent choice."

"I figure it should be, since it's marked up about three hundred percent." While Freddie struggled with a laugh and the sommelier struggled with his dignity, Nick passed the list back and lighted a cigarette. "So, any luck on finding an apartment?"

"I didn't do a lot about it today, but I think Sydney will come up with something."

"Finding one in New York isn't a snap, kid. And you can get conned. There are plenty of people out there just waiting for a chance to gobble up fresh meat. You ought to think about moving in with one of the family for the time being."

She arched a brow. "Want a roommate?"

He gaped at her, blinked, then blew out smoke. "That wasn't what I meant."

"Actually, being roomies would be handy once we start working together—"

"Hold it. You're getting ahead of yourself."

"Am I?" With a slight smile, she sat back as the sommelier presented the wine label for Nick's inspection.

"Fine," he said with an impatient wave of his hand, but there was no getting rid of the man until the ritual of the wine was completed. Nick handed the cork to

Freddie. Cork smelled like cork, and he'd be damned if he'd sniff it. To speed the business up, he took a quick sip of the sample that was poured into his glass. "Great, let's have it."

With strained dignity, the sommelier poured Freddie's wine, then topped off Nick's, before nestling the bottle into the waiting silver bucket.

"Now listen—" Nick began.

"It *was* an excellent choice," Freddie mused as she savored the first sip. Dry, and nicely light. "You know, I trust your taste in certain areas, Nicholas, without reservation. This is one of them," she said, lifting her glass. "And music's another. You may be reluctant to admit that your little Freddie's as good as you are, but your musical integrity won't let you do otherwise."

"Nobody's saying you're as good as I am, kid. But you're not bad." Giving in, just a little, he tapped his glass against hers. For a moment, he lost his train of thought. Something about the way the candlelight played in those smoky eyes. And the look in them, as if she had a secret she wasn't quite ready to share with him. "Anyhow." He cleared his throat, brought himself back. "I liked your stuff."

"Oh, Mr. LeBeck." She lowered her lashes, fluttered them. "I don't know what to say."

"You've always got plenty to say. The one number— 'It Was Ever You'? It may fit in with the score."

"I thought it would." She smiled at his narrowed eyes. "As the daughter of Spencer Kimball, I do have certain connections. I've read the book, Nick. It's wonderful. The story manages to be beautifully old-fashioned and contemporary at the same time. It has a terrific central love story, wit, comedy. And with Maddy O'Hurley in the lead—"

"How do you know that?"

She smiled again, and couldn't prevent it from leaning toward smug. "Connections. My father's done quite a bit of work for her husband. Reed Valentine's an old friend of the family."

"Connections," Nick muttered. "Why do you need me? You could go straight to Valentine. He's backing the play."

"I could." Unconcerned with the tone of annoyance, Freddie pursed her lips and studied her wine. "But that's not the way I want to do it." She lifted her gaze, met his, held it. "I want you to want me, Nick. If you don't, it wouldn't work between us." She waited a beat. Could he see that she wasn't simply talking about music, but about her life, as well? Their life. "I'll do everything I can to convince you that you do want me. Then, if you can look at me and tell me you don't, I'll live with it."

Something was stirring deep in his gut. Something skittish and dangerous and unwanted. He had an urge, a shockingly strong one, to reach out and run his fingers down that smooth ivory-and-rose cheek. Instead, he took a careful breath and crushed out his cigarette.

"Okay, Fred, convince me."

The hideous tightness around her heart loosened. "I will," she said, "but let's order dinner first."

She chose her meal almost at random. Her mind was too busy formulating what she should say, and how she should say it, to worry about something as insignificant as food. She sipped her wine, watching Nick as he completed his part of the order. When he finished and looked back over at her, she was smiling.

"What?"

"I was just thinking." Reaching over, she laid a hand over his. "About the first time I saw you. You walked into that wonderful chaos at Grandma's and looked as if you'd been hit by a brick."

He smiled back at her, on easy ground again. "I'd never seen anything like it. I never believed people lived that way—all that yelling and laughing, kids running around, food everywhere."

"And Katie marched right up to you and demanded you pick her up."

"Your little sister's always had her eye on me."

"So have I."

He started to laugh, then discovered it wasn't all that funny. "Come on."

"Really. One look at you, and my in-the-middle-of-puberty-hell heart started beating against my ribs. Your hair was a little longer than it is now, a little lighter. You were wearing an earring."

With a half laugh, he rubbed his earlobe. "Haven't done that in a while."

"I thought you were beautiful, exotic, just like the rest of them."

Initial embarrassment at her description turned to puzzlement. "The rest of who?"

"The family. God, those wonderful Ukrainian Gypsy looks, my father's aristocratic handsomeness, Sydney's impeccable glamor, Zack, the tough weather-beaten hunk."

He'd like that one, Nick thought with a grin.

"Then you, somewhere between rock star and James Dean." She sighed, exaggerating the sound. "I was a goner. Every girl's entitled to a memorable first crush. And you were certainly mine."

"Well." He wasn't sure how to react. "I guess I'm flattered."

"You should be. I gave up Bobby MacAroy and Harrison Ford for you."

"Harrison Ford? Pretty impressive." He relaxed as their appetizers were served. "But who the hell's Bobby MacAroy?"

"Only the cutest boy in my eighth-grade class. Of course, he was unaware that I planned for us to get married and have five kids." She lifted her shoulder, let it fall.

"His loss."

"You bet. Anyway, that day I just sort of looked at you, and worked on working up the courage to actually speak. Little freckled Fred," she mused. "Among all those exotic birds."

"You were like porcelain," he murmured. "A little blond doll with enormous eyes. I remember saying something about how you didn't look like your little brother and sister, and you explained that Natasha was technically your stepmother. I felt sorry for you." He looked up again, losing himself for a moment in those depthless eyes. "Because I felt sorry for me—the out-of-step stepbrother. And you sat there, so serious, and told me *step* was just a word. It hit me," he told her. "It really hit for the first time. And it made a difference."

Her eyes had gone moist and soft. "I never knew that. You seemed so easy with Zack."

"I tried to hate him for a long time. Never quite pulled it off, though I worked pretty hard at making life miserable for both of us. And then, I was hung up on Rachel."

"Hung up? But…" Diplomatically Freddie trailed off and took an avid interest in her food.

He was easy with the memory now, had been for years. "Yeah, I was barely nineteen. And because I figured she was a class act with a great figure and incredible legs, I didn't see how she could resist me. You're blushing, Fred.

"Hey, every boy's entitled to one memorable crush." He grinned at her. "I was pretty ticked when I figured out Rachel and Zack had a thing going, made an idiot out of myself. Then I got over it, because they had something special. And because it finally occurred to me that I loved her, but I wasn't *in* love with her. That's how crushes end, right?"

She eyed him levelly. "Sometimes. And in a roundabout way, what we've been talking about right here proves my point about why we should work together."

He waited while their appetizers were cleared and the second course was served. Interested, he picked up the wineglass that had just been topped off again. "How?"

To add emphasis to her pitch, Freddie leaned forward. And her perfume drifted over him so that his mouth watered. "We're connected, Nick. On a lot of levels. We have a history, and some similarities in that history that go back to before we met."

"You're losing me."

She gave an impatient shake of her head. "We don't

have to get into that. I know you, Nicholas. Better than you may think. I know what your music means to you. Salvation."

His eyes clouded, and he lost interest in his meal. "That's pretty strong."

"It's absolutely accurate," she corrected. "Success is a by-product. It's the music that matters. You'd write it for nothing, you'd play it for nothing. It's what kept you from sinking without a trace, every bit as much as the family did. You need it, and you need me to write the words for it. Because I hear the words, Nick, when I hear your music. I hear what you want it to say, because I understand you. And because I love you."

He studied her, trying to separate emotion and practicality. But she was right. He'd never been able to separate the two with his music. The emotion came first, and she'd tapped into that with the words she'd already written, and with the words she'd just spoken.

"You make a strong case for yourself, Fred."

"For us. We'll make a hell of a team, Nick. So much stronger and better than either of us could be separately."

The music he'd played that morning wound through his head, her lyrics humming with it. *It was ever you, in my heart, in my mind. No one before and no one after. For only one face have I always pined. You are the tears and the laughter.*

A lonely song, he thought, and an achingly hopeful one. She was right, he decided—it was exactly what he'd intended.

"Let's play it like this, Freddie. We'll take some time,

see how it goes. If we can come up with two other solid songs for the libretto, we'll take it to the producers."

Under the table, she tapped her nervous fingers on her knee. "And if they approve the material?"

"If they approve the material, you've got yourself a partner." He lifted his glass. "Deal?"

"Oh, yes." She tapped her glass against his, sounding a celebratory note. "It's a deal."

It was far more than the wine that had her feeling giddy when Nick walked her up to her hotel room after dinner. Laughing, she whirled, pressing her back against the door and beaming at him. "We're going to be fabulous together. I know it."

He tucked stray curls behind her ear, barely noticing that his fingertip skimmed the lobe, lingered. "We'll see how it flies. Tomorrow, my place, my piano. Bring food."

"All right. I'll be there first thing in the morning."

"You come before noon, I'll have to kill you. Where's your key, kid?"

"Right here." She waved it under his nose before sliding it into the slot. "Want to come in?"

"I've got to finish off the late shift and close the bar. So…" His words, and his thoughts, trailed off as she turned back and slipped her arms around him. The quick flash of heat stunned him. "Get some sleep," he began, and lowered his head to give her a chaste peck on the cheek.

She wasn't that giddy—or perhaps she was just giddy enough. She shifted, tilting her face so that their lips met. Only for two heartbeats, two long, unsteady heartbeats.

She savored it, the taste of him, the firm, smooth texture of his mouth, and the quick, instinctive tightening of his hands on her shoulders.

Then she drew away, a bright, determined smile on her lips that gave no clue as to her own rocky pulse. "Good night, Nicholas."

He didn't move, not a single muscle, even after she shut the door in his face. It was the sound of his own breath whooshing out that broke the spell. He turned, walked slowly toward the elevators.

His cousin, he reminded himself. She was his cousin, not some sexy little number he could enjoy temporarily. He lifted a hand to push the button for the lobby, noticed it wasn't quite steady, and cursed under his breath.

Cousins, he thought again. Who had a family history and a potential working relationship. No way he was going to forget that. No way in hell.

Chapter Three

"Hi, Rio." Freddie balanced bag, purse and briefcase as she entered through the kitchen of Lower the Boom.

"Hey, little doll." Busy with lunch preparations, Rio had both hands occupied himself. "What's doing?"

"Nick and I are working together today," she told him as she headed for the stairs.

"Be lucky if you don't have to pull him out of bed by his hair."

She only chuckled and kept going. "He said noon. It's noon." *On the dot,* she added to herself, maneuvering up the narrow, curved staircase. She gave the door at the top a sharp rap, waited. Tapped her foot. Shifted her bags. *Okay, Nicholas,* she thought, *up and at 'em.* After fighting the door open, she gave a warning shout.

In the silence that followed, she heard the faint sound of water running. In the shower, she decided, and, satisfied, carried her bundles into the kitchen.

She'd taken him seriously when he told her to bring food. Out of the bag she took deli cartons of potato salad, pasta salad, pickles and waxed-paper-wrapped sandwiches. After setting them out, she went on a search for cold drinks.

It didn't take long for her to realize they had a choice between beer and flat seltzer. And that Nick's kitchen was crying out for a large dose of industrial-strength cleaner.

When he came in a few minutes later, the sleeves of her sweater were pushed up and she was up to her elbows in steaming, soapy water.

"What's going on?"

"This place is a disgrace," she said without turning around. "You should be ashamed of yourself, living like this. I wrapped the medical experiments that were in the fridge in that plastic bag. I'd take them out and bury them if I were you."

He grunted and headed for the coffeepot.

"When's the last time you took a mop to this floor?"

"I think it was September 1990." He yawned and, trying to adjust his eyes to morning, measured out coffee. "Did you bring food?"

"On the table."

With a frown he studied the salads, the sandwiches. "Where's breakfast?"

"It's lunchtime," she said between her teeth.

"Time's relative, Fred." Experimentally, he bit into a pickle.

With a clatter, Freddie set the last of the dishes she'd found crusted in the sink aside to drain. "The least you could do is go in and pick up some of the mess in the living room. I don't know how you expect to work in this place."

The tart taste of the pickle improved his spirits, so he took another bite. "I pick it up the third Sunday of every month, whether it needs it or not."

She turned, fisted her hands on her hips. "Well, pick it up now. I'm not working in this pit, clothes everywhere, trash, dust an inch thick."

Leaning back on the table, he grinned at her. Her hair was pulled back, in an attempt to tame it that failed beautifully. Her eyes were stormy, her mouth was set. She looked, he thought, like an insulted fairy.

"God, you're cute, Fred."

Now those stormy eyes narrowed. "You know I hate that."

"Yeah." His grin only widened.

With dignity, she ripped off a paper towel from a roll on the counter to dry her hands. "What are you staring at?"

"You. I'm waiting for you to pout. You're even cuter when you pout."

She would not, she promised herself, be amused. "You're really pushing it, Nick."

"It stopped you from ordering me around, the way you do with Brandon."

"I do not order my brother around."

Nick scooted around her to get one of the coffee mugs she'd just washed. "Sure you do. Face it, kid, you're bossy."

"I certainly am not."

"Bossy, spoiledå and cute as a little button."

To prove her own control, she took one long, deep breath. "I'm going to hit you in a minute."

"That's a good one," Nick acknowledged as he poured coffee. "Sticking your chin up. It's almost as good as a pout."

For lack of something better, she tossed the balled paper towel so that it bounced off his head. "I came here to work, not to be insulted. If this is the best you can do, I'll just go."

He was chuckling as she started to storm by him. For the first time since she'd come to New York, he felt their relationship was back on the level where it belonged. Big-brotherly cousin to pip-squeak. He was chuckling still as he grabbed her arm and whirled her around.

"Ah, come on, Fred, don't go away mad."

"I'm not mad," she said, even as her elbow jabbed into his stomach.

His breath whooshed out on a laugh. "You can do better than that. You've got to put your body behind it, if you want results."

Challenged, she attempted to, and the quick tussle threw them both off balance. He was laughing as they fought for balance, as she ended up with her back against the refrigerator, his hands at her hips, hers gripping his forearms.

Then he stopped laughing, when he realized he was pressed against her. And she was so soft and small. Her eyes fired up at him. And they were so wide and deep. Her mouth, pouting now, drew his gaze down. And it was so deliciously full.

She felt the change slowly, a melting of her body, a thrumming in her blood. This was what she had been waiting for, yearning for—the man-to-woman embrace, the awareness that was like light bursting in the head. Following instinct, she slid her hands up his arms to his shoulders.

He would have kissed her, he realized as he jerked back. And it would have had nothing to do with family affection. In another instant, he would have kissed her the way a hungry man kisses a willing woman—and broken more than a decade of trust.

"Nick." She said it quietly, with the plea just a whisper in the word.

He'd scared her, he thought, berating himself, and lifted his hands, palms out. "Sorry. I shouldn't have teased you like that." More comfortable with distance, he backed up until he could reach the mug he'd set on the table.

"It's all right." She managed a smile as the warmth that had shuddered into her system drained out again. "I'm used to it. But I still want you to pick up that mess."

His lips curved in response. It was going to be all right after all. "My place, my mess, my piano. You'll have to get used to it."

She debated a moment, then nodded. "Fine. And when I get my place, and my piano, we'll work there."

"Maybe." He got a fork and began to eat potato salad out of the carton. "Why don't you get some coffee, and we'll talk about what I'm after with the score?"

"What *we're* after," she corrected. She plucked a mug out of the drain. "Partner."

They sat in the kitchen for an hour, discussing, dissecting and debating the theme and heart of the score for *First, Last and Always*. The musical was to span ten years, taking the leads from a youthful infatuation into a hasty marriage and hastier divorce and ultimately to a mature, fulfilled relationship.

Happy ever after, Freddie called it.

The perpetual rocky road, was Nick's opinion.

They both agreed that the two viewpoints would add zest to the work, and punch to the music.

"She loves him," Freddie said as they settled at the piano. "The first time she sees him."

"She's in love with love." Nick set up the tape recorder. "They both are. They're young and stupid. That's one of the things that makes the characters appealing, funny and real."

"Hmmm."

"Listen." He took his place on the piano bench beside her, hip to hip with her. "It opens with the crowd scene. Lots of movement, lights, speed. Everybody's in a hurry."

He flipped through his staff sheets and, with what Freddie decided was some sort of inner radar, unerringly chose the one he wanted.

"So I want to hit the audience with the confusion and rush." He adjusted the synthesizer keyboard on the stand beside him. "And that energy of youth in the opening number."

"When they run into each other, literally."

"Right. Here."

He started to play, a jarring opening note that would wake the senses. Freddie closed her eyes and let the music flood over her.

Quick, full, sometimes clashing notes. Oh, yes, she

could see what he wanted. Impatience. Self-absorption. *Hurry up, get out of my way.* In part of her mind, she could see the stage, packed with dancers, convoluted choreography, the noise from traffic. Horns blaring.

"Needs more brass here," Nick muttered. He'd all but forgotten Freddie's presence as he stopped to make notes and fiddle with the synthesizer.

"'Don't Stop Now.'"

"I just want to punch up the brass."

She only shook her head at him and placed her own hands on the piano keys. With her eyes narrowed on the notes he'd scribbled on the staff paper, she began, voice melding with music.

"'Don't stop now. I've got places to go, people to see. Don't know how I'm supposed to put up with anybody but me.'"

Her voice was pure. Funny, he'd almost forgotten that. Low, smooth, easily confident. Surprisingly sexy.

"You're quick," he murmured.

"I'm good." She continued to play while words and movement ran through her head. "It should be a chorus number, lots of voices, point and counterpoint, with an overlying duet between the principals. He's going one way, she the other. The words should overlap and blend, overlap and blend."

"Yeah." He picked up the fill on the synthesizer, playing with her. "That's the idea."

She slanted him a look, a smug smile. "I know."

It took them more than three hours and two pots of coffee to hammer out the basics of the opening. Not wanting to jar her system with any more of the caffeine Nick seemed to thrive on, Freddie insisted he go down to the bar and find her some club soda. Alone, she made a few minute changes to both words and music on the staff sheet. Even as she began to try them out, the phone interrupted her.

Humming the emerging song in her head, she rose to answer.

"Hello?"

"Why, hi. Is Nick around?"

The slow, sultry, Southern female voice had Freddie lifting a brow. "He'll be back in just a second. He had to run down to the bar."

"Oh, well, I'll just hang on then, if it's all right with you. I'm Lorelie."

I bet you are, Freddie thought grimly. "Hello, Lorelie, I'm Fred."

"Not Nick's little cousin Fred?"

"That's me," she said between her teeth. "Little cousin Fred."

"Well, I'm just thrilled to talk to you, honey." Warmed, honeyed molasses all but seeped through the phone line. "Nick told me he was visiting with you last night. I didn't mind postponing our date, seeing as it was family."

Damn it, she'd known it was a woman. "That's very understanding of you, Lorelie."

"Oh, now, a young girl like you, alone in New York, needs the men in her family to look out for her. I've been here myself five years, and I'm still not used to all the people. And everybody just moves so fast."

"Some aren't as fast as others," Freddie muttered.

"Where are you from, Lorelie?" she asked, politely, she hoped.

"Atlanta, honey. Born and bred. But up here with these Yankees is where the modeling and television work is."

"You're a model?" Didn't it just figure?

"That's right, but I've been doing a lot more television commercials these days. It just wipes you out, if you know what I mean."

"I'm sure it does."

"That's how I met Nick. I just dropped into the bar one afternoon, after the longest shoot. I asked him to fix me a long cool something. And he said I looked like a long cool something to him." Lorelie's laugh was a silver tinkle that set Freddie's teeth on edge. "Isn't Nick the sweetest thing?"

Freddie glanced up as the sweetest thing came back in with an armload of soda bottles. "Oh, he certainly is. We're always saying that about him."

"Well, I think it's just fine that Nick would tend to his little cousin on her first trip alone to the big city. You're a Southern girl, too, aren't you, honey?"

"Well, south of the Mason-Dixon line, at least, Lorelie. We're practically sisters. Here's our sweet Nick now."

Face dangerously bland, Freddie held out the receiver. "Your magnolia blossom's on the phone."

He set the bottles down in the most convenient place, on the floor, then took the phone. "Lorelie?" With one wary eye on Freddie, he listened. "Yeah, she is. No, it's West Virginia. Yeah, close enough. Ah, listen…" He turned his back, lowering his voice as Freddie began to noodle softly at the piano. "I'm working right now. No, no, tonight's fine. Come by the bar about seven." He cleared his throat, wondering why he felt so uncomfortable. "I'm looking forward to that, too. Oh, really?" He glanced cautiously over his shoulder at Freddie. "That sounds…interesting. See you tonight."

After he hung up, he bent down to retrieve one of the bottles. As he unscrewed the top and took it to Freddie, he wondered why it should feel like a pathetic peace offering. "It's cold."

"Thanks."

And so, he noted, was her voice. Ice-cold.

She took the bottle, tipped it back for a long sip. "Should I apologize for taking you away from Lorelie last night?"

"No. We're not— She's just— No."

"It's so flattering that you told her all about your little lost cousin from West Virginia." Freddie set the bottle down and let her fingers flow over the keys. Better there than curled around Nick's throat. "I can't believe she bought such a pathetic cliché."

"I just told her the truth." He stood, scowling and feeling very put-upon.

"That I needed to be looked after?"

"I didn't say that, exactly. Look, what's the big deal? You wanted to have dinner, and I rearranged my plans."

"Next time, just tell me you have a date, Nick. I won't have any trouble making plans of my own." Incensed, she pushed away from the piano and began stuffing her papers into her briefcase. "And I am not your little cousin, and I don't need to be looked after or tended to. Anybody but a total jerk could see that I'm a grown woman, well able to take care of herself."

"I never said you weren't—"

"You say it every time you look at me." She kicked a pile of clothes away as she stormed across the room for her purse. "It so happens that there are a few men around who would be more than happy to have dinner with me without considering it a duty."

"Hold on."

"I will not hold on." She whirled back, curls flying around her face. "You'd better take a good look, Nicholas LeBeck. I am not little Freddie anymore, and I won't be treated like some family pet who needs a pat on the head."

Baffled, he dragged his hands through his hair. "What the hell's gotten into you?"

"Nothing!" She shouted it, frustrated beyond control. "Nothing, you idiot. Go cuddle up with your Southern comfort."

When she slammed the door, Nick leaned down to open a club soda for himself. He could only shake his head. To think, he mused, she'd been such a sweet-tempered kid.

Freddie worked off a great deal of her anger with a long walk. When she felt she was calm enough to speak without spewing broken glass, she stopped at a phone booth and checked in with Sydney. The conversation did quite a bit to lift her spirits.

Afterward, armed with an address, she rushed off to view a vacant one-bedroom apartment three blocks from Nick's.

It was perfect. While Freddie wandered from room to room, she envisioned the furnishings she'd place here, the rugs she'd place there. Her own home, she thought, with room enough for a piano under the window, space enough for a pullout sofa so that her brother or sister could come and stay for visits.

And best of all, close enough that she could keep an eye on Nick.

How do you like that, Nicholas? she wondered as she grinned at her view of Manhattan. *I'm going to be looking out for you. I love you so much, you stupid jerk.*

Sighing, she turned away from the window and walked into the kitchen. It was small and needed some paint to perk it up, but she would see to that. She'd enjoy choosing the right cookware, the pots and pans and kitchen implements. She loved to cook, and even as a child had loved the big kitchen in her home in West Virginia, the wonderfully crowded kitchen at her grandmother's in Brooklyn.

She'd cook for Nick here, she thought, running a finger over the smooth butcher-block countertop, if he played his cards right. No. She smiled at herself, and at her own impatience. It was she who had to play the cards, and play them right.

She'd been too hard on him, even if he had been a jerk. She'd spent more than half her life in love with him, but he spent that same amount of time thinking of her as a little cousin—if not by blood, then by circumstance. It was going to take more than one romantic dinner and one afternoon as colleagues to change that.

And change it she would. Hands on hips, she began another tour of the apartment. Just as she would build a life here, one that reflected her own taste and grew from the solid, loving background she'd been blessed with. And before she was done, the world she created would be filled with music and color and love.

And, by God, with Nick.

It was nearly seven when Nick came down to the bar. Zack lifted a brow as he mixed a stinger. "Hot date?"

"Lorelie."

"Oh, yeah." Now Zack wiggled his brows. "Tall, willowy brunette with rose petals in her voice."

"That's the one." Nick moved behind the bar to help fill orders. "We're just going to catch some dinner. Then we'll come back here so I can relieve you."

"I can cover for you."

"No, it's no problem. She likes hanging out here. After I close up, we'll figure out something else to do."

"I bet you will. Table six needs two drafts and a bourbon and branch."

"Got it."

"Hey, did you hear about Freddie's apartment?"

Nick's hand paused on the lever. "What apartment?"

"Found one just a couple blocks from here. She's already signed the papers." Zack filled an empty bowl with beer nuts. "You just missed her. She came in to celebrate."

"Did anybody look over the place for her? Mik?"

"She didn't say. Kid's got a good head on her shoulders."

"Yeah. I guess. She should have gotten Rachel to look over the lease, though."

Chuckling, Zack laid a hand on Nick's shoulder as

he was finishing preparing the order. "Hey, the little birds have to leave the nest sometime."

With a shrug, Nick placed the drinks on the end of the bar for the waitress. "So, she went on back to the hotel?"

"Nope. Went out with Ben."

"Ben." Nick's fingers froze on the cloth he'd picked up to wipe the bar. "What do you mean, she went out with Ben?" Now Nick twisted the cloth into a semblance of a noose. His eyes went bright and hard as a dagger. "You introduced Fred to Stipley?"

"Sure." With a nod to a waitress, Zack began to fill another order. "He asked me who the pretty blonde was, so I introduced them. They hit it off, too."

"Hit it off," Nick repeated. "And you just let her walk out of here with a stranger."

"Come on, Nick, Ben's no stranger. We've known him for years."

"Yeah," Nick said grimly, imagining slipping the cloth noose around Zack's neck. "He hangs around bars."

Surprised and amused, Zack glanced over. "So do we."

"That's not the point, and you know it." Nick rattled bottles and resisted the urge to pour a stiff shot of whiskey for himself. "You can't just hook her up with some guy and let her waltz off with him."

"I didn't hook them up. I introduced them, they talked for a while and decided to catch a movie."

"Yeah, right." *Movie, my ass,* he thought. What man in his right mind would want to waste time at the movies with a woman with big, liquid gray eyes and a mouth like heaven? Oh, God, he thought, his stomach clenching as he imagined Fred at Ben Stipley's mercy. "Ben just wanted a little company at this week's box-office hit. Damn it, Zack, are you crazy?"

"Okay, I'll give it to you straight. I sold her to him for five hundred and season tickets to the Yankees. He should have her to the opium den by this time."

Nick managed to get his vivid imagination under control, but didn't have the same luck with his temper. "That's real funny, bro. Let's see how funny you are if he hits on her."

After setting the drinks aside, Zack turned to study his brother. Fury, he noted, which he'd seen plenty of times before on Nick's face. Since it seemed so incredibly out of place under the circumstances, he kept his tone mild.

"And if he does, she'll handle it or hit back. He's not a maniac."

"A lot you know about it," Nick muttered.

Baffled, Zack shook his head. "Nick, you like Ben. You've gone to Yankees games with him. He lent you his car when you wanted to drive to Long Island last month."

"Sure I like him." Incensed, Nick grabbed a beer mug from the shelf and began to polish it. "Why shouldn't I like him? But that has nothing to do with Fred picking up some strange guy in a bar and going off with him to God knows where."

Zack leaned back, tapping a finger against the bar. "You know, little brother, someone who didn't know you might think you're jealous."

"Jealous?" Terrifying thought. "That's bull. Just

bull." He slapped the mug down and chose another at random. If he didn't keep busy, he was afraid he might streak out of the bar and start searching every movie theater in Manhattan.

But a strange idea was beginning to take root in Zack's mind. He eyed Nick more cautiously now, toying with the thought of his brother falling for little Freddie Kimball.

"Then why don't you tell me what's not bull? What's going on with you and Freddie, Nick?"

"Nothing's going on." In defense, Nick concentrated on the glass he was polishing, and attacked. "I'm just trying to look out for her, that's all. Which is more than I can say for you."

"I guess I could have locked her up," Zack mused. "Or gone along with them as chaperon. Next time I see she's having a conversation with a friend of mine, I'll call the vice squad."

"Shut up, Zack."

"Cool off, Nick. Your Georgia peach just walked in."

"Great." Making an effort, Nick ordered himself to shift Freddie and her idiotic behavior to the back of his mind. He had his own life, didn't he? And, as Freddie had recently grown so fond of pointing out, she was a grown woman.

Nick glanced over, working up a smile, as Lorelie sauntered toward the bar. There she was, he thought. Gorgeous, sexy and if their last date was any indication, more than ready to let nature take its course.

She slid fluidly onto a bar stool, flipped back her shiny stream of dark hair and beamed sparkling blue eyes at him.

"Hello, Nick. I've been looking forward to tonight all day."

It was hard to keep the smile in place when it hit him—and it hit him hard—that he wasn't the least bit interested in Southern hospitality.

Chapter Four

Nick smelled coffee and bacon the minute he stepped out of the shower. It should have put him in a better mood, but when a man hadn't slept well, worrying over a woman, it took more than the possibility of a hot meal to turn the tide.

She had a lot of explaining to do, he decided as he stalked into his bedroom to dress. Out half the night with some guy she'd picked up at a bar. She'd been raised better than that. He had firsthand knowledge.

It was one of the things he counted on, he thought as he met his own annoyed eyes in the mirror over the dresser. Freddie's family, the care and attention they devoted to each other. Every time he visited them, he'd seen it, felt it, admired it.

And he was just a little envious of it.

He'd missed that kind of care and attention growing

up. His mother had been tired, and he supposed she'd been entitled to be, with the burden of raising a kid on her own. When she hooked up with Zack's old man, things had changed some. It had been good for a while, certainly better than it had been. They'd had a decent place to live, he mused. He'd never gone hungry again, or felt the terror of seeing despair in his mother's eyes.

With hindsight, he even believed that his mother and Muldoon had loved each other—maybe not passionately, maybe not romantically, but they'd cared enough to try to make a life together.

The old man had tried, Nick supposed as he tugged on jeans. But he'd been set in his ways, a tough old goat who never chose to see more than one side of things— his own side.

Still, there'd been Zack. He'd been patient, Nick remembered, carelessly kind, letting a kid trail along after him. Maybe it was the memory of that, the way Zack had taught him to play ball or just let him dog his heels, that had given Nick an affection and ease with children.

For he knew all too well what it was like, to be a kid and at the mercy of adult whims. Zack had made him feel as if he belonged, as if there were someone who would be there when you needed them to be there.

But it hadn't lasted. As soon as Zack was old enough to cut out, he had, joining the navy and shipping off. And leaving, Nick acknowledged now, a young stepbrother miserably alone.

When Nick's mother died, things had deteriorated fast. Nick's defense against the loss and the loneliness had been defiance, rebellion, and a replacement of family with the edgy loyalty of a gang.

So he'd been a Cobra, he reflected, cruising the streets and looking for trouble. Finding it. Until the old man died, and Zack came back to try to pull a bitter, hard-shelled kid out of the pit.

Nick hadn't made it easy on him. The memories of those days had a rueful smile tugging at his lips. If he could have found a way to make it harder back then, he would have. But Zack had stuck. Rachel had stuck. The whole chaotic bunch of Stanislaskis had stuck. They had changed his life. Maybe saved it.

It wasn't something Nick ever intended to forget.

Maybe it was his turn to do some paying back, he considered. Freddie might have the solid base he'd missed in his formative years, but she was flying free now. It seemed to him she needed someone to rein her in.

And since no one else was interested in overseeing Freddie's behavior, it fell to him.

He pulled his still-damp hair back and tugged a shirt over his head. Maybe she was just too naive to know better. He paused, considering the thought. After all, she'd spent most of her life snuggled up with her family in a little town where having clothes stolen off the line still made the papers. But if she was determined to live in New York, she had to learn the ropes fast. And he was just the man to teach her.

Feeling righteous, Nick strolled into the kitchen to begin the first lesson.

Freddie was standing at the stove, sautéing onions, mushrooms and peppers in preparation for the omelet she'd decided to cook as an opening apology. After a bit of reflection, she'd decided she'd been entirely too hard on Nick the day before.

It had been jealousy, she was forced to admit. Plain and simple.

Jealousy was a small, greedy emotion, she acknowledged to herself, and had no place in her relationship with Nick. He was free to see other women…for the time being.

Temper tantrums weren't going to advance her cause and win his heart, she reminded herself. She had to be open, understanding, supportive. Even if it killed her.

Catching the movement out of the corner of her eye, she turned to the doorway with a big, bright smile.

"Good morning. I thought you might want to start the day with a traditional breakfast for a change. Coffee's ready. Why don't you sit down, and I'll pour you some?"

He eyed her the way a man might a favored pet who tended to bite. "What's the deal, Fred?"

"Just breakfast." Still smiling, she poured coffee, then set the platter of toast and bacon on the table she'd already set. "I figured I owed you, after the way I acted yesterday."

She'd given him his opening. "Yeah, about that. I wanted to—"

"I was completely out of line," she continued, pouring already-beaten eggs into the sizzling pan. "I don't know what got into me. Nerves, I guess. I suppose I didn't realize how big a change I was making in my life, coming here."

"Well, yeah." Somewhat soothed, Nick sat and picked up a strip of bacon. "I can see that. But you've got to be careful, Fred. The consequences don't take nerves into account."

"Consequences?" Puzzled, she gave the fluffy eggs an expert flip. "Oh…I guess you could have booted me out, but that's a little excessive for one spat."

"Spat?" Now it was his turn to be puzzled, as she slid the omelet out of the pan. "You had a fight with Ben?"

"Ben?" She transferred the omelet to Nick's plate then stood holding the spatula. "Oh, Ben. No, why would I? Why would you think so?"

"You just said— What the hell are you talking about?"

"About yesterday. Giving you a hard time after Lorelie called." She tilted her head. "What are you talking about?"

"I'm talking about you letting some strange guy pick you up in a bar. That's what I'm talking about." Nick studied her as he forked in the first bite of his omelet. God, the kid could cook. "Are you crazy, or just stupid?"

"Excuse me?" All her good intentions began a slow slide into oblivion. "Are you talking about my going to the movies with a friend of Zack's?"

"Movies, hell." Nick fueled up on breakfast as he prepared to lecture. "You didn't get home until after one."

Her hands were on her hips now, and her fingers were tight around the handle of the spatula. "How would you know when I got home?"

"I happened to be in the neighborhood," he said loftily. "Saw you get out of a cab at the hotel. One-fifteen." The memory of standing on the street corner, watching her flit into the hotel in the middle of the night, soured his mood again, though it didn't diminish his appetite. "Are you going to try to tell me you caught a double feature?"

He reached for the jam for his toast just as Freddie brought the spatula down smartly on the top of his head. "Hey!"

"Spying on me. You've got a lot of nerve, Nicholas LeBeck."

"I wasn't spying on you. I was looking out for you, since you don't have the sense to look out for yourself." With well-conditioned reflexes, he ducked the second swipe, pushed back from the table. His body moved on automatic, tensed for a fight. "Put that damn thing down."

"I will not. And to think I felt guilty because I'd yelled at you."

"You should have felt guilty. And you sure as hell should have known better than to go off with some guy you know nothing about."

"Uncle Zack introduced us," she began, fury making her voice low and icy. "I'm not going to justify my social life to you."

That's what *she* thinks, Nick countered silently. No way in hell was he going to allow her to go dancing off with any bar bum who happened along, and he needed to make that clear. "You're going to have to justify it to somebody, and I'm the only one here. Where the hell did you go?"

"You want to know where I went? Fine. We left the bar and raced over to his place, where we spent the next several hours engaged in wild, violent sex—several acts of which are still, I believe, illegal in some states."

His eyes went hard enough to glitter. It wasn't just

her words, it wasn't just her attitude. It was worse, because he could imagine—with no trouble at all—a scenario just like the one she'd described. Only it wasn't Ben she was breaking the law with. It was Nick LeBeck.

"That's not funny, Fred."

Much too wound up to note or care about the dangerous edge to his voice, she snarled at him. "It's none of your business where I went or how I spent my evening, any more than it's mine how you spent yours with Scarlett O'Hara."

"Lorelie," he corrected, between his teeth. It didn't do his disposition any good to remember that he hadn't spent the evening with Lorelie, or anyone else. "And it is my business. I'm responsible for—"

"Nothing," Freddie snapped back, jabbing the spatula into his chest. "For nothing, get it? I'm above the age of consent, and if I want to pick up six guys at a bar, you have nothing to say about it. You're not my father, and it's about time you stopped trying to act like it."

"I'm not your father," Nick agreed. A slow, vicious buzz was sounding in his ears, warning him that his temper was about to careen out of control. "Your father might not be able to tell you what happens to careless women. He sure as hell wouldn't be able to show you what happens when a woman like you takes chances with the wrong man."

"And you can."

"Damn right I can." In a move too quick and unexpected for her to evade, he snatched the spatula out of her hand and threw it aside. Even as it crashed against the wall, her eyes were going wide.

"Stop it."

"What are you going to do to make me?" Nick's movements were smooth, predatory, as he stalked her, backing her into a corner. "You going to call for help? You think anybody's going to pay attention to you?"

He'd never looked at her like that before. No one had, with all that lust and fury simmering. Fear lapped through her until her pulse was scrambling like a rabbit's.

"Don't be ridiculous," she said, trying for dignity and failing miserably as he slapped his palms on either side of the wall, caging her. "I said stop it, Nick."

"What if he doesn't listen to you?" He stepped closer, until his body was pressed hard against hers, until she could feel the wiry strength in it, just on the edge of control. "Maybe he wants a sample—more than a sample. All that pretty skin." His eyes stayed on hers as he ran his hands up her arms, down again. "He's going to take what he wants." Now his hands were at her hips, kneading. "How are you going to stop him? What are you going to do about it?"

She didn't think, didn't question. Riding on fear jumbled with excitement, Freddie threw her arms around his neck. For an instant, the gleam in his eyes changed, darkened, and then her mouth was on his.

All her pent-up needs and fantasies poured into the kiss. She clung to him, wrapped herself around him and reveled in the wild flash of heat.

He was holding her as she'd always wanted to be held by him. Hard, possessively hard. His mouth was frantic as it took from hers. A scrape of teeth that made her head spin, a plunge of tongue that staggered her soul.

Desire. She could taste it on him. The full, ripe and

ready-to-explode desire of a man for a woman. They might have been strangers, so new was this burst of passion and need. They might have been lovers for a lifetime, so seamlessly choreographed were the fast, frenetic movements of hands, of mouths and bodies.

He lost his head. Lost himself. Her mouth was a banquet of flavors—the tart, the sweet, the spicy—and he was ravenous. There was so much there—the scent and taste and texture of her, so much more than the expected, so much richer than dreams. All of it opened for him, invited him to feast.

He didn't think of who they were, or who they had been. There was no thought at all, only a desperate leap of emotion that consumed him, even as he avidly consumed her.

More. The need for more slashed through him like a whip. He pressed her hips into the edge of the counter, then lifted her up onto it so that his hands were free to touch and take.

He heard her raspy indrawn breath when his fingers streaked under her sweater and closed over her. Then his own moan—part pain, part pleasure—when he found her, firm and soft, her nipples hard with desire against his thumbs, her heart pounding out an erotic rhythm against his palms.

She began to tremble. One quick shudder that grew and quickened until she was vibrating like a plucked string.

Shame washed over him, a cold gray mist over red-hot lust. Staggered by what he'd done, by what he'd wanted to do, he dropped his hands and slowly stepped back.

Her breath sounded more like sobbing, and her

eyes, he noted, furious with himself, were glazed. As he watched, she gripped the edge of the counter for balance, and her knuckles went white.

"I'm sorry, Fred. Are you all right?" When she said nothing, nothing at all, he used his temper to combat the shame. "If you're not, you've nobody to blame but yourself. That's the kind of treatment you're opening yourself up to," he shot at her. "If it had been anybody but me, things would have been worse. I'm sorry I scared you, but I wanted to teach you a lesson."

"You did?" Though her heart was still thudding, Freddie was recovering, slowly. Nothing she ever imagined had come close to being as wonderful, as exhilarating, as the reality of Nick. Now he was going to spoil it with apologies and lectures. "I wonder—" hoping she could trust her legs, she slid slowly from the counter to the floor "—who taught whom. I kissed you, Nicholas. I kissed you and knocked you on your butt. You wanted me."

His blood was still humming. He couldn't quite silence the tune. "Let's not confuse things, Fred."

"Oh, I agree, let's not. You weren't kissing your little cousin just now, Nick. You were kissing me." Now it was she who stepped forward, and he back, in a reversal of the dance. "And I was kissing you."

His throat had gone unbearably dry. Who was this woman? he wondered. Who was this devilish sprite with eyes full of awareness and knowledge, who was turning him inside out with a look? "Maybe things got out of hand for a minute."

"No, they didn't."

The smile was entirely too smug and female. It was

a look he recognized, and on another woman he might even have appreciated. "It isn't right, Fred."

"Why?"

"Because." He found himself fumbling over reasons he knew only too well. "I don't have to spell it out for you." He picked up his neglected coffee and drank it down stone-cold.

"I think you're having a hard time spelling it out for yourself." Empowered, Freddie tilted her head again. "I wonder, Nick, what *you* would do if I were to kiss you, right now."

Take her, he was certain, without thought or conscience, on the floor. "Cut it out, Fred. We both need to cool off."

"You may be right." Her lips curved again, sweetly. "I'd say you need some time to get used to the idea that you're attracted to me."

"I never said that." He set down his cup again.

"It isn't always easy to accept changes in people we think we know. But I've got plenty of time."

She was standing perfectly still, but he could feel her circling him. "Fred." He let out a long breath. "I'm trying to be reasonable here, and I'm not sure it's going to work." He frowned down at her. "I'm not sure any of this is going to work. Maybe some things have changed, and whatever those changes are, we don't seem to get along as smoothly as we once did. If working together means risking our friendship—"

"You're nervous about working with me?"

No button she could have chosen could have been more effective. Whatever he had made of himself through the years, there was still a remnant of the rebellious young man whose pride was a point of honor.

"Of course I'm not afraid of working with you, or anyone."

"If that's true, then we don't have a problem. Of course, if you're thinking you might not be able to stop yourself from— How did you so poetically put it? Oh, yes, sampling me—"

"I'm not going to touch you again."

The gritty fury in his voice only made her smile sweeten. "Well, then. I suggest you make the best of the breakfast you've let get cold. Then we'll get to work."

He was true to his word. They worked together for hours, and he never made any physical contact. It cost him. She had a way, he discovered, of shifting her body, tilting her head, looking up under her lashes—all of which seemed designed to make a sane man beg.

By the end of the day, Nick was no longer sure he was sane.

"That's good, good," Freddie murmured, scanning notes even as Nick played them. "Someone with Maddy O'Hurley's range is going to really kick on that."

"I didn't say this was Maddy's solo," Nick snapped. But that wasn't the point, he thought. The point was that Freddie was reading his mind, and his music, much too clearly. He had an odd and uncomfortable vision of himself as a fish nibbling at the bait. And it was Freddie holding the rod.

"Maybe I was thinking of using it for the second leads. A duet."

"No, you weren't," she said, calmly enough. "But fine,

if you want to play it that way. I've got some ideas for lyrics for their number." She slid him a sidelong look. "They don't really fit this music, but I can adjust. Maybe if you pick up the tempo."

"I don't want to pick up the tempo. It's fine as it is."

"Not for the second leads' duet. Now, for Maddy's solo, it should go something like…'You made me forget, today and tomorrow, if you—'"

Nick interrupted her. "Are you trying to tick me off?"

"No, I'm trying to work with you." She made a quick note on one of the sheets of paper propped up on the piano, then shifted enough to smile at him. "I think you need a break."

"I know when I need a break." He snatched a pack of cigarettes off the top of the piano, lighted one. "Just shut up a minute, and let me work on this."

"Sure." With her tongue in her cheek, Freddie slid off the bench. She rolled her shoulders, stretched as he fiddled with the notes. Changing them, she noted, when they both knew they needed no changing.

He was fighting her, she noted, and realized nothing could have pleased her more. If he was fighting, that meant there was something there he had to defend against. Testing, she laid her hands on his shoulders and rubbed.

His system shot immediately into overdrive. "Cut it out, Fred."

"You're all stiff and tight."

His hands crashed down on the keys. "I said cut it out."

"Touchy," she murmured, but backed off. "I'm going to get something cold. Want anything?"

"Bring me a beer."

She lifted a brow, well aware that he rarely drank anything but coffee when he worked. As she stood in the kitchen opening a beer and a soft drink, she heard the quick rap on the door, the shout of greeting.

"You're busted," Alex Stanislaski called out from the other room. "For keeping my niece chained to a piano all afternoon."

"Where's your warrant, cop?"

Alex only grinned and caught Nick in a headlock. "I don't need no stinking warrant. Where is she, LeBeck?"

"Uncle Alex! Thank God you've come!" Freddie dashed into the living room and jumped into his arms. "It's been horrible. All day long, half notes, sharps, diminished ninths."

"There, there, baby, I'm here now." He gave her a quick kiss before holding her at arm's length. "Bess said you were prettier than ever. This guy been giving you a hard time?"

"Yes." She slipped an arm around her uncle's waist and smiled smugly at Nick. "I think you should haul him in for impersonating a human being."

"That bad, huh? Well, I'm here to take you away from all this. How about dinner?"

"I'd love it. Then you can tell me all about the promotion Bess was bragging about."

"It's nothing," Alex muttered, causing Nick to stop playing long enough to look over his shoulder.

"That's not what I heard." The sneer was automatic and friendly. *"Captain."*

"It's not official." Alex gave Nick a punch on the shoulder.

"Police brutality." Since Freddie hadn't brought it out, Nick rose to get his beer, and one for Alex from the kitchen. "He's always had it in for me."

"Should have tossed away the key the night I caught you climbing out of the window of that electronics shop."

"Cops have memories like elephants."

"When it comes to punks." Comfortable, Alex leaned against the piano. "That was a nice sound you were making. You two really collaborating on this musical thing?"

"That's the rumor," Freddie answered. "Only Nick's having a hard time splitting his energy between being my partner and my surrogate father."

"Oh?"

"He trailed me on a date last night."

"I did not." Disgusted, Nick took a swallow of beer. "She has delusions of adulthood."

A little wary of the vibes scooting around in the air, Alex cleared his throat. "She looks pretty grown up to me."

"Why, thank you. Same time tomorrow, Nick?"

"Yeah, fine."

"You can come on to dinner too, you know. The invitation was general," Alex said. "Bess is calling in Italian."

"No, thanks." Nick set aside his beer and ran his fingers over the keys. "I've got stuff to do."

"Suit yourself. Come on, Fred, I'm starved. I spent a hard day catching bad guys."

"I'm out the door." Deliberately she leaned over and kissed Nick's cheek. "See you tomorrow."

Alex waited until they'd gotten outside before he went for the subject. "So, what's going on?"

"On where?"

"Between you and Nick?"

"Not as much as I'd like," Freddie said without any preamble, and, since Alex merely stood there, stepped to the curb to hail a cab herself.

"Ah, are you speaking professionally, or personally?"

"Oh, professionally, we're clicking right along. He should have something to take the producers early next week. Why don't we take the subway?" she suggested after scanning the street. "It's going to be hell catching a cab this time of day."

He walked along with her toward the subway station. "You're talking...personally, then?"

"Hmm? That's right." She smiled approvingly over at him. The dimming sunlight haloed around his dark hair, making him look, to her, like a knight just out of battle. "It's so good to be here with all of you, Uncle Alex."

"It's good to have you. What kind of personally?" he asked, not allowing himself to be sidetracked for an instant from the subject at hand.

She sighed, but there was humor in it. "Exactly what you're worried about. I love you, Uncle Alex."

"I love you, too, Fred." He hurried after her as she started down the steps to the station. "Look, I know you had a crush on Nick when you were a kid."

"Do you?" Only more amused, she dug around in her bag for change.

"Sure, it was kind of cute. We all noticed."

"Nick didn't." She let her change fall back into the bag when Alex pulled out tokens for both of them.

"So, he's slow. My point is, you're not a kid anymore."

She stopped on the other side of the turnstile, put both hands on his face and kissed him full on the mouth. "I can't tell you what it means to hear someone else say that. I *really* love you, Alexi."

"I think you're missing my point here." Taking her elbow, he guided her through the crowd waiting for the next train uptown.

"No, I'm not. You're worried that I'm going to do something that I'll regret, or that Nick will regret."

"If I thought he'd have anything to regret, he wouldn't be able to play a tune for a month."

She only laughed. "Big talk. You love him like a brother."

His golden eyes went dark. "It wouldn't stop me from breaking all the bones in his hands if he used them the wrong way."

She thought it best not to mention just where Nick's hands had been a few hours before. "I'm in love with him, Uncle Alex." She laughed, shaking back her hair. "Oh, that felt wonderful. You're the first one I've told. Dad and Mama don't even know." Her laugh leveled off to a chuckle when she saw that he was simply gaping at her. "Is it really that much of a surprise?"

He found his voice with an oath, then pulled her onto the train that had stopped at the station. "Now listen to me, Freddie—"

"No, listen to me first." Since the car was full, she snagged a pole and held on as the train jostled out of the station. "I know you're thinking I might not know the difference between puppy love and the real thing, but I do. I do," she repeated, with such quiet conviction that he remained silent. "I don't just love the boy I met all those years ago, Uncle Alex, or the one I came to know. It's the man he's become I'm speaking of. With all his faults, and his virtues, his impatience, his kindness and even his streak of mean. I love the whole person, and he might not know it yet, he may not accept it, or love me back, but that doesn't change what's inside me for him."

Alex let out a long breath. "You have grown up."

"Yes, I have. And I've had the very best examples ahead of me. Not just Mama and Dad, but you and Bess and all the rest of you. So I know when you love deep enough, and true enough, it lasts."

He couldn't argue with that. What he'd found with Bess only became more precious and more vital every day. "Nick's as important to me as anyone in the family," Alex said carefully. "Even you. So I can tell you that he's not an easy man, Freddie. He's got baggage he hasn't tossed out."

"I know that. I can't say I understand it all, but I know it. Just don't worry too much," she asked, and took one hand off the pole to touch his cheek. "And I'd appreciate it if you'd keep this between us for now. I'd like some time before the rest of the family starts looking over my shoulder."

When Freddie returned to the hotel that evening, there was a message waiting for her at the desk. Intrigued, she tore open the envelope as she took the elevator up to her floor.

Inside, Nick's handwriting was scrawled across a sheet of staff paper.

Okay, you're right. It's Maddy's solo. I want lyrics by tomorrow. Good ones. I've scheduled a meeting with Valentine and the rest of the suits. Don't mess up. Nick.

She all but danced to her room.

Two hours later, she was racing up the steps to Nick's apartment. She knew he was working the bar, and she couldn't be bothered with him. Instead, she sat at his piano and switched on the tape recorder.

"I've got your lyrics, Nicholas, and they're better than good. Just listen."

Primed by her own excitement, she sang to him as she played his melody. The words had been swimming in her head since she'd first heard the music. Refined now, polished, they melded with the notes as if they'd been born together.

After the last note died away, she closed her eyes.

"What are you doing here?"

She jolted, turning quickly toward the doorway, where Nick stood. He didn't look friendly, she noted.

"Leaving you a message. You wanted the song done before your meeting. It's done."

"I heard." And he'd suffered, listening to it, watching her as she sang for him. "Do you know what time it is?"

"About midnight, I guess. I thought you'd be busy downstairs."

"We are busy downstairs. Rio told me you were up here."

"You didn't have to come up. I just didn't want to wait until tomorrow." Her nerves came rushing back. "How much did you hear?"

"Enough."

"Well?" Impatient, she swung her legs over the bench so that she could face him. "What did you think?"

"I think they'll go for it."

"That's it. That's all you can say?"

"What do you want me to say?"

It was like pulling teeth, she thought, always. "What you feel."

He didn't know what he felt. She was somehow drawing him into areas he'd never explored. Never wanted to explore. "I think," he said carefully, "it's a stunning lyric, one that goes for the heart and the gut. And I think when people walk out of the theater, it'll be playing in their heads."

She couldn't speak. She was embarrassed when she realized that her eyes had filled. Lowering them, she stared at her linked hands. "That's a curve I didn't expect from you."

"You know the gift you have, Fred."

"Yes, I tell myself I do." Calmer, she looked up again. Her heart did one slow roll in her breast as she watched him. "I tell myself a lot of things, Nick. Things that don't always hold up when I'm alone in the middle of the night. But what you said will, whatever happens."

He couldn't take his eyes off her, hardly realized he was walking to her. "I'm going to take what we worked on so far to Valentine tomorrow. Take the day off."

"I can start on the new apartment while I'm trying not to go insane from nerves."

"Fine." As if it belonged to someone else, his hand reached down for hers, drew her to her feet. The only light in the room came from the gooseneck lamp atop the piano. Its glow fell short of them, leaving them in soft shadow. "You shouldn't have come back here tonight."

"Why?"

"I'm thinking about you too much. It's not the way I used to think about you."

"Times change," she said unsteadily. "So do people."

"You don't always want them to, and it's not always for the best. This isn't for the best," he murmured as he lowered his mouth to hers.

It wasn't frantic this time. She'd been prepared for that, but this time it was slow, and deep, and quietly desperate. Instead of revving for the storm, her body simply went limp, melting into his like candle wax left too long at the flame.

It was the innocence he felt, her innocence, fluttering helplessly against his own driving needs. The images that spun through his brain aroused him, amazed him, appalled him.

"I lied," he murmured, and pulled back with difficulty. "I said I wouldn't touch you again."

"I want you to touch me."

"I know." He kept his hands firm on her shoulders when she would have swayed toward him. "What I want is for you to go home, back to your hotel, now. I'll get in touch with you after I've seen Valentine."

"You want me to stay," she whispered. "You want to be with me."

"No, I don't." That, at least, was the truth. He didn't want it, even if he seemed so violently to need it. "We're family, Fred, and it looks as though we may be collaborators. I'm not going to ruin that. Neither are you." He set her aside, stepped away. "Now, I want you to go down and have Rio flag you a cab."

Every nerve ending in her body was on full alert. But while she might have preferred to scream in frustration, she could see that his eyes were troubled. "All right, Nick, I'll wait to hear from you."

She started for the door, then stopped and turned. "But you're still going to think about me, Nick. Too much. And it's never going to be the way it used to be again."

When the door closed behind her, he lowered himself to the piano stool. She was right, he acknowledged as he rubbed his hands over his face. Nothing was going to be quite the same again.

Chapter Five

Sunday dinner at the Stanislaski household was never a quiet, dignified affair. It began in the early afternoon, with the sounds of children shouting, adults arguing and dogs barking. Then there were always the scents of something wonderful streaming through the kitchen doorway.

As the family grew, the house in Brooklyn seemed to stretch at its joints to accommodate them all. Children tumbled over the floor or were welcomed into laps, and there were board games and toys scattered over the well-worn rugs. When it came time for the meal, leaves were added to the table and everyone sat elbow-to-elbow with everyone else in the chaos of conversation, bowls and platters being passed around.

Mikhail's and Sydney's home in Connecticut was much larger, Rachel's and Zack's apartment more accommodating, and Alex's and Bess's airy loft more spacious. No one ever considered changing the tradition from Yuri's and Nadia's overflowing home.

Because this was where the family began, Freddie mused as she squeezed between Sydney and Zack on the ancient sofa. This, no matter where any of them lived or worked or moved to, was home.

"Up," Laurel demanded, and began the climb into Freddie's lap. She had the flashing sunburst smile of her father and her mother's cool, discerning eye.

"And up you go." Freddie bounced Laurel as the toddler entertained herself with the glint of colored stones on Freddie's necklace.

"You're pleased with the apartment, then?" Sydney reached out to run a hand over her son's hair as he darted past in pursuit of a cousin.

"More than pleased. I really appreciate you helping me out. It's exactly what I was looking for—size, location."

"Good." With a mother's instinct, Sydney kept a wary eye on her oldest. Just lately, he'd taken to torturing his sister. Not that she worried about Moira overmuch. The girl had a fast and wicked left jab. "Griff," she called out, and it took no more than that along with a steely maternal look, to have the boy reconsider yanking his sister's curling ponytail, just to see what would happen.

"Are you looking for furniture?" Sydney asked as Laurel climbed determinedly from Freddie's lap to hers.

"Halfheartedly," Freddie admitted. There was a bloodcurdling war whoop from upstairs, followed by a loud thump. No one so much as blinked. "I picked up a few things over the last couple of days. I think I'll get more in the swing when I move in next week."

"Well, there's a shop downtown with good prices on rugs. I'll give you the name. Ah, Zack?"

"Hmm?" He tore his eyes from the ball game currently on the television and glanced in the direction Sydney indicated. His youngest had dragged a chair over to Nadia's breakfront and had both greedy eyes on a bag of Yuri's gumdrops, on the top shelf.

"Forget it, Gideon."

Gideon beamed, all innocence. "Just one, Daddy. Papa said."

"I'll just bet he did." Zack rose, caught his son around the waist and tossed him in the air to distract him. "Hey, Mom. Catch."

Experience and reflex had Rachel scooping her son out of the air on the fly. The new criminal court judge held her giggling child upside down as she turned to Freddie. "So, where's our temperamental Nick?"

Exactly the question Freddie had been asking herself. "I'm sure he'll be here shortly. He'd never miss a meal. I talked to him yesterday."

And he hadn't been able, or hadn't been willing, to give her an opinion on the producers' reaction to their collaboration. The wait, Freddie thought, was like sitting on one of Nadia's pin cushions.

Waiting was something she should excel at by now, she thought with a little sigh. She'd been waiting for Nick for ten years.

She let the conversation and noise flow around her before rising. Maneuvering with practiced skill around the various sprawled bodies and abandoned toys, she wandered into the kitchen.

Bess sat contentedly at the kitchen table, putting the finishing touches on an enormous salad while Nadia guarded the stove.

It was a good room, Freddie mused, looking around. A nurturing room, with its cluttered counters and its refrigerator door totally covered with wildly colorful drawings, courtesy of the grandchildren. Always there was something simmering on the stove, and the cookie jar was never empty.

Such things, she thought, such small things, made a home. One day, she promised herself, she would make such a room.

"Grandma." Freddie pressed a kiss to Nadia's warm cheek. She caught the scent of lavender weaving through the aromas of roasting meat. "Can I help?"

"No. You sit, have some wine. Too many cooks in my kitchen these days."

Bess winked at Freddie. "I'm only allowed because I'm getting lessons. Nadia thinks I should stop doing all my meals with the phone as my only cooking utensil."

"All my children cook," Nadia said with some pride.

"Nick doesn't," Freddie pointed out, and snatched a radish while Nadia's back was turned.

"I did not say they all cooked well." Nadia continued to mix the dough for her biscuits. She was a small, sturdy woman, her hair now iron gray, around a serene and timelessly lovely face. The smoothness, Freddie realized now, came from happiness. Age had scored a few lines, to be sure, but none came from discontent.

"When you learn," Nadia said, turning to wag a wooden spoon in Bess's direction, "you teach your children."

Bess gave a mock shudder. "Horrible thought. Just last week Carmen emptied an entire bag of flour over her head, then added eggs."

"You teach her right." Nadia smiled. "Your sons, too. I give you recipes my mama gave to me. Freddie, you make the chicken Kiev like I taught you?"

"Yes, Grandma." Unable to resist, Freddie gave Bess a smug smile. "When I'm settled in my new apartment, I'll cook it for you and Papa."

"Show-off," Bess muttered.

There were shouts from the other room, of greeting, of demands, of questions. As the noise level rose dramatically, Nadia opened her oven to check her roast.

"Nick is here," she announced. "Soon we eat."

In a move she hoped was casual, Freddie rose and reached for the jug wine on the counter. "Want something cold, Aunt Bess?"

"I wouldn't mind some juice." With her tongue caught between her teeth, Bess sliced cucumbers with concentration and intensity. "How's the game going?"

"I was wondering about the same myself," Freddie murmured as the door of the kitchen swung open.

And there was Nick, a huge bouquet of daisies in one hand, a toddler in his other arm, and another child clinging to his leg.

"Sorry I'm late." He presented the bouquet to Nadia with a kiss.

"You bring me flowers so I don't scold you."

He grinned at her. "Did they work?"

She only laughed. "You're a bad boy, Nicholas. Put these in water. Use the good vase."

Unhampered by the children hanging on him, Nick

opened a cabinet. "Pot roast," he said, and turned his head to nip at Laurel, on his hip. "Almost as tasty as little girls."

Laurel squealed happily and snuggled closer.

"Pick me up, Nick. Pick me up, too."

Nick looked down at the boy tugging on his jeans. "Wait until I have a hand free, Kyle."

"Kyle, let Nick finish what he's doing." Bess took the glass of juice Freddie offered.

"But, Mom, he picked Laurel up."

"Wait your turn." Nick dumped daisies into the vase, then bent to scoop the boy up. With his arms full again, he turned to look at Freddie. "Hi, kid. How's it going?"

"You tell me." She eyed him over the rim of her glass. And damned him for looking so casually beautiful, his hands full of children, his eyes impersonally friendly as they studied her. "Have you heard back from Reed?"

"It's Sunday," Nick reminded her. "He and his family are at the Hamptons, or Bar Harbor, or someplace. We'll hear something in a few days."

In a few days she would explode. "He must have had a reaction."

"Not really."

"Did he listen to the tape?"

Nick accommodated Kyle, who was squirming for attention, by tickling the boy's ribs. "Sure he listened."

In a lightning mood swing, Kyle shifted his affections and held out his arms and wailed for Freddie. The pass was completed with the fluidity of long practice, and she set him on her hip. "Well, then, what did he say when he heard it?"

"Not a lot."

She hissed through her teeth. "He must have said something. Indicated something."

Nick merely shrugged. He reached down, aiming for a slice of carrot from Bess's salad and got his hand slapped. "Jeez, Bess, who's going to notice?"

"I am. I'm working on presentation here. Color, texture, shape. Take this instead." She held out a carrot she had yet to slice.

"Thanks. Anyway, Fred, why don't you just play house for a couple days?" He bit into the carrot and chewed thoughtfully. He liked watching the way her eyes went from lake calm to stormy and the way her bottom lip seemed to grow fuller as temper took hold. "Buy your knickknacks and whatever for the new place. I'll be in touch when I hear anything."

"You just want me to wait?"

As if in sympathy, Kyle rested his head on Freddie's shoulder and scowled at Nick. "You just want me to wait?" he mimicked, and had Nick grinning.

"That's the idea. And don't get that devious brain of yours working on the idea of calling Valentine yourself. Old family friend or not, that's not how I work."

She could only steam in silence, as that was exactly what she'd been considering. "I don't see how it would hurt—"

"No," he said simply, and, handing her what was left of his carrot, walked out with Laurel.

"Stubborn, hardheaded know-it-all," Freddie grumbled.

"Know-it-all," Kyle echoed gleefully.

"Aunt Bess, when you have connections, you use them, don't you?"

Bess took a sudden, intense interest in the proper

way to slice a mushroom. "You know, I think I'm getting the hang of this. It's all in the wrist."

"Temperamental jerk," Freddie said under her breath.

"Jerk," Kyle agreed, as she strode out with him on her hip.

"They are children one minute, men and women the next," Nadia commented.

"It's rough, being a grown-up."

Thoughtfully, Nadia rolled out her biscuit dough. "He looks at her."

Bess raised her head. She hadn't been certain Nadia would notice what she had. Of course, Bess mused, she should have known better. When it came to family, Nadia missed nothing.

"She looks back," Bess said, and the two women were suddenly grinning at each other.

"She would push him to be his best."

Bess nodded. "And he'd keep her from being too driven."

"He has such kindness in him. Such a need for family."

"They both do."

"It's good."

With a chuckle, Bess lifted her glass of juice. "It's great."

That was just the first of a number of conversations that night that both Freddie and Nick would have been stupefied to hear.

In their loft, Bess cuddled against Alex, sleepy-eyed and yawning. The first trimester of her pregnancies always left her as lazy as a cat in a moonbeam at night.

"Alexi."

"Hmmm?" He stroked her hair, half listening to the news on the bedroom television, half musing about his caseload. "Need something?"

It amused them both that she was the clichéd expectant mother in her early weeks, with all the accompanying strange cravings. "I think there are still some strawberries and peanut butter in the fridge."

"Well…" She thought it over, then shook her head. "No, we seem to be holding our own tonight." She smiled as his hand skimmed lightly over her still-flat belly. "Actually, I was thinking about Freddie and Nick."

Cautious, his promise to his niece weighing heavily on him, Alex shifted. "What about them?"

"Do you think they know they're crazy about each other, or are they still at that 'I don't know what's going on around here' stage?"

"What?" He sat straight up in bed, gaping down at his sleepy-eyed, tousled-haired wife. "What?"

"I can't decide myself." With ease, she slithered, accommodating herself to his new position. "It's probably a little weird for both of them, under the circumstances."

Alex let out a long breath. Why did he continue to delude himself that Bess's freewheeling manner made her oblivious of nuances?

"Weird," he muttered. "How do you know they're crazy about each other?"

She drummed up the energy to open one eye. "How many times do I have to tell you, writers are every bit as observant as cops? You noticed it, didn't you? The way they've started to look at each other, circle around?"

"Maybe." He wasn't certain he was entirely comfortable with the idea yet. "Somebody ought to clue Natasha in."

Bess gave a lazy snort. "Alexi, compared to a mother, cops and writers are deaf, dumb and blind." She snuggled closer. "Strawberries, huh?"

Across town, Rachel and Zack made a final check on their kids. Rachel eased the headset off her daughter's ears while Zack tucked a stuffed rabbit more securely under her limp arm—a tribute, Rachel often thought, to the contrasts of a growing girl.

"She looks more like you every day," Zack murmured as they stood for a moment, watching their first-born sleep.

"Except for that Muldoon chin," Rachel agreed. "Stubborn as stone."

Arm in arm, they walked out and across the hall, into the room shared by their sons. They both let out a long, helpless sigh. You could, if you were a parent and had particularly sharp eyes, just make out the two sprawled bodies amid the debris. Clothes, toys, models, sports equipment, were scattered, piled or precariously perched on nearly every surface on the top bunk, Jake's arm and leg draped over the mattress. A devoted guardian angel or pure good luck kept him from rolling over and falling into a heap on a tumble of possessions. Below, Gideon was no more than a lump beneath the tangled sheets.

"Are you sure they're ours?" Rachel wondered as she gave her older son a nudge that had him muttering in his sleep and rolling to safety.

"I ask myself that same question every day. I caught

Gideon telling one of Mik's kids that if they tied on bed sheets like a cape, then jumped off Yuri's roof, they'd fly back to Manhattan."

Rachel closed her eyes and shuddered. "Don't tell me. Some things I'm better off not knowing." She uncovered Gideon's head on the pillow, discovered it was his feet, and tried the other side.

"I meant to ask you, how do you feel about Nick and Fred?"

"Working together? I think it's great." Zack swore as his stockinged foot stepped hard on an airplane propeller. "Damn it."

"I've told you to wear hip boots in here. And that's not what I meant. I meant how do you feel about the romance."

One hand massaging his wounded instep, Zack stopped dead. "What romance? Whose romance?"

"Nick and Fred. Keep up with the tour, Muldoon."

He straightened, very slowly. "What are you talking about?"

"About the fact that Freddie is head over heels in love with Nick. And the fact that he keeps shoving his hands into his pockets whenever she gets within arm's reach. Like he's afraid if he touches her he'll—"

"Hold on. Just hold on." Because his voice rose, she shushed him, and he grabbed her arm to pull her into the hall. "Are you telling me that the two of them are interested in—"

"I'd say they're way beyond interested." Amused, Rachel tilted her head. "What's the matter, Muldoon? Worried about your baby brother?"

"No. Yes. No." Frustrated, he dragged a hand through his hair. "Are you sure about this?"

"Of course I am, and if you weren't so used to looking at Nick as if he were still a teenager with delinquent tendencies, you'd have seen it too."

Zack let his shoulders sag against the wall behind him. "Maybe I did see it. Something about the way he acted when she went out with this friend of ours."

Rachel's sense of fun kicked into high gear. "Uh-oh—jealous, was he? Sorry I missed it."

"He was ready to strangle me for introducing them." Slowly, Zack's lips curved. Then a laugh rumbled up. "Son of a gun. Freddie and Nick. Who'd have thought?"

"Anybody with eyes. She's been mooning over him for years."

"You're right. And she may be a sweetheart, but she's no pushover. I'd say my little brother has trouble on his hands." He looked back at his wife. Her hair was loose and tumbled. She was wearing only a thin robe that tended to slip, just a little bit, off her right shoulder. His grin widened. "And speaking of romance, Your Honor, I just had a thought, may it please the court."

Leaning forward, he whispered something in her ear that had her brows shooting up and her own mouth bowing. "Well, well, that's a very interesting suggestion, Muldoon. Why don't we discuss it—in my chambers?"

"Thought you'd never ask."

In their rambling house in the Connecticut countryside, Sydney lay sprawled over her husband. Her heart was still pounding like a jungle drum, her blood singing in harmony.

Amazing, she thought. After all these years, she never quite got used to just what the man could do to her body. She hoped she never would.

"Cold?" he murmured, skimming a hand over her naked back.

"Are you kidding?" She lifted her still-glowing face to his, meeting his eyes in the flickering glow of candlelight. "You're so beautiful, Mikhail."

"Don't start that."

She chuckled and trailed a line of kisses up his chest. "I love you, Mikhail."

"That you can start." He let out a contented sigh as she settled into the curve of his shoulder. For a time, they lay in blissful silence, watching the shadows dance.

"Do you think we will plan a wedding soon?" he asked.

Sydney didn't ask what wedding. Though they hadn't yet discussed it, she understood what he meant. And who. "Nick's not sure of his moves, or his needs. I think Freddie's sure of the latter for herself, but far from sure of the former. It's sweet, watching them watch each other."

"Reminds me of another time," he mused. "Another couple."

She shifted to smile at him. "Oh, does it?"

"You were very stubborn, *milaya*."

"You were very arrogant."

"Yes." It didn't offend him in the least. "And if I had been less, you'd have been an old maid, married to your business." He barely registered the punch in the stomach. "But I saved you from that."

"Now who's going to save *you*?" She rolled on top of him.

* * *

Blissfully unaware of her family's interest, Freddie grabbed her just-hooked-up cordless phone in her new apartment. Almost dancing with excitement, she punched out the number quickly. Her father, she knew, would be in class, but her mother would be at the toy store.

"Mama." Clutching the receiver, she turned three circles, making her way across the living room toward the kitchen. "Guess where I am. Yes." Her laughter echoed through the nearly empty rooms. "It's wonderful. I can't wait for all of you to see it. Yes, I know, at the anniversary party. Everything's fabulous." She did a quick boogie over the antique Oriental she'd picked up in the shop Sydney had recommended. "I saw them all on Sunday. Grandma made pot roast. A present?" she stopped her improvised jitterbug to listen. "From Dad? Yes, I'll be here all day. What is it?"

She rolled her eyes and began a new dance. "All right, I'll be patient. Yes, I got the dishes you sent. Thank you. I even lined the kitchen cupboards to honor them. I've picked up some essentials."

She snagged a cookie from the bag on the kitchen counter and two-stepped back into the living room. "No, I'm going to buy a bed here. I really hoped you'd keep mine in my room. It makes me feel like I'm still sort of there. Oh, and tell Brandon I haven't had a chance to get to Yankee Stadium yet, but I'm hoping to take in a game next week. And I've already got tickets for the ballet."

Two tickets, she thought. She'd get Nick there, come hell or high water.

"Tell Katie I'll commit every movement, every plié

and fouettée turn to memory. Oh, and tell Dad— Oh, there's too much to tell everyone. I'll talk you all sense-less when you come up, and— Hold on, someone's buzzing me. Yes, Mama," she said with a smile. "I'll make sure I know who it is first. Just wait. Yes?" she called into her intercom.

"Miss Frederica Kimball? Delivery for you."

"Papa?"

"Who you think?" came the strongly accented voice. "Frank Sinatra?"

"Come on up, Frankie. I'm in 5D."

"I know where you are, little girl."

"Yes, it's Papa," Freddie said into the phone. "He'll want to say hello, if you've got time." She was already unlocking her door and swinging it open. "You should see, Mama—I've got this great elevator, iron grates and everything. And my neighbor across the hall's a strug-gling poet who wears nothing but black and speaks in this tony British accent with just a hint of the Bronx un-derneath. I don't think she ever wears shoes. Oh, here's the elevator. Papa!"

It wasn't only Yuri. Behind him, Mikhail came, bear-ing an enormous box.

"Pots and pans," Mikhail told her when he set the box down with a dangerous-sounding thud. "Your grandma is afraid you don't have anything to cook with."

"Thanks. Mama's on the phone."

"Let me have it." Mikhail snatched the receiver even as her grandfather gathered Freddie into a bear hug.

Yuri was a big, broadly built man who squeezed her as if it had been years, rather than days, since he'd seen her.

"How is my baby?"

"Wonderful." He smelled of peppermint, tobacco and sweat, a combination she associated with love and perfect safety. "Let me give you the grand tour."

Yuri adjusted his belt, took one long, pursed-lipped look at her living room. "You need shelves."

"Well." She snuck her arm around his waist and fluttered her lashes. "Actually, I was thinking that if I just knew a carpenter who had some time…"

"I build you shelves. Where is furniture?"

"I'm picking it up, a little at a time."

"I have table in my shop. Goes well right here."

He stalked over to the windows, checked to see that they had adequate locks and moved smoothly up and down.

"Good," he pronounced. He was checking the baseboards and the level of the counters in the kitchen when Nick strolled in. "So," Yuri said, "you come to unload boxes?"

"No." Nick shoved a large, blooming white African violet at Freddie. "Housewarming present."

She couldn't have been more thrilled if he'd come in on one knee, with a diamond ring the size of a spotlight in his hands. "It's beautiful."

"I remembered you liked plants. Figured you'd want one." With his hands already seeking the safety of his pockets, he scanned the room. "I thought you said it was just a little place."

It would fit two of his apartment, he noted, and shook his head. So went the perceptions of the rich and privileged. "You shouldn't leave your door open."

She lifted her brows. "I'm not exactly alone."

"Papa. Tash wants to talk to you. Fred, you got something to drink in here?"

"In the fridge," she told Mikhail, watching Nick. "So, did you come by to look the place over, give it the LeBeck seal of approval?"

"More or less." He wandered out of the living room, into the bedroom that held nothing more than a closet, which was already full of clothes, a few boxes and a rug that he figured probably cost the equivalent of a year's rent for him.

"Where are you going to sleep?"

"I'm expecting a sofa bed to be delivered today. I want to take my time picking out a real bed."

"Hmmm." He wandered out again. Dangerous area, he realized. Thinking of her in bed. Her bed. His bed. Any bed. "You want to keep these windows locked," he said as he strolled through. "That fire escape's an invitation."

"I'm not an idiot, Nicholas."

"No, you're just green." He glanced up in time to catch the can of soda Mikhail tossed at him. "You need a dead bolt on that door."

"I have a locksmith coming at two. Anything else, Daddy?"

He only scowled at her. He was mulling over the proper retort when her buzzer sounded again. It seemed there was another delivery for Miss Kimball.

"Probably the sofa," Freddie mused, as Nick lighted a cigarette and looked around for an ashtray. She found him a porcelain soapdish shaped like a swan.

But it wasn't a sofa. Her mouth fell open and stayed

open as three broad-shouldered men muscled in the base of a grand piano.

"Where you want it, lady?"

"Oh, God. Oh, my God. Dad." Her eyes filled to overflowing instantly.

"Put it over there," Nick told them as Freddie sniffled and wiped her cheeks. "A Steinway," he noted, thrilled for her. "Figures. Nothing but the best for our little Fred."

"Shut up, Nick." Still sniffling, she took the phone from Yuri. "Mama. Oh, Mama."

The men went about their business as she wept into the phone.

He should have left with the rest of them, Nick told himself when he found himself alone with Freddie thirty minutes later. She was busy tuning the glorious, gleaming instrument, between bouts of weeping.

"Cut it out, will you?" Shifting uncomfortably on the new bench, Nick hit middle C.

"Some of us have emotions and aren't ashamed to express them. Give me an A."

"God, what a piece," he murmured. "Makes my little spinet sound like a tin can."

She glanced over as she hit a chord. They both knew he could have replaced the spinet with an instrument every bit as magnificent as this. But he was attached to it.

"Looks like we'll be able to work here, too, if we want to." She waited a beat, flexed her fingers, tried out an arpeggio. "If we have anything to work on."

"Yeah, about that." Entranced with the piano, Nick began improvising a blues. "Listen to that tone."

"I am." As delighted as he, she picked up his rhythm and filled in on the bass. "About that?" she prompted.

"Hmm. Oh. You've got yourself a gig, Fred. You'll have contracts by the end of the week. You've lost the tempo," he complained when her hands faltered. "Pick it up."

She only sat, her hands still on the keys, staring straight ahead. "I can't breathe."

"Try sucking air in, blowing it out."

"I can't." Giving in, she swiveled, let her head fall between her knees. "They liked it," she managed as Nick awkwardly patted her back.

"They loved it. All of it. Valentine told me Maddy O'Hurley said it was the best opening number of her career, and she wanted more. She dug the love song, too. Of course, it was my melody that caught her."

"Cram it, LeBeck." But despite her sharp tone, her eyes were wet when she lifted her head.

"Don't start leaking again. You're a professional."

"I'm a songwriter." Jittery with success, she threw her arms around him and clung. "We're a team."

"Looks that way." He found his face buried in her hair. "You've got to stop wearing this stuff."

"What stuff?"

"That perfume. It's distracting."

She was too overwhelmed by possibilities to worry about taking careful steps. "I like distracting you." Heedlessly, she slid her lips up his throat until she found the vulnerable lobe of his ear and nipped.

He nearly gave in to the compelling need to turn his suddenly hungry mouth to hers, and swore. "Cut that out." Taking her firmly by the shoulders, he pushed her back. "We've got a professional relationship here. I don't want things clouded up with…"

"With what?"

"Hormones," he decided. "I'm past the age where I think with my glands, Fred, and you should be, too."

She ran her tongue over her lips. "Am I bothering your glands, Nicholas?"

"Shut up." He rose, knowing he was safer with some distance. "What we need is some ground rules."

"Fine." She couldn't stop the wide smile or the sparkle in her eyes. "What are they?"

"I'll let you know. Meanwhile, we're partners. Business partners." He decided it wasn't wise to seal the arrangement with a handshake. Not when she had those soft, narrow, incredibly sensitive hands. "Professionals."

"Professionals," she agreed. She tilted her head and crossed her legs in a slow, fluid way that had him staring carefully at a spot above her head. "So, when do we start…partner?"

Chapter Six

Nick knew Freddie's mind wasn't focused on her work. They'd cruised along smoothly enough for two weeks, but as the time approached for her family to come to New York for Nadia's and Yuri's anniversary party, her work came more in fits and starts than in a flow.

He hadn't meant to snap at her, really, but the way her mind was darting from subject to subject—a new recipe for canapés she just had to give to Rio, the art deco lamp she'd bought for her living room, the jumpy, tongue-twisting lyrics she'd come up with for a number in the second act—they weren't getting any real work done.

"Why don't you just go shopping, get your nails done, do something really important."

Freddie sent him a bland look and forced herself not to look at her watch again. Her family was scheduled to arrive in less than three hours.

"I bet Stephen Sondheim's taking an afternoon off wouldn't have sent Broadway into a crisis."

He knew that. And if she hadn't *assumed* they were taking the rest of the day off, he'd have suggested it himself. "We've got an obligation. I take obligations seriously."

"So do I. I'm only talking about a few hours."

"A few hours here, a few hours there." He refused to look at her as he reached up to change a note on the sheet of music. "You've already had plenty of those the last few days." He picked up the cigarette he'd left burning and drew deep. "It must play hell, having your social life get in the way of your hobby."

She took a careful breath, hoping it would help. It didn't. "It must play hell, having your creativity always at war with your sanctimonious streak."

That little barb stung, as she'd meant it to. "Why don't you try doing your job? I can't keep carrying you."

Now her breath hissed out. "Nobody has to carry me. I'm here, aren't I?"

"For a change." He tossed the cigarette back in the ashtray to smolder. "Now why don't you try contributing something, so we can earn our keep? Some of us don't have Daddy's money behind us, and have to work for a living."

"That's not fair."

"That's the fact, kid. And I don't want a partner who only wants to play at songwriting when it suits her busy schedule."

Freddie pushed back on the stool, swiveled—the better to glare at him. "I've been working every bit as hard as you, seven days a week for nearly three weeks now."

"Except when you had to go buy sheets, or a lamp, or wait for your bed to be delivered."

He was baiting her, and even knowing it, she swallowed the lure whole. "I wouldn't have had to take time off if you'd agreed to work at my place."

"Yeah, great. Working with all the sawdust and noise, while Yuri builds you shelves."

"I need shelves." She did her best to rein in the temper he seemed hell-bent on driving to a gallop. "And it was hardly my fault that the delivery was three hours late. I finished the chorus from the first solo in the second act while I was there."

"I told you that needs work." Ignoring her, Nick started to play again.

"It's fine."

"It needs work."

She let out a huff of breath, but she refused to lower herself to the childish level of arguing back and forth. "All right, I'll work on it. It would help if the melody wasn't flat."

That tore it. "Don't tell me the melody's flat. If you can't figure out how to write for it, I'll do it myself."

"Oh, really? And you've got such a way with words, too." Sarcasm dripped as she rose from the bench. "Go ahead, then, Lord Byron, write us some poetry."

When his eyes snapped to hers, they were dangerously sharp and ready to slice. "Don't throw your fancy education in my face, Fred. Going to college doesn't make you a songwriter, and neither do connections. I'm giving you a break here, and the least you can do is put in the time it takes."

"You're giving me a break." There was a growl

in her voice, feral and furious. "You conceited, self-important idiot. All you've given me is grief. I make my own breaks. I don't need you for this. And if you're not satisfied with my work habits, or the results, take it to the producers."

She stormed across the room, snatching up her bag en route.

"Where the hell do you think you're going?"

"To get my nails done," she tossed back, and made it to the door before he caught her.

"We're not done here. Now sit down and do what you're getting paid to do."

She would have shaken him off, but after one attempt, she decided she preferred dignity to freedom. "Let's get something straight here. We're partners. Partners, Nicholas, which means you are *not* my boss. Don't confuse the fact that I've let you call the shots so far with subservience."

"You've *let* me call the shots," Nick repeated, enunciating each word.

"That's exactly right. And I've tolerated your mercurial moods, your sloppiness and your indulgent habit of sleeping until after noon. Tolerated them because I chose to attribute them to creativity. I'll work in this sty you live in, arrange my schedule to accommodate yours, even struggle to make something worthwhile out of second-rate melodies. But I won't tolerate nasty remarks, insults or threats."

His eyes were glittering now. Another time, she might have admired the golden lights among the green. "Nobody's threatened you. Yet. Now, if you've got your little tantrum out of your system, let's get back to work."

She jabbed her elbow into his ribs, remembering his advice about putting her body behind it. He was still swearing when she yanked the door open.

"You go to hell," she suggested, and slammed the door hard in his face.

He nearly, very nearly, went after her. But he wasn't entirely sure whether he would strangle her or drag her off to bed. Either way, it would be a mistake.

What had gotten into her? he wondered as he nursed his sore ribs on the way back to the piano. The girl he'd known had always been agreeable, a little shy and as sweet-natured as a sunrise.

Showed what happened, he supposed, when little girls became women. A little constructive criticism, and they turned into shrews.

Damn it, the chorus did need work. The lyrics weren't up to her usual standard. And, as he would be the first to admit, her usual standard was stunning.

Thoughtfully, he ran a hand along the edge of the piano. Well, maybe he hadn't admitted it. Not exactly. But she knew how he felt. She was supposed to know how he felt.

Disgusted, he rubbed at a headache brewing dead center in his forehead. Maybe he'd been a little hard on her, but she needed somebody to crack the whip now and then. She'd been pampered and indulged all of her life, hadn't she? It showed in the way she would carelessly shift priorities from work to social issues.

How long did it take for anyone to set up housekeeping? After Rachel and Zack moved out, he'd been settled in fine in a couple of hours.

Frowning now, Nick turned on the bench to face the room. So it was a little messy—it was lived-in, homey.

No, the place was a sty. He'd meant to pick it up, but since it never stayed that way, what was the point? And he'd planned to paint, and maybe get rid of that chair with the broken leg at some point.

It was no big deal; he could take care of it in a weekend. He didn't need the kind of palace Freddie was setting up a few blocks away. He could work anywhere.

It was irritating that the more time she spent in these rooms, the more drab and unkempt they seemed to him. But it was his business, and he didn't need her making snide comments about the way he chose to live.

Determined to push her out of his mind, he set his fingers on the keys, began to play. After two bars, his face was grim.

Damn it, the melody was flat.

In her apartment, Freddie put the finishing touches on the welcome snack she was preparing for her family. Already she was regretting not holding out for a larger place. If she had rented a two-bedroom, everyone could have stayed with her instead of bunking in with Alex and Bess.

Still, they'd all have some time together at her place before the party, and she wanted it to be perfect.

Your problem exactly, she mused, and her shoulders slumped as she arranged fruit and cheese. Everything always has to be perfect to satisfy Fred. Good isn't enough. Wonderful isn't enough. Perfection only, or toss it out.

She'd swiped at Nick because he wasn't perfect.

He'd deserved it, though, she assured herself. Making her sound like some spoiled child who was only playing at a career. That had hurt, hurt more because she wanted his respect every bit as much as she wanted his love. The hurt continued to ache because he hadn't understood, didn't understand how very much it all meant to her.

Coming to New York was a thrill, true, but it had also been a wrench to her heart. Writing the score for the musical was a dream come true, but it was also grueling work, with the sharp terror of failure always balanced over her head like an ax.

Didn't he know that if she failed as his partner, she would have failed at everything she'd ever wanted? It wasn't just a job to her, and it certainly wasn't the hobby he'd made it sound like. It was, very simply, her life.

Because thinking of it made her eyes sting, she fought to put it out of her mind and concentrate on the evening ahead.

It would be perfect— Catching herself, she swore, and then nearly sliced her finger instead of the stalk of celery. It would be wonderful, she corrected, having the whole family in one place, celebrating the endurance and beauty of marriage. Because it was important to her, she'd taken on a great deal of the responsibility for planning Yuri's and Nadia's anniversary celebration herself. She'd chosen and ordered the flowers, helped Rio select the menu and worked out countless other details.

While Nick was sleeping that morning, she'd already been at Lower the Boom, decorating the bar. She and Rachel and Zack had scrubbed the place down first, so that every inch would shine. Bess had helped her with the balloons, and Alex had taken an hour's personal time to pitch in. Sydney and Mikhail had swung by to help Rio with kitchen duty.

Everyone had helped, she thought now. Except for Nick.

No, she wasn't going to think about him, she promised herself. She was only going to think about how they would all make the evening as special for her grandparents as it could possibly be.

When her buzzer sounded, she raced to it, her eyes darting everywhere, to make sure all was in place.

"Yes?"

"The Kimball crew, all present and accounted for."

"Dad! You're early. Come up, come on up. Fifth floor."

"On our way."

Freddie hurried to the door, dragging at locks, pulling at the safety chain. Unable to wait, she raced out to the elevator, fidgeting as she heard its mechanical whine.

She saw them behind the grate first, when the car came to a stop—her father's gold hair, with its gleaming threads of silver, her mother's dark, dancing eyes. Brandon with a Yankees cap on backward and Katie already tugging at the grate.

"Fred, what a great place." Already as tall as her sister, Katie threw her long, graceful arms around Freddie's neck. "There's a dance studio across the street. I could see them rehearsing through the window."

"Big deal," Brandon said. "Where's the food?"

"Ready and waiting," she assured him. Brandon was, she thought, a spectacular melding of their parents, gold and exotic. "Door's open." She accepted his quick, off-hand kiss as he brushed by her.

"Dad." She giggled, as she always had, when he scooped her off her feet for a hug. "Oh, it's so good to see you. I've missed you." She blinked back tears she hadn't expected as she reached out for Natasha. "I've missed you both so much."

"The house isn't the same without you." Natasha rocked in the tight embrace, then eased back. "But look at you! So sleek and polished. Spence, where's our little girl?"

"She's still in there." He bent to kiss Freddie again. "We brought you something."

"More presents?" She laughed and slipped her arms around their waists to lead them to the apartment. "I haven't gotten over the piano yet. Dad, it's beautiful."

He nodded as he stood in the doorway and studied it. The dark wood gleamed in the sunlight from the window. "You chose the right spot for it."

She started to tell him that Nick had chosen the spot, then shook her head instead. "There couldn't be a wrong one."

"You got anything but rabbit food?" Brandon demanded as he strolled out of the kitchen gnawing on a celery stick.

"That's all you're getting here. You can stuff yourself at the party."

"Mama, Dad," Katie called out from the bedroom. "Come here. You've got to get a load of this!"

"My bed," Freddie explained to her puzzled parents. "It just came yesterday."

It was, if she said so herself, utterly fabulous. The

spacious room had allowed her to indulge in king-size, and she'd chosen a head and footboard of iron, painted a soft green, like copper patinated over time. The rods curved in a graceful semicircle, and were accented by metal flowers and small exotic birds in flight.

"Wow" was all Brandon could say with his mouth full of the scorned rabbit food.

"Great, isn't it?" Lovingly Freddie ran her fingers over the bars, and along the ivory-toned lace of the spread she'd chosen.

"Like sleeping in a fairy tale," Natasha murmured.

"Exactly." Freddie beamed. If anyone would understand and appreciate the sentiment, she knew it would be her mother. "And Papa built the shelves here for the carvings Uncle Mik made me over the years. I picked up this mirror at an antique shop downtown." She glanced at the ornately framed glass, its long oval shape accented by twisting brass-and-copper calla lilies, then grimaced at the cardboard boxes beneath.

"I haven't found the right bureau yet."

"You've accomplished a lot in less than a month," Spence pointed out. There was a little ache, just under his heart. He expected it would always be there when he thought of his baby living away from him. But there was pride, as well, and that was what showed in his eyes as he draped an arm around her shoulders. "I hear you and Nick are making progress on the score."

"It comes and goes." Forcing a smile, she walked back to the living room, where Brandon was already sprawled on the sofa and Katie was darting from window to window, hoping for another glimpse of the dance rehearsal.

"I still need to change for the party," Freddie said a little later, after they made a thorough inspection and caught each other up on their current events. "We'll need to get there early. You have the tickets, Dad?"

"Right here." He patted the breast of his jacket. "Two to Paris, open-dated, with a certificate for a stay at the honeymoon suite at the Ritz."

"Mama and Papa in Paris," Natasha murmured. "After all these years, for them to go back to Europe like this."

Gently Spence brushed a hand over her dark corkscrew curls. "Not quite as exciting as traveling through the mountains in a wagon."

"No." She smiled. The memory of their escape from the Ukraine, the fear and the bitter, bitter cold, had never faded. "But I think they'll prefer it." She noted, as she had several times over the past hour, the trouble lurking in Freddie's eyes. "I think you and the kids should go over now, Spence, see if Zack and Nick need any help." She smiled again, sending a silent message to her husband. "I'll stay here and primp with Freddie."

Curiosity came and went in his eyes before he nodded. "Sounds like a plan. Save the first dance for me," he added, kissing his wife.

"Always." Natasha waited, nudging her younger children along, then accepting Freddie's offer of a glass of wine. "Show me what you'll wear tonight."

"When I bought it I figured wearing it tonight would make me the sexiest woman there." Pride glowed on her face as she studied her mother, exotic as a Gypsy in flowing carmine silk. "After seeing you, I guess I'll have to settle for the second sexiest."

With a quick, throaty laugh, Natasha led the way into the bedroom. "Don't mention looking sexy around your father. He isn't quite ready for it."

"But he's all right, isn't he? About the move?"

"He misses you, and sometimes he looks in your room as if he still expects to see you there—in pigtails. So do I," Natasha admitted, and sat on the edge of the bed. "But yes, he's all right with it. More than. He—both of us are so proud of you. Not just because of the music, but because of who you are."

No one was more surprised than Natasha when Freddie dropped on the bed beside her and burst into tears.

"Oh, my love, my baby, what is it?" Drawing Freddie close, Natasha stroked and soothed. "There, sweetheart, tell Mama."

"I'm sorry." Giving up, Freddie pressed her face into Natasha's soft, welcoming shoulder and wept. "I guess this has been building up all day—all week. All my life. Maybe I am spoiled and indulged."

Instantly insulted, Natasha leaned back to look at Freddie. "Spoiled? You're not spoiled, and not indulged! What would put such nonsense in your head?"

"Not what, who." Disgusted with herself, Freddie dug around in her pocket for a tissue. "Oh, Mama, I had such an awful fight with Nick today."

Of course, Natasha thought with a little inward sigh. She should have suspected it. "We often fight with those we care about, Freddie. You shouldn't take it so hard."

"It wasn't just a spat, not like we've had before. We said awful things to each other. He doesn't have any respect for who I am, or what I'm trying to do. As far as he's concerned, I'm just here to kick up my heels, knowing if I trip, you and Dad will be there to catch me."

"And so we would, if you needed us. That's what family is for. It doesn't mean you're not strong and self-reliant, just because you have someone who would reach out if you needed help."

"I know. I know that." But it helped enormously to hear it, all the same. "He just thinks— Oh, I wish I didn't care what he thought," Freddie added bitterly. "But I love him. I love him so much."

"I know," Natasha said gently.

"No, Mama." Taking a steadying breath, Freddie shifted so that her eyes were level with Natasha's. "It's not like with Brandon and Katie, or the rest of the cousins. I love him."

"I know." The ache in Natasha's own heart swelled as she smoothed back Freddie's tumbled hair. "Did you think I wouldn't see it? You stopped loving him as a child loves years ago. And it hurts."

Comforted, Freddie rested her head on Natasha's shoulder again. "I didn't think it was supposed to. It was always so easy to love him before." She sniffled. "Now look at me, crying like a baby."

"You have emotions, don't you? You have a right to express them."

She had to smile, as her mother's words so closely echoed the ones she herself had thrown at Nick days before. "I certainly expressed them this afternoon. I told him he was sloppy and self-important."

"Well, he is."

With a watery chuckle, Freddie got up to pace. "Damn right he is. He's also kind and generous and loving. It's just hard to see it sometimes, through that shell he's still got covering him."

"His life hasn't been simple, Freddie."

"And mine has." She reached out to trace the carving of a sleeping princess Mikhail had made her with her finger. "Dad worked hard to give me the kind of home every child should have. And then you came and completed the circle. You and the whole family. I know Nick was already a man when we came into his life, and that the years before left scars. It's the whole person I'm in love with, Mama."

"Then you'll have to learn to accept and deal with the whole person."

"I'm beginning to understand that. I had it all worked out," she said, turning with a wry smile on her face. "I had a carefully outlined plan. But it's not a simple thing, convincing a man to fall in love with you."

"Do you really want it to be simple?"

"I thought I did. Now I don't know what I want or what to do about it."

"You can make one part simple." Rising, Natasha took the tattered tissue from Freddie's hand and dried her daughter's tears herself. "Be yourself. Be true to that, to your heart. Patience." She laughed when Freddie rolled her eyes. "I know that's difficult for you. But patience, Freddie. See what happens if you step back instead of bounding forward. If he comes to you, you'll have what you want."

"Patience." More settled, Freddie heaved an exaggerated sigh. "I guess I could try it." She cocked her head. "Mama, am I bossy?"

"Perhaps a little."

"Stubborn?"

Natasha tucked her tongue in her cheek. "Perhaps more than a little."

Amused at herself, Freddie smiled. "Flaws or virtues?"

"Both." Natasha kissed Freddie's nose. "I wouldn't change either trait. A woman in love needs to be a little bossy, and more than a little stubborn. Now go wash your face. You're going to make yourself beautiful— and make him suffer."

"Good idea."

Nick decided he wouldn't hold a grudge. Since it was Yuri's and Nadia's night, he wouldn't spoil it by sniping at Fred. However much she deserved it.

And maybe, just maybe, he felt a little guilty. Especially after coming downstairs and seeing firsthand how much time and effort she'd put into making the place festive. If someone had bothered to wake him up, he'd have given her a hand. With a flick of his finger, he sent the lacy white wedding bells over the bar spinning.

He wouldn't have thought of wedding bells, he admitted. Or of the baskets and buckets of flowers that filled the room with color and scent. He wouldn't have come up with the feathery doves hanging from the ceiling or the elegant candles in silver holders at the tables.

It would have taken her a lot of time to track down the decorations, he supposed. So maybe he should have been a little more patient with her dashing out on him, or dashing in with her mind so obviously elsewhere.

He'd forgive her, and let bygones be bygones.

"Hey, Nick, did you try those meatballs?"

He turned, cocked a smile at Brandon. "I saw them, and nearly got my hand chopped off reaching for a sample."

"Rio likes me better." Smug, Brandon slid a meatball from a toothpick into his mouth. "Hey, did you get a load of Freddie's bed?"

"Her bed?" Guilt, fear and secret lust sharpened his voice. "Of course not. Why would I?"

"It's a real piece of work, big as a lake." Brandon slid onto a stool and tried his most charming smile. "So, Nick, how about a beer?"

"Don't mind if I do."

"I meant for me," Brandon complained when Nick helped himself.

"Sure, kid. In your dreams." He glanced over as the door opened. And was very grateful he'd already swallowed.

Natasha was striking, an elegant Gypsy in swirling red silk, but Nick's gaze was riveted to Freddie.

She looked as though she'd draped herself in moonlight. He tried to tell himself the dress was gray, but it glinted and danced with silver lights. And she was poured into it. The simple scooped neckline and snugly cinched waist enhanced her slim, fragile build. And the way her hair was left loose and tousled made it appear she'd just gotten out of that lake-size bed Brandon had just told him about.

Natasha immediately walked over to hug him, and Freddie offered him a quick, distant smile but avoided meeting his eyes.

"New suit?" Freddie asked at random, realizing she had to say something and she'd been staring at his lapel for several seconds. She approved of the tailored lines of the black jacket, but certainly wasn't going to say anything about it.

"I figured the occasion called for it."

But not for a tie, she noted. The open collar of the black shirt suited him—as did the beer in his hand and the challenging glint in his eyes when she finally looked up. She hoped her careless shrug masked her thoughts of just how dangerous—and exciting—he looked. The man didn't deserve her compliments, after his behavior that day.

"You look very handsome," Natasha put in.

"Thanks."

"Everything looks perfect. I had a wonderful time arranging it all," Freddie said, turning a slow circle to be certain everything was in place.

"You did a good job in here." It was, Nick thought, a suitable white flag. But she only tossed him a carefully bland look over her shoulder. "It looks great," he continued, wishing he'd kept his mouth shut in the first place. "Must have taken a lot of time."

"I've got nothing but time, according to some people. Brandon, how about giving me a hand? Uncle Mik will be bringing Papa and Grandma along any time."

"He's not bringing them," Nick muttered into his beer.

"What do you mean, he's not bringing them? Of course he is. I arranged it."

"I unarranged it," Nick shot back, then added, "they're coming in a limo."

She blinked. "A limo?"

"I got the idea from someone," he said, and sent her

a sneer. "It's their anniversary after all. It's not like they're just going out to dinner."

Freddie made a sound in her throat that had Brandon wiggling his eyebrows at his mother.

"Battle stations," he murmured, and leaned forward to enjoy the fray.

"That was very considerate of you, Nicholas." Freddie's voice was cool and controlled again, causing her brother to sigh in disappointment. "I'm sure they'll appreciate it. And, of course, it takes hardly any time and effort at all to pick up the phone and order a car. I'm going to help Rio."

She sashayed out. Or so Nick described it to himself. Muttering, he pushed aside his beer. It looked as though it was going to be a very long night.

Chapter Seven

Freddie hated the fact that she couldn't stay mad at Nick. Aloof, maybe. The bar was crowded with so many bodies, the room filled with so much noise, that it wasn't difficult to stay aloof from one man.

But she just couldn't hold on to her temper, not after what Nick had done for her grandparents.

In any case, there wasn't time to brood over it, or over him. There were toasts to be drunk, food to be eaten, dances to be danced.

Not that Nick asked her to dance. He partnered her aunts, her mother, Nadia, family friends and relations. And, of course, the stupendously sexy Lorelie.

Well, if he was playing the aloof game, she would play harder.

"Great party!" Ben shouted near her ear.

"It is." She managed to work up a smile for him as

he awkwardly led her around the crowded dance floor. "I'm glad you could make it."

"Wouldn't have missed it. I've known Zack's in-laws for years. Terrific people."

"The best." Her smile bloomed a bit when she spotted Alex twirling his mother. "The very best."

"I was thinking..." Ben missed a step, and barely missed her toes. "Sorry. Failed my dance class."

"You're doing fine." Though he was in danger of breaking her wrist as he pumped her arm like a well handle to keep his time. She grabbed the first distraction she could think of to save herself. "Have you tried the food? Rio's really outdone himself."

"Then let's get some plates."

Look at her, Nick thought darkly, scowling at Freddie as Lorelie draped herself over him. Flirting with Ben. Anyone—even Ben—should have the sense to see that she wasn't interested. Just leading him on. Typical female.

"Nick, honey." Lorelie's creamy voice invaded his thoughts. She sent him a melting look. "You're not paying attention. I feel like I'm dancing by myself."

He sent her a quick, charming smile that made even the savvy Lorelie almost believe he thought of no one but her. "I was just wondering if I should check the bar."

"You checked it five minutes ago." Lorelie pouted prettily. She knew when she didn't have a man's full attention—and how to take it philosophically. As attractive as Nick was, there were always other fish to fry. "Well, why don't you get me a glass of champagne, then?"

"Sure, coming right up." Relieved, he left her. She'd

been clinging to him all night, like poison ivy on an oak, Nick thought. That kind of possessiveness always made him determined to shake loose.

The truth was, they just weren't clicking. He didn't think he was going to break her heart or anything quite so melodramatic, but Nick had learned through sad experience that women didn't always take even the most compassionate breakup well.

He'd have to let her down gently. No doubt, the sooner he backed off, the better it would be. For her.

The idea made him feel so altruistic, and relieved, that he opened a fresh bottle of champagne with a celebratory pop.

"How come we get music only from that box?" Yuri caught Nick in a headlock that would have felled a grizzly. "Are you a piano player or not?"

"Sure, but I'm kind of tied up here."

"I want music from my family. It's my party, yes?"

The man who could deny a request from Yuri was a tougher man than Nick LeBeck.

"You bet, Papa. I'll get right on it. Here take this." He handed Yuri the glass of champagne. "No, don't drink it." With a quick laugh, Nick gestured across the room. "See the brunette over there? The one with the big…personality?"

Yuri grinned lavishly. "Who could miss?"

"Take it to her, will you? Explain I'll be playing for a while. And don't lay on too much charm."

"I'm very controlled." Then he rhumbaed over to Lorelie.

Prepared to enjoy himself, Nick made his way through the crowd to the piano. His smile dimmed considerably when he spotted Freddie already sitting on the bench.

"You're in my spot."

She shot him a look that said in no uncertain terms that she was no more pleased with the arrangement than he. "They want both of us."

"It only takes one."

"It's Papa's party, yes?"

He caught himself struggling with a grin at her imitation. "Looks that way. Move over."

He sat, deliberately shifting to avoid touching her tempting, creamy shoulder and angled toward the keyboard beside the piano.

"What do they want?"

"Cole Porter, maybe, or Gershwin."

With a grunt, Nick began the opening bars of "Embraceable You."

Freddie shrugged and flowed with him into the tune.

Twenty minutes later, she was too pleased with the partnership to attempt to be aloof. "Not too shabby."

"I can hold my own with forties stuff."

"Hmm." Automatically she picked up on the boogie-woogie he'd slid into.

He was enjoying, too much, the way she always seemed to anticipate him in any improvisation.

And her perfume was driving him insane.

"You can take five if you want. I can handle this. Ben's probably getting lonely."

"Ben?" Blank, she glanced up again. "Oh, Ben. I think he can survive without me. But you go ahead and take a break. I'm sure Lorelie misses you."

"She's not the possessive type." To cover the lie, he

switched tempos, trying to catch her. But she kept pace with him easily.

"Really? Couldn't prove that by me, the way she was hanging all over you. Of course, some men—" She broke off as applause erupted. "Look at them." She laughed, everything inside her warming as she watched Yuri and Nadia jitterbugging. "Aren't they great?"

"The best. Why don't we— Son of a bitch."

"What?" She blinked, then refocused. It appeared the lonely Ben and Lorelie were finding solace with each other. If *solace* was quite the word, Freddie mused, for the way they were nuzzling in the corner. "She's sitting in his lap."

"I see where she's sitting."

"So much for letting him down easy," Freddie muttered, just as Nick echoed the same sentiments, applied to Lorelie.

He snapped back first. "What? What did you say?"

"Nothing. I didn't say anything. What did you say?"

"Nothing."

Suddenly they were grinning at each other.

"Well…" Freddie let out a quick breath as her fingers continued to move over the keys. "Don't they make a cute couple?"

"Adorable. Now they're going to dance."

"Too bad for her," Freddie said, with feeling. "Ben's a nice guy, but he dances like he's drilling for oil. I think he dislocated my shoulder."

"She can handle it. But let's slow this down before Yuri kills himself."

He segued into "Someone To Watch Over Me."

Freddie sighed, yearned. Romantic tunes always

tugged at her heart. Flowing with it, she looked over at Nick. Maybe, while she was feeling so in tune with him, the taste of crow wouldn't stick in her throat.

"It was lovely, what you did for Grandma and Papa."

"No big deal. I just made a phone call, like you said."

"Truce," she murmured, and touched a hand to his for a moment. "It wasn't just the limo, Nick, though that was wonderful. Stocking it with all those white roses, caviar, iced vodka. It was very thoughtful."

"I figured they'd get a kick out of it." As usual, her simple sweetness layered guilt over his black mood.

Pass the crow.

"I came down pretty hard on you earlier. I should have taken into consideration all the time and effort you put into getting things ready for tonight and setting up your apartment. Though why it took you so long to look for a lamp is beyond me."

Her art deco lamp was her current pride and joy. "Why don't you stick with the apology?"

"You did a nice job on the party."

"Thanks." Pleased with the small victory, she signaled to her father to take over for her. "And since you talk so sweet," she added, leaning over to give him a kiss, "I forgive you."

"I wasn't asking you—" But she was already up and gone. Nick scowled when Spence took his daughter's place. "Women."

"Couldn't have put it better myself. She's certainly grown into an attractive, independent one."

"She was a nice kid," Nick mused. "You shouldn't have let her grow up."

Spence noted, with a glance at Nick's face, that Natasha's theory on romance probably was on the mark. There was an ache around his heart. Spence supposed there always would be, at the idea of his little girl moving into her own separate life. But there was pride, as well.

Seamlessly he meshed with Nick on a Ray Charles classic.

"You know," he continued, "boys are already coming by the house, flirting with Katie."

"No way." Shock raced into Nick's eyes first, then the uncomfortable feeling of, at thirty, actually beginning to feel old. "No way. If I had a daughter, no way I'd let that happen."

"Reality's tough," Spence agreed, then let the devil take over. "You know, Nick, it certainly eases my mind to know that you're around to look after Freddie. I'd worry a lot more if I didn't have someone I trusted keeping an eye out."

"Yeah." Nick cleared his throat. "Right. Listen, I'd better take over at the bar for a while."

Spence grinned to himself and added a flourish to the notes.

"You shouldn't tease him," Natasha said from behind him, laying a hand on her husband's shoulder.

"It's my job, as a father, to make his life a living hell. And just think, with the practice I have, how good I'll be at it when it's Katie's turn."

"I shudder to think."

It was after two before the party broke. Now only Nick and Freddie and a few straggling family members remained. With a satisfied look, Freddie glanced around the bar.

It looked as though an invading army had suddenly pulled up stakes and gone off to another battle.

Tattered crepe paper hung drunkenly, so that white doves flew at half-mast. The tables that had been loaded with food had been thoroughly decimated, and all that was left of Rio's pièce de résistance, the five-tiered wedding cake, were crumbs and a few smears of silvery icing.

There were glasses everywhere. Some enterprising soul had built a fairly impressive pyramid of lowball glasses in the corner. She saw a forest of crumpled napkins littering the floor, and, oddly, a single gold shoe with a stiletto heel.

She wondered how its owner had managed to walk out without lurching.

Leaning against the bar, Zack took his own survey and grinned. "Looks like everybody had a good time."

"I'll say." Rachel picked up a cloth and gave the bar a halfhearted swipe. "Papa was still dancing on his way out, and my ears are ringing from Ukrainian folk songs."

"You belted out a few yourself," Zack reminded her.

"Vodka does that to me. Wasn't it wonderful, seeing their faces when we gave them their gift?"

"Grandma just cried," Freddie murmured.

"And Papa stood there telling her not to," Nick put in. "While he was crying himself."

"It was a wonderful idea, Freddie." Rachel's eyes filled again as she thought of it. "Lovely, romantic. Perfect."

"I knew we wanted to give them something special. I'd never have thought of it if Mama hadn't mentioned it."

"You couldn't have come up with better." Rolling her weary shoulders, Rachel took another look around. "Look, I vote we leave this mess and tackle it in the morning."

"I'm with you." More than willing to turn his back on the destruction, Zack took her hand and drew her around the bar. "Abandon ship."

"You two go ahead," Freddie said casually. She didn't want the night to end. And if prolonging it meant dealing with dirty dishes, so be it. "I just want to make a dent."

Guilt had Rachel hesitating. "I suppose we could—"

"No." Freddie aimed a quiet, meaningful look. "Go home. You've got a baby-sitter to deal with. I don't."

"Another hour won't matter," Zack said, squaring his shoulders.

"But we'll leave it to you," Rachel said, stepping hard on her husband's foot.

"But—"

Zack finally caught the drift, and the ensuing kick in the shin. "Oh, right. You kids get a start on it. I'm exhausted. Can hardly keep my eyes open." To add emphasis, he tried an exaggerated yawn. "We'll finish up what you don't tomorrow. Night, Freddie." Not sure if he should wink or issue a sharp warning in Nick's direction, Zack merely stared. "Nick."

"Yeah, see you." After the door closed, Nick shook his head. "He was acting weird."

"He was just tired," Freddie said as she loaded glasses onto a tray.

"No, there's tired and there's weird. That was weird." Which, Nick realized, was pretty much how he felt, now that he and Freddie were alone. "Listen, they've got the right idea. It's late. Why don't we pretend this is done, and go away? It'll still be here tomorrow."

"Go on up if you're tired." Freddie marched toward the kitchen with her loaded tray. "I couldn't sleep knowing I'd left all this. Not that it would bother you," she said over her shoulder as the door swung behind her.

"It's not like I made this mess myself," Nick muttered, loading another tray. "I think I spotted one or two other people using glasses around here tonight."

"Did you say something?" Freddie called out.

"No. Nothing."

He carted his tray into the kitchen, where she was already filling the dishwasher, and set it down with a clatter.

"You don't go to hell for leaving dishes in the sink."

"You don't win any prizes, either. I said go on up to bed. I can handle it."

"I can handle it," he mimicked in a mumble as he dragged out a pail. He stuck it in the sink, added a hefty dose of cleaner and a hard spray of hot water.

When he stalked out moments later, she was grinning.

For the next twenty minutes, they worked in silence that became more and more companionable. It pleased her to see the food cleared away, the bar gleaming again. And, she thought, while Nick wasn't exactly whistling while he worked, his mood was definitely clearing up.

"I noticed that Ben and Lorelie left together," Freddie began.

"You don't miss much." But his lips twitched. "They had a fine old time. Everybody did."

"You're not upset."

He shrugged. "It wasn't serious. Lorelie and I never…" *Whoops, watch your step.* "We just didn't click."

She couldn't prevent the overwhelming sense of glee, but she did manage to conceal it. Humming a little, she picked up a chair, upended it onto a table in the area Nick had already mopped.

He swabbed a bit closer. Since she was being so easy about things, he thought it was time to clear the decks.

"Fred, I wanted to talk to you about this afternoon."

"All right. You know, if we clean up any more, Zack will think we don't need him. I don't want to hurt his feelings."

But she wandered over to the jukebox, loitered over the choices. Inspired, she pushed buttons, turned. "You didn't dance with me tonight, Nick."

"Didn't I?" He knew very well he hadn't, and why.

"No." She walked to him as the slow, shuffling notes seeped out. "'If I Didn't Care,'" she thought. The Platters.

Perfect.

"You don't want to hurt my feelings, do you, Nicholas?"

"No, but—"

But she was already slipping her arms around him. He laid his hand on the small of her back and led her into the dance.

His movements were smooth and surprisingly stylish. Always had been, she remembered as she rested her head on his shoulder. The first time she danced with him, she'd thrilled to them.

But there was a different kind of thrill now, for the woman, rather than the adolescent girl.

She fit so well, he thought. Always had, he remembered as he drew her closer. But she'd never smelled like this before, and he couldn't remember her hair teasing him into brushing his lips over it.

They were alone, and the music was right. He'd always been susceptible to music. It tempted him now to rub his lips over her temple, nibble lightly at her ear.

Catching himself, he swung her out in a slow spin that made her laugh. Her eyes were glowing when she turned back into his arms.

She followed his every move as though she'd been born in his arms. Seemed to anticipate him as he walked her, circled her, twirled her again. In a move as gracefully choreographed as the dance, she lifted her head.

And his mouth was waiting.

He simply slid into her. Into the kiss, the warmth, the simplicity of it. Her arms came up, encircled his neck, her fingers skimming up threading into his hair.

He didn't hear the music end, for it was playing in his head. Their own intimate symphony. He thought he could absorb her if she would let him. Her skin, her scent, that wonderfully generous mouth.

As the kiss deepened, lengthened, he imagined how perfectly simple it would be to pick her up, carry her upstairs. To his bed.

The clarity of the vision shocked him enough to have him pulling her back. "Fred—"

"No, don't talk." Her eyes were clouded, dreamily. "Just kiss me, Nick. Just kiss me."

Her mouth was on his again, making him long to forget all the reasons why it shouldn't be. However confused those reasons were becoming, he put his hands firmly on her shoulders and stepped back.

"We're not doing this."

"Why?"

"You're on dangerous ground here," he warned her. "Now get your things, your purse, whatever. I'm taking you home."

"I want to stay here, with you." Her voice was calm, even if her pulse rate wasn't. "I want to go upstairs with you, to bed."

The knot in his stomach tightened like a noose. "I said get your purse. It's late."

Her experience might be limited, but she thought she knew when to advance and when to retreat. On legs that weren't quite steady, she walked behind the bar to get her purse.

"Fine. We'll play it your way. But you don't know what you're missing."

Afraid he did, he dragged a hand through his hair. "Where did you learn this stuff?"

"I pick it up as I go along," she said over her shoulder as she yanked open the door. "Coming?"

It had just occurred to him that it might be a better—safer—idea to get her a cab. But she was already outside.

"Just hold on." He slammed the bar door behind him and locked it.

Freddie began to stroll down the street. "Beautiful night."

Nick muffled his muttering and methodical cursing. "Yeah, just dandy. Give me your purse."

"What?"

"Just give it to me." He snatched the glittery fancy and shoved it into his jacket pocket. For the first time, he noticed her earrings. "I bet those rocks are real."

"These?" Automatically she lifted a hand to the sapphire-and-diamond clusters. "Yes, why?"

"You should know better than to walk around with a year's rent on your earlobes."

"It's no use having them if I'm not going to wear them," she pointed out with perfect logic.

"There's a time and a place. And walking on the Lower East Side at 3:00 a.m. doesn't qualify for either."

"Want to put them in your pocket, too?" Freddie said dryly.

Before he could tell her it was just what he had in mind, someone called his name.

"Yo, Nick!"

Glancing across the deserted street, Nick saw the shadow, recognized it. "Just keep walking," he told Freddie, automatically shifting her to his far side. "And don't say anything."

Breathless from the short jog, a thin-faced man in baggy pants fell into step beside them. "So, Nick, how's it hanging?"

"Can't complain, Jack."

Freddie opened her mouth, but only a muffled squeak came out when Nick crushed all the major bones of her hand.

"Fancy stuff." Jack winked at Nick and gave him an elbow dig. "You always had the luck."

The man was too pitiful to bother decking. "Yeah, I'm loaded with it. We've got places to go, Jack."

"Bet. Thing is, Nick, I'm short until payday."

When wasn't he? Nick thought. "Come by the bar tomorrow, I'll float you."

"Appreciate it. Thing is, I'm short now."

Still walking, Nick dug into his pocket, pulled out a twenty. He knew exactly where it would go, if Jack could link up with his dealer at this hour.

"Thanks, bro." The bill disappeared into the baggy pants. "I'll get it back to you."

"Sure." When icicles drip in hell. "See you around, Jack."

"Bet. Once a Cobra, always a Cobra."

Not, Nick thought, if he could help it. Furious at being forced into the encounter, and that Freddie had been touched by the slimy edge of his past, he quickened his pace.

"You know him from the gang you used to belong to," Freddie said quietly.

"That's right. Now he's a junkie."

"Nick—"

"He hangs around the neighborhood, sometimes during the day. Odds are he won't remember you, he was already buzzed, but if you run into him, just keep running. He's bad news."

"All right." She would have reached for him, tried to comfort him somehow, drive away the misery lurking just behind his eyes. But they had reached her building, and he was pulling her purse out of his pocket.

Nick took out her keys himself and unlocked the front door, then stepped inside and pressed the button for the elevator. "Go upstairs. Lock your door."

"Come up with me. Stay with me."

He wanted to touch her, just once more. But his fingers still felt soiled where they had brushed Jack's over a crumpled twenty-dollar bill.

"Do you have any idea what happened just now?" Nick demanded. "We just ran into part of my life, and if I hadn't been along, he would have taken more from you than your pretty earrings."

"He isn't part of your life," she said calmly. "He isn't your friend. But you gave him money."

"So maybe he won't mug the next person he sees."

"You're not one of them anymore, Nick. I doubt you ever really were."

He was suddenly so weary, so horribly tired. Giving in, he rested his brow against hers. "You don't know what I was, what I still might be. Now go upstairs, Fred."

"Nick—"

To silence her, he gripped her shoulders and brought his mouth down hard on hers. When she could breathe again, she would have staggered, but his hands steadied her as he pushed her into the elevator. She could only stare, system sizzling, as he snapped the grate closed.

"Lock your door," he said again, and walked out.

He took a careful look up the street, down, then turned and waited until he saw her light flash on.

He took the long way home.

Chapter Eight

She'd had incredible dreams. True, she'd gotten only a few hours' sleep, but she saw no reason to complain. In fact, Freddie had awakened early, feeling wonderful. Since she had time to spare, she walked over to the Village and spent the morning haunting some of the more interesting shops, picking up what Nick liked to call her knickknacks.

By the time she'd cabbed home, dropped off her newest treasures and walked out again, she was running a little behind.

But the day was too gorgeous for her to worry about it.

Spring was in full swing now, with just a hint of the summer to come teasing the edges. It made the day balmy and bright, with none of the horrendous heat that could plague the city during the dog days.

She was, Freddie decided, one of the luckiest women

in the world. She lived in an exciting city, was embarking on a new, equally exciting career. She was young and in love. And, unless her female intuition was faulty, she was very close to convincing the man she loved that he loved her right back.

Every step of her plan was falling into place.

Since she was feeling generous, she stopped by a sidewalk vendor to buy both herself and Nick a jumbo pretzel.

As she was slipping her change back into her pocket, she spotted the man leaning on the front of the building across the street.

The thin face, the baggy clothes. With a little inward shiver, she recognized the man Nick had called Jack from the night before. He was smoking, bringing a cigarette to his lips in quick, greedy puffs as his eyes darted right and left like wary birds.

Even though those eyes lingered a moment on her before passing on, she saw no recognition in them. Relieved, she turned away. Not that she would have spoken to him unless it was unavoidable, Freddie thought. Still, she wouldn't have cared to explain to Nick about any interaction she had with one of his old gang comrades.

She quickened her pace, heading toward the bar without looking back. Though the back of her neck prickled.

She pushed Jack out of her mind as she stepped into the kitchen, and loitered there a few moments to praise Rio for his success with last night's food.

Nibbling on her pretzel, she started upstairs. Her sunny mood didn't cloud over, even when Nick yanked open the door and scowled at her.

"You're late."

So much, she thought, *for loverlike greetings.*

"I wasn't even sure you'd be up yet. We had a late night."

He didn't care to be reminded of it. "I'm up, and I'm working, which is more than I can say for you."

He'd had much worse than a late night. He hadn't slept more than an hour, and even that had been restless and sweaty. Old dreams and new ones had plagued him.

He'd been raw then, and he was raw now, suffering from a combination of emotional and physical frustration he'd never experienced before.

And he knew just where to lay the blame for it.

She was standing right in front of him, looking as bright and golden as a sunbeam.

Though she was well aware of his foul mood, Freddie smiled at him, tilted her head. He hadn't bothered to shave, she noted, but she didn't object to the look. The angry eyes and stubbled chin gave him a sort of reckless and dangerous edge that was appealing, in its way.

She had a feeling he'd had trouble sleeping, and couldn't have been happier.

"Rough night, Nick? Have a pretzel."

Since she all but shoved it into his mouth, he had little choice but to take a bite. But he didn't have to like it.

"Where's the mustard?"

"Get your own." She crossed to the piano and sat. "Ready to work?"

"I've been working." What else was there to do, when you couldn't sleep? "What have you been doing?"

"Shopping."

"Figures."

"And before you start hammering me, I happened to

have finished the lyrics to 'You're Not Here.'" Pleased to be able to put him in his place, she opened her brief-case and pulled them out. "I polished them up before the shops opened."

He muttered something, but joined her on the bench. In spite of himself, his mood began to lift as he read them. He should have known they'd be perfect.

Still, there was no use indulging her vanity. "They're not too bad."

She rolled her eyes. "Thank you, Richard Rodgers."

His mouth quirked. "You're welcome, Stephen Sond-heim."

Now that he looked at her, really looked, his gaze narrowed. "What did you do to your hair?"

Instinctively she reached up to pat it. "I pulled it back and put it up. It gets in the way."

"I like it in the way." To prove it, he started yank-ing out pins.

"Stop it." Flustered, she batted at his hands. He sim-ply caught her wrists, bracketing them with one hand while he used the other to pull her careful hairdo apart.

By the time the damage was to his liking, he was laughing and she was swearing at him. "There," he de-cided. "Much better."

"Now you're a fashion consultant."

"You look cute when it sort of sproings all over the place."

She blew it out of her face. "Sproings. Thanks." Now her eyes gleamed. "Maybe I'll do some rearranging on yours."

She made her dive, but he was quicker. It had always been a disappointment to her that she couldn't quite outmaneuver him. He just wrestled her backward until she was breathless and giggling.

It took her a moment to realize he wasn't smiling anymore, but was staring at her. Staring with a sharp, focused intensity that had her pulse stuttering and her throat going dry. Her legs had gotten tangled with his, so that she was all but sitting on his lap.

A tug, a sweet, gradual pull, stretched from her heart down to her center.

"Nick."

"We're wasting time." He let his hands fall away, untangled himself. He just had to get on the right track, he was sure of it, and he'd stop having these sudden, voracious cravings for her. "We'll run through the number you just finished, see how it plays."

Patience, she reminded herself, and wiped her damp palms on her trousers. "Fine. Whenever you're ready."

After a rocky start, the work smoothed out. Both of them became focused on the music, so that they could sit hip to hip as collaborators, as friends.

One hour passed into two, and two into three, and more. At one point, Rio brought up some leftovers from the party, and stayed awhile to listen, with a smile on his wide face.

They nibbled at food, polished, argued over small points and nearly always agreed on the big ones.

Nearly.

"It should be romantic."

"Comedic," Nick disagreed.

"It's their wedding night."

"Exactly." He took time out for a cigarette, secretly pleased that he was cutting down on his tobacco intake daily. "They've rushed headlong into marriage. They've known each other three days."

"They're in love."

"They don't know what they are." Thoughtfully, he took a slow drag, setting the scene in his head. "They've just rushed off to a JP for a ridiculous ceremony, now they're in a broken-down hotel room, wondering what they've gotten into. And what the hell they're going to do about it."

"That may be, but it's still their wedding night. You're writing a dirge."

He only grinned. "Ever really listened to the Wedding March, Fred?" To prove his point, he crushed the cigarette out and began to play it.

Freddie had to admit it was solemn, serious, and a little scary. "Okay, you've got a point. Play it again and let me think."

She got up to pace, letting Nick's music run through her. And she watched him, and wondered.

What was it about him that pulled her so? His looks? Perhaps that had been true years ago, when a young girl first saw those restless green eyes. But she looked deeper now.

His manner? That made her smile. Hardly that. However kind and loving Nick could be, he could be equally brusque and careless of feelings. Not that he meant to hurt others' feelings, she thought. He simply forgot about them.

It was his heart, she decided, that had always called to hers, and always would.

But what if she had met him only yesterday? What

if they had come together as strangers and she had simply, irrevocably lost that heart to him?

Would she be frightened, unsure? Excited?

"Who is this man," she murmured, "who calls me his wife? It takes more than a gold ring to change a girl's life."

She wrinkled her nose when Nick glanced back. "Needs to be sharper," she said.

Thinking, she took another turn around the room. "Till death do us part? That's a deal with no heart. Love, honor and cherish, from now till I perish?"

He turned and grinned. "I like it. Marriage and death. Quite a pair."

"I can do better. Who is this man, waiting outside the door? What's he want me to be? A wife, a lover, a whore? He's going to see me naked. There's no way I can fake it…"

She stopped, laughed, rubbed the back of her neck. "I'm getting punchy."

"It's the right theme," he told her. "Panic."

"Maybe…maybe." She walked back to him. "What if we started out the way you have it, slow, funereal— a cello-and-organ thing. Then we pick up the tempo, faster, then faster. Panic building."

"With a key change."

"Good. Try here." To demonstrate, she leaned over his shoulder, putting her hands over his on the keys.

"Yeah, I got the picture." He wished to God her breasts weren't pressing into his back. "You're crowding me, Fred."

The strain in his voice alerted her. "Am I? Sorry." But she wasn't, not a bit. She eased back a little, listening to him work. "I think we've got it." Gently she laid her hands on his shoulders and began to rub. "You're tight."

His fingers fumbled, infuriated him. "You're still crowding me."

"I know."

Her hair brushed his cheek, and that damned perfume she wore shot straight to his loins. Intending on snarling at her, he turned his head—his first mistake—and ended up staring into those wide gray eyes.

"Am I making you nervous, Nicholas?" she murmured, as she slid onto the stool beside him.

The simple truth came out before he could stop it. "You're making me crazy."

"Good." She leaned forward, and pressed a soft, lascivious kiss with just a hint of tongue full on his lips before he could evade. "You've been making me crazy for years. It's about time I had a turn."

His breath was backing up in his lungs. He thought he understood exactly how a man feels when he goes down for the third time. Choking, floundering. And fighting a losing battle with fate.

His voice hardened in defense. "This isn't a game, Fred, and you don't know the rules."

She slid her hands up his forearms, rested them on his shoulders, then moved in slowly, until her mouth was nearly on his. "I imagine you could teach me."

He was holding on to control by a thread, a slippery, frayed thread that kept dancing out of his hands. "If you knew what I'd like to teach you, you'd run, and run fast, all the way home to Daddy."

That statement had pride kicking in. Her chin shot up, and her eyes dared him. "Try me."

It was insane, he knew it was insane, to drag her against him, to plunder that teasing, tormenting mouth with his. He told himself he'd wanted to frighten her, to make her leap up and race for the door, for her own good.

But it was a lie.

When her body quivered against his, then strained, then melted, that thin thread snapped and sent him tumbling.

"Damn it. Damn both of us." He dragged her off the stool, caught her up in his arms in a gesture every woman dreams of. "You're not walking away this time."

Her breath might have come in shallow gasps, but she met his eyes levelly. "I'm not the one that's been walking away, Nick. And you're not going to get me to run, either."

"Then God help you. God help us both."

His mouth was on hers again, wild and free, as he whirled her into the bedroom.

The sheets were in tangles on the unmade bed, a testament to his restless night. The late-afternoon sun beat on the windows so that the light was harsh and unforgiving. Another time, he might have given some thought to ambience, to the romantic trappings she might have hoped for.

But now he simply fell with her onto the bed, and plundered.

His hands were already dragging at her blouse, and his lips were everywhere. She didn't protest the speed, or the urgency, but met it, beat for beat. After waiting for him for so long, it seemed right to hurry. Perhaps there was a small seed of panic lodged inside her. The fear that she would fumble when it counted most.

Would there be pain? she wondered. Humiliation?

Then his mouth was hot on hers again, and the seed died, withered by the heat, before it had the chance to grow.

She'd never imagined it could be like this. So violent and intense a need. So exciting. All her fantasies, her long-held dreams and quiet hopes, paled against the brilliance of reality.

He couldn't get enough of her. It seemed as if he'd waited all his life for this one moment. She was a banquet of flavors, tart, sweet, tangy, and he a starving man.

Her skin was ivory-pale, with a fire just underneath that seduced and enraptured. Each small movement she made, as fluid as the dance they'd shared the night before, aroused him beyond belief.

Part of his brain understood that she was innocent. He knew she was small, delicate. He could feel that fragile skin, those subtle curves, under his hands. So without even realizing it, he slowed his pace. And began to savor.

There was sweetness in her. The shape of her mouth, the curve of her shoulder. Gently he skimmed his lips down her throat, calling on patience now to allow her to adjust to each new level of pleasure. So he played her with care, with skill. Adding notes and small flourishes, letting them linger, sustain. And as he felt each response shiver through her, saw it mirrored on her face, he found there was no need to hurry after all.

She couldn't keep her eyes open. They were too heavy. Odd, how light the rest of her felt. Like thin, fragile glass. And he stroked and cupped her in those wonderful artist's hands, as if he knew she might break.

Then his mouth moved down, circling, teasing, then capturing, her breast. The pleasure arrowed into her and quivered there.

To touch him, she thought hazily. At last to touch him. To feel that wiry strength, those muscles covered by taut skin. Murmuring her approval, she ran her hands over him freely, delighted with each new discovery.

Those soft, testing caresses had the blood pounding in his head. When his mouth came back to hers again, he demanded just a little more—just a little deeper, a little longer.

He thought she looked like a princess under glass, with her eyes closed, her skin glowing and her hair like a sunburst over his pillow.

But she was trembling beneath him, her lips were full and swollen from his patient, relentless assault, and her breath was quickening. Focused on her, only her, he eased her gently toward the next level.

When he cupped her, she was hot and wet and irresistible.

Her eyes flew open at the new intimacy. And the pressure, the unbearable pressure that seemed to press outward through her body, threatening to shatter her, promising to overwhelm. Even as she shook her head in denial, she arched against him.

He took her flying toward the first peak so that she cried out, shocked, staggered by the impact. Her nails bit heedlessly into his back in response to the violence that gripped her, held her helpless. And made her crave.

Then the tension spurted out of her, leaving her limp. She thought she heard him groan, felt him shudder even as she shuddered. But he was taking her high again, so quickly, so skillfully, that she could only cling and let him lead.

His hands were balled into fists as he eased himself into her, slowly, so slowly that sweat sprang to his skin and his body seemed to scream out for release.

He knew he would hurt her. Damage her. Invade her.

But she opened for him fluidly, as if she'd been waiting all along.

He would burn in hell for what he'd done. Nick cursed himself over and over, but he couldn't find the strength to move. He was still sprawled over her, still inside her, trying to recover from the climax of his life.

He'd had no right to take her. Less to find any pleasure in it.

He wished she would say something, anything, so that he would have some clue as to how to handle the situation. But she only lay there, limply, with one hand resting lightly on his back.

His responsibility, he reminded himself. And it was time to face the music.

As gently as possible, he shifted, rolled off her. She made some sound, vaguely feline, as he moved, then simply curled to him.

He would certainly burn in hell, he thought, for wanting her all over again.

"There's nothing I can do to make up for this."

"Nothing," she said with a sigh, and rested her hand on the old scar above his heart.

He stared fiercely at a spot on the ceiling. "Can I get you something? Brandy, maybe?"

"Brandy?" Puzzled, she drummed up enough energy to move her head and look at him. "I haven't been in an accident or been caught in an avalanche. Why would I need brandy?"

"For the…shock," he supposed. "Water, then," he said, disgusted with himself. "Something."

The lovely pink mists were clearing from her brain. Clearing enough that she could see the regret and self-condemnation in his eyes. "You're not going to tell me you're sorry this happened."

"Damned right I'm sorry, for whatever good it does. I should never have touched you. Never have let things get this far. I knew it was your first time."

Pride wobbled. "How?"

He finally shot her a look. "Let's just say it was obvious."

"I see." Perhaps, after such stunning pleasure, there could be humiliation. "Was I inadequate?"

"In—" He let out a breath, then a curse. The woman had turned him inside out, now she wanted to know if she was inadequate. "No, you weren't inadequate. You were amazing."

"I was?" Her lips began to curve. "Amazing?"

He recognized that smug tone and wondered how, at such a time, it could amuse him. "That's not the point."

"I think it's a good one, though." Understanding, and sorry for the torment she heard in his voice, she shifted until she could look down at his face. "I always knew you'd be my first, Nicholas. I always wanted you to be."

He wondered why the thrill that sent through him didn't shame him. "I took advantage—"

She cut him off with a delighted laugh. "No way. Maybe you want to delude yourself that you ravished the virgin, Nicholas, but I seduced you, and I worked damned hard at it."

"I'm trying to take responsibility here," he said patiently. "You're making it tough."

"You made me happy," she murmured, and lowered her mouth lightly to his. "I hope we made each other happy. Why should knowing that make you sad?"

It didn't seem to make much sense, but he found himself smiling at her. "You're supposed to be weepy and trembling and shocked."

"Oh." She pursed her lips. "Well, maybe if we take it from the top—so to speak—I'll get it right the next time."

Later, he left her in his bed and went down to the bar for his shift. For the first time in years, he caught himself watching the clock. Though he drew drafts and mixed drinks with the ease of experience, he nearly snarled at the few customers who lingered through last call.

The minute the last one was out the door, he locked up. He gave the bar no more than a cursory cleanup before rushing back upstairs.

She was sleeping, her head nestled in his pillow, her arm thrown out over the space where he would soon be. He found himself grinning, delighted just to watch her, to listen to the slow, even sound of her breathing, the little catch in it when she shifted in sleep and rustled the sheet.

Then an idea began to form in his brain that had him grinning and unbuttoning his shirt.

He left his clothes in a heap on the floor, then eased down at the edge of the bed. He tugged the sheet aside and picked up her foot.

Freddie drifted awake on a tingle of pleasure. It seemed to creep along her skin, seep into her blood. She heard herself sigh with it, a lovely dream. Then she shot fully awake and into a sitting position when Nick scraped his teeth along her instep.

"Nick?" Disoriented, pulse pumping, she pushed the hair out of her eyes and blinked at the shadow at the bottom of the bed. "What are you doing?"

"Waking you up."

His eyes, well adjusted to the dark, gleamed like a cat's. A wolf's. He found it endearing, arousing, that when she discovered she had no sheet to cover herself, she crossed an arm over her breasts and looked flustered.

"Too late," he murmured. "I've already seen you naked."

Feeling foolish, she lowered her arm. A little.

"I had this interesting fantasy, about nibbling on your toes and working my way up. I'm indulging myself."

"Oh." The idea had heat rushing through her. "Come to bed."

"Eventually."

"I want to…" She trailed off, sliding bonelessly back down as his tongue did amazing and wicked things to her ankle.

"I figured since you seduced me—" he progressed, inch by devastating inch, up her calf "—it was only right that I return the favor."

Who would have thought, she wondered, that the back of a knee could be so wonderfully sensitive? "Well…" Her voice was weak. "Fair's fair."

When Freddie let herself into her apartment the next morning, she was singing. Not only was she in love, she thought, but Nick LeBeck was her lover. And she was his.

She did three quick pirouettes across her living room, buried her face in the tiny white blooms of the violet he'd given her, then spun away again.

Everything in her life was suddenly and absolutely perfect.

She would have deserted her beautiful new apartment and moved into the pigsty he lived in in an instant, bag and baggage. But she could easily imagine Nick's face if she brought up the idea.

Total shock, she acknowledged. And a good dose of fear.

Well, there was no need to rush, she reminded herself. Not now.

But if he didn't make a move before too much longer, she would have to take the initiative herself. And propose.

Still, at the moment, she was more than content. All she wanted was a shower—the one she'd taken with Nick that morning didn't count—and a change of clothes. She was due back at Nick's in an hour.

They still had a score to finish.

She was just stepping, dripping, out of the shower when her buzzer sounded.

"Coming, coming, coming." Tugging on a robe as she ran, she rushed to the intercom. "Yes?"

"Fred, open up."

The sound of his voice still had the power to thrill her. "Nick, you've got to stop following me."

"Ha-ha. Now open up. I wouldn't have had to run all the way over here if you'd answered your phone."

"I was in the shower." She pressed the buzzer to admit him, then undid her locks before dashing back to the bathroom. She managed to tuck her hair into a towel, and slather on some moisturizer before he walked in.

"Don't *ever* leave your door unlocked like that."

Always the sweet-talker, she thought. "You were on your way up."

"Ever," he repeated, then eyed her. "Didn't you just take a shower an hour ago?"

She tilted her head, then shoved the towel back into place as it tipped. "I put that more in the class of water games than grooming. What are you, the water police?"

Distracted, he reached out to toy with her lapel. "What do you call this thing?"

She glanced down at her short plum-colored silk robe. "A robe. What do you call it?"

"An invitation, but we haven't got time. Get packed."

Her brows shot up. "I'm leaving?"

"We're leaving. Maddy O'Hurley called five minutes after you left. She wants us to come to her house for a few days up at the Hamptons. In the Hamptons. Whatever."

Since the towel refused to stay in place, Freddie pulled it off. "Now?"

"That's the idea. Her weekend home's there, and she's got the family with her." Idly he reached out and tugged one of her wet curls. "She thought it would be an opportunity for us to work together, and have a little R and R while we're at it."

"Sounds like a plan."

"So hurry up, will you?" Impatience was shimmering around him now. "I've got to get back and do my own packing, rent a car and arrange for someone to take over my shift at the bar."

"Okay, go get busy. I'll be ready when you are."

"You wouldn't want to put any money on it, would you? Holy hell!" He'd backed into the bedroom as he spoke, and now stood gaping. "What is that?"

"A bed," she told him, stepping forward to run a loving hand over the curved footboard. "My bed. Fabulous, isn't it?"

He grinned. "Arabian Nights or Sleeping Beauty. I can't decide which."

"Something in between." She arched a brow. "It's bigger than yours."

"It would make three of mine." He fingered the lace of the spread. He would have banked on her choosing lace. Slowly, he turned his head, looked back at her with a gleam in his eyes, and lust in his heart. "So, Fred, just how fast can you pack?"

"Fast enough," she promised, and leaped onto the bed with him.

Chapter Nine

Freddie didn't see why she couldn't drive. The snappy convertible Nick had rented for the trip was a pleasure, and she enjoyed having the wind rush through her hair, the blast of the radio. But she'd have preferred being behind the wheel.

"How come you get to drive?" she demanded.

"Because I've driven with you, Fred. You poke."

"I do not poke. I simply obey the law."

"Poke." Enjoying himself, he increased the pressure on the gas pedal. There was nothing like driving full-out with Ray Charles pumping out of the stereo. "If you were driving, we wouldn't get there until next week."

"You've already managed to get one ticket," she reminded him primly.

Ten miles out of the city, Nick thought in disgust, and he'd been busted. "Traffic cops have no sense of adventure." But Nick did, and proved it by taking a turn fast. "This baby handles," he murmured. "Okay, navigator, check when our next turn's coming. I think we're almost on it."

Freddie glanced down at the directions, snickered. "You passed it, hotshot, about a half a mile back."

"No problem." He zipped the car into a tight U-turn that had Freddie caught between a scream and laughter.

"The general population can sleep easy, knowing you live in Manhattan and don't own a car. Make a left," she instructed. "And slow down. I'd like to get there in one piece."

He eased back—a little—and scanned the big, rambling houses they passed. Lots of lawn, he mused, lots of glass. Lots of money.

Big rooms, he imagined, filled with Oriental rugs and pricey antiques. Or glossy floors and stunning modern furnishings. Swimming pools with sparkling water and cushy lounge chairs set around them.

Though, of course, those would be sheltered by trimmed shrubbery and grand old trees.

Just the sort of neighborhood he would have been barred from a decade or so before. Now, he was here by invitation.

"It's that one." Freddie leaned forward. "The cedar with the weeping cherries in the front. Oh, aren't they beautiful?"

The blossoms were just past their peak, already littering the ground with fragile pink petals, but they did make a show. Nick couldn't claim to know a lot about horticulture, but he thought the scent tickling his senses was lilac.

When he turned into the sloping driveway, he was rewarded by the sight of a majestic bush loaded with lavender-hued spikes.

"Not bad for a weekend getaway," he murmured, studying the multileveled structure of glass and wood. "It must have twenty rooms."

"Probably. I wonder if—" Freddie broke off as a horde of children raced around from the far side of the house. Though of varying sizes and shapes, they appeared as a mass.

Until a slim, dark-haired boy took another child out with a flying tackle that was likely to jar internal organs.

Taking the cue, the rest of them piled on, shouting and wrestling.

"I see Maddy meant it literally when she told you the family would be here. The whole family, from the looks of it," Freddie observed. "That's Maddy's oldest boy trying to murder one of Trace's kids. I think."

She smiled as a pixie-size girl with wild red curls and an unidentifiable smear on her cheek spotted them, and waved.

"Mom!" the girl shouted. "Hey, Mom, company." As an afterthought, she gave the cousin she held in a headlock one last jab in the ribs, then scrambled up and raced to the car.

"Hi, I'm Julia. Remember me?"

"Of course I do." After she'd climbed out of the car, Freddie gave Maddy's youngest daughter a welcoming kiss. "Nick, this is Julia Valentine. I won't try to sort the others out for you quite yet."

"Hi, Julia." She had the look of her mother, he

thought. If Maddy O'Hurley really looked like the woman he'd seen on stage and on billboards. "You've got quite a war going on."

"Hi." Julia beamed a smile at him. "We like to fight. We're Irish."

Nick had to grin. "That accounts for it."

"There's a lot of us, 'cause most everybody had twins. Trace had *two* sets of twins. But Aunt Chantel had triplets." She wrinkled her nose. "All boys. Come in. I'll take you inside."

Being female, if only seven, Julia focused on Nick. "I'm going to be a dancer on Broadway. Like Mom. You can write my music."

"Thanks."

As Julia opened the door, they were greeted by a small, towheaded boy with a maniacal gleam in his eye and a croaking frog in his hands.

"Put Chauncy back, Aaron," Julia ordered, with the perfect disdain of older sibling for younger. "He doesn't scare anybody."

"He will when he gets teeth," Aaron said darkly, and scrambled out.

"That's my little brother. He's a pain."

Before anyone could comment, a red-haired rocket fired down the stairs. She was wearing ragged cutoff shorts, no shoes and an oversize, faded T-shirt that claimed she loved New York.

Maddy O'Hurley, Broadway's baby, made her entrance with style.

"Aaron, you little beast. Where are you? Didn't I tell you to keep this lizard in the aquarium?"

Spotting her visitors, she screeched to a halt, holding a very annoyed-looking silvery reptile by the middle.

"Oh." She blew the hair out of her eyes. "So much for elegant entrances. Freddie." She started to leap forward for a hug, remembered, and held the lizard out to her daughter.

"Julia, do me a favor and put this thing back where it belongs." That disposed of, she caught Freddie in a hard embrace. "It's so good to see you. I'm glad you could come."

"So am I."

"And you're Nick." With an arm still around Freddie's shoulders, she held out a hand. "It's great to meet you, at last. I've admired your work for a long time."

Nick knew he was staring, and didn't care. She did look like the woman he'd seen on the stage, on billboards. Porcelain skin, expressive face. And despite being the mother of four, a dancer's gracefully athletic build.

"My first Broadway show," he said. "Ten, eleven years ago. You were headlining. I've never seen anything like you before, or since."

"Well." Maddy decided a handshake wasn't enough, and kissed him instead. "I'm going to like you. Let's go see who else is around. We can take your stuff upstairs later."

The house wandered and was full of light, from wide glass doors, bow windows, skylights. There were occasional obstacles—toy trucks, a baseball mitt, someone's disreputable sneakers. Those touches of home melded easily with the elegance of the architecture.

In a spacious sun room, decked with exotic flowers and lacy ferns, a Hollywood legend lounged.

Chantel O'Hurley had her feet up, and her eyes closed. Nearby stood a man whose tough build and stance shouted *cop* to Nick's well-schooled brain.

"Brent's holding his own," Quinn Doran said, watching the children through the glass. "He may be the runt of our litter, angel, but he's game."

"Monsters," Chantel murmured, but there was a mother's indulgence in the word. "Why, if I was going to have triplets, couldn't they have been nice, well-mannered little girls?"

"They'd have bored you to death. Besides, who showed them how to use a slingshot?"

She smiled to herself. Of course, she had. Her boys, she thought. Hers. After years of longing, being afraid to hope, she'd netted three at one time.

Lazily she held out a hand, the way a woman does when she knows it will always be taken. "Come over here, Quinn, before someone finds us."

"Too late," Maddy announced. "Company. Nick, my sister Chantel, doing her Cleopatra impression, and her husband, Quinn Doran."

"Freddie." Chantel shifted fluidly to kiss Freddie's cheek, but her gaze lifted to Nick. "What excellent taste you have, darling."

"I think so."

Now Nick wasn't just staring. He was goggling. The blonde goddess aimed her sizzling blue eyes at him and smiled. Every nerve ending in his body went on full alert.

"You're writing the score for Maddy's new musical.

From what I'm told, you've enough talent to make her sound professional."

Maddy simply sniffed. "She's just jealous because I have two Tonys and she only has one measly Oscar." Satisfied, Maddy signaled. "Come on, we'll see who else we can find."

"Just a minute," Freddie murmured as she and Nick passed out of the room through the doorway. She dabbed lightly at the corner of his mouth.

"What is it?"

"Oh, nothing. Just a little drool."

"Funny." But he didn't resist one last look over his shoulder at the vision lounging on the floral chaise. "She's even better in person."

"Pull yourself together, Nicholas. I'd hate to have Quinn kill you in your sleep. Rumor is he'd know how to do it, quickly and quietly." Before he could comment, Freddie let out a shout. "Trace!"

While Nick watched, narrow-eyed, she launched herself into the well-muscled arms of a tawny man with a boxer's build.

"Freddie." Trace kissed her lavishly. "How's my pretty girl?"

"I'm fine." Slinging an arm around Trace's neck, she beamed back at Nick. "Trace O'Hurley, Nick LeBeck."

"Nice to meet you."

Though he was friendly enough, his eyes skimmed over Nick in a way that shouted *cop* again. Odd, Nick mused, he'd thought the guy was a musician. He'd even admired his work. But a cop's eyes were a cop's eyes.

"Most everybody else is in the kitchen," Trace continued. "Abby's cooking."

"Thank God," Maddy put in. "She's the only one we can trust. Are you hungry?"

"Well, I—"

"You must be hungry." She linked an arm through Nick's and barreled on, before he could finish the thought. "I'm always frantic to eat after a trip."

She led the way down a zigzagging hall. Nick noted that Trace didn't bother to set Freddie back on her feet, but carried her along, like some kind of white knight with a damsel.

The noise reached them first, and then Maddy swung open a door.

The kitchen was huge, but so crowded with bodies and motion that it seemed cozy. Only the blonde woman stirring something at the stove appeared at rest.

A scrawny man with thinning hair was whirling a middle-aged woman around the room. Their steps meshed almost magically, and they miraculously avoided—through some internal radar, Nick supposed—collisions with chairs, counters and onlookers.

"Then when we went into the last number," Frank announced as he spun Molly in three tight circles, "we brought the house down."

With impressive grace, he whipped his wife into the arms of the man leaning against the kitchen counter, then picked himself up a redhead.

"Molly knows I've got two left feet." Dylan Crosby chuckled and passed his mother-in-law to his oldest son. "Here, Ben, dance with your grandmother before I damage her."

Spotting Trace, Frank grinned widely. "I've got your wife, Tracey! The girl would have a career on the boards if she'd just give up science." He dipped Gillian fluidly, then spun her back. "Hi, there, Freddie girl."

Seamlessly Trace passed Freddie to Frank, so that she was caught up in surprisingly ropey arms and became part of the dance. "You dance, boy?" he shouted at Nick.

"Actually, I—"

"Dad, let them catch their breath." Chuckling, Abby turned from the stove and moved to Nick. "Welcome to bedlam. I'm Abby Crosby."

"You were an O'Hurley first," her father reminded her.

"Abby O'Hurley Crosby," she corrected. "And if you sit down quickly enough, Dad won't be able to make you learn to do a time step."

They were quite a crew, Nick discovered. Before he fell into his own extended family, he hadn't really believed people lived this way. But, like the Stanislaskis, this confusing, noisy group was a family.

And Nick had learned that such families often talked over each other, around each other and very often through each other. They picked petty fights, argued over nothing, chose sides. And united like steel against any outside foe.

He knew he was going to enjoy them, could already tell some of the kids apart by the time the chaotic meal they shared was over. Twins and triplets abounded, just to confuse things. But it was no surprise, he supposed, as Maddy and her sisters were triplets themselves.

After the kitchen was cleared, both Freddie and Nick had agreed willingly with Maddy's suggestion that they run through a few numbers.

It didn't take long for Nick to adjust himself to the household's jumpy rhythm. They even managed to get a little work done between distractions.

"Mom." Maddy's oldest girl came to the music room doorway. "Douglas is being a jerk again." Cassandra's gaze was dark as she complained about her twin.

"He's just a male, honey," Maddy told her. "You have to be patient."

Reed shot his wife a bland look over her opinion of his species. "Cassie, your mother's working, remember?"

"I remember." Cassie heaved a sigh. "No interruptions unless there's blood. Maybe there will be," she muttered before moving off.

"Why don't we take it from the second verse?" Maddy suggested, obviously unconcerned about the possibility of fratricide. "Don't stop now. I've got places to go, people to see."

"From the diaphragm, Maddy," Frank instructed as he strolled in three measures later. "You won't reach the back row that way. It's a nice tune," he told Nick and Freddie. "Had me whistling. In fact, I was thinking about the movements. You know, if we—"

"Dad, we really need to get the vocals before we worry about choreography. Where's Mom?" Maddy asked, before he could tell her why she was wrong.

"Oh, off with some of the kids. Now, I was thinking—"

"Probably went for ice cream." If her mother wasn't around to jerk his chain, Maddy knew, she had to resort to dirty tactics. "I heard a rumor about fudge ripple."

"Oh?" Frank's eyes glazed, then gleamed. "Well,

then I'd better go find them. Can't have the children overindulging. Dentist's bills, you know."

"Sorry." Maddy lifted a hand as her father scooted out. "My family."

"No problem." Nick tried a new chord. "I've got one of my own. Second verse," he said, then lost every thought in his head as Chantel sauntered in.

"Oh, don't mind me," she purred. "I'll just sit over in the corner, quiet as a mouse."

"A rat," Maddy muttered. "Go away, Chantel, you're distracting my composer."

Amused that it was no less than the truth, Chantel shrugged her creamy shoulders. "Well, if you're going to be temperamental, I'll go out by the pool. Maybe some of the kids want to take a dip." She aimed a last melting smile at Nick, and glided away.

"Don't worry." Maddy patted Nick's shoulder as he stared blankly at the keys. "She affects men that way. Testosterone poisoning."

"Second verse, Nick." Freddie helped the reminder along with an elbow to his ribs.

"Right, I was just…thinking."

He made the effort, managed to complete the verse, move into the chorus, but then Abby raced by the music room window, screaming with laughter as she was pursued by her husband with a very large water gun.

"The children," Reed said, and shook his head. "Why don't we consider this a successful day's work and take a break? A swim sounds like a good idea."

"A brilliant one," Maddy agreed.

"You go ahead." Freddie picked up a sheet of music. "I'd like to fiddle with this for a few minutes."

"Come out when you're done, then." Maddy reached for Reed's hand. "If you can face it."

Nick craned his neck to try to get a glimpse of the pool. "Do you think she'll wear a bikini?"

Freddie lifted a brow. "Maddy?"

They both knew who he'd meant, but the alternative wasn't an image a man would sneeze at, either. Seeing that Nick was lost in consideration of numerous bikini-clad O'Hurleys, Freddie laughed.

"Animal."

He ran his tongue over his teeth. "You think Abby's going swimming, too?"

"I think you can get in trouble ogling married women. Now, if you can get your hormones under control, I'd like to run through 'You're Not Here.' Maddy might like to work on it later."

"It's rough yet."

"I know, but the core's there."

True enough, he thought. And it might smooth out the edges if they could work on it with Maddy, face-to-face. "Okay. I was thinking, if we tried it this way…"

Freddie closed her eyes, listened as the first notes drifted out. Nodding to herself, she added her voice to his music.

On the patio, Maddy held up a hand, then laid it on Abby's shoulder. "Listen."

"It's lovely," Abby murmured as her eyes misted. "Sad and lovely. She doesn't hide it very well when she sings. Being in love with him."

"No." Chantel slipped an arm around Abby's waist, so that the three of them stood together. "I guess they'll muddle through it."

"We did." With the music floating over them, Maddy gazed out over the lawn, toward the pool.

There was Dylan, coaching one of Trace's girls in a back flip. And Chantel's triplets, in a heated lap race, with Gillian and Cassie playing referee. Douglas was being the jerk his twin considered him, splashing Trace's other daughter.

Her father sat, eating fudge ripple ice cream with Trace's twin boys on either knee.

Ben and Chris, the boys Abby had raised alone for a time, were tall, handsome young men, arguing about which cassette to put into the portable stereo.

Quinn and Trace sat in the shade, sharing a beer and war stories, while Molly applauded Abby's only daughter, Eva, on her underwater somersaults.

Aaron and Abby's youngest boy searched the grass for anything with more than two legs. Julia turned cartwheels to annoy them.

My family, she thought as she lifted a hand to wave to Reed. *All present and accounted for.*

"I feel good." Maddy drew in a deep breath, threw her face back to the sun. "And I have a strong feeling that those two at the piano are going to help me cop another Tony."

Unable to resist, Chantel slid her gaze toward her sister. "Oh, darling, do you have one already?"

With a rollicking laugh, Chantel ran, with Maddy inches behind.

Late, late at night, when the house was finally quiet, Nick drew Freddie to him, so that her head rested on his shoulder. Since Maddy had been considerate enough to give them adjoining rooms, he'd felt no guilt about sneaking into Freddie's bed.

It was good to simply lie there, with his heartbeat leveling toward normal, and his body sated from the slow, quiet love they'd made. She felt so natural curled up against him, he wondered how he'd ever slept without her.

"Tired?" he asked her.

"Hmm. Relaxed. It's been a terrific day. I loved seeing all of them again, how much the kids have grown. Everything."

"They're quite a group."

"They are that. I think it's great the way they all juggle their schedules so they can have a week or two each year with everyone in the same place. Sometimes they go to Dylan and Abby's farm in Virginia." She sighed sleepily and cuddled closer when his fingers began to stroke along her shoulder. "We visited there once. It's beautiful, all rolling hills, horses grazing. Space."

"You'd need a lot of room with all these kids. Abby has the twin girls, right?"

"No, that's Trace and Gillian. Abby has four—Ben, Chris, Eva and Jed. And she had them one at a time."

"Four." He shuddered.

"You love kids." She shifted, turning her head so that she could study his face. It was beautiful in the splash of moonlight, dreamy and heroic, like something out of an Arthurian legend.

"Sure I do. But it always amazes me that some people can handle so many, want to handle so many."

She was caught up in the way he looked, that cool,

sculpted face, the sea-green eyes. The way it felt to press against him, warm, exciting and right.

"I like big families. I was an only child for a few years. I wasn't lonely, because Dad was always there. But everything just clicked into place when Natasha came into our lives. I wanted a baby sister," she remembered. "But Brandon came first, and that suited me fine."

Nick had been an only child himself. But he'd had no father to be there. "I used to wish for a brother. Then I had Zack." He shrugged. "He went to sea, and I didn't."

Her generous heart ached for the boy he'd been. "It was hard on you, his leaving."

"He did what he had to do. At the time, it seemed like he was leaving me. Just me. I got over it."

The wave of love rolled over her, making her careless with words. "So now you have a brother again, and an enormous family. You never have to be alone, unless you want to. That's why I'd like at least three children myself."

A little warning blip sounded in his brain. He glanced down at her, then focused carefully on the ceiling. "Well."

Succinctly put, Freddie thought, but she didn't allow herself to sigh. It was much too soon to think about children. Their children.

It was a good time, as Nick saw it, to change the subject. "Chantel doesn't look like anyone's mother."

Now Freddie lifted a brow. "Well, she is. And, if you don't mind a little friendly advice, you really should try to keep your tongue from hanging out every time she walks into the room."

He looked at her again, leered. "Jealous?"

She surprised, and insulted, him by bursting into delighted laughter. It rocked her hard enough that she was forced to sit up and try, unsuccessfully, to catch her breath.

Looking down at his scowling face only started her up again.

"You're overdoing it," he complained.

"Jealous." Gasping for air, she pressed a hand to her stomach. "Oh, right, Nicholas. I'm green. No doubt she'd toss Quinn aside in a heartbeat to run off with you. Anyone can see they only tolerate each other. That's why the air starts to sizzle when they're in the same room together."

His pride was injured, a little. "So she's stuck on her husband. Anyway, how do you figure he handles those steamy love scenes she plays on the screen?"

"By knowing she's not playing a scene when she's with him, I imagine." Unable to resist, she brushed her fingers through his hair. "That's what marriage is all about, isn't it? Trust and respect, as well as love and passion?"

Another warning blip. "I suppose," he said, and let it stop there. "Zack's going to drop his teeth when I get back and tell him about meeting her. He's seen some of her movies enough times to recite the dialogue."

"So, you'll gloat."

"Damn right."

Relaxed again, he glanced down at her. She looked so pretty, so...magical, he supposed, in the streams of moonlight that poured through the skylight. Her hair was a mess, the way he liked it best, and her lips were barely curved, as if she were thinking of something that pleased her.

"Not tired, huh?"

More than interested, she walked her fingers up his chest. She had been thinking of something that pleased her. She'd been thinking of him.

"I wondered if you'd get back to that."

"Just building up my strength."

"Good." Laughing, she rolled on top of him. "'Cause you're going to need it."

Chapter Ten

"You're telling me you met Chantel O'Hurley. *The* Chantel O'Hurley."

"That's what I said." It was a big charge for Nick to pull one off on Zack. It was no secret that the blonde goddess was one of "Zack's little fantasies," as Rachel dryly put it. "The same Chantel O'Hurley whose movies you buy on video the minute they hit the stands." He hefted another crate of club soda into the storeroom.

"Wait a minute. Just a minute." Going in behind Nick empty-handed, Zack tugged on his sleeve. "You mean you met her, in the flesh?"

"She's got some terrific flesh, too, let me tell you." It didn't hurt to gloat. "I had dinner with her, a couple of times." Nick made sure it sounded offhand, added a shrug for good measure. "Of course, her sisters aren't chopped liver, either. They're both—"

"Yeah, yeah, we'll talk about her sisters later. You had dinner, I mean, like dinner? With her?" Zack found he had to clear his throat. "Together. With her."

"That's right." Of course, the meal had been shared by an entire household, kids included, but there was no need to mention those small details. "I told you I was going to spend a couple of days with Maddy and Reed."

"I wasn't thinking," Zack muttered. "Didn't put it together. If you really met her, had dinner with her, what's she like?"

Nick turned, pursed his lips in an exaggerated kiss.

"Come on, you're killing me." A victim of his own fantasies, Zack hurried out after Nick. "I mean, how does she look, just hanging around?"

"She filled out her bikini just fine."

"Bikini." Overcome, Zack pressed a hand to his heart. "You saw her in a bikini."

"We took a couple swims together, sure." Actually, he and Freddie had been entertaining her triplets with water polo. But why get technical?

"Swam with her." Zack swallowed hard. "Got...wet."

"Usually do, swimming."

Mindful of his blood pressure, Zack decided to ease back from that particular image. He'd save it for later. "And you talked to her. Had conversations?"

"All the time. She's got a sharp brain. That sort of adds to the appeal, I think. After all, *I'm* not an animal."

"I'm just asking." It was a harmless diversion, Zack thought, for a happily married man who adored and lusted after his own wife. "You really met her." He sighed, lifted a crate of soft drinks.

"I not only met her. I kissed her."

"Get out of town."

"No, you're right, I didn't kiss her."

Zack snorted. "No kidding."

"*She* kissed *me.*" Nick leaned on a dolly of crates, tapping his finger to his lips. "She planted one on me. Right here."

"You're standing there telling me Chantel O'Hurley kissed you—on the mouth."

"Hey, would I lie to you?"

Zack thought about it. "No," he decided. "You wouldn't." Before Nick had a clue of his intention, Zack grabbed him, jerked him forward and kissed him—as Chantel had—full on the mouth.

"Damn it, Zack!" Another flurry of oaths followed as Nick grimaced and rubbed his mouth with the back of his hand. "Are you crazy?"

"Hey, I figure it's as close as I'll ever get." Satisfied, Zack carried in the next case. "A man has his dreams, pal."

"Well, keep your dreams away from me." Nick gave his mouth another swipe for good measure. "Man, what if somebody saw you do that?"

"Just us here, bro. And I do appreciate you coming in to give me a hand so soon after you got back in town."

"Don't mention it. And I mean don't mention it."

"So, how did Freddie like her trip to the rich and famous?"

"She's used to it." Nick scratched his neck as a line of sweat began to dribble. "It's her kind of background."

"I guess you're right. It's hard to tell. She's just Freddie around here."

They finished unloading the cases, and finished off

by having tall glasses of the iced tea Rio had stored in the refrigerator. "Hot for June," Zack commented. "You're going to have to hook the air conditioner up in the apartment."

"Before long."

It seemed a good opening, Zack mused, for something that had been preying on his mind. "I was thinking, with the way your career's moving, and everything…" *Everything* was Freddie, but it didn't seem quite the time to bring that up. "You might not want to stay on here."

"Upstairs?"

"Yeah, that, and here. Working at the bar."

Puzzled, Nick set down his glass. "Are you firing me?"

"Hell, no. The truth is, I don't know what I'd do without you right now. But I was beginning to worry that you're feeling obligated. Bartending wasn't your dream for your future."

"It wasn't yours, either," Nick said quietly.

"That's different," Zack began, then shook his head when he caught Nick's look. "Okay, maybe it wasn't. I had my shot, made my choice. And the fact is, I love this place. It makes me happy now. I don't want either one of us to lose sight of the fact that you've got something else going."

"Still looking out for me?"

"Habit."

Nick's lips curved. "Well, let's put it this way. Sooner or later you're going to have to find yourself another bartender and part-time piano player. But for the present, working the night shift doesn't interfere with my composing. And if the play's a bomb, I need a backup."

"It won't be a bomb."

"You're right, it won't. But let's just let things float the way they are for a while." He glanced at the clock, swore. "Damn, I'm late. I told Freddie we'd start a half hour ago. See you later."

Alone, Zack wandered back into the bar. No, he thought, it wasn't the deck of a ship, and he wasn't at the helm. And Rachel wasn't a blonde movie queen.

He grinned and gulped down the rest of his iced tea. And he was a very, very happy man.

For another change of scenery, Nick had decided it was time they gave Freddie's piano a try. Despite the distractions, the noise and the temptation to spend their time playing, instead of working, while visiting the O'Hurleys, they had managed to buckle down long enough to make some real progress.

Nick's tendency might have been to float on that for a day or two, but Freddie couldn't wait to get back to it.

So they settled in her apartment for the afternoon, putting the finishing touches on act 1's closing chorus number.

"It pops," Nick decided. "It's a good thing we didn't finish this when Frank was around. He'd already be working on the choreography."

"Well, I like it. But I think—"

"Nope, time to stop thinking." He snagged her, pulling her into his arms as he rose.

"Put me down. We haven't even started on the opening for act 2."

"Tomorrow."

"Today," she said, laughing as she tried to wiggle free. "Nick, it's the middle of the day."

"Even better."

"You're the one who always says we have work to do."

"That was when I was trying to avoid doing just what I'm going to do right now." He dropped her onto the bed, from a height designed to make her bounce.

"We haven't finished our quota for the day." When he grinned at her and began to unbutton his shirt, she pushed herself up. "That's not the quota I meant."

"Going to make me seduce you, huh?"

"No." Instantly, she thought better of it. Tilting her head, she gave him a long, considering look. "Well, maybe…if you think you can."

He'd already unbuttoned his shirt. The idea of a challenge put a new spin on the easy pleasure he'd anticipated. She slid her gaze away, then back to him when he sat on the side of the bed.

"Just looking at me isn't very seductive."

"I like looking at you, now and again."

Her brows lowered even as he smiled. "That's very smooth, Mr. Romance."

"You have to remember, you're not really my type— according to an unimpeachable source." He merely caught her around the waist and pinned her when she started to spring off the bed in a huff.

"I'm not interested," she said coolly. "Let me up."

"Oh, you're interested. This little pulse in your throat…" He lowered his lips to it, grazed over. "It's hammering."

"That's annoyance."

"No. When you're really annoyed, you get this line right here." With a fingertip, he traced between her brows, smiling when the line formed. "Yeah, like that." He kissed her forehead, as well, satisfied when it smoothed.

"I don't want you to—" Her words slipped down her throat when his mouth cruised teasingly over hers.

"What?"

"To...mmmm."

"That's what I thought."

How could any man resist that slow melt she did? That quiet purr in the back of her throat when a kiss drew out, long and lazy?

And it was that way he wanted to make love with her now. Lazily, so that his system could absorb every small and subtle change in hers. A touch, and she shifted to him. A murmur, and she sighed out her pleasure.

It seemed there was nothing he could do, or ask, that she didn't respond to willingly.

He wanted to see her, all of her, while the sun streamed in the windows and the spurting sound of midday traffic rattled against the panes. His hands were patient and slow as he flicked open the buttons of her blouse, one by one.

Beneath, she wore clinging cotton, with a fuss of lace at the bodice. He traced a fingertip along the edge, dipped under it, while her breath caught and quickened.

It was always this way, she thought hazily. Effortless and lovely. Whether they came together frantic or teasing, quiet or with shock waves, it was always so simple.

So perfect.

She could feel her own arousal blossom inside her,

like a rose, petal by petal. It was just that easy to open for him, to bring him to her so that their mouths met and their bodies fit.

The faint breeze from the open windows drifted over her, as lazily as his hands, so that her skin was warmed, then cooled, warmed, then cooled. Dreamlike, the sounds from the street below, the streak of sunlight, all faded into a background, a kind of stage set for the fantasy.

She arched to help him when he drew the cotton away, when he loosened her trousers. In concert, she slipped his open shirt from his shoulders, letting her hands glide along the wiry strength of his arms.

She wasn't sure when the pace began to quicken, or the heat to build. The underlying urgency seeped into her like a drug, then shot straight through her bloodstream.

Now she was clinging to him, moving frantically beneath him.

"I want you now, Nick." The explosive spurt of energy had her rolling over the bed, struggling, even as he struggled to possess.

The pleasure was suddenly dark, dangerous, careening from misty dreams into a rage of greed. The hunger stabbed, so sharp, so voracious, that both of them shuddered.

No one had ever given him this.

"Now," she said, gasping out the word as she mounted him, crying out in triumph as she enclosed him.

Stunned by the lightning change in her, staggered by the force of his own appetite, he gripped her hips hard and let her ride him.

* * *

It was later when he thought of it. Later when they lay together, exhausted as children after a romp. He'd never given her the slightest hint of romance. None of the pretty trappings—the candles and wine, the quiet corners and long walks.

She deserved better. Then again, he'd tried to convince her right from the start that she deserved better than what he had to offer. Since she hadn't listened, the least he could do was give her something back.

He wished he could give her everything.

Where had that thought come from? he wondered, and let out a quiet, careful breath. Emotion whirled through him, buffeting him like a storm, he thought. Warming him like light. Calling to him like music.

When had he gone from enjoying her to craving her? To loving her?

Back up, back up, he warned himself. It would be disastrous for both of them if he let whatever was bubbling inside him get out of control.

Better to move on the initial idea, he decided, and pretend he'd never thought any further than giving her a special evening.

"You've got a lot of fancy duds in that closet."

It amused her that he would have taken notice of her wardrobe. "Even in West Virginia, we manage to shop, and wear something other than overalls occasionally."

"Don't get testy—I like West Virginia."

It was where she'd grown up, in a big house, with antique furniture and a live-in housekeeper. And he'd grown up over a bar, and on the streets, with a stepfather who liked his whiskey just a little too much. *Best to remember that, LeBeck, before you get any crazy* ideas.

"I was just thinking you could pick out something jazzy, and we'd go out."

"Go out?" Intrigued now, she sat up, blinking sleepily. "Where?"

"Wherever you like." He wished she wouldn't look at him as if he'd just conked her on the head with a bat. They'd gone out before. More or less. "I've got some connections, I could get tickets for a show. Not mine," he added before she could speak. "I don't want my own tunes competing inside my head."

She shifted again, foolishly delighted by the idea of a date. "It's kind of late in the day to snag tickets for anything."

"Not if you know who to call." He trailed a finger lightly down her arm in a way that made her want to sigh. She wondered if he knew he touched her just like that now and again, without thinking about it. "We could have a late supper afterward. At that French place you like."

Not just a date, she thought, dazed. A power date. "That would be nice." She wasn't sure how to react, and before she could, he was up and tugging on his clothes.

"Get spruced up, then. I'll go make some calls and meet you at my place. An hour."

He leaned over to give her a quick kiss, then was gone, leaving her staring after him.

Maybe he wasn't Sir Lancelot, she thought with a shake of her head. But, tarnished armor or not, he had his moments.

* * *

It took her every bit of an hour to pull herself together. She hoped Nick would consider the off-the-shoulder plum silk jazzy enough. She did wish they'd arranged to meet at her place, however, when she narrowly avoided getting her heel caught in the sidewalk.

She breezed past Rio with a wave, and a quick pirouette when he whistled at her. A quick knock at the top of the stairs, and she walked in.

"This time you're late," she called out.

"Had to help Zack with a delivery."

"Oh." She nibbled on her lip. "I didn't even think about your shift."

"It's my night off." He strolled out of the bedroom, still tugging on his jacket. He gave her a long look and a nod of approval. "Very nice."

"You've got such a way with compliments, Nicholas."

"How about this?" He grabbed her, lifted her to her toes and kissed her until her head threatened to blow off her shoulders.

"Okay," she said when she could breathe again. "That's pretty good."

Abruptly nervous, he let her go again. "We've got enough time before curtain for a drink. Why don't I play your personal bartender?"

"Why don't you, then? A little white wine—bartender's choice."

"I think I've got something you'll approve of." He'd snagged the bottle of Cristal from Zack's stash.

"Well." Freddie's eyes widened. "This is certainly turning into a night to remember."

"That's the idea." He decided he liked surprising her.

Doing something out of the ordinary for her. He popped the cork with an expert's flourish, and poured it into two flutes he'd commandeered from the bar. "To family ties," he said, and touched his glass to hers.

She smiled as she lifted her own glass. "What kind of a mood are you in? I can't quite pin it down."

That stirring was going on again, needs and longings tangling together in his stomach, just around his heart. "I'm not so sure myself."

And the fact that he wasn't didn't make him as nervous as it should have. Because he was happy. Incredibly, completely happy. And he only got happier every time he looked at her.

He was certain he could go on looking at her for a lifetime.

And when that unexpected curve rounded like a fastball in his stomach, his breath caught and wheezed out slowly.

"Are you all right?" Solicitous, Freddie thumped him on the back.

"I'm fine." *Love. A lifetime.* "I'm...fine."

Now it was her turn for nerves, so she took a small step back. "Why are you looking at me like that?"

"Like what?"

"Like you've never seen me before."

"I don't know." But that was a lie. He hadn't seen her before, not through the eyes of a man flustered by love.

He had, he realized, done the most amazing thing. He'd fallen head over heels in love with his closest friend.

"Let's sit down." He needed to.

"All right." Cautious, she settled on the sofa. "Nick,

if you're not feeling well, we can take a rain check on the show."

"No, I'm fine. Didn't I say I was fine?"

"You don't look fine. You're pale."

He supposed he was. He'd never been in love before. He'd danced around it, toyed with it, teased the edges of it. But now it looked as though he'd fallen headfirst into the pit.

With Fred.

He was just getting used to the fact that he could make love to her. But being in love was going to take a lot more thought. It was a pity he couldn't wrap his brain around anything that wasn't sheer emotion.

"Fred...things have moved pretty fast between us."

She lifted a brow. "Do you call a decade-plus fast?"

He waved that away. "You know what I mean. I was thinking that I might be hemming you in, between the work and everything else."

The shiver that ran up her spine was icy and full of fear. But her voice was calm enough. "Are you trying to let me down gently, Nick?"

"No." The very thought appalled him. Losing her now—it was unthinkable. "No," he repeated, and gripped her hand so tightly she jolted. "I want you, Fred. I'm just beginning to realize how much."

Her heart turned slowly over in her breast, and swelled. "You have me, Nick," she said quietly. "You always have."

"Things have changed." He wasn't sure how to phrase it, not in a way that would satisfy them both. But he had to let her know something of what he was feeling. "Not just because we've gone to bed together.

Not just because what I have with you there is different, stronger than anything I've ever had before."

"Nick." Swamped with love, she lifted their joined hands to her cheek. "You've never said anything like that to me before. I never thought you would."

Neither had he. Now, all at once, he was afraid he wouldn't get the words, the right ones, out fast enough. "I don't want to push things, Fred, for either of us, but I think you should know—"

The thud of heavy footsteps on the stairs had Nick swearing and Freddie cursing fate. Neither of them moved when Rio opened the door, looking grim.

"Nick, you'd better come downstairs."

A hard fist of fear rammed into his throat. "Zack?"

"No, it's not Zack." Rio glanced apologetically at Fred. "But you'd better come."

"Stay here," Nick ordered Fred, but Rio counter-manded him.

"No, she should come, too. She can help." As Nick passed him, Rio clamped a hand on his shoulder. "It's Marla."

Nick hesitated, looked back at Freddie. There was no way to keep her out of it. "How bad is she?"

Rio only shook his head and waited for Nick and Freddie to precede him.

The name meant nothing to Freddie. She thought it might be some old flame who'd stormed into the bar in a jealous or, worse, drunken rage.

But the tableau that greeted her in the kitchen wiped that image out of her head.

The woman was dark, thin and had probably been pretty once, before trouble and fatigue dug lines into her face. But it was hard to tell much of anything, because of the bruises.

She sat absolutely still, a young, hollow-eyed boy gripping the back of her chair, a smaller girl sitting at her feet, with her thumb in her mouth. In the woman's lap, a baby of perhaps three months cried thinly.

Nick wanted to shout at her, to rage. He wanted to shake this woman, this girl he had once known and nearly loved, until she lost that empty, hopelessly beaten look. Instead, he went to her, gently lifted her chin. The first tear spilled over onto her cheek as she looked at him.

"I'm sorry, Nick. I'm so sorry. I didn't know where else to go."

"You never have to be sorry for coming here. Hey, Carlo." He tried a smile on the boy. Though he laid a hand very lightly on the boy's shoulders, Carlo still stiffened and drew inward.

Big hands, the child knew, were never to be trusted.

"And who's this big girl. Is this Jenny?" Nick picked the girl up, set her on his hip. With her thumb still in her mouth, she rested her head on his shoulder.

"Rio, why don't you grill up some burgers for the kids?"

"Already on."

"Jenny, want to sit on the counter and watch Rio cook?" When she nodded, Nick settled her there. It only took a look to have Carlo creeping over, and out of the way.

"I don't want to be any trouble to you, Nick," Marla began, rousing herself to rock the baby.

"Want some coffee?" Without waiting for her assent, he walked to the pot. "The baby's hungry, Marla."

"I know." With what seemed like a terrible effort, she shifted, reaching for the paper bag at her feet. "I can't nurse her. I'm dried up. But I got some formula."

"Why don't I fix it?" With a bolstering smile, Freddie held out her arms. "Is it all right if I hold her?"

"Sure. She's a good baby, really. It's just that…" She trailed off and began to weep without a sound.

"You're going to be all right now," Freddie murmured as she slipped the baby out of Marla's hold. "Everything's going to be all right now."

"I'm so tired," Marla managed. "It's just that I'm tired."

"Don't." The order was quick and harsh as Nick set the coffee in front of her. "He knocked you around again, didn't he?"

"Nick." Freddie sent a warning glance at the children.

"You think they don't know what's going on?" But he lowered his voice. "Welcome to reality." He sat beside Marla, took her hands and set them around the cup. "Are you going to call the cops this time?"

"I can't, Nick." His snort of disgust seemed to shrink her. "I don't know what he'd do if I did. He gets crazy, Nick. You know how crazy Reece gets when he's drinking."

"Yeah." Absently he rubbed a hand over his chest. He had the scars to remind him. "You told me you were going to leave him, Marla."

"I did. I swear I did. I wouldn't lie to you, Nick. I've been in that apartment you helped me get before the baby was born. I wouldn't take him back, not after the last time."

The last time, Nick recalled, Reece had knocked her down the stairs. She'd been six months pregnant.

"So how'd you get the split lip, the black eye?"

She looked wearily down at her coffee, lifted it mechanically to drink. Rio set a plate in front of her.

"I'm going to take the kids inside to eat."

"Thanks." She swiped at another tear. "You two be good, you hear? Don't make any trouble for Mr. Rio." She nearly smiled as Freddie sat down to feed the baby. "Her name's Dorothy—like in *The Wizard of Oz*. The kids picked it out."

"She's a lovely baby."

"Good as gold. Hardly ever cries, and sleeps right through the night."

Nick interrupted her, patience straining. "Marla."

In response, Marla took one shuddering breath. "He's been calling me, wanting to see the kids, he said."

"He doesn't give a damn about those kids."

"I know it." Marla's lip trembled, but she managed to firm it. "So do they. But he sounded so sad on the phone, and he came by once and bought them ice cream. So I hoped, maybe, this time…"

She trailed off, knowing that hope was more than foolish. It was deadly.

"I wasn't going to take him back, or anything. It just seemed as if I should let him see the kids now and again. As long as I was right there to make sure he didn't drink or get mean. But tonight, when he came around, I was in the bedroom with the baby, and Jenny let him in. It was too late, Nick. I could see right away he was drunk, and I told him to get out. But it was too late."

"Okay. Take it slow." He rose to wrap some ice for her swollen lip.

But she couldn't take it slow, not now that it was pouring out of her. Like poison she'd been forced to drink. "He just started smashing things and screaming. I got the kids into the bedroom, got them away so he wouldn't hurt them. That only made him madder. So he went after me. I don't know how I got away from him, but I got into the bedroom with the kids, locked the doors. We got out by the fire escape. And we ran."

"Nick," Freddie murmured. "Take the baby." She rose, passing him the dozing infant. "Let's clean you up," she said briskly, and ran water on a cloth. With gentle hands, she smoothed it over Marla's face.

As she tried to soothe the bruises, clean the cuts, she talked softly. About Marla's children, caring for a new baby. When she felt Marla begin to respond, she sat again, took the woman's hand.

"There are places you can go. Safe places, for you and your children."

"She needs to call the cops." However fierce his voice, Nick cradled the sleeping baby tenderly on his shoulder.

"I don't disagree with him." Freddie picked up the wrapped ice, offered it to Marla. "But I think I understand being afraid. They'd help you at a women's shelter. Help your children."

"Nick said I should go before, but I thought it was better to handle it on my own."

"Everybody needs help sometime."

Marla closed her eyes and tried to find some tattered rag of courage. "I can't let him hurt my kids, not anymore. I'll go if you say it's right to, Nick."

It was more than he'd expected. He knew he owed part of the win to Freddie's quiet support. "Fred, upstairs, in the drawer under the kitchen phone, there's a number. It says *Karen* over it. Call it, ask for her and explain the situation."

"All right." As she walked away, she heard Marla begin weeping again.

She'd hardly completed the arrangements when Nick came in.

He took a moment to study her—the slim woman in the elegant dress. "I'm going to dump on you, Fred. I'm sorry our whole evening is shot, and it's not over yet."

"It's all right, but I don't know what you mean. Oh, Nick, that poor woman."

His eyes only darkened. "I want you to take her and the kids to the shelter. They're not too happy having a man come around there in the first place. Small wonder. I'd feel better knowing you were with her, saw her settled in."

"Of course, I'd be glad to. I'll come back as soon as—"

"No, go home." The order snapped out. "Just go home when you're done. I've got something to do."

"But, Nick…"

"I don't have time to argue with you." He strode out, slamming the door behind him.

He had something to do, all right. And Nick figured it would take very little legwork to locate his old gang captain. Reece still ran in the same circles they had when they were teenagers. He still haunted the same streets and the same dingy rooms where a few dollars would buy anyone of any age drugs, liquor or a woman.

He found Reece huddled over a whiskey in a dive less than fifteen blocks from Lower the Boom.

The atmosphere wasn't designed to draw a discerning clientele. The air was choked with smoke and grease, the floors littered with butts and peanut shells. And the drinks were as cheap as the single hooker at the end of the bar, staring glassily into her gin.

"Reece."

He'd put on weight over the years. Not the muscle of maturity, but the heaviness of the drunk. He turned slowly on the stool, the sneer already in his eyes before it twisted his mouth.

"Well, well, if it isn't the upstanding LeBeck. Bring my friend a gentleman's drink, Gus, and hit me again. Put 'em both on his tab." The thought struck Reece so funny, he nearly rolled off the stool.

"Save it," Nick told the bartender.

"Too good to have a drink with an old friend, Le-Beck?"

"I don't drink with people who shoot me, Reece."

"Hey, I wasn't aiming at you." Reece tossed back his whiskey and slapped the empty glass on the bar as a signal for another. "And I served my time, remember? Five years, three months, ten days." He took out a crumpled pack of cigarettes and pulled one out with his teeth. "You're not still sore I hooked up with Marla, are you? She always had a thing for me, old buddy. Hell,

I was doing her back when you thought she was your one and only."

"A smart man learns to forget about yesterday, Reece. But you were never too smart. But it's Marla we're going to deal with. Here and now."

"My old lady's my business. So are the brats."

"Was, maybe." The wolf was in Nick's eyes now, as he leaned closer to Reece. And the wolf had fangs. "You're not going near them again. Ever. If you do, I'll have to kill you." It was said quietly, with a casualness that made the bartender check for his Louisville Slugger, just under the cash register.

Reece only snorted. He remembered Nick from the old days. He'd never had the guts to follow through on a threat with any real meat. "The bitch come running to you again?"

"I guess you figure she got off easy—a split lip, a few bruises. She didn't have to go into the hospital this time."

"A man's got a right to show his wife who's in charge." Brooding over it, Reece swirled his liquor. "She's always asking for it. She knew I didn't want that last brat. Hell, the first one ain't even mine, but I took her on, didn't I? Her and that damn little bastard. So don't you come around telling me I can't teach my own woman what's what."

"I'm not going to tell you. I'm going to show you." Nick rose. "Stand up, Reece."

Reece's reddened eyes began to gleam at the possibility of spilling blood. "Going to take me on, bro?"

"Stand up," Nick repeated. Seeing the bartender make a move out of the corner of his eye, Nick reached for his wallet. He pulled out bills, tossed them on the bar. "That should cover the damages."

The bartender scooped up the money, counted it and nodded. "I got no problem with that."

"You've been needing the high-and-mighty beat out of you, LeBeck." Reece slid off his stool, crouched. "I'm just the one to do it."

It wasn't pretty. At first blood, the hooker deserted her gin and crept out the door. The few others who inhabited the bar stood back and prepared to enjoy.

Drunk he might be, but the whiskey only made Reece more vicious. His meaty fist caught Nick at the temple, shooting jagged lights behind his eyes, and then another fist plowed into his gut. Nick doubled over, but as he came up again, his fist drove hard into Reece's jaw.

He followed through methodically, cold-bloodedly, concentrating on the face. Blood spurted out of Reece's nose as he tumbled back against a table. Wood splintered under his weight.

With a roar of outrage, Reece charged Nick like a bull, head lowered, fists pumping. Nick evaded the first rush, landed a fresh blow. But in the narrow confines of the bar, there was little room to maneuver. Outweighed, he went down hard under Reece's lunge.

He felt Reece's hands around his neck, choking off air. Ears buzzing, he pried at them, sucking in air and gathering strength to drive a short-armed punch. Reece's teeth tore his knuckles, but he continued to hammer, almost blindly now, until the stranglehold loosened.

There was an animal in him. It eyed Reece ferally, wrestled the bigger man over the floor. There was the sound of smashed glass, the sting of it pricking and biting at skin. Hate made him strong and wild and merciless.

He could smell the blood, and taste it. Even as Reece's eyes rolled back and his body sagged, Nick continued to pound.

"Enough." It took the bartenders and two others to drag Nick up. "I don't want nobody beat to death in my place. You done what you come to do, now get out."

Nick staggered once, wiped the blood off his mouth with the back of his hand. "You tell him when he comes to, if he raises his hand to a woman again, I'll finish the job."

Chapter Eleven

Freddie considered going home after delivering Marla and her family to the abuse shelter. God knew she was drained, as emotionally and physically exhausted as she'd ever been in her life. She'd gone no farther than the entryway of the shelter herself, but she'd been relieved that it didn't seem like an institution.

Nick had done his research well.

There'd been children's drawings tacked up on the wall, and a small sitting room off to the side, where the furnishings were spare, but comforting.

The woman who greeted them had seemed weary, yet her voice had been soothing. Freddie's last glimpse of Marla had been watching her being led up the stairs, with the woman murmuring to her.

So she didn't go home, despite Nick's insistence, but went back to wait for him.

"Figured you'd be back," Rio said when she stepped into the kitchen. "You got Marla and the kids away okay?"

"Yes." She sat, let her shoulders sag against the chair. "It seemed like a good place. A safe one. I don't think she even realized where she was. She just followed along, like the children."

"You've done all you can do." Rio set a plate in front of her. "You eat something now. No arguments."

"I won't give you any." Freddie picked up her fork and dipped into the chicken and rice. "Who is she, Rio?"

"A girl Nick used to know. He didn't see much of her for a while, after he got settled down here with Zack and Rachel. When she got pregnant with the boy, Carlo, her family booted her out."

"Heartless," Freddie murmured. "How can people be so heartless? What about the father?"

"Wasn't interested, I guess." Rio shrugged, caught himself and turned to her. "The boy isn't Nick's."

"You don't have to tell me that, Rio. He'd never have left them to fend for themselves." Setting her fork aside, she rubbed her hands over her face. "This man, the one who did this to her. He isn't Carlo's father?"

"Nope. She didn't get tangled up with him until about four years ago. He was doing time when the boy was born."

"A real prince."

"Oh, Reece is a royal bastard, all right." Rather than the coffee she'd expected, Rio set a cup of herbal tea in front of her. "I guess the name isn't ringing any bells with you."

"No." She frowned, sniffed the tea. Chamomile. It almost made her smile. "Should it?"

"He nearly killed Nick." Rio's dark eyes went grim. "A little over ten years ago, he broke in here with a couple of his Cobra slime buddies, juiced up and armed to the teeth. Figured on robbing the place. He was going to shoot Zack."

The blood drained out of her face. "I remember. Oh, God, I remember. Nick pushed Zack away."

"And took the bullet," Rio finished. "I thought we were going to lose him. But he's tough. Nick's always been tough."

Very slowly, as if her bones might shatter from the movement, she rose. "Where is he, Rio? Where's Nick?"

He could have lied to her. But he chose to tell her straight. "I gotta figure he went looking for Reece. And I gotta figure he found him."

She had to fight to get the air out of her lungs, to pull it back again. "We have to tell Zack. We have to—"

"Zack's out looking right now. So's Alex." He set a huge and gentle hand on her shoulder. "There's nothing to do but wait, honey."

So she waited, eventually going upstairs to pace Nick's apartment. Every sound on the street, from the bar below, had her holding her breath. Every wail of a siren had her trembling.

He's tough. Nick's always been tough.

She didn't give a damn how tough he was. She wanted him home, whole and safe.

Tormented by the images rolling through her brain,

she kept her hands busy. She began to tidy the room, then to dust, then to scrub.

When she heard footsteps on the stairs, she was down on her knees washing the kitchen floor. She scrambled up, raced toward the door.

"Nick. Oh, God, Nick." All but shattered with relief, she threw her arms around him.

He let her cling for a moment, though the pressure had the aches in his body singing. When he found the energy, he peeled her away.

"I told you to go home, Fred."

"I don't care what you told me, I was— Oh, you're hurt."

Her eyes went huge as relief jerked into shock. His face was bloody, one eye nearly swollen shut. His clothes were torn and stained with more blood.

"You need to go to the hospital."

"I don't need a damn hospital." He lurched away from her, gave in to his weakened legs and sank into a chair. And prayed to any god that might be listening that he wouldn't be sick. "Don't start on me. I've already been through this with Zack. Go away, Fred."

Instead, she said nothing, walked into the bathroom and gathered up every first aid supply she could find. Armed with antiseptic, bandages and dampened cloths, she came back to find him sitting as she'd left him.

He took one look, would have scowled if his face hadn't felt as though it would crack open at the movement. "I don't want you nursing me."

"Just be quiet." Her hands were a great deal steadier than her voice when she dabbed at the blood. "I imagine I'm supposed to ask how the other guy looks. You had no business going after him."

"It is my business. She meant something to me once." He hissed, then settled, when she pressed the cool cloth to his swollen eye. "And even if I'd never seen her before, any man who knocks a woman around, tosses kids around, deserves a beating."

"I don't disagree with the sentiment," she murmured. "Only with your method. This is going to sting some."

More than some, he discovered, and swore ripely. "I wish to hell you'd go away."

"Well, I'm not." She tried to comfort herself with the thought that the cuts on his face weren't deep enough for stitches. Then she saw his hands. White-hot fury erupted inside her. "Your hands. Look what you've done to your hands. You idiot. Why can't you use your head instead of your glands?"

She could have wept with grief. His beautiful, talented artist's hands were torn and bleeding. Dark, ugly bruises had already formed, marring them, swelling them.

"They ran into his teeth a few times."

"Isn't that just like you? Isn't that just typical? Nicholas LeBeck's first rule of order. If you can't solve the problem, batter it down." She was wrapping cold cloths around his hands as she spoke. "You could have called Alex."

"Don't hassle me, Fred. You heard her. She isn't going to file charges."

"She's in the shelter, isn't she? She and the children?"

"And he just walks? Not this time." Experimentally Nick flexed his fingers. They were stiff and painful, but it was the torso Freddie had yet to see that was agonizing. "He tried to kill my brother once, and did less than six years for it. The system says he's rehabilitated, so he gets out and starts hammering on Marla. So, screw the system. My way works."

"He nearly killed you before." Her lips trembled as she rose. "He could have done it again."

"He didn't, did he? Now back off."

He dragged himself to his feet and limped into the kitchen. He managed to locate the aspirin quickly enough, but with his injured hands he found he couldn't pry off the lid.

Her own movements stiff from a different kind of pain, Freddie took the bottle from him. She opened it, set it on the counter for him, then poured him a glass of water.

"How far, Nick?" Her voice was controlled, too controlled. "How far do you want me to back off?"

He didn't turn, only stayed where he was, his hands braced on the counter, his body throbbing with a thousand hurts. "I can't talk about this now. If you want to do something for me, you'll go home. Leave me alone. I don't want you here."

"Fine. I should have remembered, the lone wolf prefers to slink off on his own to lick his wounds. I'll just leave you to it." As wounded as he now, she spun on her heel. She was halfway across the living room when Zack came in. Brushing an impatient hand over her damp cheek, she kept walking. "Be careful," she warned. "I think he's rabid."

"Freddie—" But she was moving fast, her heels already clattering on the stairs. Zack marched into the kitchen. "What did you do to make her cry?"

Nick only swore and dumped four aspirin on the counter. "Stay out of it." He winced as the water he swallowed burned his abused throat. "I'm not in the mood for company, Zack."

"You aren't getting company. Sit down, damn it, before you keel over."

That, at least, seemed like a reasonable idea. With careful movements, Nick lowered himself into a kitchen chair.

Standing back, Zack took a survey. Freddie had done some good, he supposed, but his brother still looked like the wrong end of a punching bag. "Did a number on you, didn't he?"

"He got in a few."

"Let's get what's left of that shirt off and take a look."

"I'm not much interested in seeing." But he couldn't drum up the energy to object as Zack began removing the torn material. Zack's slow, vicious oaths confirmed the worst. "That bad?"

"He got in more than a few. Damn it, Nick, did you have to go looking for trouble?"

"I didn't have to look far, did I?" He looked up then, met Zack's eyes coolly. "It was a long time coming. Now it's done."

Zack merely nodded, began to open cupboards. "Is that liniment still around here?"

"Someplace. Under the sink, maybe."

Once he located it, Zack came back to finish what Freddie had started. "You're going to feel worse tomorrow."

"Thanks, just what I needed to hear. Got a cigarette on you? I lost mine."

Zack took one out, lighted it, placed it between Nick's swollen fingers. "I hope he looks as bad as you."

"Oh, worse." The sour grin hurt. "A lot worse."

"That's something, then. I'm surprised you had the energy left to fight with Freddie."

"I wasn't fighting with her. I just wanted her out. She shouldn't have been around this. Any of it."

"Maybe not. But I'd say she can handle herself."

She was sure of it. It seemed clear after two days that Nick was determined to avoid her. Still licking his wounds, she imagined as she walked back from Nick's apartment yet again.

Still, she hadn't expected the locked door. Her only consolation was that Zack had assured her Nick was healing.

She was tired of worrying about him, she decided. And since work wasn't an option until his hands were better, she'd found other ways to fill her time.

She'd enjoyed taking toys over to the shelter more than anything else. Marla still seemed nervous and strained, but the children were already relaxing. The highlight of Freddie's day had been when the solemn-eyed Carlo smiled at her.

Time, she thought. They only needed time and care.

And what, she wondered, did Nick need? Apparently he didn't think it was Freddie Kimball. At least not at the moment. So she'd give him the distance he wanted right now. But sooner or later, she was going to get sick of standing back and waiting.

Love shouldn't be so complicated. She brooded, looking down at the sidewalk. It all had seemed so simple when she left home to come to New York. Everything she'd planned and hoped for had slowly come to be.

Now, because of some blip from his past, it was falling apart on her.

With a sigh, she opened the security door of her building. The sudden jab from behind had her stumbling. She would have fallen, if an arm hadn't come around her, jerking her back.

"Keep walking," the voice ordered. "And keep quiet. Feel that? It's a knife. You don't want me to use it."

Calm, she ordered herself. *Don't panic.* It was broad daylight. "There's money in my purse. You can have it."

"We'll talk about that. Open the elevator."

The idea of being closed in with him, with the knife, had her struggling. She bit back a cry when the blade pierced.

"Open the elevator or I'll cut you open right here."

Fighting to keep part of her mind cool, free from the panic that had her body shuddering, she obeyed. Once they were inside and moving, he shifted her, and she could see him.

The thin face, the glazed eyes. It was the man Nick had called Jack.

"You're a friend of Nick's." She managed to keep her voice level. "I was with him the night he gave you money. If you need more, I'll give it to you."

"You're going to give me more than money." Jack lifted the knife, running the flat of the blade over her cheek. "It's a matter of honor, baby."

"I don't understand." Her wild hope of rushing out ahead of him, screaming, when they reached her floor was smashed when he twisted her arm behind her back.

"Not a peep," he warned. "We're going to walk straight to your place, and I know which one it is. I've seen your light come on. Then you're going to unlock the door, and we'll go inside."

"Nick wouldn't want you to hurt me."

"Too bad about Nick. You pull anything out of that bag but your keys, baby, and you'll be bleeding."

She took out her keys, her movements deliberately sluggish. If she stalled long enough, someone would see. Someone would help.

"Move it." Jack yanked her arm higher, so that she whimpered when the last lock opened. He was sweating when he shoved her inside. "Now then, it's just you and me." He pushed her into a chair. "Nick shouldn't have gone after Reece. Once a Cobra, always a Cobra."

"Reece put you up to this." A new glimmer of hope tormented her. "Jack, you don't have to do this. Reece is just using you."

"Reece is my friend, my bro." His eyes began to glitter. "Lots of the others, they forgot what it was like in the old days. But not Reece. He keeps the faith."

Freddie might have felt pity—for surely the man *was* pitiful—if fear hadn't had its bony fingers clutched around her throat. "If you hurt me, you'll be the one to pay. Not Reece."

"Let me worry about that. Now take off your clothes."

Now the fear screamed in her eyes. Seeing it, Jack grinned. He was flying now. He'd used the money Reece had given him for a nice solid hit of coke.

"We might as well have a little fun first. Strip, baby. I've got a feeling Nick's picked himself another winner."

He would rape her, she thought, and as hideous as that was, she felt she could survive it. But she knew, in some cold corner of her brain, that he couldn't intend for her to survive. He would rape her, then he would kill her.

And he'd enjoy both.

"Please, don't hurt me." She let the terror ring in her voice. She would use it, to fight back.

"You do what I tell you, you're nice to me, nobody has to get hurt." He licked his lips. "Stand up and strip, or I'll have to start cutting you."

"Don't hurt me," she said again. She braced herself. She would need momentum, and a great deal of luck. If she didn't follow through, she wouldn't get a second chance. "I'll do anything you want. Anything."

"I'll bet. Now get up."

He gestured with the knife, grinned. She let her eyes slide toward the bedroom door, go wide. Jack was just stupid enough to follow her glance.

And she sprang.

The keys he hadn't bothered to take away from her were clamped between her tensed knuckles like daggers. Without a moment's hesitation or regret, she went straight for the eyes.

He screamed. She'd never heard a man scream like that, high and wild. With one hand clutching his eyes, he swung out blindly with the knife. With every ounce of her strength, Freddie struck him over the head with her prized art deco lamp.

The blade clattered to the floor as he crumpled.

Breathing hard, she stared down at him for several seconds. As if in a dream, she walked to the phone.

"Uncle Alex? I need help."

She didn't faint. She'd been terrified she would, but she managed to follow Alex's instructions and leave the apartment. She was outside, swaying at the curb, when the first cop car pulled up.

Alex was thirty seconds behind it.

"You're all right? You're okay?" His arms came around her hard, and the veteran cop buried his face in her hair. "Did he hurt you, baby?"

"No. I don't think. I'm dizzy."

"Sit down, honey. Sit right here." He helped her to the building's stoop. "Head between the knees, that's a girl. Take it slow. Get upstairs," he ordered the uniform. "Get that lowlife out of my niece's apartment. Book him on assault with a deadly, attempted rape. I want the knife measured. If it's over the legal limit, slap him with that, too."

"He said Reece told him to," Freddie said dully.

"Don't worry, we'll take care of it. I'll take you to the hospital. I won't leave you alone there."

"I don't need the hospital." She lifted her head again. The wavering dizziness had passed, but she still felt oddly light-headed. "He cut me a little, I think." Testing, she brushed her fingers over her side, stared dumbly at the smear of red.

In a flash, she was cradled in Alex's arms. "The hospital," he said again.

"No, please. It's not deep. It stings some, but it's almost stopped bleeding. It just needs a bandage."

At the moment, he would have indulged her in anything. Still holding her, he looked up as two of his men carried out a limp and bleeding Jack.

He couldn't take her back upstairs, Alex thought. And he wanted her away from the perp and the crime scene. "Okay, honey. The bar's close by. I'll take you there, and we'll have a look. If I don't like what I see, your next stop's the ER."

"All right." She let her head rest on his shoulder, discovering that all she really wanted to do was sleep.

"This creep needs a doctor," one of the officers told Alex. "He needs one bad."

"Take him in, then, see that he gets fixed up. I want him in shape when I lock him in a cell."

All Freddie remembered from the short trip to Lower the Boom was Alex's soothing voice. It reminded her of being rocked when she was a child and had the chicken pox.

"I didn't let him hurt me, Uncle Alex."

"No, baby, you took care of yourself. Just let me take over now."

Rio let out a shout of alarm when Alex pushed the kitchen door open. "Sit her down, sit her down right here! Who hurt my baby? Who hurt my sweetheart? Nick!" He bellowed it out before either Alex or Freddie could answer. "Get your ass down here, now!" Moving like a bulldozer, he shoved open the door between the kitchen and bar. "Muldoon, I want the good brandy in here, pronto. You just sit easy, honey," he continued, in a voice that had lowered by several decibels and softened like silk.

"I'm all right, Rio. Really." Already soothed, she turned her face into the wide paw he'd laid on her cheek.

"Looks shallow." Alex sighed with relief. He'd expected the worst when he tugged Freddie's blouse out of her waistband to examine the cut. "We'll patch it up for you."

"What the hell's all the commotion?" Obviously annoyed by the shouted orders, Zack came in, holding a bottle of brandy. One look at Freddie had him darting over and crouching in a position that mirrored Alex's.

"Give her room to breathe." Though shaken, Rio snatched the bottle and poured a hefty two fingers into a tumbler. "Drink it down, Freddie."

She would have obeyed, if Nick hadn't come stalking down the stairs. His injured eye was more open than closed now, but a rainbow of bruises and scrapes had bloomed on his face.

When he saw her, the blood drained out of it.

"What happened? Were you in an accident? Fred, are you hurt?"

He snagged her free hand, nearly crushing the bones.

"Give her a minute," Alex ordered. "Drink the brandy, Freddie. Take your time."

"I'm okay." But the jolt of brandy as it hit her system cleared the fog and brought on the trembling.

"Is that blood?" Nick stared, horrified, at the stain on her blouse. "For God's sake, she's bleeding!"

"We're taking care of it." Alex took the antiseptic Rio passed him and dabbed it on gently. "I want you to come home with me, Freddie. When you're feeling better, I'll take your statement."

"I can do it now. I'd rather do it now."

"What do you mean, statement? Were you mugged?" Nick demanded. "Damn it, Fred, how many times have I told you to be careful?"

"She wasn't mugged," Alex snapped out. "Your old pal, Jack, wasn't interested in her money."

As soon as he said it, Alex cursed himself. Pale as death, Nick dropped Freddie's hand and stepped back.

"Jack." As fury filled the hole shock had dug, his eyes turned to hard green slits. "Where is he?"

"In custody. What's left of him." Alex stroked a hand over Freddie's hair before taking out a pad and switching into cop mode. "Tell me from the beginning, everything you remember."

"I was going home," she began.

Nick listened, the bitterness burning his throat, the impotence dragging at him.

Because of him, he thought. All of it. Every instant of terror she'd been through was because of him. His need to settle debts, to handle a problem his own way, could have cost Freddie her life.

"Then I called you," Freddie finished. "I could see he was bleeding. His eyes…" She had to swallow.

"Let me worry about him," Alex told her. "I want you to put it all out of your mind for now. I'll go back to your place and get some things for you. You can stay with us as long as you like."

"I appreciate that, really I do, but I need to go home." She took his hand before he could protest. "I can't be afraid to stay in my own home, Uncle Alex. He'd have gotten to me then, don't you see? I'm not going to let that happen."

"Hardhead." He kissed her gently. "If you change

your mind, it only takes a call." He rose then, skimmed his gaze over the three men standing by. "You look after her. I've got to get to the station and take care of this." In a mute apology, he laid a hand on Nick's shoulder. "Make her rest. She'll listen to you."

When he left, Freddie felt three pairs of eyes on her. "I'm not going to fall apart," she said.

Nick said nothing, simply stepped to her, scooped her off the chair.

"I don't need to be carried."

"Shut up. Just shut up. I'm taking her upstairs. She's going to lie down."

"I can lie down at home."

Ignoring her, he started up the steps.

"You don't want me here." As if to complete the day, tears began to burn her eyes. "Do you think I can't tell you don't want me here?"

"Here's where you're staying." He carried her inside and straight to the bedroom. "You're going to rest until you get some color back in your face."

"I don't want to be with you."

A quick stab in the heart made him wince. But he couldn't blame her. "I'm going to leave you alone, don't worry." His voice was quiet, distant. "Don't fight me on this, Fred. Please."

He drew the rumpled spread over her, neglecting to take off her shoes. "I'm going downstairs." He stepped back, dipped his hands into his pockets. "Do you want anything? Want me to call Rachel, or one of the others?"

"No." She closed her eyes. Now that she was horizontal, she wasn't sure she could get up again. "I don't want anything."

"Try to sleep for a while." He moved over to tug down the shades on the window and plunged the room into soft gloom. "If you need anything, just call down to the bar."

She kept her eyes closed, wishing him to leave, willing it. Even when she heard the soft click of the door closing, she didn't open them again.

He hadn't offered the loving compassion Alex had, or the quick, forceful concern of Rio or Zack. Oh, he'd been angry, she thought, furious over what had nearly happened to her. She knew he cared. They'd been part of each other's lives for too long for him not to.

But he hadn't held her. Not the way she so desperately needed him to.

She wondered if he ever would.

Chapter Twelve

She hadn't thought she would sleep. It was a surprise to wake, groggy, in the half-light. Freddie wasn't certain if it was a good sign or a bad one that she remembered immediately, and clearly, what had happened and why she was alone in Nick's bed in the middle of the day.

Wincing a little as the bandage on her side pulled, she tossed the spread aside. She was unbearably thirsty, and the brandy she was only vaguely aware of having drunk had left her a head full of cotton.

At the kitchen sink, she filled a glass of water to the rim and drank it down. It was odd, and annoying, she thought, that she still felt so shaky. Then it occurred to her that she hadn't eaten since breakfast, and that hadn't been much of a meal.

Without much hope, she opened Nick's refrigerator. She had her choice of a chocolate bar and an apple.

Feeling greedy, she took them both. She was just pouring another glass of water when Nick walked in, carrying a tray.

His heart lurched when he saw her standing there, so small, so delicate. And when he thought of what might have happened to her. In defense, he kept his voice neutral. "So, you're up."

"It appears so," she said in the same distant tone.

"Rio thought you might want to eat something." He set the tray on the table. "Your color's back."

"I'm fine."

"Like hell."

"I said I'm fine. You're the one who looks like he's been run over by a truck."

"I went looking for my fight," he said evenly. "You didn't. And we both know where the blame lands in this one."

"With Reece."

In an attempt to keep himself calm, he took out a cigarette. "Reece wouldn't have given two damns about you if it hadn't been for me. And if you hadn't been with me in the first place, Jack wouldn't have known where to find you."

She took a moment to steady herself. "So, I see, this is all about you. In your twisted logic, I was threatened with a knife and rape because I happened to have walked down the street with you one night."

The knife. Rape. It froze his blood. "There's nothing twisted about the logic. Reece wanted to pay me back, and he found a way. I can't do much about it, since Alex—"

"Do?" she repeated, interrupting him. "What would

you do, Nick? Go beat Reece up again, pound on Jack? Is that supposed to make it come out right?"

"No. I can't make it come out right." And that was the worst of it. There was nothing he could do to change what had happened. Only what might happen next. He crushed out the cigarette he found he didn't want. "You and I have to settle things, though. I think you should work at home, when you feel up to it again. I can send the music over to you."

"What exactly does that mean?"

"Just what I said. I figure we've reached a point in the score where it's just as constructive, maybe more so, to work separately." His eyes shot to hers, hardened. "And I don't want you around here."

"I see." She needed her pride now, every ounce of it. "I take that to mean on both professional and personal levels."

"That's the idea. I'm sorry."

"Are you? Isn't that nice. 'Sorry, Fred, time's up.'" She whirled on him. "I've loved you all my life."

"I love you, too, and this is the best for both of us."

"I love you, too," she repeated, snagging him by the shirtfront. "How dare you come back with some watered-down pat-on-the-head response when I tell you that!"

Very slowly, very firmly, he pried her fingers from his shirt. "I made a mistake." He'd convinced himself of it. "And now I'm trying to fix it. I understand that you might get emotions confused with sex."

She shocked them both by slapping him, and putting her weight behind it. For a motionless moment, there was only the sound of her unsteady breathing. Then she exploded. "Do you think it was just sex? That what happened between us was just heat and flash? Damn you, it wasn't. You know it wasn't. Maybe it was the only way I could get to you, the only way I could think of. But it mattered, it all mattered. I worked every step of the way to make you see it, see me. I planned it out, step by step, until—"

"Planned?" He cut her off with one searing look. "You planned it? You came to New York, convinced me to work with you, had me take you to bed? And it was all part of some grand scheme?"

She opened her mouth, closed it again. It sounded so cold, so calculated, that way. It hadn't been, hadn't been meant to be. Not when you added love.

"I thought it through," she began.

"Oh, I bet you did." The slip had given him the outlet he needed for his rage and distance. "I bet you figured it all out in that sharp little head of yours. You wanted something, and did whatever it took to get it."

"Yes." She sat down now, weakened by shame. "I wanted you to love me."

"And what's the rest of the plan, Fred? Tricking me into marriage, family, white picket fences?"

"No. I wouldn't trick you."

"You wouldn't think of it that way, but that was the goal, wasn't it?"

"Close enough," she murmured.

"I can see it," he snarled out as he stormed around the kitchen. "Freddie's list of goals. Move to New York. Work with Nick. Sleep with Nick. Marry Nick. Raise a family. The perfect family," he added, in a tone that made her wince. "It would have to be perfect, right? You always want everything neat and tidy. Sorry to disappoint you. Not interested."

"That's clear enough." She started to rise, but he pressed a hand to her shoulder and held her down.

"You think it's that easy? I want you to take a look, a good long one, at what you were fishing for. I'm two steps away from the guy who held a knife on you. I know it. The family knows it—the family you're basing all these half-baked fantasies on. Isn't that the way you saw it, Fred? Like the Stanislaskis?"

"Why wouldn't I?" she tossed back, humiliated that she was close to tears. "Why wouldn't you?"

"Because I've been around, and you haven't. How many people do you think there are out there like them? You're using top-grade for your yardstick."

"There's nothing wrong with that. It works. It can work."

"For them. A few others. Is that what started cooking in your head when we were with the O'Hurleys? Another big, happy family?"

She lifted her chin. "It should prove my point. It can work."

"For them." He slapped his palms on the table, forcing her to stare into his face. "Take another look here. What's happened in the last few days is my world, Fred. Battered women, frightened kids, drunks who brawl in bars. Men who think rape is an entertaining pastime. And you want to start a family on that? You need to be committed."

"You're not responsible for what happened to Marla. Or to me."

"No?" His lip curled. "Look at the thread. I'm the thread. Maybe I've been pulled out of that whole world," he said. "But it only happened because of the family. What do you think they'd say if they knew I've been sleeping with you?"

"Don't be ridiculous. They love you."

"Yeah, they do. And I owe them, plenty. Do you think I'm going to pay them back by shacking up with you over a bar? Do you think I'm crazy enough to think about marriage and kids. Kids, for God's sake, where I come from? I don't even know who my father was. But I know who I am, and I'm not passing it on. I care about you, sure I do—enough to get you the hell out."

"You care," she said slowly, "so you're breaking it off."

"That's exactly right. I was out of my mind to let it get this far, and I nearly—" Now he broke off, remembering how close he'd come, only a few days before, to declaring himself. "What matters is, you worked on me, and I let things get temporarily out of hand. It ends here. For the sake of the family, we'll try to forget any of it happened."

"Forget?"

"All of it. I'm not going to risk hurting you any more, and I sure as hell don't want to hurt the rest of the family. They're all I've got—the only people who ever wanted me or cared about me."

"Poor, poor Nick," she said, with ice. "Poor lost, unwanted Nick. You really think you're the only one who's faced that kind of rejection, or wondered just what lack might have been passed onto him. Well, it's time you learned to live with it. I have."

"You don't know anything about it."

"My mother never wanted me."

"That's bull. Natasha's—"

"Not Mama," she said coldly. "My biological mother."

That stopped him. It was so easy to forget Spence had been married before. "She died when you were a kid, a baby. You don't know how she felt."

"I know exactly." There was no bitterness in her voice. That was what tugged at him. There was no emotion at all. "Dad would have kept it from me. I doubt he has a clue I ever overheard him talking to his sister. Or with Mama. I was nothing more than a mistake she'd made, then decided to forget. She left me when I was an infant, without a second thought. And her blood's in me. That coldness, that callousness. But I've learned to live with it, and to overcome it."

He couldn't imagine her harboring that kind of pain, that kind of doubt. "I'm sorry. I didn't know. No one's ever talked about her." He wished he could have held her then, offered comfort, until her body lost that uncharacteristic rigidness. He didn't dare offer her anything. "But that doesn't change what's here."

"No, it doesn't. You won't let anything change." Freddie was crying now, but the tears were hot, more of anger than of grief. "You knew I was in love with you. And you knew, in the end, I would have made any compromise, any adjustment, to make you happy. But you don't make compromises, Nick LeBeck."

"You're too upset to handle this now. I'm going to get you a cab."

"You're not going to get me a cab." She shoved at him. "You're not going to send me anywhere. I'll go when I'm ready to go, and I can take care of myself. I proved that today, didn't I? I don't need you."

She let the words hang, closed her eyes on them a moment. When she opened them again, they were fierce. "I don't need you. What a concept in my life. I can live without you, Nicholas, so you needn't worry that I'll come around mooning over you. I thought you could love me."

Her breath came out steady, strengthening her. "My mistake. You aren't capable of loving that way. I wanted so pitifully little from you. So pitifully little, I'm ashamed."

He couldn't stop himself from reaching out. "Fred."

"No, damn you, I'll finish this. Not once did you ever tell me you loved me. Not the way a man tells a woman. And not once did you try to show me, except in bed. And that's not enough. Not one soft word. Not one. You couldn't even drum up the effort to pretend and tell me, even once, that you thought I was beautiful. No flowers, no music unless we made it for someone else. No candlelight dinners, except when I arranged them myself. I did all the courting, and that makes me pathetic. I was willing to settle for crumbs from you, and that's exactly what I got."

"It wasn't like that." It appalled him that she should think so. "Of course I think you're beautiful."

"Now who's pathetic?" she snapped back.

"If I didn't think about romance, it was because things got confused so fast." That was a lie, and he knew it. Yet he wondered why he was defending himself, why he felt such panic at the steely, disinterested look she sent him, when he'd been so hell-bent on pushing her away. "I can't give you what you need."

"That's very clear. I'm better off without you. That's very clear, too. So, we'll do just as you suggested. We'll forget it."

He put a hand on her arm as she started to walk out. "Fred, wait a minute."

"Don't touch me," she said, in such a low, furious voice that his fingers dropped. "We'll finish our commitment to the musical. And we'll make polite conversation around the family. Other than that, I don't want to see you."

"You live three damn blocks away," he called after her.

"That can be changed."

"Running home after all?"

She shot one frigid look over her shoulder. "Not on your life."

He thought about getting drunk. It was an easy escape, and would hurt no one but him. But he just couldn't work up any enthusiasm for it.

He got through the night, though he didn't sleep. The music he tried to write in the dawn hours was flat and empty.

He'd done what he needed to do, he told himself. So why was he so miserable?

She'd had no right to attack him. Not after she told him that everything that had happened since she'd come to New York was part of some plot. He was the victim here, and still he'd done his best to protect her in the end.

Imagine him, married, trying to raise kids. He snorted, then dropped into a chair, because the whole picture was suddenly so appealing.

Insane maybe, he mused, but appealing. A family of his own, a woman who loved him. Surely that was insane.

Insane or not, it was hopeless now. The woman who had walked out the day before didn't love him. All she felt for him was disdain.

Saw to that, didn't you, LeBeck? You idiot.

He'd had a shot. It was all so clear, now that it was over. He'd had a chance to love and be loved, to make a life with the only woman who had ever really meant anything to him.

How could he have been so stupid, so blind? It had always been her. If he had good news, she was the first one he wanted to share it with. If he was down, he knew it would only take her voice over the phone to bring him up again.

Friends. He supposed that was what had thrown him all along. They'd been friends. And when he felt more than friendship for her, he'd tried to block it, ignore it, deny it. He'd used every excuse available to hide the real one.

He hadn't believed he deserved her.

Even when their relationship changed, he'd held part of himself back. She'd been right. He'd never given her soft words. He'd never shared the reins of courtship.

Now he'd lost her.

He let his head fall back, closed his eyes. She was better off without him. He was sure of that. Had been sure.

The knock on the door had him springing up. She'd come back, was all he could think.

All the pleasure died from his face when he saw Rachel.

"Well, that's quite a greeting."

"Sorry." Dutifully he pecked her cheek. "I was… Nothing. What you are doing here?"

"Paying you a visit. I don't have to be in court for another couple of hours." She walked over to a chair, sat, gestured to another. "Sit down, Nick. I want to talk to you."

It was her lawyer's voice that put him on guard. "What's the problem?"

"You are, I believe. Sit." When he did, she laid a hand on his. "I love you."

"Yeah, I know. So?"

"I just wanted to get that out of the way, so I can tell you what an absolute jerk you are." The hand that had rested so gently over his balled into a fist and rapped his shoulder. "What a stupid, idiotic, inconsiderate, blind male boob you are."

"What's the deal?" he said between clenched teeth, as she'd squarely hit a spot that was still raw from Reece. He supposed he deserved the pain.

"I stayed with Freddie last night. She didn't want me to, but we ganged up on her."

"Oh." He let out a careful breath. "So how is she?"

"As far as the attack on her, she's holding up. As far as your attack, she's pretty hurt."

"Hold on. I didn't attack her."

"Objection overruled. I pried most of what happened out of her. It's bad enough that you've broken her heart, Nick, but to mess up your own life while you were at it takes real skill."

His defense mechanism clicked in before he could stop it. "Look, we slept together a few times. I realized it was a mistake and put the brakes on."

"Don't insult me, Nick," she said coolly. "Or Freddie. Or yourself."

He let his eyes close with an oath. The hell with it, he thought. The hell with defending himself, with pride, with anything else that blocked the way. "I love her, Rachel. I didn't realize how much, how bad it was, until she walked out the door."

It was hard, but Rachel restrained herself from offering the comfort, the sympathy, that stirred inside her. "Have you bothered to tell her you love her?"

"Not the way she needed. It's one of the things I neglected."

"So I gathered."

"I wasn't prepared for it." He pushed himself up to prowl the room. "She had it all worked out in her head. One of her step-by-steps."

"And you found that insulting," Rachel put in. "Which proves you're a fool. Some more intelligent men might have found being found attractive and desirable by an attractive, desirable woman a compliment."

"It threw me, okay? It all threw me. Everything I was feeling for her hit me like a wall. I didn't know it could be like this."

"So to fix it, you tossed her out."

"She walked."

"Do you want her to keep on walking? She will. And if you dare tell me that you're not good enough, that you haven't got what it takes to make her happy, I'll really hit you next time. There's only part of the boy I got stuck with all those years ago left in you, Nick. And it's the best part."

He wanted to believe it. He'd tried for more than a decade to make it true. "I don't know if I can give her what she wants."

"Then you won't," Rachel snapped back, without sympathy. "And she'll survive. She's cried herself dry, and she's purged most of the rage. The woman I left a little while ago was very controlled, and determined to forget you."

"I want her back." The thought wasn't as frightening as he'd assumed it would be. In fact, it felt incredibly right. "I want it all back."

"Then you'd better get to work, pal." She rose, took him by the shoulders and gave him a quick kiss on the cheek. "My money's on you, LeBeck."

Nick wasn't sure he'd take the bet himself. The odds were long, he decided as he carted his bags toward Freddie's building. It was going to take some pretty fancy footwork to squeeze an entire courtship into one crowded balcony scene.

Nick glanced up to the fifth floor of Freddie's apartment building, and headed for the fire escape.

"And where do you think you're going, LeBeck?"

The beat cop Nick had known half his life strolled up, tapping his baton.

"How's it going, Officer Mooney?"

But the wily veteran eyed Nick's bags suspiciously. "My question was, where are *you* going?"

"I need a break here, Mooney."

"Do you now? Well, why don't you tell me about it?"

"See that window?" Nick pointed, waited until Mooney's eyes lifted and focused. "The woman I love lives up there."

"Captain Stanislaski's niece lives up there. And the girl's had a spot of trouble."

"I know. She's the one I'm in love with. She's a little annoyed with me at the moment."

"Do tell."

"I messed up, and I want to fix it. Look, she's not going to let me in the front."

"You think I'm going to let you climb up to the lady's window?"

Nick shifted his bags. "Mooney, how long have you known me?"

"Too long." But he smiled a little. "What have you got in mind?"

By the time Nick finished telling him, Mooney was grinning. "Tell you what I'm going to do, since I've watched you grow from a snot-nosed punk into an upstanding citizen. I'm going to stand right down here and let you give it your best shot. If the lady isn't receptive, you're coming right back down."

"Deal. Listen, it could take a little time. She's pretty stubborn."

"Aren't they all? I'll give you a leg up, boy."

With Mooney's help, Nick managed to yank down the ladder. After a climb that reminded him that his bruises were still very much around, he tapped on Freddie's window.

Moments later, she jerked it open.

Her eyes were a little swollen, and that cheered him. Even if the expression in them wasn't welcoming.

"Fred, I want to—"

She slammed the window down and flipped the lock.

"Strike one, Nick!" Mooney called up. A man came out of the bakery behind him and paused next to the cop.

"What's going on?"

"The boy up there's trying to charm the lady."

Nick prayed it was just temper. If she'd finally written him off, he'd lose everything that mattered. He only had to get her attention, he assured himself, and wiped a damp, nervous hand on his jeans. He pulled the flowers out first. They'd gotten a little crushed, but he didn't think she'd notice.

He rapped again, harder. "Open up, Fred. I brought you flowers. Look." More than a little desperate, he waved the bouquet when her face appeared on the other side of the glass. "Yellow roses, your favorite."

Her answer was to yank the drapes smartly shut.

"Strike two, Nick!"

"Shut up, Mooney," he muttered.

He was drawing a crowd now, but he ignored it as he pulled out his next weapon. After arranging the candles in their holders, he lighted them. He turned to the blank window and tried to pitch his voice loud enough so Fred would have to hear him, but not so loud that he'd get commentary from below.

"Hey, I've got candlelight out here, Fred.... Did I ever tell you how beautiful you look in candlelight? The way your eyes sparkle and your skin kind of glows? You look beautiful in any light, really, sunlight or moonlight. I should have told you that. I should have told you a lot of things."

Nick shut his eyes a moment, took a breath. "I was afraid I'd mess up and ruin your life, Fred, so I messed up anyway and nearly ruined both our lives." His hands were pressed against the window glass now, as if he could will her to open it. "Let me fix it. I've got to fix it. Just let me tell you everything I should have told you. Like the way the smell of you haunts me. I breathe you for hours, even when you're not there, like you're inside me."

"That's pretty good," Mooney noted to several people who'd stopped to watch. They all agreed with him.

"Open the window, Fred. I need to touch you."

He wasn't even sure if she was listening. All he could see was the insulated barrier of draperies. He set up the portable keyboard, to the hoots and calls of encouragement of the crowd below.

"We wrote this song for each other, Fred, and I didn't even know it."

He played the opening chord from "It Was Ever You" and, tossing pride away, sang.

He was into the second verse before she snapped the drapes aside and tossed up the window.

"Stop it," she demanded. "You're making a fool out of yourself and embarrassing me. Now I want you to—"

"I love you."

That stopped her. He saw tears swim into her eyes before she fought them back. "I'm not putting myself through this again. Now go away."

"I've always loved you, Freddie," he said quietly. "That's why there was never anyone else who meant anything, or could. I was wrong, stupid, to think I had to let you go. I need you to forgive me, Fred, to give me another chance, because there's nothing without you."

The first tear fell. "Oh, why are you doing this? I'd made up my mind."

"I should have done it a long time ago. Don't leave me, Fred. Give me a chance." Nick picked up the flowers again and offered them.

After a moment's hesitation, she took them. "It isn't just flowers, Nick. I was angry then. It's—"

"I was afraid to love you," he murmured. "Because it was so big, so huge, I thought it might swallow me whole. And I was afraid to show you."

Her gaze lifted from the flowers, held his. She'd once dreamed about seeing that look in his eyes. The tenderness, the strength, and the love. "I never wanted you to be anything but what you are, Nick."

"Come on out." His eyes never left hers when he held out his hand. "Welcome to my world."

She sniffled, then shook her head with a laugh. "All right, but we'll probably be arrested for arson."

"No problem. I've got a cop watching."

Even as she stepped out on the crowded platform, she looked down. Besides the uniform, there were several others in the audience. Someone waved at her.

"Nick, this is ridiculous. We can talk this through inside."

"I like it out here." She'd wanted romance. By God, he was going to give it to her. "And there's not much to talk about—just tell me you still love me."

"I do." Swamped with it, she lifted a hand to his cheek. "I do love you."

"Forgive me?"

"I wasn't going to. Ever. I was going to live without you, Nick."

"That's what I was afraid of." He laid a hand over the one resting on his cheek. "And now?"

"You haven't left me much choice." She brushed a tear away. "What were you thinking of, candles and music before noon?"

She'd already forgiven him, he realized, humbled. "I thought it was time I did the courting. Do you want me to go to the next step in my master plan?"

"I want to apologize about that."

"I hope you won't." He lifted her hand and kissed it, in a gesture that made her blink. "I intend to remind you, for the rest of your life, that you came gunning for me. I'm glad you did." He kissed her hand again. "I'm going to need a long time to show my gratitude." Watching her, he shifted and took a small box out of his pocket. "I'm hoping you'll give it to me. Marry me, Fred." He flipped the top on the box to reveal an elegantly simple, traditional diamond. "No one's ever loved you the way I do. No one ever will."

"Nick." She pressed her hand to her mouth. This wasn't a dream, she realized. Not a fantasy, not a stage in some careful plan. It was real and wrenching.

And perfect.

"Yes. Oh, yes." On a watery laugh, she threw herself into his arms.

"Looks like the boy hit a home run after all," Mooney observed. He gave himself the pleasure of watching the couple five stories up kiss as if they'd go on that way through eternity.

Then he tapped his stick. "Okay, let's move along. Give them some privacy."

Whistling, Mooney sauntered away. He glanced back once, smiled as he saw the pretty woman toss her bouquet high in the air.

Nick LeBeck, Mooney thought. The boy had come a long way.

Epilogue

BROADWAY RHYTHM
By Angela Browning

After last night's wildly successful opening of *First, Last and Always*, starring the luminous Maddy O'Hurley and the delicious Jason Craig, there's no doubt about these two stellar performers' niche on the Great White Way. The audience, including yours truly, adored them from the dynamic, colorful opening scene to the wryly romantic closing number. Miss O'Hurley in particular proved her range and scope in her captivating portrayal of Caroline from quirky ingenue to mature woman.

While these two stars and the inspired supporting cast lit up the stage, it was the music that drove the production. Take it from me—as of last night, Broadway has two new darlings. The team of Nicholas LeBeck and Frederica Kimball have created a score that soared and dipped, that raised the roof and touched the heart. Believe me, there were few dry eyes in the house last night when the two leads reprised the haunting "It Was Ever You." Notes and lyrics are certainly the heartbeat of any musical, and this heart pumped with fresh energy and spirit. Mr. LeBeck's debut score for *Last Stop* earned him rave reviews, and sang with potential. With *First, Last and Always* he's proven himself.

His partner is every bit his match. Miss Kimball's lyrics range from the gently poetic to the smugly cynical to the brashly funny, slipping so truly into LeBeck's notes that it's not possible to tell which came first. Like all great collaborations, this one appears seamless.

Perhaps this is due to the fact that the team of LeBeck and Kimball are not only musical partners, but newlyweds. Married only three months, the bride and groom had plenty of reason to smile after last night's smash opening. I, for one, wish them a long, happy and productive partnership.

"How many times are you going to read that?"

Freddie sighed. She sat cross-legged in the middle of the rumpled bed, copies of all the early reviews spread around her. And over Nick. Her hair had long since fallen out of the sophisticated twist she'd worn to the opening. The sleek black gown she'd spent days shopping for was tossed carelessly on the floor—where it had landed when Nick peeled it off of her.

They'd come in giggling sometime past dawn, high on celebratory champagne, success and healthy lust.

"It was wonderful."

He grinned. "Thanks."

With a laugh, she swatted him with the newspaper and watched her wedding ring glint in the sunlight that streamed through the window. It still gave her a wonderful jolt to see it on her finger. "Not that—but that wasn't bad, either. The night," she said, closing her eyes to bring it all back. "The crowds, the people, the lights and music. The applause. God, I loved the applause. Remember how people stood up and cheered at the end of 'I'm Leaving You First'?"

He folded his arms behind his head and continued to grin. She looked so cute, so pretty, sitting there in one of his T-shirts, her hair curling everywhere, her eyes glowing.

She looked so…his.

"Did they? I didn't notice."

"Sure. That's why you broke all the fingers in my hand squeezing it."

"I was just trying to keep you from leaping on stage and taking a bow."

"I felt like it," Freddie admitted. "I wanted to jump up and dance. They loved it, Nick. They loved what we made together."

"So did I. I loved sitting front-row center and hearing what we created over the bar on my old piano. And remembering what happened to us while we wrote the words and music."

She laid a hand over his, linked fingers. "It was the most exciting time of my life. And last night just made it all the more special. Everyone looked so wonderful. All the family. It was almost like our wedding day, with everyone dressed up and beaming. And you were almost as nervous."

"You were every bit as beautiful." Nick watched her color come up, her smile spread. She wasn't used to him remembering to tell her, he knew, or being able to say it so easily. "Mrs. LeBeck." He sat up to comb his fingers through her hair, to meet her mouth with his. "I love you."

"Nick." She pressed her cheek to his and held tight. "It's all so perfect. I knew it would be if I waited long enough. And somehow I know it's only going to get better. We're a team."

"And we're a hit. LeBeck and Kimball. Broadway's new darlings."

She chuckled, then nuzzled his neck. "You read it this time."

His hands had already slipped under the T-shirt. "Now?"

"After," she murmured, then with a laugh, rolled over the rave reviews with him.

* * * * *

CONSIDERING KATE

To my guys

Chapter One

It was going to be perfect. She was going to see to it. Every step, every stage, every detail would be done precisely as she wanted, as she envisioned, until her dream became her reality.

Settling for less than what was exactly right was a waste of time after all.

And Kate Kimball was not a woman to waste anything.

At twenty-five, she had seen and experienced more than a great many people did in a lifetime. When other young girls had been giggling over boys or worrying about fashion, she'd been traveling to Paris or Bonne, wearing glamorous costumes and doing extraordinary things.

She had danced for queens, and dined with princes.

She had sipped champagne at the White House, and wept with triumph and fatigue at the Bolshoi.

She would always be grateful to her parents, to the big, sprawling family who'd given her the opportunities to do so. Everything she had she owed to them.

Now it was time to start earning it herself.

Dance had been her dream for as long as she could remember. Her obsession, her brother, Brandon, would have said. And not, Kate acknowledged, inaccurately. There was nothing wrong with an obsession—as long as it was the *right* obsession and you worked for it.

God knew she'd worked for the dance.

Twenty years of practice, of study, of joy and pain. Of sweat and toe shoes. Of sacrifices, she thought. Hers, and her parents. She understood how difficult it had been for them to let her, the baby of the family, go to New York to study when she'd been only seventeen. But they'd never offered her anything but support and encouragement.

Of course, they'd known that though she was leaving the pretty little town in West Virginia for the big city, she'd be surrounded—watched over—by family. Just as she knew they had loved and trusted—believed in her enough—to let her go in any case.

She'd practiced and worked, and had danced, as much for them as for herself. And when she'd joined the Company and had appeared on stage the first time, they'd been there. When she'd earned a spot as principal dancer, they'd been there.

She'd danced professionally for six years, had known the spotlight, and the thrill of *feeling* the music inside her body. She'd traveled all over the world, had become Giselle, Aurora, Juliet, dozens of characters both tragic and triumphant. She had prized every moment of it.

No one was more surprised than Kate herself when

she'd decided to step out of that spotlight and walk off that stage. There was only one way to explain it.

She'd wanted to come home.

She wanted a life, a real one. As much as she loved the dance, she'd begun to realize it had nearly absorbed and devoured every other aspect of her. Classes, rehearsals, performances, travel, media. The dancer's career was far more than slipping on toe shoes and gliding into the spotlight—or it certainly had been for Kate.

So she wanted a life, and she wanted home. And, she'd discovered, she wanted to give something back for all the joy she'd reaped. She could accomplish all of that with her school.

They would come, she told herself. They would come because her name was Kimball, and that meant something solid in the area. They would come because her name was *Kate Kimball,* and that meant something in the world of dance.

Before long, she promised herself, they would come because the school itself meant something.

Time for a new dream, she reminded herself as she turned around the huge, echoing room. The Kimball School of Dance was her new obsession. She intended it to be just as fulfilling, just as intricate, and just as perfect as her old one.

And it would, no doubt, entail as much work, effort, skill and determination to bring to life.

With her hands fisted on her hips, she studied the grime-gray walls that had once been white. They'd be white again. A clean surface for displaying framed posters of the greats. Nuryev, Fontayne, Baryshnikov, Davidov, Bannion.

And the two long side walls would be mirrored

behind their *barres*. This professional vanity was as necessary as breathing. A dancer must see each tiny movement, each arch, each flex, even as the body felt it, to perfect the positioning.

It was really more window than mirror, Kate thought. Where the dancer looked through the glass to see the dance.

The old ceiling would be repaired or replaced—whatever was necessary. The furnace…she rubbed her chilly arms. Definitely replaced. The floors sanded and sealed until they were a smooth and perfect surface. Then there was the lighting, the plumbing, probably some electrical business to see to.

Well, her grandfather had been a carpenter before he'd retired—or semiretired, she thought with affection. She wasn't totally ignorant of what went on in a rehab situation. And she'd study more, ask questions, until she understood the process and could direct the contractor she hired appropriately.

Imagining what would be, she closed her eyes, dipped into a deep plié. Her body, long and wand-slim, simply flowed into the movement until her crotch rested on her heels, rose up again, lowered again.

She'd bundled her hair up, impatient to get out and take another look at what would soon be hers. With her movements, pins loosened and a few locks of glossy black curls spilled out. Freed, they would fall to her waist—a wildly romantic look that suited her image on stage.

Smiling, a bit dreamy, her face took on a quiet glow. She had her mother's dusky skin and high, slashing cheekbones, her father's smoky eyes and stubborn chin.

It made an arresting combination, again a romantic

one. The gypsy, the mermaid, the faerie queen. There had been men who'd looked at her, taken in the delicacy of her form, and had assumed a romanticism and fragility—and never anticipated the steel.

It was, always, a mistake.

"One of these days you're going to get stuck like that, then you'll have to hop around like a frog."

Kate sprang up, eyes popping open. "Brandon!" With a full-throated war whoop, she leaped across the room and into his arms.

"What are you doing here? When did you get in? I thought you were playing winter ball in Puerto Rico. How long are you staying?"

He was barely two years her senior—an accident of birth he'd used to torment her when they'd been children, unlike her half sister, Frederica, who was older than both of them and had never lorded it over them. Despite it, he was the love of her life.

"Which question do you want me to answer first?" Laughing, he held her away from him, taking a quick study of her out of tawny and amused eyes. "Still scrawny."

"And you're still full of it. Hi." She kissed him smackingly on the lips. "Mom and Dad didn't say you were coming home."

"They didn't know. I heard you were settling in and figured I'd better check things out, keep an eye on you." He glanced around the big, filthy room, rolled his eyes. "I guess I'm too late."

"It's going to be wonderful."

"Gonna be. Maybe. Right now it's a dump." Still, he slung his arm around her shoulders. "So, the ballet queen's going to be a teacher."

"I'm going to be a wonderful teacher. Why aren't you in Puerto Rico?"

"Hey, a guy can't play ball twelve months a year."

"Brandon." Her eyebrow arched up.

"Bad slide into second. Pulled a few tendons."

"Oh, how bad? Have you seen a doctor? Will you—"

"Jeez, Katie. It's no big deal. I'm on the Disabled List for a couple of months. I'll be back in action for spring training. And it gives me lots of time to hang around here and make your life a living hell."

"Well, that's some compensation. Come on, I'll show you around." And get a look at the way he moved. "My apartment's upstairs."

"From the looks of that ceiling, your apartment may be downstairs any minute."

"It's perfectly sound," she said with a wave of the hand. "Just ugly at the moment. But I have plans."

"You've always had plans."

But he walked with her, favoring his right leg, through the room and into a nasty little hallway with cracked plaster and exposed brick. Up a creaking set of stairs and into a sprawling space that appeared to be occupied by mice, spiders and assorted vermin he didn't want to think about.

"Kate, this place—"

"Has potential," she said firmly. "And history. It's pre-Civil War."

"It's pre-Stone Age." He was a man who preferred things already ordered, and in an understandable pattern. Like a ballpark. "Have you any clue what it's going to cost you to make this place livable?"

"I have a clue. And I'll firm that up when I talk to the contractor. It's mine, Brand. Do you remember when we were kids and you and Freddie and I would walk by this old place?"

"Sure, used to be a bar, then it was a craft shop or something, then—"

"It used to be a lot of things," Kate interrupted. "Started out as a tavern in the 1800s. Nobody's really made a go of it. But I used to look at it when we were kids and think how much I'd like to live here, and look out these tall windows, and rattle around in all the rooms."

The faintest flush bloomed on her cheeks, and her eyes went deep and dark. A sure sign, Brandon thought, that she had dug in.

"Thinking like that when you're eight's a lot different than buying a heap of a building when you're a grown-up."

"Yes, it is. It is different. Last spring, when I came home to visit, it was up for sale. Again. I couldn't stop thinking about it."

She circled the room. She could see it, as it would be. Wood gleaming, walls sturdy and clean. "I went back to New York, went back to work, but I couldn't stop thinking about this old place."

"You get the screwiest things in your head."

She shrugged that off. "It's mine. I was sure of it the minute I came inside. Haven't you ever felt that?"

He had, the first time he'd walked into a ballpark. He supposed, when it came down to it, most sensible people would have told him that playing ball for a living was a kid's dream. His family never had, he remembered. Any more than they'd discouraged Kate from her dreams of ballet.

"Yeah, I guess I have. It just seems so fast. I'm used to you doing things in deliberate steps."

"That hasn't changed," she told him with a grin. "When I decided to retire from performing, I knew I wanted to teach dance. I knew I wanted to make this place a school. My school. Most of all, I wanted to be home."

"Okay." He put his arm around her again, pressed a kiss to her temple. "Then we'll make it happen. But right now, let's get out of here. This place is freezing."

"New heating system's first on my list."

Brandon took one last glance around. "It's going to be a really long list."

They walked together through the brisk December wind, as they had since childhood. Along cracked and uneven sidewalks, under trees that spread branches stripped of leaves under a heavy gray sky.

She could smell snow in the air, the teasing hint of it.

Storefronts were already decorated for the holidays, with red-cheeked Santas and strings of lights, flying reindeer and overweight snowpeople.

But the best of them, always the best of them, was The Fun House. The toy store's front window was crowded with delights. Miniature sleighs, enormous stuffed bears in stocking caps, dolls both elegant and homely, shiny red trucks, castles made of wooden blocks.

The look was delightfully jumbled and…fun, Kate thought. One might think the toys had simply been dropped wherever they fit. But she knew that great care, and a deep, affectionate knowledge of children, had gone into the design of the display.

Bells chimed cheerfully as they stepped inside.

Customers wandered. A toddler banged madly on a xylophone in the play corner. Behind the counter, Annie Maynard boxed a flop-eared stuffed dog. "He's one of my favorites," she said to the waiting customer. "Your niece is going to love him."

Her glasses slid down her nose as she tied the fuzzy red yarn around the box. Then she glanced up over them, blinked and squealed.

"Brandon! Tash! Come see who's here. Oh, come give me a kiss, you gorgeous thing."

When he came around the counter and obliged, she patted her heart. "Been married twenty-five years," she said to her customer. "And this boy can make me feel like a co-ed again. Happy holidays. Let me go get your mother."

"No, I'll get her." Kate grinned and shook her head. "Brandon can stay here and flirt with you."

"Well, then." Annie winked. "Take your time."

Her brother, Kate mused, had been leaving females puddled at his feet since he'd been five. No, since he'd been born, she corrected as she wandered through the aisles.

It was more than looks, though his were stellar. Even more than charm, though he could pump out plenty when he was in the mood. She'd long ago decided it was simply pheromones.

Some men just stood there and made women drool. Susceptible women, of course. Which she had never been. A man had to have more than looks, charm and sex appeal to catch her interest. She'd known entirely too many who were pretty to look at, but empty once you opened the package.

Then she turned the corner by the toy cars and very nearly turned into a puddle.

He was gorgeous. No, no, that was too female a term. Handsome was too fussily male. He was just...

Man.

Six-two if he was an inch, and all of it brilliantly packaged. As a dancer she appreciated a well-toned body. The specimen currently studying rows of miniature vehicles had his packed into snug and faded jeans, a flannel shirt and a denim jacket that was scarred and too light for the weather.

His work boots looked ancient and solid. Who would have thought work boots could be so sexy?

Then there was all that hair; dark, streaky blond masses of it waving around a lean, sharp-angled face. Not rugged, not classic, not anything she could label. His mouth was full, and appeared to be the only soft thing about him. His nose was long and straight, his chin, well, chiseled. And his eyes...

She couldn't quite see his eyes, not the color, with all those wonderful lashes in the way. But they were heavy-lidded, so she imagined them a deep, slumberous blue.

She shifted her gaze to his hands as he reached for one of the toys. Big, wide-palmed, blunt-fingered. Strong.

Holy cow.

And while indulging in a moment's fantasy—a perfectly harmless moment's fantasy—she leaned and knocked over a small traffic jam of cars.

The resulting clatter slapped her out of her daydream, and turned the man's eyes—his surprising and intense green eyes—in her direction.

"Oops," she said. And grinning at him, laughing

at herself, crouched down to pick up the cars. "I hope there were no casualties."

"We've got an ambulance right here, if necessary." He tapped the shiny red-and-white emergency vehicle, then hunkered down to help her.

"Thanks. If we can get these back before the cops get here, I may just get off with a warning." He smelled as good as he looked, she decided. Wood shavings and man. She shifted, deliberately, and their knees bumped. "Come here often?"

"Yeah, actually." He glanced up at her, took a good long look. She recognized the stirring of interest in his eyes. "Guys never outgrow their toys."

"So I've heard. What do you like to play with?"

His eyebrows shot up. A man didn't often come across a beautiful—provocative—woman in a toy store on a Wednesday afternoon. He very nearly stuttered, then did something he hadn't done in years—spoke without thinking first.

"Depends on the game. What's yours?"

She laughed, pushed back a tendril of hair that tickled her cheek. "Oh, I like all kinds of games—especially if I win."

She started to rise, but he beat her to it, straightening those yard-long legs and holding out a hand. She gripped it, discovered to her pleasure it was as hard as she'd imagined, and as strong.

"Thanks again. I'm Kate."

"Brody." He offered the tiny blue convertible he was still holding. "In the market for a car?"

"No, not today. I'm more or less browsing, until I see what I want...." Her lips curved again, amused, flirtatious.

Brody had to order himself not to whistle out a breath. He'd had women come on to him from time to time, but never quite like this. And he'd been in a self-imposed female drought for... For what was beginning to seem entirely too long.

"Kate." He leaned on a shelf, angled his body toward her. Funny, how the moves came back, how the system could pick up the dance as if it had never sat one out. "Why don't we—"

"Katie. I didn't know you'd come in." Natasha Kimball hurried across the shop, carting an enormous toy cement mixer.

"I brought you a surprise."

"I love surprises. But first here you are, Brody, as promised. Just came in Monday, and I put it aside for you."

"It's great." The cool-eyed, flirtatious expression had vanished into a delighted grin. "It's perfect. Jack'll flip."

"The manufacturer makes its toys to last. This is something he'll enjoy for years, not just for a week after Christmas. Have you met my daughter?" Natasha asked, sliding an arm around Kate's waist.

Brody's eyes flicked up from the truck in its open-fronted box. "Daughter?"

So this is the ballerina, he thought. Doesn't it just figure?

"We just met—over a slight vehicular accident." Kate kept the smile on her face. Surely she had imagined the sudden chill. "Is Jack your nephew?"

"Jack's my son."

"Oh." She took a long step back in her mind. The nerve of the man! The nerve of the *married* man flirting with her. It hardly mattered who had flirted first after all. *She* wasn't married. "I'm sure he'll love it," she said, coolly now and turned to her mother.

"Mama—"

"Kate, I was just telling Brody about your plans. I thought you might like him to look at your building."

"Whatever for?"

"Brody's a contractor. And a wonderful carpenter. He remodeled your father's studio last year. And has promised to take a look at my kitchen. My daughter insists on the best," Natasha added, her dark gold eyes laughing. "So naturally, I thought of you."

"I appreciate it."

"No, I do, because I know you do quality work at a fair price." She gave his arm a little squeeze. "Spence and I would be grateful if you looked the building over."

"I don't even settle for two days, Mama. Let's not rush things. But I did run into something annoying in the building just a bit ago. It's up in the front charming Annie."

"What…Brandon? Oh, why didn't you say so!" As Natasha rushed off, Kate turned to Brody. "Nice to have met you."

"Likewise. Give me a call if you want me to look at your place."

"Of course." She placed the little car he'd handed her neatly back on the shelf. "I'm sure your son will love his truck. Is he your only child?"

"Yes. There's just Jack."

"I'm sure he keeps you and your wife busy. Now if you'll excuse me—"

"Jack's mother died four years ago. But he keeps me

plenty busy. Watch those intersections, Kate," he suggested, and tucking the truck under his arm, walked away.

"Nice going." She hissed under her breath. "Really nice going."

Now maybe she could run out and see if there were any puppies she could kick, just to finish off the afternoon.

One of the best things about running your own business, in Brody's opinion, was being able to prioritize your time. There were plenty of headaches—responsibilities, paperwork, juggling jobs—not to mention making damn sure there were jobs to juggle. But that one element made up for any and all of the downside.

For the last six years he'd had one priority.

His name was Jack.

After he'd hidden the cement truck under a tarp in the back of his pickup, had run by a job site to check on progress, called on a supplier to put a bug in their ear about a special order and stopped at yet another site to give a potential client an estimate on a bathroom rehab, he headed home.

Mondays, Wednesdays and Fridays, he made a point to be home before the school bus grumbled to the end of the lane. The other two school days—and in the case of any unavoidable delay—Jack was delivered to the Skully house, where he could spend an hour or two with his best pal Rod under the watchful eye of Beth Skully.

He owed Beth and Jerry Skully a great deal, and most of it was for giving Jack a safe and happy place to be when he couldn't be home. In the ten months Brody had been back in Shepherdstown he was reminded, on an almost daily basis, just how comforting small towns could be.

Now, at thirty, he was amazed at the young man who had shaken that town off his shoes as fast as he could manage a little more than ten years before.

All for the best, he decided as he rounded the curve toward home. If he hadn't left home, hadn't been so hardheadedly determined to make his mark elsewhere, he wouldn't have lived and learned. He wouldn't have met Connie.

He wouldn't have Jack.

He'd come nearly full circle. If he hadn't completely closed the rift with his parents, he was making progress. Or Jack was, Brody corrected. His father might still hold a grudge against his son, but he couldn't resist his grandson.

He'd been right to come home. Brody looked at the woods, growing thick on either side of the road. A few thin flakes of snow were beginning to drift out of the leaden sky. Hills, rocky and rough, rose and fell as they pleased.

It was a good place to raise a boy. Better for them both to be out of the city, to start fresh together in a place Jack had family.

Family who could and would accept him for what he was, instead of seeing him as a reminder of what was lost.

He turned into the lane, stopped and turned off the truck. The bus would be along in minutes, and Jack would leap out, race over and climb in, filling the cab of the truck with the thrills and spills of the day.

It was too bad, Brody mused, he couldn't share the spills and thrills of his own with a six-year-old.

He could hardly tell his son that he'd felt his blood move for a woman again. Not just a mild stir, but a full leap. He couldn't share that for a moment, a bit longer than a moment, he'd contemplated acting on that leap of blood.

It had been so damn long.

And what harm would it have done, really? An attractive woman, and one who obviously had no problem making the first move. A little mating dance, a couple of civilized dates, then some not-so-civilized sex. Everybody got what they wanted, and nobody got hurt.

He cursed under his breath, rubbed at the tension that had settled into the back of his neck.

Someone always got hurt.

Still, it might have been worth the risk…if she hadn't been Natasha and Spencer Kimball's pampered and perfect daughter.

He'd gone that route once before, and had no intention of navigating those pitfalls a second time.

He knew plenty about Kate Kimball. Prima ballerina, society darling and toast of the arty set. Over and above the fact that he'd rather have his teeth pulled— one at a time—than sit through a ballet, he'd had his fill of the cultured class during his all-too-brief marriage.

Connie had been one in a million. A natural in a sea of pretense and pomp. And even then, it had been a hard road. He'd never know if they'd have continued to bump their way over it together, but he liked to believe they would have.

As much as he'd loved her, his marriage to Connie had taught him life was easier if you stuck with your own. And easier yet if a man just avoided any serious entanglements with a woman.

It was a good thing he'd been interrupted before he'd followed impulse and asked Kate Kimball out. A good thing he'd learned who she was before that flirtation had shifted into high gear.

A very good thing he'd had the time to remember his priority. Fatherhood had kicked the stuffing out of the arrogant, careless and often reckless boy. And had made a man out of him.

He heard the rumble of the bus, and sat up grinning. There was no place in the world Brody O'Connell would rather be than right here, right now.

The big yellow bus groaned to a stop, its safety lights flashing. The driver waved, a cheerful little salute. Brody waved back and watched his lightning bolt shoot out the door.

Jack was a compact boy, except for his feet. It would take some years for him to grow into them. At the end of the lane, he tipped back his head and tried to catch one of those thin snowflakes on his tongue. His face was round and cheerful, his eyes green like his father's, his mouth still the innocent bow of youth.

Brody knew when Jack stripped off his red ski cap— as he would at the first opportunity—his pale blond hair would shoot up in sunflower spikes.

Watching his son, Brody felt love swarm him, fill him so fast it was a flood of the heart.

Then the door of the truck opened, and the little boy clambered in, an eager puppy with oversize paws.

"Hey, Dad! It's snowing. Maybe it'll snow eight feet and there won't be any school and we can build a million snowmen in the yard and go sledding." He bounced on the seat. "Can we?"

"The minute it snows eight feet, we start the first of a million snowmen."

"Promise?"

Promises, Brody knew, were always a solemn business. "Absolutely promise."

"Okay! Guess what?"

Brody started the engine and drove up the lane. "What?"

"It's only fifteen days till Christmas, and Miss Hawkins says tomorrow it'll be fourteen and that's just two weeks."

"I guess that means one from fifteen is fourteen."

"Yeah?" Jack's eyes went wide. "Okay. So it's Christmas in two weeks, and Grandma says that time flies, so it's practically Christmas *now.*"

"Practically." Brody stopped the truck in front of the old three-story farmhouse. Eventually he'd have the whole thing rehabbed. Maybe by the time he was eligible for social security.

"So okay, if it's almost practically Christmas, can I have a present?"

"Hmm." Brody pursed his lips, wrinkled his brow and appeared to give this due consideration. "You know, Jacks, that was good. That was a really good one. No."

"Aw."

"Aw," Brody echoed in the same sorrowful tone. Then he laughed and snatched his son off the seat. "But if you give me a hug, I'll make O'Connell's Amazing Magic Pizza for dinner."

"Okay!" Jack wrapped his arms around his father's neck.

And Brody was home.

Chapter Two

"Nervous?" Spencer Kimball watched his daughter pour a cup of coffee. She looked flawless, he thought. Her mass of curling hair was tied neatly into a tail that streamed down her back. Her stone-gray jacket and trousers were trim and tailored in an understated chic he sometimes thought she'd been born with. Her face—Lord, she looked like her mother—was composed.

Yes, she looked flawless, and lovely. And grown up. Why was it so hard to see his babies grown?

"Why should I be nervous? More coffee?"

"Yeah, thanks. It's D-Day," he added when she topped off his cup. "Deed Day. In a couple hours, you'll be a property owner, with all the joys and frustrations that entails."

"I'm looking forward to it." She sat to nibble on the half bagel she'd toasted for breakfast. "I've thought it all through very carefully."

"You always do."

"Mmm. I know it's a risk using so much of my savings, and a good portion of my trust fund in this investment. But I'm financially sound and I know I can handle the projected expenses over the next five years."

He nodded, watching her face. "You have your mother's business sense."

"I like to think so. I also like to think I'll have your skill for teaching. After all, I'm an artist, who comes from two people who are artists. And the little bit of teaching I did in New York gave me a taste for it." She picked up the cream, added a little more to her coffee. "I'm establishing my business in my hometown, where I have solid contacts with the community."

"Absolutely true."

She set the bagel aside and picked up her coffee. "The Kimball name is respected here, and my name is respected in dance circles. I've studied dance for twenty years, sweated and ached my way through thousands of hours of instructions. I should have learned more than how to execute a clean *tour jeté*."

"Without question."

She sighed. There was no fooling her father. He knew her inside and out. He was all that was solid, she thought, all that was steady. "Okay. You know how you get butterflies in your stomach?"

"Yeah."

"Mine are frogs. Big, fat, hopping frogs. I wasn't this nervous before my first professional solo."

"Because you never doubted your talent. This is new ground, honey." He laid a hand over hers. "You're entitled to the frogs. Fact is, I'd worry about you if you didn't have the jumps."

"You're also worried I'm making a big mistake."

"No, not a mistake." He gave her hand a squeeze. "I've got some concerns—and a father's entitled to the jumps, too—that in a few months you might miss performing. Miss the company and the life you built. Part of me wishes you'd waited a bit longer before making such a big commitment. And the other part's just happy to have you home again."

"Well, tell your frogs to settle down. Once I make a commitment, I keep it."

"I know."

That was one of the things that concerned him, but he wasn't going to say that.

She picked up her bagel again, grinning a little. She knew just how to distract him. "So, tell me about the plans to remodel the kitchen."

He winced, his handsome face looking pained. "I'm not getting into it." As he glanced around the room he raked a hand through his hair so the gold and silver of it tangled. "Your mother's got this bug over a full redo here. New this, new that, and Brody O'Connell's aiding and abetting. What's wrong with the kitchen?"

"Maybe it has something to do with the fact it hasn't been remodeled in twenty-odd years?"

"So what's your point?" Spencer gestured with his coffee cup. "It's great. It's perfectly comfortable. But then he had to go and show her sample books."

Her lips twitched at the betrayal in her father's voice, but she spoke with sober sympathy. "The dog."

"And they're talking about bow and bay windows. We've got a window." He gestured to the one over the sink. "It's fine. You can look through it all you want. I tell you, that boy has seduced my wife with promises of solid surface countertops and oak trim."

"Oak trim, hmm. Very sexy." Laughing, she propped an elbow on the table. "Tell me about O'Connell."

"He does good work. But that doesn't mean he should come tear up my kitchen."

"Has he lived in the area long?"

"Grew up not far from here. His father's Ace Plumbing. Brody left when he was about twenty. Went down to D.C. Worked construction."

All right, Kate thought. She'd have to pry if that was all she could shake loose. "I heard he has a little boy."

"Yeah, Jack. A real pistol. Brody's wife died several years ago. Cancer of some kind, I think. My impression is he wanted to raise his son closer to family. Been back about a year, I guess. He's established a nice business, with a reputation for quality work. He'll do a good job for you."

"If I decide to hire him."

She wondered what he looked like in a tool belt, then reminded herself that was not only *not* the kind of question a woman should ask her doting father, but also one that had nothing to do with establishing a business relationship.

But she bet he looked just fine.

It was done. The frogs in her stomach were still pretty lively, but she was now the owner of a big, beautiful, dilapidated building in the pretty college town of Shepherdstown, West Virginia.

A building that was a short walk from the house where she'd grown up, from her mother's toy shop, from the university where her father taught.

She was surrounded by family, friends and neighbors. Oh, God.

Everyone knew her—and everyone would be watching to see if she pulled it off, stuck it out, or fell flat on her face. Why hadn't she opened her school in Utah or New Mexico or someplace she was anonymous, somewhere with no expectations hovering over her?

And that, she reminded herself, was just stupid. She was establishing her school here because it was home. Home, Kate thought, was exactly where she wanted to be.

There would be no falling, flat or otherwise, Kate promised herself as she parked her car. She would succeed because she would personally oversee every detail. She would take each upcoming step the way she'd taken all the others that had led here. Carefully, meticulously. And she would work like a Trojan to see it through.

She wouldn't disappoint her parents.

The important thing was that the property was now hers—and the bank's—and that those next steps could be taken.

She walked up the steps—her steps—crossed the short, slightly sagging porch and unlocked the door to her future.

It smelled of dust and cobwebs.

That would change. Oh, yes, she told herself as she set her bag and keys aside. That would begin to change very soon. In short order, the air would smell of sawdust and fresh paint and the sweat of a working crew.

She just had to hire the crew.

She started to cross the floor, just to hear her footsteps echo, and saw the little portable stereo in the center of the room. Baffled, she hurried to it, picked up the card set on top of the machine and grinned at her mother's handwriting.

She ripped open the envelope and took out the card fronted with a lovely painting of a ballerina at the *barre*.

Congratulations, Katie!
Here's a small housewarming gift so you'll always have music.
Love, Mom, Dad and Brandon

"Oh, you guys. You just never let me down." A little teary-eyed, she crouched and turned the stereo on.

It was one of her father's compositions, and one of her favorites. She remembered how thrilled, and how proud she had been, when she had danced to it the first time on stage in New York.

Kimball dancing to Kimball, she thought, and shrugged out of her coat, kicked off her shoes.

Slow at first—a long extension. The muscles tremble, but hold, and hold. A bend at the knee to change the line. Turning, beat by beat.

Lower. A gentle series of pirouettes, fluid rather than sharp.

She moved around the dingy room, sliding into the well-remembered steps. Music swelled into the space, into her mind, into her body.

Building now, from romance toward passion. *Arabesque,* quick, light triple pirouette and into *ballottes*.

The joy of it rushed into her. The confining band flew out of her hair. *Grande jeté*. And again. Again. Feel like you could fly forever. Look like you can.

End it with flair, with joy, in a fast rush of *fouetté* turns. Then set! Snap like a statue, one arm up, one back.

"I guess I'm supposed to throw roses, but I don't have any on me."

Her breath was already coming fast, and she nearly lost it completely as the statement shoved her out of dance mode. She pressed a hand to her speeding heart, and panting lightly, stared at Brody.

He stood just inside the door, hands in his pockets and a toolbox at his feet.

"You can owe me," she managed to say. "I like red ones. God, you scared the life out of me."

"Sorry. Your door wasn't locked, and you didn't hear me knock." Or wouldn't have, he decided, if he'd thought to knock.

But when he'd seen her through the window, he hadn't thought at all. He'd just walked in, dazzled. A woman who looked like that, who moved like that, was bound to dazzle a man. He imagined she knew it.

"It's all right." She turned and walked over to turn down the music. "I was initiating the place. Though the dance looks better with the costumes and lights. So." She pushed at her tumbled hair, willing her speeding heart to settle. "What can I do for you, Mr. O'Connell?"

He walked toward her, stopping to pick up her hair band. "You lost this during a spin."

"Thanks." She tucked it into her pocket.

He wished she'd pulled her hair back into it. He didn't care for his reaction to the way she looked just now, flushed and tousled and…available. "I get the feeling you weren't expecting me."

"No, but I don't mind the unexpected." Especially, she thought, when it comes with fabulous green eyes and a sexy little scowl.

"Your mother asked me to come by, take a look at the place."

"Ah. You're another housewarming present."

"I beg your pardon?"

"Nothing." She angled her head. Dancers, she mused, knew as much about body language as a psychiatrist. His was stiff, just a little defensive. And he was certainly careful to keep a good, safe distance between them. "Do I make you nervous, O'Connell, or just annoy you?"

"I don't know you well enough to be nervous or annoyed."

"Want to?"

His belly muscles quivered. "Look, Ms. Kimball—"

"All right, don't get huffy." She waved him off. A pity, she thought. She preferred being direct, and he, obviously, didn't. "I find you attractive, and I got the impression you were interested, initially. My mistake."

"You make a habit of coming on to strange men in your mother's toy store?"

She blinked, a quick flicker of temper and hurt. Then she shrugged. "Oh, well. Ouch."

"Sorry." Disgusted with himself, he held up both hands. "Way out of line. Maybe you do annoy me after all. Not your fault. I'm out of practice when it comes to…aggressive women. Let's just say I'm not in the market for any entanglements right now."

"This is a blow—I'd already picked the band for the wedding, but I expect I'll recover."

His lips curved. "Oh, well. Ouch."

He had a great smile when he used it, Kate thought. It was a damn shame he was so stingy with it where she was concerned. "Now that we have all that out of the way. What do you think?" She spread her arms to encompass the room.

Since here he was on solid ground, Brody relaxed. "It's a great old place. Lots of atmosphere and potential. Solid foundation. Built to last."

The little prickle of annoyance that still chilled her skin faded away. Warmth radiated. "That's it. Now I love you."

It was his turn to blink. He'd already taken a defensive step in retreat when Kate laughed. "Boy, you *are* out of practice. I'm not going to throw myself into your arms, Brody—though it's tempting. It's just that you're the first person who's agreed with me on this. Everyone else thinks I'm crazy to sink so much time and money into this building."

He couldn't remember having a woman make him feel like an idiot so often in such a short space of time. He shoved his hands into his pockets again. "It's a good investment—if you do it right and you're in for the long haul."

"Oh, I'm in. Why don't you tell me how you'd do it right?"

"First thing I'd do is have the heating system looked at. It's freezing in here."

She grinned at him. "We may just get along after all. The furnace is in the basement. Want to take a look?"

She came down with him—which he didn't expect. She didn't bolt when they came across a startled mouse—or the old shedded skin of a snake that had likely dined on the rodent's relatives. And that he had expected.

In his experience, women—well, intensely female women types—generally made a quick retreat when they came across anything that slithered or skittered. But Kate just wrinkled her nose and took a little notebook out of her jacket pocket to jot something down.

The light was poor, the air thick and stale, and the ancient furnace that squatted on the original dirt floor, a lost cause.

He gave her that bad news, then explained her options, the pros and cons of electric heat pumps, gas, oil. BTU's, efficiency, initial cost outlay and probable monthly expenses.

He imagined he'd do just as well speaking in Greek and offered to send brochures and information to her father.

"My father's a composer and a college professor," she said with cool politeness. "Do you assume he'd understand all of this better than I would because we have different chromosomes?"

Brody considered for a moment. "Yeah."

"You assume incorrectly. You can send me your information, but at this point I'm more inclined to the steam heat. It seems simpler and more efficient as the pipes and radiators are already in place. I want to keep as much of the building's character as possible, while making it more livable and attractive. Also, I'll have secondary heat sources, if and when I need them, when the chimneys are checked—repaired if necessary."

He didn't much care for the icy tone, even if he did agree with the content. "You're the boss."

"There, you're absolutely correct."

"You have cobwebs in your hair. Boss."

"So do you. I'll need this basement area cleaned, and however authentic the dirt floor might be, I'll want cement poured. And an exterminator. Better lighting.

As it is, it's virtually wasted space. It can be put to use for storage."

"Fine." He took a notepad and pencil out of his breast pocket and began scribbling notes.

She walked to the stairs, jiggling the banister as she started up. "The stairs don't have to be pretty, but they have to be safe."

"You'll get safe. All the work will be up to code. I don't work any other way."

"Good to know. Now, let me show you what I want on the main level."

She knew what she wanted. Maybe a little too precisely for his taste. Still, he had to give her points for not intending to simply gut the building, but to make use of its eccentricities and charm.

He couldn't see a ballet school, but she apparently could. Right down to the bench she envisioned built in under the front windows, and the canned ceiling lights.

She wanted the kitchen redone, turning it into a smaller, more efficient room and using the extra space for an office.

Spaces that had metamorphosed over the years from bedrooms to storage rooms to display rooms would become dressing areas with counters and wardrobes built in.

"It seems a little elaborate for a small-town dance school."

She merely lifted an eyebrow. "It's not elaborate. It's correct. Now these two bathrooms." She stopped in the hall beside two doors that were side by side.

"If you want to enlarge and remodel, I can open the wall between them."

"Dancers have to forgo a great deal of modesty along the way, but let's draw the line at coed bathrooms."

"Coed." He lowered the notebook, stared at her. "You're planning on having boys?" His grin came fast. "You think you're going to get boys in here doing what's it? Pirouettes? Get out."

"Ever hear of Baryshnikov? Davidov?" She was too used to the knee-jerk reaction to be particularly offended. "I'd put a well-trained dancer in his prime up against any other athlete you name in a test of strength and endurance."

"Who wears the tutu?"

She sighed, only because she was perfectly aware this was the sort of bias she'd be facing in a rural town. "For your information, male dancers are real men. In fact, my first lover was a *premier danseur* who drove a Harley and could execute a *grande jeté* with more height than Michael Jordan can pull off for a slam dunk. But then Jordan doesn't wear tights, does he? Just those cute little boxers."

"Trunks," Brody muttered. "Basketball trunks."

"Ah, well, it's all perception, isn't it? The bathrooms stay separate. New stalls, new sinks, new floors. One sink in each low enough for a child to reach. White fixtures. I want clean and streamlined."

"I got that picture."

"Then moving right along." She gestured toward the stairs at the back end of the corridor. "Third floor, my apartment."

"You're going to live here—over the school?"

"I'm going to live, breathe, eat and work here. That's how you turn a concept into reality. And I have very specific ideas about my living quarters."

"I bet you do."

* * *

Specific ideas, Brody thought an hour later, and good ones. He might have disagreed with some of the details she wanted on the main level, but he couldn't fault her vision for the third floor.

She wanted the original moldings and woodwork restored—and added that she'd like whoever had painted all that gorgeous oak white caught, dragged into the street and horsewhipped.

Brody could only agree.

Portions of the woodwork were damaged. He liked the prospect of crafting the replacement sections himself, blending them in with the old. She wanted the floors sanded down, and coated with a clear seal. He'd have done precisely the same.

As he toured the top rooms with her, he felt the old anticipation building. To make his mark on something that had stood for generations, and to preserve it as it was meant to be preserved.

There had been a time when he'd done no more than put in his hours—do the job, pick up the pay. Pride and responsibility had come later. And the simple pleasure they gave him had pushed him to better himself, to hone his craft—to build something more than rooms.

To build a life.

He could make a difference here, Brody thought. And he wanted, badly, to get his hands on this place and make that difference. Even if it meant dealing with Kate Kimball, and his irritating reaction to her.

He hoped—if he got the job—she wouldn't be one of those clients who hovered. At least not while she was wearing that damn perfume.

Then they were back to bathrooms. The old cast iron

tub stayed. The beige wall hung sink went, and Brody was directed to find a suitable white pedestal sink to replace it.

The boss also wanted ceramic tile—navy and white—though she agreed to look at product samples before making the final decision.

She was just as decisive in the kitchen, but there he stopped her.

"Look, are you actually going to cook in here, or just heat up takeout?"

"Cook. I do know how."

"Then you want solid work space there, instead of breaking it up." Brody gestured. "You want efficient traffic flow, so you work from the window. You want your sink under the window instead of on that wall. You move the refrigerator there, the stove there. See, then you've got flow instead of zigzagging back and forth. Wasted effort, wasted space."

"Yes, but there—"

"That's for your pantry," he interrupted, the room clear in his mind. "It gives you a nice line of counter. You angle it out here..." He pulled out his measuring tape. "Yeah, angle it out and you've got room for a couple of stools, so you get work space and seating space instead of dead space."

"I was thinking of putting a table—"

"Then you'll always be walking around it, and crowding yourself in."

"Maybe." She thought of the kitchen table where she'd sat with her father only that morning. And had sat with her family on countless mornings. Sentimental, she decided. And in this case probably impractical.

"Let me get the measurements, and I'll draw it up for you in the next few days. You can think about it."

"All right. Plenty of time. The main level's my priority."

"It'll take me some time to work it up and get you a bid. But I can tell you now, you're cruising toward six figures and a good four months work for the complete rehab."

She'd come to that conclusion herself, but hearing it was still a jolt. "Work it up, draw it up, whatever it is you do. If I decide to hire you for the job, when would you be able to start?"

"I can get the permits pretty quick. And put in a materials and supply order right off. Probably start work first of the year."

"Those are magic words. If I go with you, I want to get started right away. Get me a bid, Mr. O'Connell, and we'll see if we can do business."

She left him to measure and calculate, and went down to stand on her little front porch.

She could hear the light traffic from the main street, only a half block over. And smell the smoke from someone's fireplace or woodstove. Her bumpy little front lawn was a disgrace of dead and dying weeds and a sad and ugly stump of what had once been a regal maple.

Across the narrow side street was another brick building that had been converted into apartments. It was old, tidy and utterly quiet at this midday hour.

Another hundred thousand, she thought. Well, it could be done. Fortunately she hadn't lived extravagantly over the past few years. And she did, indeed, have her mother's head for business. Her savings had been carefully invested—and the trust fund was there as a cushion.

If she felt too much was going out, while nothing was coming in, she could agree to do a few guest appearances with the company. That door had been left open.

The fact was, with all the weeks of construction ahead, it would make sense to do so—and not only for financial reasons.

She was used to working, used to being busy. Once the work began on the building there would be nothing for her to do but wait until each stage was complete.

It was an easy trip to New York, and the simplest thing in the world to stay with family there. Rehearse, train, perform, come home again. Yes, that might be the best solution all around.

But not yet. Not quite yet. She wanted to see her plans get off the ground first.

"Kate?" Brody stepped out, her coat in his hand. "It's cold out here."

"A bit. I was hoping it would snow. We got teased the other day."

"As long as it's not eight feet."

"Hmm?"

"Nothing." He laid her coat over her shoulders, automatically lifting her hair out of the collar. There was so damn much of it, he thought. Soft, curling miles of it.

His hands were still caught in it when she turned, when she looked up, met his eyes. Interested after all, she realized with a lovely liquid tug in the belly. "Why don't we walk around the corner. You can buy me a cup of coffee." She moved in, a deliberate test for both of them. "We can discuss…counter space."

She clogged his brain, his lungs, and did a hell of a job on his loins. "You're coming on to me again."

Her smile was slow, devastatingly female. "I certainly am."

"You're probably the most beautiful woman I've ever seen."

"That's the good fortune of birth, but since I look a great deal like my mother, thank you. I particularly like your mouth." She shifted her gaze to it, lingered. "I just keep coming back to it."

His throat was dry as the Sahara. What had happened with women since he'd been out of the game? he wondered. When had they started seducing men on the front porch in the middle of the afternoon?

He could feel the chill December wind whipping against his face. And the heat swarming into his blood. "Look." In self-defense, he took her by the arms. Her coat slid off her shoulders, and he felt the taut sculpted muscle beneath her suit jacket.

"I've been looking." Her gaze flicked up to his again. So male, she thought. So frustrated. "I just happen to like what I see."

Her eyes were pure gray, he thought. Mysterious as smoke. He had only to lower his head, or better, yes better, to yank her to her toes. Then his mouth would be on those sultry, self-satisfied lips of hers.

He had a feeling, a bad one, it would be like barehanding a live wire. Thrilling, and potentially deadly.

"I told you I wasn't interested."

"Yes, you did. But you lied." To prove it, she rose up to her toes and took a quick, hard nip into his bottom lip. His hands tightened like vises on her arms. "See?"

she whispered when he held her there, only a breath away. "You're very interested."

Amused at both of them, she lowered to the flats of her feet, eased back. "You just don't want to be."

"It comes down to the same thing." He let her go, bent to pick up his toolbox. Damn it, his hands weren't even close to steady.

"I don't agree, but I won't push it. I'd like to see you socially, if and when that suits you. Meanwhile, since we have similar views on this building, and I liked most of your ideas, I hope we'll be able to work together."

He hissed out a breath. Cool as January, he noted. While he was flustered, heated up and churning. "You're a real piece of work, Kate."

"I am, that's true. I won't apologize for being what I am. I'll look forward to getting the brochures and information we discussed, and your bid on the job. If you need to get back in for more measurements or whatever, you know how to reach me."

"Yeah, I know how to reach you."

She stayed where she was, watched him stride down to the curb, climb into his truck. He'd have been surprised if he'd heard the long shaky breath she expelled as he drove away.

Surprised as well if he'd seen her slowly lower herself to the top step.

She was nowhere near as cool as January. She sat in the brisk breeze waiting to cool off. And for the frogs in her belly to settle down again.

Brody O'Connell, she thought. Wasn't it strange and fascinating that a man she'd only met twice should have such a strong effect on her? It wasn't that she was shy around men—far from it. But she was selective. The lover she'd tossed in Brody's face had been one of the three men—all of whom she'd cared for deeply—that she'd allowed into her life, and into her bed.

Yet, after two meetings—no, she thought, ordering herself to be brutally honest—after *one* meeting, she'd wanted Brody in her bed. The second meeting had only sharpened that want into a keen-edged desire she wasn't prepared for.

So she would do the logical and practical thing. She'd settle herself down, clear her mind. Then she'd begin to plan the best way to get him there.

Chapter Three

Jack sat at the partner's desk in what he and his dad called their office and carefully printed out the alphabet. It was his job. Just like Dad was doing his job, on his side of the desk.

The drafting paper and rulers and stuff looked like a lot more fun than the alphabet. But Dad had said, if he got it all done, he could have some paper to draw with, too.

He thought he would draw a big, giant house, just like their house, with the old barn that was Dad's workshop. And there would be lots of snow, too. Eight whole feet of snow and millions and billions of snowmen.

And a dog.

Grandpa and Grandma had a dog, and even though Buddy was sort of old, he was fun. But he had to stay at Grandma's. One day he'd have a dog all of his own and its name would be Mike and he'd chase balls and sleep in the bed at night.

He could have one as soon as he was old enough to be responsible. Which could even be tomorrow.

Jack peeked up to study his father's face and see if it was maybe time to ask if he was responsible yet.

But his dad had that look where he was kind of frowning but not mad. His working look. If you interrupted the working look, the answer was almost always: Not now.

But the alphabet was boring. He wanted to draw the house or play with his trucks or with the computer. Or maybe just look outside and see if it was snowing yet.

He butted his foot against the desk. Squirmed. Butted his foot.

"Jack, don't kick the desk."

"Do I have to write the *whole* alphabet?"

"Yep."

"How come?"

"Because."

"But I got all the way up to the *P*."

"If you don't do the rest, you can't say any words that have the letters in them you left out."

"But—"

"Can't say 'but.' *B-U-T*."

Jack heaved the heavy sigh of a six-year-old. He wrote the next three letters, then peeked up again. "Dad."

"Hmm."

"Dad, Dad, Dad, Dad. *D-A-D*."

Brody glanced up, saw his son grinning at him. "Smart aleck."

"I know how to spell Dad and Jack."

Brody narrowed his eyes, lifted a fist. "Do you know how to spell knuckle sandwich?"

"Nuh-uh. Does it have mustard?"

The kid, Brody thought, was sharp as a bucket of tacks. "How'd you get to be such a wise guy?"

"Grandma says I got it from you. Can I see what you're drawing? You said it's for the dancing lady. Are you drawing her, too?"

"Yes, it's for the dancing lady, and no, you can't see it until you're finished your job." However much he wanted to set his own work aside and just *be* with his son, the only way to teach responsibility was to be responsible.

That was one of those sneaky circles of parenthood.

"What happens when you don't finish what you start?"

Jack rolled his eyes. "Nothing."

"Exactly."

Jack heaved another sigh and applied his pencil. He didn't see his father's lips twitch.

God, what a kid. Brody wanted to toss his own pencil down, snatch Jack up and do whatever this major miracle of his life wanted to do for the rest of the evening. The hell with work, with responsibility, with what needed to be done.

There was only one thing he wanted more than that. To finish what he started. There was no job more vital than Jack O'Connell.

Had his own father ever looked at him and wondered, and worried? Probably, Brody thought. It had never showed, but probably. Still, Bob O'Connell hadn't been one for wrestling on the rug or foolish conversations.

He'd gone to work. He'd come home from work. He'd expected dinner on the table at six.

He'd expected his son to do his chores, stay out of trouble, and to—above all—do what he was told without question. One of those expectations had been to follow, precisely, in his father's footsteps.

Brody figured he'd disappointed his father in every possible area. And had been disappointed by him.

He wasn't going to put those same demands and expectations on his own son.

"Zee! Zee, Zee, Zee!" Jack picked up the paper, waved it madly. "I finished."

"Hold it still, hotshot, so I can see." A long way from neat, Brody noted when Jack held the paper up. But it was done. "Good job. You want some graph paper?"

"Can I come over there and help work on yours?"

"Sure." So he'd stay up an extra hour and work, Brody thought as Jack scrambled down from his stool. It would be worth it to have this time with his son. He reached down, hauled Jack up on his lap. "Okay, so what we've got here is the apartment above the school."

"How come they wear those funny clothes when they dance?"

"I have no idea. How do you know they wear funny clothes?"

"I saw a cartoon, and there were elephants in funny skirts. They were dancing on their toes. Do elephants really have toes?"

"Yeah." Didn't they? "We'll look it up later so you can see. Here, take the pencil. You can draw this line here, right against the straight edge."

"Okay!"

Father and son worked, heads close together, with the big hand guiding the small.

When Jack began to yawn, Brody shifted him, laying Jack over his shoulder as he rose.

"I'm not tired," Jack claimed even as his head drooped.

"When you wake up, it'll only be five days till Christmas."

"Can I have a present?"

Brody smiled. His son's voice was thick, his body already going limp. He paused in the living room, by the tree, swaying slightly as he had when Jack had been an infant, and fretful in the night. As Christmas trees went, Brody mused, this one wasn't pretty. But it was festive. The mix of ornaments covered every available inch. Wads of tinsel shone in the multicolored lights Jack had wanted.

Rather than an angel or a star, there was a grinning Santa at the top. Jack still believed in Santa Claus. Brody wondered if he would this time the following year.

Thinking of that, of the years passed and passing still, he turned his face into his son's hair. And just breathed him in.

After he'd carried Jack up to bed, he came down and brewed a fresh pot of coffee. Probably a mistake, Brody thought even as he poured the first cup. It would very likely keep him awake.

Still he stood, looking out the dark window, sipping it black. The house was too quiet with Jack asleep. There were times, God knew, when the boy made so much noise, caused so much chaos, it seemed there would never be a moment of peace and quiet.

Then when he got it, Brody wanted the noise.

Parenting, he thought, had to be the damnedest business going.

But the problem now was restlessness. It was a feeling he hadn't experienced for quite some time. With parenting, establishing a business, making a home, soliciting jobs, he hadn't had much excess time.

Still don't, he thought, and began to pace the kitchen while he drank his coffee.

There was enough work to be done on the house to keep him busy for…probably the rest of his life. Should have bought something smaller, he thought, and less needy. Something more practical—and he'd heard variations on those thoughts from his father since he'd dug up the down payment.

Trouble was, he'd fallen head over heels for the old place, and so had Jack. And it was working, he reminded himself, glancing around the completed kitchen with its glass-fronted cabinets and granite counters.

Still, work was the bottom line, and he really had to carve out the time to deal with the rooms he'd put off.

Hard to find time when there were only days left until Christmas.

Then, there was the job due to be completed the next afternoon. And on the heels of that came the school holiday. He should have lined up a babysitter—he'd meant to. But Jack disliked them so much, and the guilt was a slow burn.

He knew Beth Skully would take Jack at least part of the time. But after a while, it felt like imposing. In an emergency, he could call on his mother. But that was a tricky business. Whenever he passed Jack off in that direction, he felt like a failure.

He'd make it work. Jack could come along with him some of the time, go to his pal Rod's some of the time. And in a pinch, he'd visit his grandmother.

And that wasn't the problem at all, Brody admitted. That wasn't the distraction, lodged like a splinter in his mind.

The splinter was Kate Kimball.

He didn't have the time nor the inclination for her.

All right, damn it, he didn't have the time. Whatever he did have for her was a hell of a ways up from inclination. He dragged a hand through his mass of sun-streaked hair and tried to ignore the sheer sexual frustration eating at his gut.

Had he ever felt this much pure physical hunger for a woman before? He must have. He just didn't remember clearly, that was all. Didn't remember being churned up this way.

And it really ticked him off.

It was only because it had been a long time. Because she was so openly provocative. So unbelievably beautiful.

But he wasn't a kid anymore who could grab pretty toys without considering the consequences. He was no longer free to do whatever he liked, when he liked. And he wouldn't want it any other way.

Not that taking her up on her obvious invitation had to have consequences. In the long run. Even in the short. They were both adults, they both knew the ropes.

And that kind of thinking, he decided, would only get him in trouble.

Do your job, he told himself. Take her money. Keep your distance.

And stop thinking about that amazing, streamlined body of hers.

He poured a second cup of coffee—knowing he was damning himself to a sleepless night—then went back to work.

The next afternoon, Kate opened the door to find Brody on her doorstep. Her pleasure at that was side-tracked by the bright-eyed little boy at his side.

"Well, hello, handsome."

"I'm Jack."

"Handsome Jack. I'm Kate. Come in."

"I'm just dropping off the drawings, and the bid." Brody held them out, kept a hand firm on Jack's shoulder. "My card's in there. If you have any questions or want to discuss the drawings or the figures, just get in touch."

"Let's save time and look them over now. What's your hurry?" She barely looked at him, but beamed smiles at Jack. "*Brr.* It's cold out there. Cold enough for cookies and hot chocolate."

"With marshmallows?"

"In this house, it's illegal to serve hot chocolate without marshmallows." She held out a hand. Jack's was already in it as he bolted inside.

"Listen—"

"Oh, come on, O'Connell. Be a sport. So, what grade are you in, Handsome Jack?" She crouched down to unzip his coat. "Eighth, ninth?"

"No." He giggled. "First."

"You're kidding. This is such a coincidence. We happen to be running a special today for blond-haired boys in first grade. Your choice of sugar, chocolate chip or peanut butter cookies."

"Can I have one of each?"

"Jack—"

"Ah, a man after my own heart," Kate said, ignoring Brody. She straightened, handed Brody Jack's coat and cap and muffler, then took the boy's hand.

"Are you the dancing lady?"

She laughed as she started back with him toward the kitchen. "Yes, I am." With that sultry smile on her lips, she glanced back over her shoulder at Brody. Gotcha, she thought. "Kitchen's this way."

"I know where the damn kitchen is."

"Dad said damn," Jack announced.

"So I hear. Maybe he shouldn't get any cookies."

"It's okay for grown-ups to say damn. But they're not supposed to say sh—"

"Jack!"

"But sometimes he says that, too," Jack finished in a conspirator's whisper. "And once when he banged his hand, he said *all* the curse words."

"Really?" Absolutely charmed, she pulled a chair out for the boy. "In a row, or all mixed up?"

"All mixed up. He said some of them lots of times." He gave her a bright smile. "Can I have three marshmallows?"

"Absolutely. You can hang those coats on the pegs there, Brody." She sent him a sunny smile, then got out the makings for the hot chocolate.

And not a little paper pack, Brody noted. But a big hunk of chocolate, milk. "We don't want to take up your time," he began.

"I have time. I put in a few hours at the store this morning. My mother's swamped. But Brandon's taking the afternoon shift. That's my brother's ball mitt," she told Jack, who instantly snatched his hand away from it.

"I was only looking."

"It's okay. You can touch, he doesn't mind. Do you like baseball?"

"I played T-ball last year, and I'm going to play Little League when I'm old enough."

"Brand played T-ball, too, and Little League. And now he plays for a real major league team. He plays third base for the L.A. Kings."

Jack's eyes rounded—little green gems. "For real?"

"For real." She crossed over, slipped the glove onto the delighted Jack's hand. "Maybe when your hand's big enough to fit, you'll play, too."

"Holy cow, Dad. It's a real baseball guy's mitt."

"Yeah." He gave up. He couldn't block anyone who gave his son such a thrill. "Very cool." He ruffled Jack's hair, smiled over at Kate. "Can I have three marshmallows, too?"

"Absolutely."

The boy was a jewel, Kate thought as she prepared the hot chocolate, set out cookies. She had a weakness for kids, and this one was, as her father had said, a pistol.

Even more interesting, she noted, was the obvious link between father and son. Strong as steel and sweet as candy. It made her want to cuddle both of them.

"Lady?"

"Kate," she said and put his mug of chocolate in front of him. "Careful now, it's hot."

"Okay. Kate, how come you wear funny clothes when you dance? Dad has no idea."

Brody made a small sound—it might have been a groan—then took an avid interest in the selection of cookies.

Kate arched her eyebrows, set the other mugs on the table, then sat. "We like to call them costumes. They help us tell whatever story we want through the dance."

"How can you tell stories with dancing? I like stories with talking."

"It's like talking, but with movement and music. What do you think of when you hear 'Jingle Bells,' without the words?"

"Christmas. It's only five days till Christmas."

"That's right, and if you were going to dance to Jingle Bells, the movements would be happy and fast and fun. They'd make you think of sleigh rides and snow. But if it was 'Silent Night,' it would be slow and reverent."

"Like in church."

Oh, aren't you quick, she thought. "Exactly. You come by my school sometime, and I'll show you how to tell a story with dancing."

"Dad's maybe going to build your school."

"Yes, maybe he is."

She opened the folder. Interesting, Brody thought, how she set the bid aside and went straight to the drawings. Possibilities rather than the bottom line.

Jack got down to business with the hot chocolate, his eyes huge with anticipation as he blew on the frothy surface to cool it. Kate ignored hers, and the cookies. When she began to ask questions, Brody scooted his chair over so they bent over the drawings together.

She smelled better than the cookies, and that was saying something.

"What is this?"

"A pocket door—it slides instead of swings. Saves space. That corridor's narrow. I put one here, too, on your office. You need privacy, but you don't have to sacrifice space."

"I like it." She turned her head. Faces close, eyes locked. "I like it very much."

"I drew some of the lines," Jack announced.

"You did a fine job," Kate told him, then went back to studying the drawings while Brody dealt with the tangle of knots in his belly.

She looked at each one carefully, considering changes, rejecting them, or putting them aside for future possibilities. She could see it all quite clearly—the lines, the angles, the flow. And noted the details Brody had added or altered. She couldn't find fault with them. At the moment.

More, she was impressed with his thoroughness. The drawings were clean and professional. She doubted she'd have gotten better with an architect.

When she was done, she picked up the bid—meticulously clear—ran down the figures. And swallowed the lump of it.

"Well, Handsome Jack." She set the paperwork down again. "You and your dad are hired."

Jack let out a cheer, and since nobody told him not to, took another cookie.

Brody didn't realize he'd been holding his breath, not until it wanted to expel in one great whoosh. He controlled it, eased back. It was the biggest job he'd taken on since moving back to West Virginia.

The work would keep him and his crew busy all through the winter—when building work was often slow. There'd be no need to cut back on his men, or their hours.

And the income would give him a whole lot of breathing room.

Over and above the vital practicalities, he'd wanted to get his hands on that building. The trick would be to keep them there, and off Kate.

"I appreciate the business."

"Remember that when I drive you crazy."

"You started out doing that. Got a pen?"

She smiled, rose to get one out of the drawer. Leaning over the table, she signed her name to the contract, dated it. "Your turn," she said, handing him the pen.

When he was done, she took the pen back, looked over at Jack. "Jack?"

"Huh?" Crumbs dribbled from the corner of his mouth. Catching his father's narrow stare, he swallowed. "I mean, yes, ma'am."

"Can you write your name?"

"I can print it. I know all the alphabet, and how to spell Jack and Dad and some stuff."

"Good. Well, come on over here and make it official." She tilted her head at his blank look. "You drew some of the lines, didn't you? You want to be hired, or not?"

Pure delight exploded on his face. "Okay!"

He scrambled down, scattering more crumbs. Taking the pen, he locked his tongue between his teeth and with painful care printed his name under his father's signature.

"Look, Dad! That's me."

"Yeah, it sure is."

Stupefied by emotion, Brody looked up, met Kate's eyes. What the hell was he going to do now? She'd hit him at his weakest point.

"Jack, go wash your hands."

"They're not dirty."

"Wash them anyway."

"Right down the hall, Jack," Kate said quietly. "Count one door, then two, on the side of the hand you write your name with."

Jack made little grumbling sounds, but he skipped out of the room.

Brody got to his feet. She didn't back off. No, she wouldn't have, he thought. So their bodies bumped a little, and his went on full alert.

"That was nice. What you did, making him feel part of it."

"He is part of it. That is clear." And so was something else that needled into her heart. "It wasn't a strategy, Brody."

"I said it was nice."

"Yes, but you're also thinking—at least wondering if—it was also clever of me. A slick little ploy to get to you. I want to sleep with you, and I'm very goal oriented, but I draw the line at using your son to achieve the desired end."

She snatched up his empty mug, started to turn. Brody laid a hand on her arm. "Okay, maybe I wondered. Now I'll apologize for it."

"Fine."

He shifted, gripped her arm until she turned to face him. "Sincerely apologize, Kate."

She relaxed. "All right. Sincerely accepted. He's

beautiful, and he's great. It's tough not to get stuck on him right off the bat."

"I'm pretty stuck on him myself."

"Yes, and he on you. It shows. I happen to like children, and admire loving parents. It only makes you more attractive."

"I'm not going to sleep with you." He wasn't gripping her arm now, but sliding his hands down the length.

She smiled. "So you say."

"I'm not going to mess up this job, complicate it and my life. I can't afford…"

He'd had something definite to say. Decisive. But she slid her hands up his chest, over his shoulders.

"You're not on the clock yet," she murmured and lifted her mouth to his.

He closed the gap and lights exploded inside his head. Eruptions blasted inside his body. Her mouth was warm, tart, persuasive. The sensations simply took control of the two of them. Of him.

He meant to take her by the shoulders, pull her back. He meant to. He could hold her at arm's length. And would.

In a little while.

But for now, for right now, he wanted to just lose himself in the sheer sensation. He wanted to have to hold her to keep his balance. She smelled dark. And dangerous.

It was irresistible. He was irresistible. He kissed like a dream, she thought, letting out a throaty little purr. As if it was all he'd ever done, all he ever wanted to do.

His mouth was soft, and hot. His hands hard, and strong. Was there anything sexier in a man than strength? The strength that came from muscles and from the heart.

He made her mind spin a dozen lazy pirouettes, with her pulse throbbing thick to keep the beat.

She wanted to send that rhythm speeding. Wanted it more than she'd anticipated. And floating on that lovely mix of anticipation, sensation and desire, she let her head fall back.

"That was nice." Her fingers slid up into his hair. "Why don't we do that again?"

He wanted to—to start and finish in one huge gulp. And his six-year-old son was splashing in the sink down the hall. "I can't do this."

"I think we just proved you could."

"I'm not going to do this." Now he did hold her at arm's length. Her eyes were dark, her mouth soft. "Damn, you muddle a man's brain."

"Apparently not enough. But it's a beginning."

He let her go. It was the safest move. And stepped back. "You know, it's been a long time since I...played this game."

"It'll come back to you. You may have been on the bench for a while, but it'll come back. Why don't we go out to dinner and start your training?"

"I washed both sides," Jack announced as he hopped back into the room. "Can I have another cookie?"

"No." He couldn't take his eyes off hers. Couldn't seem to do anything but stare and want. And wonder. "We have to go. Say thank you to Kate."

"Thanks, Kate."

"You're welcome, Jack. Come back and see me, okay?"

"Okay." He grinned at her as his father bundled him into his coat. "Will you have hot chocolate?"

"I'll make sure of it."

She walked them to the door, stood in the opening to watch them climb into the truck. Jack waved enthusiastically. Brody didn't look back at all.

A cautious man, she thought as they drove off. Well, she could hardly blame him. If she'd had something as precious as that little boy to worry about, she'd have been cautious, too.

But now that she'd met the son, she was even more interested in the man. He was a good father, one who obviously paid attention. Jack had been warmly dressed, healthy, friendly, happy.

It couldn't be easy, raising a child alone. But Brody O'Connell was doing it, and doing it well.

She respected that. Admired that. And, was attracted to that.

Maybe she'd been a little hasty, acting on pure chemistry. But she pressed her lips together, remembering the feel and taste of his and wondered who could blame her.

Still, it wouldn't hurt to take more time, to get to know him better.

After all, neither of them were going anywhere.

Chapter Four

"Earthquakes," Kate said.

"Ice storms," Brandon countered.

"Smog."

"Snow shovels."

She tossed back her hair. "The joy of the changing seasons."

He pulled her hair. "The beach."

They'd been having the debate for years—East Coast versus West. At the moment, Kate was using it to take her mind off the fact that Brandon was leaving in under an hour.

Just the post-Christmas blues, she assured herself. All that excitement and preparation, then the lovely warmth of a traditional Christmas at home had kept her so busy, and so involved.

The Kimballs had followed their Christmas Day celebrations with a two-day trip to New York, rounding everything off with all the chaos and confusion of their sprawling family.

Now it was nearly a new year. Freddie, her sister, was back in New York with her husband, Nick, and the kids. And Brandon was heading back to L.A.

She glanced out at the tidy, quiet main street as they walked. And smiled thinly. "Road rage."

"Hard-bodied blondes in convertibles."

"You are *so* shallow."

"Yeah." He hooked his arm around her neck. "You love that about me. Hey, check it out. You got men with trucks."

Still pouting, she looked down the street and saw the work trucks and laborers. Brody, she mused, didn't waste any time.

They circled around, picked their way over rubble and hillocks of winter dry grass to the rear of the building where the activity seemed to be centered. There was noise—someone was playing country music on a portable radio. There were scents—dirt, sweat and, oddly enough, mayonnaise.

Kate walked around a wheelbarrow, stepped cautiously down a ramp and peered into her basement.

Thick orange extension cords snaked to portable work lights that hung from beams or posts. Their bare-bulb glare made her basement resemble some archeological dig, still in its nasty stages.

She spotted Brody, in filthy jeans and boots, hammering a board into place on a form. Though his breath puffed out visibly as he worked, he'd stripped off his jacket. She could see the intriguing ripple of muscle under flannel.

She'd been right, Kate noted, he looked extremely good in a tool belt.

A laborer shoveled dirt into another wheelbarrow. And Jack was plopped down, digging with a small shovel and dumping his take—or most of it—into a bucket.

The boy spotted her first. Hopped up and danced. "I'm digging out the basement! I get a dollar. I get to help pour concrete. I got a truck for Christmas. You wanna see?"

"You bet."

She had taken another step down the ramp before Brody came over and blocked her. "You're not dressed to muck around down here."

She glanced down at his work boots, then her own suede sneakers. "Can't argue with that. Can you spare a minute?"

"All right. Jack, take a break."

Brody came up the ramp, squinting against the flash of winter sunlight, with his son scrambling behind him.

"This is my brother, Brandon. Brand, Brody O'Connell and Jack."

"Nice to meet you." Brody held up a grimy hand rather than offering to shake. "I've watched you play. It's a pleasure."

"Thanks. I've seen your work, same goes."

"Are you the baseball player?" Eyes huge, Jack stared up at Brandon.

"That's right." Brandon crouched down. "You like baseball?"

"Uh-huh. I saw your mitt. I've got one, too. And a bat and a ball and everything."

Knowing Brandon would keep Jack entertained, Kate

moved a few steps away to give them room. "I didn't realize you were starting so soon," she said to Brody.

"Figured we'd take advantage of the break in the weather. Warm spell's supposed to last a few more days. We can get the basement dug out, formed up and poured before the next cold snap."

Warm was relative, she thought. It would be considerably chillier in the old stone walled basement, and considerably damper than out here in the sunlight. "I'm not complaining. How was your Christmas?"

"Great." He shifted so that his crew could muscle the next barrow of dirt up the ramp. "Yours?"

"Wonderful. I see you've expanded your crew. Was that dollar a day in my bid?"

"School's out," he said shortly. "I keep him with me. He knows the rules, and the men don't mind him."

She lifted her brows. "My, my. *Sensitivo.*"

Brody hissed out a breath. "Sorry. Some clients don't like me having a kid on a job site."

"I'm not one of them."

"Hey, O'Connell, can you spare this guy for a bit?"

Brody glanced over, noted Jack's grimy hand was clasped in Brandon's. "Well…"

"We've got a little business up at the house," Brandon went on. "I'll drop him back down on my way to the airport. Half hour."

"*Please,* Dad. Can I?"

"I—"

"My brother's an idiot," Kate said with an easy smile. "But a responsible one."

No, Brody thought, *he* was the idiot, getting the jitters every time Jack went off with someone new. "Sure. Wash your hands off in the water bucket first, Jacks."

"Okay! Wait just a minute, okay? Just a minute." Jack raced off to splash some of the dirt away.

"I'll try to stop through on my way to spring training."

"Yeah. Okay." She wouldn't cry. She would *not* cry. "Stay away from those hard-bodied blondes."

"Not a chance." Brandon snatched her up, held tight. "Miss you," he murmured.

"Me, too." She pressed her face into the curve of his neck, then stepped back with a bright smile. "Take care of that leg, slugger."

"Hey, you're talking to Iron Man. Take care of your own. Let's go, Jack." He took the boy's marginally clean and wet hand, shot a salute to Brody, and started off.

"Bye, Dad! Bye. I'll be back."

"Your brother got a problem with his leg?"

"Pulled some tendons. Bad slide. Well, I'll let you get back to work." She kept the smile on her face until she'd rounded to the front of the house. Then she sat on the steps and had a nice little cry.

When Brody walked out to his truck ten minutes later, she was still there. Tears had dried on her cheeks. A few more sparkled in her lashes.

"What? What's the matter?"

"Nothing."

"You've been crying."

She sniffled, shrugged. "So?"

He wanted to leave it at that. Really wanted to just get his…what the hell had he come out for? The problem was he'd never been able to walk away from tears. Resigned, he crossed the sidewalk and sat beside her.

"What's wrong?"

"I hate saying goodbye. I wouldn't have to say goodbye if he didn't insist on living three thousand miles away in stupid California. The dope."

Ah, her brother. "Well…" Because a fresh tear had spilled over, Brody yanked a bandanna from his pocket. "He works there."

"Excuse me, but I'm not feeling particularly logical." She took the bandanna. "Thanks."

"Don't mention it."

She dabbed at tears, then stared across the street. "Do you have any siblings?"

"No."

"Want one? I'll sell him cheap." She sighed, leaned back on the steps. "My sister's in New York. Brand's in L.A. I'm in West Virginia. I never thought we'd end up so scattered."

He remembered the way she and her brother had embraced, that natural flow of love. "You don't look scattered to me."

Kate looked back at him. In a moment, her eyes cleared. "You're right. You're absolutely right. That was exactly the right thing to say. So." She drew in a breath, handed him back his bandanna. "Take my mind off all this for a minute. What'd you do for Christmas? The big, noisy family thing?"

"Jack makes plenty of noise. He got me up at five." Remembering made Brody smile. "I think I peeled him off the ceiling around two that afternoon."

"Did he make it through Christmas dinner?"

Brody's smile faded. "Yeah, barely." He moved his shoulder. "We went over to his grandparents' for that. We live in the same town," he said. "But you could say we're scattered."

"I'm sorry."

"They dote on Jack. That's the important thing."

And why the hell did he bring it up? Maybe, he thought, maybe because it was stuck in his craw. Maybe because his father continued to dismiss everything he'd done with his life, everything he wanted to do.

"I'm having the dirt dumped around the other side of the house. You might want to have it spread there, start a garden or something in the spring."

"That's a good thought."

"Well." He got to his feet. "I've got to get back to work, before the boss docks my pay."

"Brody—" She wasn't sure what she meant to say, or how she meant to say it. Then the moment passed as Brandon pulled up to the curb in his spiffy rental car.

"Dad!" Jack was already fighting to free himself from the seat belt. "Wait till you see! Brand gave me his mitt, and a baseball with his name wrote on it and everything."

"Written on it," Brody said automatically, then caught the bullet of his son as Jack shot toward him. "Let's have a look." He examined the mitt and ball, both warm from Jack's tight grip. "These are really special, and you'll have to take special care of them."

"I will. I promise. Thanks, Brand. Thanks! I'm going to keep them forever. Can we show the guys now, Dad?"

"You bet." Brody hitched Jack higher on his hip, looked down at Brandon. "Thanks."

"My pleasure. Remember, Jack. Keep your eye on the ball."

"I will! Bye."

"Safe trip," Brody added, and carted Jack around to show off his treasures to the crew.

Kate let out a little sigh, leaned down into Brandon's open window. "Maybe you're not such a jerk after all."

"Hell of a kid." He pinched Kate's chin. "You got an eye on the dad, I noticed."

"No. I've got both eyes on the dad." Laughing, she leaned in to give him a kiss. "You go ahead after those California girls, pal. I like country boys."

"Behave yourself."

"Not a chance."

He laughed, turned on the engine again. "See you, gorgeous."

She stepped back, waved. "Fly safe," she murmured.

It was traditional for Natasha to close the shop on New Year's Eve. She spent the day in the kitchen, preparing the myriad dishes she'd set out for the open house she held every New Year's Day. Family, friends, neighbors would crowd the house for hours.

"Brand should have stayed until after the party."

"I wish he could have." Natasha checked the apricots and water she was boiling for kissel, turned the mixture down to simmer. "Don't sulk, Katie. There were times your life and your work kept you away."

"I know." Kate continued to roll out pastry dough as she'd been taught. "I just need a little more sulk time. I miss the jerk, that's all."

"So do I."

On the stove, pots puffed steam. In the oven, an enormous ham was baking. Years ago, Natasha thought, she'd have had three children underfoot while she was juggling these chores. There would have been squabbling, giggling, spills to mop up. Her patience would have been sorely tried a dozen times.

It had been wonderful.

Now she only had her Kate, pouting over the pastry dough.

"You're restless." Natasha tapped a spoon on the side of a pot, set it on its holder. "You don't have enough to fill your time while the building is going on."

"I'm making plans."

"Yes, I know." She poured two cups of tea, brought them to the table. "Sit."

"Mama, I'm—"

"Sit. So, you're like me," Natasha continued as they both took seats at the crowded table. "Plans, details, goals. These are so important. We want to know what happens next, because if we know, we can have control."

"What's wrong with that?"

"Nothing. When I came here to open my store, it was very hard. Hard to leave the family. But I needed to. I didn't know I'd meet your father here. That wasn't planned."

"It was fate."

"Yes." Natasha smiled. "We plan, you and I, and we calculate. And still, we understand fate. So maybe fate, for all your plans, brought you back."

"Are you disappointed?" She blurted it out, and felt both relief and dread that it had finally been asked.

"In what? You? Why would you think so?"

"Mama." Searching for words, Kate turned her cup around and around. "I know how much you and Dad sacrificed—"

"Wait." Dark eyes kindling, Natasha tapped her fingers hard on the table. "Maybe, after all these years my

English is failing. I don't understand the word *sacrifice* when it comes to my children. You have never been a sacrifice."

"I meant, you and Dad did so much, supported me in every way when I wanted to dance. Please, Mama," Kate said when Natasha started to speak. "Just let me finish this. It's been on my mind. All the lessons, all those years. The costumes, the shoes, the travel. Letting me go to New York when I know Dad would have preferred I'd gone to college. But you let me have what I needed most. I always knew that. I wanted you to be proud of me."

"Of course we were proud of you. What nonsense have you put in your head?"

"I know you were. I know. I could feel it, see it. When I was dancing and you were there, even when I couldn't see you through the footlights, I could *see*. And now I've tossed it away."

"No, you've set it aside. Kate, do you think we're only proud of you when you dance? Only proud of the artist, of that skill?"

Her eyes were brimming. She couldn't help it. "I worried that you might be disappointed that I gave it up to teach."

"Of all my children," Natasha said with a shake of her head, "you are the one forever searching in corners to see if there's a speck of dust. Even when there isn't, you can't help but poke in with the broom. Answer me this, do you want to be a good teacher?"

"Yes, very much."

"Then you will be, and we'll be proud of that. And between these times, between the dancer and the teacher, we're proud of you. Proud that you know what you want, and how to work for it. Proud that you're a lovely young woman with a kind heart and a strong mind. If you doubt that, Katie, you will disappoint me."

"I don't. I won't. Oh." She let out a long breath and blinked at the tears. "I don't know what's wrong with me. I'm so weepy lately."

"You're changing your life. It's an emotional time. And you give yourself too much time to think and worry. Kate, why aren't you out with your friends? You have so many still in the area. Why aren't you going out to a party tonight, or with some handsome young man, instead of staying home on New Year's Eve to bake a ham with your mama?"

"I like baking hams with my mama."

"Kate."

"All right." But she got up to finish the pastry. She needed to keep her hands busy. "I thought about going to one of the parties tonight. But most of my friends are married, or at least coupled off. But I'm not a couple and I'm not really...shopping around. You know?"

"Mmm. And why aren't you...shopping around?"

"Because I've already seen something that appeals to me."

"Ah. Who?"

"Brody O'Connell."

"Ah," Natasha said again, and lifted her tea to sip and consider. "I see."

"I'm very attracted to him."

"He's a very attractive man." Natasha's eyes began to dance. "Yes, very attractive, and I like him very much."

"Mama—you didn't send him down to look at the job to throw us together, romantically?"

"No. But I would have if I'd thought of it. So, why aren't you out with Brody O'Connell for New Year's Eve?"

"He's scared of me." Kate laughed when her mother made a dismissing noise. "Well, *uneasy* might be a better word. I might have come on a little strong, initially."

"You?" Natasha deliberately rounded her eyes. "My shy little Katie?"

"Okay, okay." Laughing now, Kate set aside the rolling pin. "I definitely came on too strong. But when I ran into him the first time in the toy store when he was getting a toy for Jack, and we were flirting, I thought we were on the same wavelength."

"In the toy store," Natasha murmured. She and Spence had met the first time in the toy store, when he had been picking out a doll for his daughter, Freddie.

Fate, she thought. You could never anticipate it.

"Yes, then when I realized he was buying that truck for his son, I assumed he was married. So I was annoyed he'd flirted back."

"Of course." Natasha was grinning now. It just got better and better.

"Then, of course, I found out he wasn't, and the field was open. He's interested, too," she muttered and banged the rolling pin. "Just stubborn about it."

"He's lonely."

Kate looked up, and the little spark of temper she'd hoped to fan into flame flickered out. "Yes, I know. But he keeps stepping back from me. Maybe he does that with everyone, but Jack."

"He's very warm and friendly with me. Yet when

I asked him to come by tomorrow, he made excuses. You should change his mind," Natasha decided. She rose to get back to work. "Yes, you should go by his house later, take him a dish of the black-eyed peas for luck in the new year, and change his mind about coming by tomorrow."

"It's pretty presumptuous, dropping by a man's house on New Year's Eve," Kate said, then grinned. "It's perfect. Thanks, Mama."

"Good." Natasha dipped a finger into the pastry filling, licked it off. "Then your father and I will have a little New Year's Eve party of our own."

Brody nursed a beer and wished he hadn't eaten that last slice of pizza. He was sprawled on the couch, with Jack, in the center of the disaster that had been their living room. Some B horror flick involving giant alien eyeballs was on TV.

He loved B movies—couldn't help himself.

In a couple of hours, he'd switch it over to the coverage of Time's Square. Jack wanted to see the ball drop—and had insisted he could stay awake until midnight.

He'd done everything but prop his eyelids open with toothpicks to make it, which explained the state of the house. He'd finally dropped, snuggled into the crook of Brody's arm.

Brody would hold the fort until five minutes before midnight, then wake Jack up to see the new year in.

Brody sipped his beer and watched the giant eye menace the humans.

And nearly jumped out of his skin when the knock sounded at his door.

Cursing, he slid Jack down onto the couch so he could lever himself off. The odds of someone coming to his door after ten at night, he figured, were about the same as giant alien eyeballs threatening the Earth.

He stepped over and around toys, shoes, socks, and headed for the door. Somebody lost or broken down, he decided. Everyone he knew was celebrating the new year, one way or the other.

Not everyone, he realized with a jolt as he opened the door to Kate.

"Hi. I took a chance you'd be home. My mother sends this."

He found the small covered bowl thrust into his hands. "Your mother?"

"Yes. You hurt her feelings saying you were too busy to come by tomorrow."

"I didn't say I was too busy, I..." What the hell had he said? He'd made it up on the spot, and for the life of him couldn't remember.

"The black-eyed peas are for luck," Kate told him. "Mama really hopes you'll change your mind and stop by. There'll be plenty of kids for Jack to hang out with. Is he up? I'll say hi."

She slipped past him into the house. He'd been too distracted to stop her. Or even try to. But he was already hurrying after her across the little foyer and into the big, messy living room where the TV blared.

Mortified, he snatched up toys and debris in her wake.

"Oh, don't start that." She waved a hand impatiently. "I know what houses with children look like. I grew up in one. What a great tree!"

Arms full, he stared at it. He'd seen the one in her

parents' living room. Beautiful ornaments, placed with care. His and Jack's looked like it had been decorated by drunk elves.

"We had one that looked like this. Freddie, Brand and I nagged Mama until she agreed to let us do the tree one year. We made a hell of a mess. It was great."

There was a fire snapping in the hearth so she walked over to warm her hands. She'd spent over an hour dressing, so that she could look completely casual. The deep purple sweater was lightly tucked into gray trousers. Tiny gold hoops glinted at her ears. She'd left her hair loose after a heated self-debate, so that it streamed down to her waist.

She imagined he'd taken less than ten minutes to look fabulous in his jeans and sweatshirt. "Terrific house," she commented. "Native stone, right? Such a quiet spot. Must be great for Jack, all this running room. You'll need to get him a dog."

"Yeah, he's made noises in that area." What the hell was he supposed to do? Now? With her? "Thank your mother for the peas."

"Thank her yourself." Kate turned, then spotted Jack facedown on the couch, one arm dangling. "Conked out, did he?" she went to the boy, automatically lifting his arm back on the cushion, draping the ancient afghan over him. "Trying to stay awake till midnight?"

"Yeah."

He looked baffled, Kate thought. Baffled, rumpled and mouthwatering standing there with her mother's bowl and Jack's toys piled in his arms. "I love this movie," she said easily, glancing at the TV. "Especially the part where they open up that doorway and it's full of alien eyeballs and tentacles. Why don't you offer me a drink? It's traditional."

"Beer's it."

"Oh, major calories. Okay, I'll live dangerously." She walked over, took her mother's bowl. "Where's the kitchen?"

"It's…" She was wearing perfume—something just sliding toward hot. The room had never experienced that sort of seductive female scent before. He glanced to the left, dropped a toy car on his foot.

"I'll find it. Want a refill?"

"No, I've got—" For God's sake, he thought, dumping the toys and going after her again. "Look, Kate, you caught me at a bad time."

"Boy, look at these ceilings. Have you been doing the rehab yourself?"

"When I have some spare time. Listen—"

He broke off, swore, when she strolled into the kitchen. "Wow." She scanned the room. Granite countertops, slate floor, oak cupboards and a charming little stone hearth.

And every inch covered with dishes, pots, school papers, newspapers, discarded outerwear.

"Wow," she said again. "This took some real effort." She stepped over to the counter where what was left of the pizza had yet to be put away. Broke off a corner. Nibbled. "Good."

The drunk elves, he thought, had nothing on the war-crazed monkeys that had invaded his kitchen. "It's usually not this bad."

"You had a party with your son. Stop apologizing. Beer in the fridge?"

"Yeah, yeah." Hell with it. "Why aren't you at a party?"

"I am. I just came late." She handed him the beer. "Open that for me, will you?" She sniffed the air while he twisted off the cap. "I smell popcorn."

"We pretty much finished that off."

"Well, that's what I get for being late." She leaned back against the counter, took a sip of beer. "Want to go sit on the couch, watch the rest of the movie and make out?"

"Yeah. No."

"No to which, the movie or the making-out?"

She was laughing at him. He wanted to be enraged. But was only aroused. "You keep getting in my way."

"So what are you going to do about it?"

With his eyes on hers, he closed the distance between them. Took the bottle from her hand, set it aside.

New Year's Eve, he thought. Out with the old. In with the...who knew?

"Well." Pulses thrumming, she started to slide her hands up his chest, but he caught them in his.

"No. My turn."

He lowered his head, and his mouth began to whisper over hers.

"Dad?"

"Oh God." It came out on a low moan as Brody stepped back.

Jack stood in the doorway, rubbing sleepy eyes. "What are you doing, Dad?"

"Nothing." And the doing of nothing with Kate was very likely to kill him.

"Actually your dad was going to kiss me."

"Kate." He said it in precisely the same tone he'd used when Jack said something unfortunate.

"Nah." Jack, in his oldest Power Ranger pajamas,

studied them owlishly. His hair stood up in pale spikes, and his cheeks were still flushed from sleep. "Dad doesn't kiss girls."

"Really?" Before Brody could back too far away, Kate simply grabbed ahold of his shirt. "Why not?"

"Because they're *girls*." To emphasize the point, Jack rolled his eyes. "Kissing girls is yuck."

"Oh, yeah." She bumped the father aside, crooked a finger to the son. "Come here, pal."

"How come?"

"So I can kiss you all over your face."

"Nuh-uh!" His eyes widened, and danced. "Yuck-o."

"Okay." She peeled off her coat, tossed it to Brody, then pushed up her sleeves. "That's it. You're doomed."

She made a grab, giving him enough time to yelp and run for cover. She played dodge and dart for a few minutes, surprising Brody at how easily she avoided trampling on toys. Jack squealed for help, obviously having a great time.

She caught him, wrestled him to the couch, pinned him while he laughed and screamed for mercy.

"Now...the ultimate punishment." She dashed kisses over his cheeks, punctuating them with loud smacks. "Say yummy," she ordered.

"Nuh-uh!" He was breathless and his belly was wild with laughter and delight.

"Say yummy, yummy, yummy or I'll never stop."

"Yummy!" he shouted, choking on giggles. "Yummy, yummy."

"There." She sat back, whistled out a breath. "My work is done."

Jack crawled right into her lap. She wasn't soft like Grandma, or hard like Dad. She was different, and her hair was soft and tickly. "Are you going to stay till midnight when it's new year?"

"I'd love to." She glanced over her shoulder at Brody. "If your dad says it's okay."

Some battles, he thought, were lost before they were waged. "I'll get your beer."

Chapter Five

"Now." Frederica Kimball LeBeck dragged her sister into Kate's bedroom, firmly closed the door. That would, she calculated, insure them approximately five minutes of quiet and privacy. "Tell me everything—from the beginning."

"Okay. According to scientific evidence, there was a great explosion in space."

"Ha-ha. About Brody O'Connell." Eight years Kate's senior—light where Kate was dark, petite where Kate was willowy, Freddie flopped on the bed. "Mama told me you've got him in your crosshairs."

"He's not a rabbit." Kate flopped on the bed in turn. "Gorgeous, though, huh?"

"Oh, yeah. Excellent shoulders. So what's the deal?"

"The deal is he's a widower, doing a bang up job raising a terrific boy. You saw Jack right?"

"Can't miss him. He's giving my Max a run for his money," she added, speaking of her own six-year-old son. "They're bonding over video games."

"Great, that'll push Brody into the social mix. I don't think he's given himself much chance to play."

"He's getting one now, whether he wants it or not. Grandpa and Uncle Mik shanghaied him. I saw them shoving him out the door so they could all go look at your building and make manly carpenter-guy noises over it."

"Perfect."

"So, is it just glands, or is it more?"

"Well, it started with glands. My glands are very susceptible to big, strong men—and their tool belts."

While Freddie snorted with laughter, Kate rolled over on her back, studied the ceiling. "Could be more. He seems like—I don't know, just a very nice man—solid, responsible, loving. The kind of man I haven't seen much of. Gun-shy, too, in a really sweet way, which makes him a wonderful challenge."

"And nobody likes a challenge more than you."

"True. Unless it's you. And I wouldn't mind pursuing the whole thing at that level. But every time I see him with Jack, there's this little…tug inside. You know?"

"Yeah." Freddie had started experiencing those tugs where her own husband, Nick, was concerned at approximately the age of thirteen. "Are you falling for him?"

"Too soon to know. But I really like him on all the important levels, which balances out nicely with all this wild lust."

She lifted her leg, pointed her toe at the ceiling. "I really want to get him alone somewhere and rip his clothes off. But I know I can also have a good conversation with him. Last night we watched the last part of that movie about the giant eye from space."

"Yeah. I love that movie."

"Me, too. That's what I mean. It was really comfortable and easy." And sweet, she thought with a long, lazy stretch. Absolutely sweet. "Even though he gives me that zing in the blood, it's nice to just sit on the couch and watch an old movie. Most of the guys I dated, it was either dancing, partying, dancing, art shows, dancing. There was never any let's just stay home for a night and relax. I'm really ready to do that."

"Small town, ballet school, a romance with a carpenter. It suits you, Katie."

"Yeah." Delighted Freddie could think so, she rolled over again. "It really does."

Yuri Stanislaski, a bull of a man with a fringe of stone-gray hair, stood in the center of the room destined to be a dance studio.

"So, this is good space. My granddaughter, she knows the value of space. Strong foundation." He walked over, gave the wall a punch with the side of his fist. "Good bones."

Mikhail, Yuri's oldest son, stood at the front windows. "She'll relive her childhood out here. It's good for her. And—" he turned, flashed a smile "—people look in, see the dancers. Advertisement. My niece is a clever girl."

There were pounding feet on the steps. Brody had no idea how many of the young people had come down with them. He thought most of them belonged to Mik, but it was impossible to keep track when there were so many of them, and all almost ridiculously good-looking.

He wasn't used to large families, all the byplay and interaction. And he had a feeling the Stanislaskis were about as big as a family could get without just bursting at the seams.

"Papa! Come on up. You gotta see this place. It's ancient. It's great!"

"My son, Griff," Mik said with a twinkle. "He likes old things."

"So, we go up." Yuri gave Brody a pat on the back that could have toppled an elephant. "We see what it is you do with this ancient great place to make my little girl safe and happy. She is a beauty, my Katie. Yes?"

"Yes," Brody said, cautiously.

"And strong."

"Ah." Unsure of his ground, he glanced toward Mikhail for help and got only that thousand-watt grin. "Sure."

"Also good bones." Yuri let out another hearty laugh, and twinkling at his son in what was an unmistakable inside joke, started up the stairs.

Brody didn't know how it happened. He'd meant to do no more than drop in on the Kimballs. To be polite, to thank Natasha for thinking of him and Jack.

He'd gotten swept in. Swallowed was more like it, he decided. He wasn't sure he'd ever seen that many people in one place at one time before. And most of them were related in one way or the other.

Since his own family consisted of himself and Jack, his parents—with three aunts and uncles and six cousins scattered down south—the sheer number of Stanislaskis had been an eye-opener.

Frankly he didn't see how they kept track of each other.

They were loud, beautiful, boisterous, full of questions, stories and arguments. The house had been so full of people, food, drink, music, that although he'd ended staying until nearly eight, he'd had no more than a few snatches of conversation with Kate.

He'd been dragged off to the building, grilled over his plans—and he wasn't dim enough to have been fooled that the grilling had been exclusively on rehab.

Kate's family had been sizing him up. Connie's had done the same, he remembered. Certainly not with this good humor or affection or, well, sheer amusement, Brody decided. But the bottom line was identical.

Was this guy good enough for their princess? In Connie's case the answer had been an unqualified no. The resentment on both sides had tainted everything that had happened afterward with shadows.

His impression was the Stanislaski verdict was still pending. Nothing he'd done to tactfully demonstrate he wasn't looking to sweep the ballerina off her toe shoes had stopped them from cornering him—good-naturedly. Asking questions—politely. Or giving him the old once-over—without the least bit of subtlety.

It was more than enough to make a man glad he was single, and intended to stay that way.

Now the party was over. The holidays were, thank the Lord, behind him. He could get back to work, remembering that Kate Kimball was a client. And not a lover.

* * *

He spent a week tearing out, cleaning out, prepping walls, checking pipes.

She never came by.

Every day when he arrived on the site, he imagined she'd stroll down at some point and check the progress. Every evening when he loaded his tools back into his truck he wondered what she was up to.

Obviously she was busy, had other things to deal with. Didn't care as much as she'd indicated about the job. Very obviously, she wasn't as interested in him as she'd pretended to be.

Which was why he'd been very smart to avoid getting tangled up with some sort of fling with her. She was probably staying out half the night living it up, and spending the other half with some slick New Yorker. He wouldn't be surprised at all. Not one bit. He wouldn't be surprised if she was already making plans to sell the property and shake the small-town dust off her dancing shoes.

But he was surprised to find himself striding up the steps to her front door and banging on it.

He paced the porch. She was the one who'd wanted to nail down every detail, wasn't she? He strode back to the door, banged again. The least she could do was maintain some pretense of interest in the project for a lousy week.

He zigzagged back and forth across the porch again. What the hell was he doing? This was stupid. It was none of his business what she did or how she did it, as long as she paid the freight. He drew a deep breath, let it out slowly and had nearly calmed himself down when the door opened.

There she was, looking all heavy-eyed and sleepy, her face flushed, her hair just a little tumbled. Like a woman who'd just slid herself out of bed, and had plans to slide right back in again.

Damn it.

"Brody?"

"Yeah. Sorry to wake you up. After all it's only four in the afternoon."

Her brain was too fuzzy to register the insult, so she gave him a sleepy smile. "It's all right. If I go down for more than an hour in the afternoon, I don't sleep well at night. Come on in. I need coffee."

Assuming he'd follow, she turned and walked back toward the kitchen. She heard the door slam, but since it often did in this house, she didn't think anything of it. "I just got in a couple of hours ago." She started a fresh pot, willed it to hurry. To stretch out fatigued muscles, she automatically moved into the first position. "How are things going on my job?"

"Your interest in stuff always blow hot and cold?"

"Hmm? What?" Third position, rise to toes. Get coffee mugs from cupboard.

"You haven't been to the site in a week."

"I was out of town. You take it black, right? A little emergency in New York."

Instantly his annoyance shifted into concern. "Your family?"

"Oh, no. They're fine." She arched her back, twisted a little, winced. "Can you...I've got this spot right back..."

She curved her arm over her back, trying to reach a sore muscle between her shoulder blades. "Just press in there with your thumb for a minute. A little lower," she said when he complied. "Oh. Mmm, that's it. Harder." She let out a low, throaty groan, tipped her head back, closed her eyes. "Oh, yes. Yes. Don't stop."

"The hell with this." Viciously aroused, he spun her around, slammed her back against the counter and crushed his mouth to hers.

Heat flashed through her logy system, lights slashed through her sleep-dulled brain. Her lips parted on a gasp of surprise, and he took the kiss deep. Took her deep before she could find her balance. She lifted her hands, a helpless flutter, as she tried to catch up.

She was trapped between his body and the counter, two unyielding surfaces. All the fatigue, the vague aches, burned away in the sudden fireball of sensation.

Frustration, need, temper, lust. They'd all been bottled up inside him since the first moment he'd seen her. Now that the cork was popped, the passion poured out. He took what he hadn't allowed himself to want, ravaging her mouth to feed the hunger.

And when she gripped his shoulders and began to tremble, he took more.

They were both breathless when he tore his mouth from hers. For a long moment they stayed as they were, staring at each other, with his hands fisted in her hair, and her fingers digging into his shoulders.

Then their mouths were locked again, a reckless war of lips and tongues and teeth. Her hands tugged at his shirt, his rushed under her sweater. Groping, gasping, they struggled to find more. His back rapped against the refrigerator; her teeth scraped along his neck. He circled around until they bumped the kitchen table. He molded her hips, was about to lift them onto that hard, flat surface.

"Katie, is that fresh coffee I…" Spencer Kimball stopped short in the doorway, slapped hard in the heart by the sight of his baby girl wrapped like a vine around his carpenter.

They broke apart, with the guilty jerk of a child caught with its hand in the cookie jar.

For an awkward, endless five seconds no one spoke nor moved.

"I, ah…" Dear God, was all Spencer could think. "I need to…hmm. In the music room."

He backed out, walked quickly away.

Brody dragged his hands through his hair, fisted them there. "Oh, God. Get me a gun. I'd like to shoot myself now and get it over with."

"We don't have one." She gripped the back of a ladder-back chair. The room was still spinning. "It's all right. My father knows I kiss men on occasion."

Brody dropped his hands. "I was about to do a hell of a lot more than kiss you, and on your mother's kitchen table."

"I know." Wasn't her pulse still banging like a kettle-drum? Couldn't she see the blind heat of desire in those wonderful eyes of his? "It's a damn shame Dad didn't have late classes today."

"This is not good." He hissed out a breath, turned on his heel and yanked a glass out of a cupboard. He filled it with cold water from the tap, considered splashing it in his face, then gulped it down instead. It didn't do much in the way of cooling him off, but it was a start. "This wouldn't have happened if you hadn't ticked me off."

"Ticked you off?" She wanted to smooth down all that streaky hair she'd mussed. Then she wanted to muss it all again. "About what?"

"Then you get me to touch you and you start making sex noises."

The hell with coffee, she decided, she wanted a drink. "Those weren't *sex* noises." She wrenched open the fridge, took out a bottle of white wine. "Those were muscle relief noises, which, I suppose, could amount to roughly the same thing. Get me down a damn wineglass, because now *I'm* ticked off."

"You?" He slammed open another cupboard, plucked out a simple stemmed glass, shoved it at her. "You go traipsing off to New York for a damn week. Don't tell anybody where you are."

"I beg your pardon." Her voice cut like ice. "Both my parents knew exactly where I was." She poured the wine, slammed the bottle down on the counter. "I was unaware I was required to check my schedule with you."

"You hired me to do a job, didn't you? A big, complicated job which you stated—clearly—you intended to be involved in, step by step. It so happens several steps have been taken during this week while you pulled your vanishing act."

"It couldn't be helped." She took a long sip of wine and tried to find the control button on her temper. "If you'd had any problems, any questions, either my mother or father could have put you in touch with me. Why didn't you ask them?"

"Because..." There had to be a reason. "My clients are usually old enough to leave me a contact number and not expect me to hunt them down through their parents."

"That's lame, O'Connell," she said, though the statement stung a bit. "However, in the future, you are directed to consult with either of my parents should you not be able to contact me. All right?"

"Fine." He jammed his hands into his pockets. "Dandy."

"And keen," she finished. It was a ridiculous argument, she decided. And though she didn't mind a good fight, she did object to being ridiculous. "Listen, I had to go to New York. When I left the company, I gave the director my word that should I be needed, and it was possible, I would fill in. I keep my word. Several of the dancers, including principals, were wiped out with the flu. We dance hurt, we dance sick, but sometimes you just can't pull it off. I gave him a week. Eight performances, while sick dancers recovered—and a couple more dropped."

She leaned back against the counter to take the weight off her legs. "My partner and I were unfamiliar with each other, which meant long, intense rehearsals. I haven't danced professionally in nearly three months. I was out of shape, so I took some extra morning classes. This didn't leave me a lot of time or energy to worry about a project I assumed was in capable hands. It didn't occur to me you'd need to reach me this early in the project, after we'd just spoken. I hope that clears things up for you."

"Yeah, that clears it up. Can I borrow a knife?"

"What?"

"You don't have a gun handy, but I can use a knife to slit my throat."

"Why don't you wait until you get home?" She sipped

her wine again, watching him over the rim. "My mother hates blood on the kitchen floor."

"Your father probably doesn't like his daughter having sex on the kitchen table, either."

"I don't know. The subject's never come up before."

"I didn't mean to grab you that way."

"Really." She held out her glass. "Which way did you mean to grab me?"

"Not." With a shrug he took the wine from her hand, sampled it. "You can see this is already getting complicated and jumbled up. The job, you, me. Sex."

"I'm very good at organizing and compartmentalizing. Some consider it one of my best—and most annoying—skills."

"Yeah, I bet." He handed her back the glass. "Kate."

She smiled. "Brody."

He laughed a little, and with his hands back in his pockets, roamed the room. "I've done a lot of screwing up in my life. With Connie—my wife—and Jack. I worked really hard to change that. Jack's only six. I'm all he's got. I can't put anything ahead of that."

"If you could, I'd think a great deal less of you. If you could, I wouldn't be attracted to you."

He turned back, studying her face. "I can't figure you."

"Maybe you should see if you can organize your schedule, so you can spend a little time on that problem?"

"Maybe we should just rent a motel room on Route 81 some afternoon and pretend there isn't a problem."

To his surprise, she laughed. "Well, that's another alternative. Personally, I'd like to do both. Why don't I leave it up to you, for the moment, as to which part of the solution we approach first?"

"Why don't we…" He glanced at the clock on the stove, swore. "I've got to go pick up Jack. Maybe you could come down to the job tomorrow at lunchtime. I'll buy you a sandwich and show you what we're doing."

"I'll do that." She tilted her head. "Want to kiss me goodbye?"

He glanced at the kitchen table, back at her. "Better not. Your father might have a weapon in the house you don't know about."

Spencer Kimball wasn't loading a shotgun. Kate found him in his studio going over his lesson plans for the current semester. He'd been going over the same page for the last ten minutes.

She crossed to where he sat at his desk looking out the window. She set a cup of coffee at his elbow, then wrapped her arms around him and propped her chin on his shoulder. "Hi."

"Hi. Thanks."

She rubbed her cheek against his and studied his view of their pretty backyard. She would ask her mother to help her plan the gardens for the school.

"Brody seems to be concerned you may shoot him."

"I don't have a gun."

"That's what I said. I also told him that my father knows I've kissed men. You do know that, don't you, Daddy?"

She only called him Daddy when she was trying to charm him. They both knew it. "What I know intellectually is a far cry from walking in on… He had his hands on your…" Spencer set his teeth. "He had his hands on my little girl."

"Your little girl had her hands on him, too." She scooted around, wiggled into her father's lap.

"I hardly think the kitchen is the proper place for you to…" What? Exactly what?

"You're right, of course." She made her voice very prim, very proper. "The kitchen is for cooking. I've certainly never seen you and Mama kissing in the kitchen. I'd have been horrified."

His lips wanted to twitch, but he overcame the urge. "Shut up."

"I always knew, if I happened to walk into the room and you and Mama *appeared* to be kissing, you were really practicing lifesaving techniques. Can't be too careful."

"You're going to need lifesaving techniques in a minute."

"Until then, let me ask you this. Do you like Brody, as a man?"

"Yes, of course, but that doesn't mean I'm going to do handsprings of joy when I walk into my kitchen and see…what I saw."

"Well, there's a possibility of a motel room on Route 81 in my future."

"Ah." Spencer dropped his forehead to hers. "Kate."

"You and Mom taught me I never had to hide anything from you. My feelings, my actions. I have feelings for Brody. I'm not completely sure what those feelings entail, but my actions are going to reflect them."

"Your actions have always reflected your feelings, with a stiff dose of logic tossed in."

"This won't be any different."

"What about his feelings?"

"He doesn't know. We'll figure it out."

"Doesn't know?" His eyes, so like hers, went to smoky slits. "Well, the boy better make up his mind in a hurry, or—"

"*Oooh,* Daddy." Kate blinked rapidly, shivered. "Are you going to go beat him up for me? Can I watch?"

"*Really* going to need those lifesaving techniques," Spencer muttered.

"I love you." She pressed a kiss to his cheek. "You raised a child, on your own, for a number of years. You know what it means when you do that, when you love the child, when you're committed to the child."

His Freddie. His first baby, now with babies of her own. "Yes, I do."

"How could I not be attracted to that part of him, Daddy, that I love so much in you?"

"And how am I supposed to argue with that?" He cuddled her closer, sighed. "You can tell Brody I don't plan to buy a gun. Yet."

She went down for lunch the next day. Then made a habit of dropping by, taking pastries and coffee, subs or sandwiches, to Brody and his crew.

Some might have called it a bribe. In fact, Brody called it exactly that, as the offerings tended to make his men more cooperative when Kate skewered them with questions, or asked for changes to the original plan.

It didn't stop him from anticipating her visits, or gauging his time so he could spare twenty minutes or a half hour to walk with her around town, or share a cup of coffee with her in the little café up the street.

He knew his men were wiggling their eyebrows or

giving each other elbow nudges whenever he walked off with Kate. But since he'd gone to high school with most of them, he took it in the spirit it was meant.

And if he caught one of them, occasionally, checking out her butt or her legs, it only took one hard stare to have that individual getting busy elsewhere.

He still couldn't figure her. She sauntered down to the job looking, always, like something clipped from the glossy pages of a magazine. Perfect and female. But she poked around the dust and grime of the site as if she were one of the crew, asking pointed questions about things like the wiring.

He'd come across her having a heated debate with one of his men over baseball. And an hour later, he overheard her on her cell phone, chatting away in precise and fluent French.

No, after two weeks of this easy routine, he still couldn't figure her. But neither could he stop thinking about her.

Now, as she wandered the main studio, he couldn't stop looking at her.

She wore some soft sweater in deep blue over gray leggings. Her hair was bundled up in some fascinating way that left her nape bare and sexy.

The room was warm thanks to the new heating system. The plaster work was well underway, and he'd brought in the first samples of the woodwork he had molded himself to match the original.

His father had left only a short time before, after putting in six hours on plumbing. A difficult and tense six hours, Brody thought now. It was a pleasure to put that aside and look at Kate.

"The plasterer's doing a great job," she said after

touring the walls. "I almost feel guilty that we're going to cover so much up with mirrors."

"Your glass is on order. It'll be in middle of February."

She picked up the sample of woodwork. "This is beautiful, Brody. You'll never be able to tell it from the original."

"That's the idea."

"Yes, it is." She set the wood down again. "You're moving along, right on schedule. Jobwise. But..." She started toward him. "In the personal department, you're lagging."

"Takes a while to lay the groundwork."

"Depends what you're planning on building, Brody." She laid her hands on his shoulder. "I want a date."

"We had lunch."

"A grown-up date. The sort reasonable, unattached adults indulge in from time to time. Dinner, O'Connell. Maybe a movie. You may not be aware, but many restaurants stay open after the lunch shift."

"I've heard that. Look, Kate." He backed up, but she moved forward with him. "There's Jack, and school nights, and complications."

"Yes, there's Jack. I enjoy spending time with him, but I'd like a little one-on-one with Jack's father. I don't think your son will be scarred for life if you go out one evening. In fact, here's what we're going to do. You, me, Friday night. Dinner. I'll make the arrangements. Pick me up at seven. You, me, Jack, Saturday afternoon. Movies. My treat. I'll pick you both up at one. Settled."

"It's not that simple. There's the whole babysitter deal. I don't know who I'd—"

He turned, desperately relieved when the door jangled open.

"Dad!" And the man of the hour shot in like a bullet. "We saw your truck, so Mrs. Skully said we could stop. Hi, Kate." He dumped his Star Wars backpack on the floor, grinned. "Listen, it echoes. Hi, Kate!"

She had to laugh, and even before Brody could, scooped Jack off his feet. "Hi, Handsome Jack. Ready to kiss me?"

"Nah." But it was obvious he was half hoping she'd kiss him again.

"That's a real problem with the men in your family." She put him on his feet as a woman, a boy and a girl came through the door. The woman blew spiky bangs out of her eyes.

"Brody, saw your truck. I thought I'd drop Jack off, save you a trip. Unless you want me to take him home awhile yet."

"No, this is great, thanks. Ah, Beth Skully, Kate Kimball."

"Kate and I sort of know each other. Rod, no running in here. You probably don't remember me," she continued without missing a beat. "My sister JoBeth was friends with your sister, Freddie."

"JoBeth, of course. How is she?"

"She's great. She and her family live in Michigan. She's a nurse-practitioner. I hope you don't mind me dropping in with the troops this way. I've been wondering what you're doing in this old place."

"Mom." The little girl, blonde and big-eyed tugged on sleeve.

"All right, Carrie, just a minute."

"I'll give you a tour," Kate offered. "If you can stand it."

"Actually, I'd love it, but we're still on the run. Having kids turns you into a bus driver. I guess you don't know, right yet, when you'll be opening your dance school?"

"I hope to start taking afternoon and evening students in April." She glanced down at Carrie, recognized the hope in those big eyes. "Are you interested in ballet, Carrie?"

"I want to be a ballerina."

"Ballerinas are sissies." Her brother sneered.

"Mom!" Carrie wailed.

"Rod, you just hush. I'm sorry about my little moron here, Kate."

"No, don't apologize. Sissies?" she said, turning to Rod, who looked pleased with himself.

"Yeah, uh-huh, 'cause they wear dopey clothes and go around like this." Rod boosted himself on tiptoe and took several small, rather mincing steps.

The result had his sister wailing for her mother yet again.

Before Beth could speak, Kate smiled and shook her head. "That's interesting. How many sissies do you know who can do this?"

Kate brought her leg up, braced a hand on her thigh and bringing her leg tight against the side of her body, pointed her toe at the ceiling.

Oh, my God, was the single thought that tumbled around in Brody's mind.

"Bet I can." Challenged, Rod grabbed his ankle, tried to pull his leg up, lost his balance and tumbled onto his butt.

"Rod, you'll snap yourself like a turkey wishbone," his mother warned, and with an arm around Carrie's shoulder smiled at Kate. "Doesn't that hurt?"

"Only if you think about it." She lowered her foot to the floor. "How old are you, Carrie?"

"I'm five. I can touch my toes."

Five, Kate thought. The bones were still soft. The body still able to learn to do the unnatural. "If you and your mama decide you should come to my school next spring, I'll teach you to dance. And you'll show your brother that ballet isn't for sissies."

She winked at Carrie, then let her body flow back into a smooth back-bend. She kicked her legs gracefully to the ceiling, held there a moment, then simply flowed upright again.

"Wow," Rod whispered to Jack. "She's cool."

Brody said nothing. Saliva had pooled in his mouth.

"Ballet is for athletes." Tossing back her hair, she angled her head at Rod. "A number of professional football players take rudimentary ballet, to help them move fast and smooth on the field."

"No way," Rod said.

"Way. Come with your sister a few times, Rod. I'll show you."

"Now, that's asking for a headache." With a laugh, Beth signaled her son. "Come on, trouble."

Brody slapped himself out of a particularly detailed fantasy that involved that stupendously flexible body. "Thanks for seeing to Jack, Beth."

"Oh, you know it's no bother. Happy to have old Jack anytime."

"Really?" Kate murmured, sending Brody a long look.

"Sure, he's…" Beth shifted her eyes between Brody

and Kate, then bit down on a grin. Well, well, well. It was about damn time the man started looking past his nose. "He's a pure pleasure," Beth went on. "In fact, I was thinking about cooking up a big pot of spaghetti one night this week and seeing if Jack wanted to have dinner with Rod."

"Friday's a great night for spaghetti," Kate said sweetly. "Don't you think, Brody?"

"I don't know. I—"

"You know, Friday's just perfect." Thrilled to help Kate execute the squeeze play, Beth nudged her kids to the door. "We'll count on that then. Jack'll just come over after school, and stay for dinner. He and the kids can watch a video after. Maybe you should plan on him spending the night. That'll work out. Just send him to school Friday with a change of clothes. Nice to see you again, Kate."

"Very nice seeing you."

"I get to have a sleepover at Rod's." Thrilled, Jack plopped down to do some somersaults. "Thanks, Dad."

"Yeah." Kate trailed a finger down Brody's chest, chuckled at his shell-shocked expression. "Thanks, Dad."

Chapter Six

Friday was not turning out to be a terrific cap to the work week. One of his men called in sick, felled by the flu that was gleefully making the rounds. Brody sent another man home at noon who was too sick to be out of bed much less swinging a hammer.

Since the other half of his four-man crew was finishing up a trim job across the river in Maryland, that left Brody to deal with the plumbing inspector, to hang the drywall for the partition between Kate's office and the school's kitchen, and to finish stripping the woodwork in those two areas.

Most of all, and most stressful, was that it left him alone on the job with his father for the best part of the day.

Bob O'Connell was under the sink to his waist. His ancient work boots had had their soles glued back in place countless times. He'd staple them back on, Brody thought, before he'd spring for another pair.

Don't need what I don't need, the old man would say. About every damn thing.

His business, his way, Brody reminded himself and wished he could stop digging up reasons to be resentful.

They rubbed each other raw. Always had.

Bob clanged pipes. Brody measured drywall.

"Turn that damn noise off," Bob ordered. "How's a man supposed to work with that crap ringing in his ears?"

Saying nothing, Brody stepped over and snapped off the portable stereo. Whatever music he'd listened to was considered noise to his father's ear.

Bob swore and muttered while he worked. Which was, Brody thought, exactly why he'd had the music on.

"Damn stupid idea, cutting this kitchen up this-a-way. Waste of time and money. Office space, my ass. What's anybody need office space for to teach a buncha twinkle-toes?"

Brody had put off working on the kitchen side of the partition as long as possible. Now he hefted the drywall section he'd measured and cut, set it into place. "I've got the time," he said and plucked a drywall nail out of his pouch. "The client's got the money."

"Yeah, the Kimballs got plenty of money. No point in tossing it away, though, is there? You shoulda oughta told her she's making a mistake sectioning this kitchen off."

Brody hammered wall to stud. Told himself to keep his mouth shut. But the words just wouldn't stay down. "I don't think she's making a mistake. She doesn't need a kitchen this size down here. It was designed to cook up bar food. What's a dance school going to do with a small restaurant kitchen?"

"Dance school." Bob made a sound of disgust. "Open and close inside a month. Then how's she going to sell this place all cut up like this? Kid-height sinks in the bathrooms. Just have to pull them out again. Surprised the plumbing inspector didn't bust his gut laughing at the rough-in."

"When you teach kids, you have to have accommodations for kids."

"We got the elementary school for that, don't we?"

"Last I heard they weren't teaching ballet at the elementary school."

"Ought to tell you something," Bob muttered, rankled by his son's tone.

Bob told himself to keep his mouth shut, to mind his own business. But, like Brody, the words just wouldn't stay down. "You're supposed to do more than take a customer's money, boy. You're supposed to know enough to point them in the right direction."

"As long as it's your direction."

Bob wormed out from under the sink. His faded blue gimme cap sat askew on a head topped with short, grizzled gray hair. His face was square and lined deep. It had once been sternly handsome. His eyes were as green as his son's.

At times they seemed to be the only thing father and son shared.

"You want to watch that mouth of yours, boy."

"Ever think about watching yours?" Brody felt the band tightening around his head. A temper headache. A Bob O'Connell headache.

Bob tossed down his wrench, got to his feet. He was

a big man, but had never run to fat. Even at sixty he was mostly muscle and grit. "When you got the years I got of living and working in the trade, you can say your piece as you please."

"Really." Brody muscled another sheet of drywall onto the sawhorses, marked his measuring cuts. "You've been saying the same damn thing to me since I was eight. I'd say I've got enough years behind me by now. This is my job—sited, designed, bid and contracted. It goes the way I say it goes."

He picked up his scoring knife, lifted his gaze to meet his father's. "The client gets what the client wants. And as long as she's satisfied there's nothing to discuss."

"From what I hear you're doing a lot more than satisfying your client on the job."

He hadn't meant to say that. Holy God, he hadn't meant to say that. But the words were out. Damn it, the boy always riled him so.

Brody's hand clenched on the knife. For a moment, too long a moment, he wanted to punch his fist into that hard, unyielding face. "What's between me and Kate Kimball is my business."

"I live in this town, too, and so does your ma. People talk about my blood, it washes over on me. You got a kid to raise, and no business running around with some fancy woman stirring gossip."

"Don't you bring Jack into this. Don't bring my son into this."

"Jack's my kin, too. Nothing's going to change that. You kept him down in the city all that time so you could do your running around and God knows, but you're here now. My home. I'm not having you shame me and that boy in my own front yard."

Running around, Brody thought. To doctors, hospitals, specialists. Then running around, trying to outrace your own grief and do what was right for a motherless two-year-old.

"You don't know anything about me. What I've done, what I do. What I am." Determined to hold his temper, he began to score the drywall along his mark. "But you've sure always managed to find the worst of it and rub it in my face."

"If I'd've rubbed it harder, maybe you wouldn't be raising a kid without his ma."

Brody's hand jerked on the knife, bore down and sliced it over his own hand.

Bob let out an oath over the bright gush of blood and grabbed for his bandanna. His shocked concern came out in hot disapproval. "Don't you know better'n to watch what you're doing with tools?"

"Get the hell away from me." Clamping a hand over the gash, Brody stepped back. He couldn't trust himself now. Wasn't sure what he might do. "Get your tools and get off my job."

"You get on out in my truck. You're gonna need stitches."

"I said get off my job. You're fired." The rapid beat of his own heart pumped blood through his fingers. "Pack up your tools and get out."

Shame warred with fury as Bob slammed his wrenches into his kit. "We got nothing to say to each other, from here on." He hauled up his tools and stalked out.

"We never did," Brody murmured.

* * *

Brody O'Connell was going to get an earful. If he ever showed up. He was going to learn, very shortly, that seven o'clock meant seven o'clock. Not seven-thirty.

She was sorry she'd convinced her parents to have an evening out. Now she had no one to complain to. She prowled the living room, glared at the phone.

No, she would not call him again. She'd called at seven-twenty and had gotten nothing but the annoyance of his answering machine.

She had a message for him, all right. But she was going to deliver it in person.

And when she thought of the trouble she'd gone to for tonight. Selecting just the right restaurant, the perfect dress. Now they'd be lucky to keep their reservation. No, she was canceling the reservation, and right this minute. If he thought she'd waltz out to dinner with a man who didn't have the common courtesy to be on time, he was very much mistaken.

She reached for the phone just as the doorbell rang. Kate squared her shoulders, lifted her chin to its haughtiest angle and took her sweet time going to the door.

"I'm late. I'm sorry. I got hung up, and should have called."

The icy words she'd planned went right out of her head. Not discourtesy, she realized after one look at his face. Upheaval. "Is something wrong with Jack?"

"No, no, he's fine. I just checked. I'm sorry, Kate." He lifted a hand in flustered apology. "Maybe we can do this another time."

"What did you do to your hand?" She grabbed it by the wrist. She could see the white gauze and bandage and the faint stain of antiseptic at the edges.

"Just stupidity. It's nothing really. A couple stitches. The ER was slow, and I got hung up."

"Are you in pain?"

"No, it's nothing," he insisted. "Nothing."

Oh, yes, she decided. It was something—and more than a physical injury. "Go home," she told him. "I'll be there in thirty minutes."

"What?"

"With dinner. We'll do the restaurant part some other time."

"Kate, you don't have to do this."

"Brody." She cupped his face in her hands. Oh, you poor thing, she thought. "Go home, and I'll be right along. Scram," she ordered when he still didn't move. And shut the door in his face.

She was, as always, precisely on time. When he opened the door, she breezed by him, hauling a huge hamper. "You're going to have a steak," she announced. "Lucky for you my parents had one thawing out in the fridge before I convinced them to go out for a romantic dinner."

She headed straight back to the kitchen as she spoke, and setting the hamper on the counter, shrugged out of her coat, then began to unpack. "Can you open the wine, or will your hand give you trouble?"

"I can handle it." He took the coat—it smelled of her—and hung it on one of the kitchen pegs. It didn't belong there, he thought, looking all female and smooth next to his ancient work jacket.

She didn't belong there, he decided, looking amazing in some little blue number that looked like it might have been painted on by some creative artist who'd been delightfully minimalist and stingy with the brush.

"Look, Kate—"

"Here."

He took the bottle, the corkscrew she held out. "Kate. Why? Why are you doing this?"

"Because I like you." She took two enormous potatoes to the sink to scrub. "And because you looked like you could use a steak dinner."

"How many men fall on their face in love with you?"

She smiled over her shoulder. "All of them. Open the wine, O'Connell."

"Yeah."

He put on music, fiddling with the radio dial until he found the classical he thought she'd like. He dug out the good dishes he hadn't seen in months and set them on the trestle table in the formal dining room where he and Jack had their celebratory meals.

He had candles—for emergency power outages. But nothing fancy and slick. He debated just plunking them down on the table anyway, then decided they'd just look pitiful.

When he came back in the kitchen, she was putting a salad together—and there were two white tapers in simple glass holders on the counter.

She didn't miss a trick, he decided.

"You know you have a severe deficiency of fresh vegetables in your crisper."

"I buy those salad things that are all made up and in a bag. Then you just, you know, dump it in a bowl."

"Lazy," she said and made him smile.

"Efficient." Because her hands were full, he picked up her wine, lifted it to her lips.

"Thanks." She sipped, watching him. "Very nice."

He set the glass down, and after a moment's hesitation, lowered his head to touch his lips to hers.

"Mmm." She touched her tongue to her top lip. "Even better. And, since you're injured, you're allowed to sit down and relax while I finish this. You'll have time to call and check on Jack one more time before dinner."

He winced. "Shows, huh."

"It looks good on you. Tell him I said hi, and I'll see him tomorrow."

"You really want to do that? The movie thing?"

"I do things I don't want, but I never volunteer to do them. Go call your boy. You're getting your steak medium rare in fifteen minutes."

She liked fussing with the meal. Liked fussing over him. Maybe it was because he so clearly didn't expect it, and was so appreciative of the little things other people tended to take for granted.

And though she'd never considered herself a nurturer, it made her feel good to be needed.

She waited until they were at the table, until he was well into his meal and on his second glass of wine. "Tell me what happened."

"Just a lousy day. What did you do with these potatoes? They're amazing."

"Secret Ukrainian recipe," she told him in a thick and exaggerated accent. "If I tell you, then I must kill you."

"I couldn't do it anyway. My kitchen wizardry with potatoes ends with my poking a few holes into one and tossing it into the mike. You speak Ukrainian? I heard you speaking French the other day."

"Yes, I speak Ukrainian, more or less. I also speak and understand English very well. So talk to me, Brody. What happened in your lousy day?"

"One thing, then the other." He moved his shoulders. "I got two guys out sick—your ballet flu's making an appearance in West Virginia. Since I had the rest of the crew on another job, it left me pretty shorthanded. Then I mistook my own hand for a sheet of drywall, bled all over the damn place, fired my father and spent a couple hours waiting to get sewn back together in the ER."

"You had a fight with your father." She laid a hand over his uninjured one. "I'm sorry."

"We don't get along—never have."

"But you hired him."

"He's a good plumber."

He slid his hand out from under hers, reached for his glass. "Brody."

"Yeah, I hired him. It was a mistake. It's tolerable when the other guys are around, but when it's just the two of us like it was today, it's asking for trouble. I'm a screwup, always was, always will be. The job's not being done right, my life isn't being done right. I'm chasing around after a fancy woman instead of seeing to my own."

"Now I'm a fancy woman?"

Brody pressed his fingers to his eyes. "I'm sorry. That was stupid, and typical. Once I start on him, I can't seem to stop."

"It's all right. I don't mind being a fancy woman." She stabbed a bite of steak. Her temper was on slow burn, but a rant wasn't what Brody needed right now.

"He's probably as miserable and frustrated about what happened as you are. He doesn't know how to talk to you any more than you know how to talk to him. But that's not your fault. I hope you can make it up with him, in your own way."

"He doesn't see me."

Her heart broke for him. "Honey, that's not your fault, either. I wanted my parents to be proud of me, maybe wanted it too much, so I worked, sometimes brutally hard, to be sure they would. That wasn't their fault."

"My family's not like yours."

"Few are. But you're wrong. You and Jack—the family you've made—it's a lot like mine. Maybe, Brody, your father sees that, and wonders why he never made that connection with his own son."

"I was a screwup."

"No, you weren't. You were a work-in-progress."

"Really rough work. I couldn't wait to get through—to get through high school, to get through my eighteenth birthday. To get through so I could get out. That's what I did, on my eighteenth birthday. I packed up and headed down to D.C. Had about five hundred dollars, no job, no nothing. But I was out of there."

"And you made it work."

"I lived by the skin of my teeth for three years. Working construction, blowing my pay on beer and… fancy women," he said with a sudden grin. "Then I was twenty-one, broke, careless, stupid. And I met Connie. I was on the crew doing some work on her parents' guest house. I hit on her, and much to my surprise we started seeing each other."

"Why to your surprise?"

"She was a college girl—conservative daughter of a conservative family. She had money and class, education, style. I was the next step up from a bum."

She studied him. Strong face, she thought. Strong hands. Strong mind. "Obviously she didn't think so."

"No, she didn't. She was the first person who ever told me I had potential. Who ever believed in me. She made me believe in myself, made me want to, so I could be what she saw when she looked at me. I stopped screwing up, and I started to grow up. You don't want to hear this."

"Yes, I do." To keep him talking, she topped off his wine. "Did she help you start your business?"

"That came later." He'd never talked about this with anyone, Brody realized. Not his parents, not his friends, not even Jack. "I was good with my hands, and I had a good eye for building. I had a strong back. I'd just never put them all to use at the same time. Then I figured out I liked myself a whole lot better when I did."

"Of course, because then you respected yourself."

"Yeah." Nail on the head, he thought. Did she ever miss? "Still, I was skilled labor, not a doctor or a lawyer or a business exec. Her parents objected to me— strongly."

She toyed with her potatoes, much more interested in what he told her than in the meal. "Then they were shortsighted. Connie wasn't."

"It wasn't easy for her to buck them, but she did. She was going to Georgetown, studying law. I was working full days and going to school at night, taking business classes. We started making plans. Couple of years down the road, we'd get married. She'd stay in school till she passed the bar, then I'd start my own business. Then she got pregnant."

He studied his wineglass, turned it around and around, but didn't lift it to drink. "We both wanted the baby. She more than me at first, because the whole thing didn't seem real to me. We got married. She kept up with her studies, and I took some extra jobs. Her parents were furious. This was what she got for throwing herself away on somebody like me. They cut her off, and that twisted her up pretty bad."

She could imagine it very well, because, she thought, she'd always had just the opposite in terms of a family that was there for her. "They didn't deserve her."

Brody lifted his eyes, met Kate's. "Damn right they didn't. The rougher it got, the more we dug in. We made it work. She made it work. A thousand times I panicked, and some of those thousand times I saw myself walking away. She'd go back to her parents, and everyone would be better off."

"But you didn't. You stuck."

"She loved me," he said simply. "The day Jack was born, I was in the delivery room, wanting to be pretty much anywhere else in the world. But she wanted me there, it was really important to her. So I pretended I wanted to be there, too. All I could think was get this over with, get this the hell over with because it's too hard. Nobody should have to do this. Then…there was Jack. This little, squirmy person. Everything changed. Everything clicked. I never knew you could love like that, in an instant, in a heartbeat, so it was everything. Every damn thing. I wanted, had to be, whatever he needed me to be. They made a man out of me, right there, in that moment. Connie and Jack made me."

Tears were flooding her cheeks, continued to spill over. She couldn't stop them, and didn't try.

"I'm sorry." He lifted his hands, let them fall again. "I don't know what got into me."

"No." She shook her head, could say nothing else quite yet. You stupid idiot, she thought. You've gone and made me fall in love with you. Now what? "That was lovely," she managed to say. "Just give me a minute." She got to her feet, and dashed off to the bathroom to compose herself.

As an alternative to banging his head on the table, Brody got up and paced. He'd come to the same conclusion as Kate—he was an idiot—but for different reasons. He'd taken her very nice gesture of a casual meal at home, one he imagined was supposed to be at least marginally romantic, and he'd turned it into a marathon on his troubles and his past.

He'd made her cry.

Great going, O'Connell, he thought in disgust. Maybe you can round on the evening by talking about how your dog died when you were ten. That would really jazz things up.

He imagined she'd want to take off as soon as possible, so began to clear the table to give her a way out.

"Sorry," he began when he heard the light click of her footsteps. "I'm an imbecile, dumping all that on you. I'll take care of this, and you can…"

He trailed off, froze, when her arms slid lightly around him and her head rested on his back.

"O'Connell, I come from strong Slavic blood. Strong and sentimental. We like to cry. Did you know my grandparents escaped from the Soviet Union when my mother was a child? My aunt Rachel is the only one who was born here in America. They went on foot, with three babies, over the mountains into Hungary."

"No, I didn't know that." He turned, cautiously, until he was facing her.

"They were cold and hungry and frightened. And when they came to America, a strange country with a strange language and strange customs, they were poor and they were alone. But they wanted something enough to fight for it, to make it work. I've heard the story dozens of times. It always makes me cry. It always makes me proud."

She turned away to stack dishes.

"Why are you telling me this?"

"Courage comes in different forms, Brody. There's strength—that's the muscle. But love's the heart. When you put them together, you can do anything. That's worth a few sentimental tears."

"You know, I figured this was the kind of day you just crossed off your list, but you've changed that."

"Well, thank you. Tell you what. We'll deal with these dishes, then you can dance with me." Time to lighten things up, she decided. "The way a man dances tells me a lot, and I haven't tested you out in that area yet."

He took the dishes out of her hands. "Let's dance now."

"Can't. Call it a character flaw, but if I don't tidy up first, I'll keep seeing unwashed dishes in my head."

He set them aside, took her hands to draw her out of the room. "That's anal."

"No, it's organized. Organized people get more done and have less headaches." She looked over her shoulder as he tugged her toward the living room. "Really, it'll only take a few minutes."

"It'll only take a few minutes later, too." Maybe he was rusty in the romance department, but he still remembered a few moves.

"Here's what we'll do. You pick out the music while I clear up the dishes."

He laughed and pulled her into the living room. "You really are compulsive." He switched the stereo to CD. "Funny, I was listening to this last night. And thinking about you."

"Oh?" The music flowed out, slow and sultry. A sexy little shuffle that spoke to the blood.

"Must've been fate," he said and slid her into his arms.

Her heart jerked once. "I'm a strong believer in fate." She ordered herself to relax, then realized she already was. Snugged up against him, moving with him, her heels making it easy—almost mandatory—to rest her cheek on his.

"Very smooth, O'Connell," she murmured. "Major points for smooth."

"Like you said, some things come back to you." He spun her out, made her laugh. Spun her back and had her breath catching.

"Nice move." Oh-oh. Oh-oh. It was getting hard to think. She'd come to the conclusion when she'd dealt with her tears that she really needed to do some serious thinking about Brody, and where this was all going.

She couldn't drive this train if she didn't have her wits about her.

She hadn't expected him to dance quite so well. If he'd fumbled a bit, she could have taken charge. Kept her balance. There were entirely too many things that were unexpected about him. And fascinating. And oh, it felt wonderful to glide around the room in his arms.

Her hair smelled fabulous. He'd nearly forgotten all the mysterious and alluring facets there were to a woman. The shape, the softness, the scents. Nearly forgotten the sensation of moving with one, slow and close. The images it had winding through a man's mind.

His lips brushed over her hair, trailed along her cheek, found hers.

She sighed into the kiss, wallowing in the sensation of her bones melting. So when the song ended and the next began, they just stood swaying together.

"That was perfect." Her mind was foggy, her heartbeat thick. And the needs she'd thought she had under control were tumbling in her belly. "I should go."

"Why?"

"Because." She lifted a hand to his cheek, eased away, just a little. "It's bad timing. Tonight you needed a friend."

"You're right." His hands slid down her arms until their fingers lightly linked. "The timing's probably off. The smart thing is to take this slow."

"I believe in doing the smart thing."

"Yeah." He walked her toward the doorway. "I've been careful to try to do the smart thing for quite a while myself."

He paused, turned her back to face him. "I did need a friend tonight. Do need one," he added, drawing her a little closer. "And I need you, Kate. Stay with me."

He lowered his head, kept his eyes on hers when their lips brushed. "Be with me."

Chapter Seven

The walls of his room were unfinished. A coil of electrical wire sat on a drywall compound bucket that stood in the corner. There were no curtains at his windows. He'd removed the closet doors, and they were currently in his shop waiting to be planed and refinished.

The floors were a wonderful random-width oak under years of dull, dark varnish. Sanding them down, sealing them clear, was down on the list of projects—far down.

The bed had been an impulse buy. The old iron headboard with its slim, straight bars had appealed to him. But he'd yet to think about linens, and habitually tossed a mismatched quilt over the sheets and considered the job done.

It wouldn't be what she was used to. Trying to see it through her eyes, Brody winced. "Not exactly the Taj Mahal."

"Another work in progress." She roamed the room, grateful to have a minute to settle the nerves she hadn't expected to feel. "It's a lovely space." She ran her fingers over the low windowsill he'd stripped down to its natural pine. "I know potential when I see it," she said, and turned back to him.

"I wanted to finish Jack's room first. Then it made more sense to work on the kitchen and the living areas. I don't do anything but sleep here. Up till now."

A quick thrill spurted through her. She was the first woman he'd brought to this room, to this bed. "It's going to be lovely." She walked to him as she spoke, every pulse point hammering. "Will you use the fireplace in here?"

"I use it now. It's a good heat source. I thought about putting in an insert, for efficiency, but..." What the hell was he doing? Talking about heat sources and inserts when he had the most beautiful woman in the world in his bedroom?

"It wouldn't be as charming," she finished, and with her eyes on his began unbuttoning his shirt.

"No. Do you want me to start a fire?"

"Later. Yes, I think that would be lovely, later. But for now, I have a feeling we can generate enough heat on our own."

"Kate." He curled his fingers around her wrists, and wondered that the need pumping through him didn't burn through the tips and singe her flesh. "If I fumble a little, blame it on this, okay?" He turned his injured hand.

He was nervous, too, she realized. Good. That put them back on even ground. "I bet a man as clever with his hands as you can manage a zipper, no matter what the handicap." She turned, lifted her hair. "Why don't we see?"

"Yeah. Why don't we?"

He drew it down slowly, exposing pale gold skin inch by inch. The curve of her neck and shoulder enticed him, so he lowered his head, brushed his lips just there. When she shivered, arched, he indulged himself, nibbling along her spine, her shoulder blades.

When he turned her to face him, her breath had already quickened.

His mouth cruised over hers, a long, luxurious savoring that liquefied the bones. And while he savored, his hands roamed lightly over her face, into her hair, down her back as if she were some exotic delicacy to be enjoyed slowly. Thoroughly.

She'd expected a repeat of the blast of passion that had exploded between them in her mother's kitchen. And was undone by the tenderness.

"Tell me..." He nibbled his way across her jaw. "If there's something you don't like."

Her head fell back, inviting him to explore the exposed line of her throat. "I don't think that's going to be an issue."

His hands, strong, patient, skimmed up her sides to the shoulders of her dress. "I've imagined touching you. Driven myself crazy imagining it."

"You're doing a pretty good job of driving me crazy now." She pushed the flannel shirt aside, reached out to tug the thermal shirt he wore beneath it out of the waistband of his jeans, sliding over the hard muscles of his stomach.

But he eased her back. It had been a long time since

he'd been with a woman. He had no intention of rushing it.

He brought her hands to his lips, kissed her fingers, her palms. And felt her pulse leap, then go thick.

"Let me do this," he murmured. He nudged the dress from her shoulders, watched it slide down her body to the floor.

She was so slender, so finely built a man could forget those tensile muscles beneath all that silky gold-dust skin. Her curves were subtle—a sleek female elegance that fascinated *and* demanded his touch.

Her breath snagged in her throat when he skimmed his fingertips along the curve of her breast, along the lace edging of her bra, then under it as if memorizing shape and texture. The hard pad of callus brushed her nipple and turned her knees to jelly.

Intrigued by her tremble, he shifted his gaze back to her face, watched her as his hands roamed down her torso, along her hips, stroked up her thighs.

"I think about your legs a lot," he told her, and flirted his fingertips along the top of her stocking. "Ballerina legs, you know?"

"Just don't pay any attention to my feet. Dancers have incredibly unattractive feet."

"Strong," he corrected. "Strong's really sexy to me. Maybe you can show me some of the things you can do later, like you did for Rod that day. I nearly swallowed my tongue."

Though she laughed, her hands were far from steady when she drew the shirt over his head, let her own fingers explore that tough wall of muscle.

"Sure. I can do even more interesting things."

They both quivered when he lifted her and laid her on the bed.

If it had been a dance, she'd have called it a waltz. Slow, circling steps in a match rhythm. The kiss was long and deep, warming the body from the inside out. She sighed into it, into him, and her arms encircled.

This, she thought, dreaming, this was something—someone—she wanted to hold. Love was a quiet miracle that bloomed in her like a rose. And loving, she would give.

Then his mouth was on the curve of her breast, rubbing along that edge of lace. Arousing, inciting, and bringing the first licks of heat toward the warmth. She moaned as his tongue slid over that swell of flesh, teasing the point then tugging on it through the thin barrier of lace. Her hips arched, and her fingers dug into his.

Waltz became tango, slow and hotly sexual.

His mind was full of her, the scents, the textures, the sounds. All of it, all of her seemed to whirl inside his brain, making him dizzy and drunk. She was carved clean as a statue, the long, hot length of her beautifully erotic. He wanted to touch, to taste everything. All of her.

Absorbed with her, he did as he pleased while she rose and rolled and shuddered with him. And when he took her up the first time, when that lovely body tensed and her breath came and went on a sob, the thrill of it coursed through him like a drug.

More and still more. A little greedier, a little faster. He tugged away those barriers of lace. Now he wanted only flesh. Hot and wet and soft.

She matched him, step for step, rising to him, opening herself. Her mouth found his as they rolled over the quilt, diving heedlessly into the kiss while her hands pleased them both.

As desperation increased, she tugged open the button of his jeans, dragged them impatiently down his hips. "Oh, I love your body. I love what you do to mine. Hurry, hurry. I want—"

Her system erupted; her mind blanked. Even as she went limp, his fingers continued to stroke her. "I want to do more."

He used his mouth. Sliding down her, breast, torso, belly. She began to move again. And then to writhe while pleasure and need pounded together inside her. Her eyes were blind, her body quaking when he rose over her.

With his heart hammering, and his mind crowded with her, he filled her with one long stroke. With a low sound of pleasure he held himself there, sustaining the moment, letting the thrill of it batter his system.

Her hips lifted, then fell away to draw him with her. Beat for beat they moved together, eyes locked, breath tangled and ragged. Her hands groped for his, gripped. The slide of flesh to flesh, slow and silky, the pulse of heart to heart, solid and real.

And when the wave rose up to swamp them both, he lowered his mouth to hers and completed the joining.

She lay limp as melted wax, eyes closed, lips curved and enjoyed the sensation of Brody collapsed on top of her. His heart continued to knock—hard, fast raps— that told her his system had been as delightfully assaulted as hers.

It had been a wonderful way to discover they were compatible in bed.

It was so fascinating to be in love. Really in love. Not like the couple of times she'd been enchanted with the *idea* of love. This was so unexpected. So intense.

She drew a long, satisfied breath and told herself she'd give the matter—and the consequences of it—a great deal of careful thought later. For the moment, she was going to enjoy it. And him.

No one had ever made her feel quite like this. No one had ever opened her up to so many *feelings*. Fate, she thought. He was hers. She'd known in some secret place inside her, the first instant she'd seen him.

And she was going to make certain he understood, when the time was right, that she was his.

She'd found him, she thought, utterly content as she stroked his back. And she was keeping him.

"For a man who claims to be out of practice, you certainly held your own."

He was trying to decide if he had any brain cells left, and if so, when they would begin to work again. He managed a grunt. That response seemed to amuse her, as she laughed and locked her arms around him.

He managed to find the energy to turn his head, found his face buried in her hair and decided that was a fine place to be. "Want me to move?"

"No."

"Good. Just give me an elbow if I start to snore."

"O'Connell."

"Just kidding." He lifted his head, levered some of his weight off her and onto his elbows. The green of his eyes was blurry with satisfaction. "You're incredible to look at."

"So are you." She lifted a hand to play with his hair. Not really blond, she thought idly. Not really brown.

But a wonderful mix of tones and textures. Like the man himself.

"You know, I wanted you here from the first time I saw you." She lifted her head just enough to bite lightly at his jaw. "Total lust at first sight—that's not usual for me."

"I had pretty much the same reaction. You jump-started parts of my system that had been on idle for a long time. Ticked me off."

"I know." She grinned. "I kind of liked it—the way you'd get all scowly and turned on at the same time. Very sexy. Very challenging."

"Well, you got me where you wanted." He lowered his head to give her a quick, nipping kiss. "Thanks."

"Oh, my pleasure."

"And since I'm here…" He moved his lips to the side of her throat, nuzzled.

Her laughing response turned to a gasp as she felt him harden inside her. Begin to move inside her.

"Hope you don't mind. I've got a lot of lost time to make up for."

"No." Her body woke, and pulsed. "Be my guest."

It wasn't easy, Brody discovered, to have a relation-ship—at least the physical part of it—with a woman when you had a child. Not that he'd change anything, but it took considerable ingenuity to juggle the demands of the man and the demands of the father.

He was grateful that Kate seemed to enjoy Jack, and didn't appear to resent spending time with him, or the time Brody devoted to him. The fact was, if she hadn't accepted the boundaries and responsibilities that went along with Jack, there wouldn't have been a relationship—physical or otherwise—to explore for long.

He guessed he was having an affair. That was a first. He'd never considered his relationship with Connie as an affair. Kids didn't have affairs at twenty-one. They had romances. He had to remind himself not to romanticize his situation with Kate.

They liked each other, they wanted each other, they enjoyed each other. Neither of them had indicated anything more than warm feelings, and lust. And that was for the best, he decided.

He was, first and last, a father. He didn't imagine most young women—career women with dozens of options ahead of them—generally chose to settle down with a man and his six-year-old son.

In any case, he wasn't looking for anything more than what there was. If he had been, he'd have to start tackling the problem of changes, adjustments and compromises for all three of them. That was bound to be messy.

Certainly a grown man was entitled to a simple affair with a like-minded woman without crowding it in with plans for a future.

Everybody was happy this way.

He stepped back, lowering his nail gun to examine the trim he'd just finished on Kate's office. It was a rich, elegant look, he decided. Classy. And it suited the woman.

He wondered where she was, what she was doing. And if they could manage to steal an hour alone before he had to go home and tackle the dinosaur poster Jack had to do for a school project.

Sex, carpentry and first grade, he thought as he

moved over to start trimming the window. A man never knew what kind of mix was going to stir up his life.

"He'll love this." Kate examined the fierce, snapping jaws of the plastic predator.

"Dinosaurs are a no-fail choice." Annie rearranged toys that didn't need rearranging, and slid her gaze toward Kate. "That Jack O'Connell's as cute as they come."

"Mmm."

"His father's not shabby, either."

"No, they both ring the bell on the cute scale. And yes, we're still seeing each other."

"I didn't say a word." Annie folded her lips. "I never pry."

"No, you just poke." She tucked the dinosaur under her arm. "That's what I love about you. Now, I'm going to go back and say hi to Mama before I go."

"Want me to wrap that beast up for you?"

"No. Wrapped it's a gift. Unwrapped I can sneak it in as a research tool for his school project."

"You always were a smart one, Katie."

Smart enough, Katie thought, to know what she wanted and how to get it. It had been two weeks since she'd made love with Brody for the first time. Since then they'd had one other evening alone and a handful of hours here and there.

She wanted a lot more than that.

They'd taken Jack to the movies, shared a few meals as a trio, and had engaged in the mother of all snowball battles the previous Saturday when a solid foot of snow had fallen.

She wanted a lot more than that as far as Jack was concerned, too.

She knocked on her mother's office door, poked her head in.

Natasha was at her desk, her hair scooped up and the phone at her ear. She curved her finger in a come-ahead gesture. "Yes, thank you. I'll expect delivery next week."

She tapped a few keys at her computer, hung up and sighed. "Perfect timing," she told Kate. "I need a cup of tea and a conversation that doesn't involve dolls."

"Happy to oblige. I'll even make the tea." Kate set the dinosaur on her mother's desk before turning to the teapot.

Natasha eyed the toy, then her daughter. "For Jack?"

"Mmm. He has a school project. I figured this might earn him some extra points, and be fun."

"He's a delightful little boy."

"Yes, I think so." Kate poured the hot water into cups. "Brody's done a wonderful job with him—though he had terrific material to work with."

"Yes, I agree. Still, it's never easy to raise a child alone."

"I don't intend for him to finish the job alone." Kate set her mother's cup on the desk, sat down with her own. "I'm in love with Brody, Mama, and I'm going to marry him."

"Oh, Kate!" Tears flooded Natasha's eyes even as she leaped up to embrace her daughter. "This is wonderful. I'm so happy for you. For all of us. My baby's getting married."

She crouched down to kiss both of Kate's cheeks. "You'll be the most beautiful bride. Have you set the date? We'll have so much planning to do. Wait until we tell your father."

"Wait, wait, wait." Laughing, Kate set her tea aside to grab Natasha's hand. "We haven't set a date, because I haven't convinced him to ask me yet."

"But—"

"I'm certain a man like Brody—he's really a traditional guy under it all—wants to do the asking. All I have to do is give him a nudge to the next stage so he'll ask, then we can get on with it."

As worry strangled the excitement, Natasha sat back on her heels. "Katie. Brody isn't a project that has stages."

"I didn't mean it exactly like that. But still, Mama, relationships have stages, don't they? And people in them work through those stages."

"Darling." Natasha straightened, sat on the corner of her desk. "I've always applauded your logic, your practicality and your sheer determination to earn a goal. But love, marriage, family—these things don't always run on logic. In fact, they rarely do."

"Mama, I love him," Katie said simply, and tears swam into her mother's eyes again.

"Yes, I know you do. I've seen it. And believe me, if you want him, I want him for you. But—"

"I want to be Jack's mother." Now Kate's voice thickened. "I didn't know I'd want that so much. At first he was just a delightful little boy, as you said. I enjoyed him, but I enjoy children. Mama, I'm falling in love with him. I'm just falling head over heels for that little boy."

Natasha picked up the dinosaur, smiled as she turned it in her hands. "I know what it is to fall in love with a child who didn't come from you. One who walks into your life already formed and makes such a difference in your life. I don't question that you would love him as your own, Katie."

"Then why are you worried?"

"Because you're my baby," Natasha said as she set the toy aside. "I don't want you to be hurt. You're ready to open your heart and your life. But that doesn't mean Brody is."

"He cares for me." She was sure of it. She couldn't be mistaken. But the worry niggled at her. "He's just cautious."

"He's a good man, and I have no doubt he cares for and about you. But, Katie, you don't say he loves you."

"I don't know if he does." Frustrated, Kate got to her feet. "Or if he loves me, if he knows it himself. That's why I'm trying to be patient. I'm trying to be practical. But, Mama, I ache."

"Baby." Murmuring, Natasha drew Kate into her arms, stroked her hair. "Love isn't tidy. It won't be, not even for you."

"I can be patient. For a little while," she added on a watery laugh. "I'm going to make it work." She closed her eyes tight. "I can make it work."

It was hard not to go over to the job site. She'd had to stop herself a half a dozen times from strolling over and seeing the progress. And seeing Brody. She made it easier on herself by spending part of the afternoon making and receiving calls in response to the ad she'd taken for her school.

The Kimball School of Dance would open in April, and she already had six potential students. There was an interview scheduled for the following week for an article in the local paper. That, she was sure, would generate more interest, more calls, more students.

A few more weeks, she thought as she pulled up behind Brody's truck in his driveway, and a new phase of her professional life would begin. She didn't intend for the next phase of her personal life to lag far behind.

He came to the door in his bare feet and smelling of crayons. The fact that she could find that both sexy and endearing in a grown man showed her just how far gone she was already.

"Hi. Sorry to drop by unannounced, but I have something for Jack."

"No, that's okay." He wiped at the magic marker staining his fingertips. "We're just in the middle… In the kitchen," he said, gesturing. "But it isn't pretty."

"The process of school projects rarely is."

It surprised him that she'd remembered the project. Had he talked about it too much? Brody wondered as he followed her back to the kitchen. He was pretty sure he'd only mentioned it—maybe moaned a little—in passing.

She stepped into the kitchen ahead of him. Surveyed the scene.

Jack was kneeling on a chair at the kitchen table, hunkered over a sheet of poster board and busily applying his crayon to the inside of an outline that resembled a large pig—as seen by Salvador Dalí.

Several picture books on dinosaurs were open on the table, along with illustrations probably printed off the computer. There was a scatter of plastic and rubber toys as well, and a forest of crayons, markers, pencils.

A pair of work boots and a pair of child's sneakers were kicked into a corner. A large pitcher half full of some violently red liquid sat on the counter. As Jack's mouth was liberally stained the same color, Kate assumed it was a beverage and not paint.

As she stepped in, her shoe stuck to the floor, then released with a little sucking sound.

"We just had a little accident with Kool-Aid," Brody explained when she glanced down. "I guess I missed a couple spots on the cleanup."

"Hi, Kate." Jack looked up and bounced. "I'm making dinosaurs."

"So I see. And what kind is this?"

"It's a Stag-e-o-saurous. See? Here he is in the book. Me and Dad, we don't draw very good."

"But you color really well," she said, admiring the bright green head on his current drawing.

"You gotta stay inside the lines. That's why we drew them really thick."

"Very sensible." She rested her chin on the top of his head and studied the poster.

She saw the light pencil marks where Brody had drawn straight lines for the lettering of the header. Jack had titled his piece A Parade Of Dinosaurs. She found it apt, as his drawings marched over the poster in a long squiggly dance.

"You're doing such a good job, I don't think you're going to need the tool I brought along for you."

"Is it a hammer?"

"Afraid not." She reached into her bag, pulled it out. "It's a deadly predator."

"It's a T-Rex! Look, Dad. They ate everybody."

"Very scary," Brody agreed and laid a hand on his son's shoulder.

"Can I take it into school? 'Cause look, its arms

and legs move and everything. His mouth goes chomp. Can I?"

"I think it'd be a good visual aid to your project, don't you, Dad? And there's this little booklet here that talks about how he lived, and when, and how he ate everybody."

"Couldn't hurt. Jack, aren't you going to thank Kate?"

"Thanks, Kate." Jack marched the dinosaur across the poster. "Thanks a lot. He's really good."

"You're welcome a lot. How about a kiss?"

He grinned and covered his face with his hands. "Nuh-uh."

"Okay, I'll just kiss your dad." She turned her head before Brody could react and closed her mouth firmly over his.

He avoided kissing her, touching her, when Jack was around. That, Kate decided, deliberately sliding her arms around Brody's waist, would have to change.

Jack made gagging noises behind his hands. But he was watching carefully, and there was a funny fluttering in his stomach.

"A woman's got to take her kisses where she finds them," Kate stated, easing back while Brody stood flustered. "Now, my work is done, I have to go."

"Aw, can't you stay? You can help draw the dinosaurs. We're going to have sloppy burgers for dinner."

"As delightful as that is, I can't. I have an appointment in town." Which was true. But she thought the ambush—the drop-by, she corrected—would be more effective if she kept it brief and casual. "Maybe, this weekend if you're not busy, we can go to the movies again."

"All right!"

"I'll see you tomorrow, Brody. No, no," she said when he turned. "I know the way out. Get back to your dinosaurs."

"Thanks for coming by," he said, and said nothing else, not even when he heard her close the front door.

"Dad?"

"Hmm."

"Do you like kissing Kate?"

"Yeah. I mean…" Okay, Brody thought, here we go. Because Jack was watching him carefully, he sat. "It's kind of hard to explain, but when you get older… Most guys like kissing girls."

"Just the pretty ones?"

"No, well, no. But girls you like."

"And we like Kate, right?"

"Sure we do." Brody breathed a sigh of relief that the discussion hadn't deepened into some stickier area of sex education. Not yet, he thought. Not quite yet.

"Dad?"

"Yeah."

"Are you going to marry Kate?"

"Am I—" His shock was no less than if Jack had suddenly kicked his chair out from under him. "Jeez, Jack, where did that come from?"

"'Cause you like her, and you like kissing her, and you don't have a wife. Rod's mom and dad, sometimes they kiss each other in the kitchen, too."

"Not everybody…people kiss without getting married." Oh, man. "Marriage is a really important thing. You should know somebody really well, and understand them, and like them."

"You know Kate, and you like her."

Brody distinctly felt a single line of sweat dribble

down his spine. "Sure I do. Yeah. But I know a lot of people, Jacks." Feeling trapped, Brody pushed away from the table and got down two clean glasses. "I don't marry them. You need to love someone to marry them."

"Don't you love Kate?"

He opened his mouth, closed it again. Funny, he thought, how much tougher it was to lie to your son than it was to lie to yourself. The simplest answer was that he didn't know. He wasn't sure what was building inside him when it came to Kate Kimball.

"It's complicated, Jack."

"How come?"

Questions about sex, Brody decided, would have been easier after all. He set the glasses down, came back to sit. "I loved your mother. You know that, right?"

"Uh-huh. She was pretty, too. And you took care of each other and me until she had to go to heaven. I wish she didn't have to go."

"I know. Me, too. The thing is, Jack, after she had to go, it was really good for me to just concentrate on loving you. That worked really well for me. And we've done all right, haven't we?"

"Yeah. We're a team."

"You bet we are." Brody held out his hand so Jack could give him a high five. "Now let's see what this team can do with dinosaurs."

"Okay." Jack picked up his crayon. His eyes darted up to his father's face once. He liked that they were a team. But he liked to pretend that maybe Kate was part of the team, too.

Chapter Eight

Brody set the first base cabinet in place, checked his level. He could hear, if he paid attention, the whirl of the drill from downstairs as one of his crew finished up the punch-out work on the main level. Up here there was the *whoosh* and *thunk* of nail guns and the whirl of saws, as other men worked in the bedroom of Kate's apartment.

It was going to be a hell of a nice space, Brody thought. The perfect apartment for a single, or a couple without children. It was a little too tight to offer a family a comfortable fit, he thought as he crouched to adjust his level.

Then he just stayed there, staring into space.

Are you going to marry her?

Why the devil had Jack put that idea into the air? Made everything sticky. He wasn't thinking about marriage. Couldn't afford to think about it. He had a kid to consider, and his business was just getting off the ground. He had a rambling, drafty old house that was barely half finished.

It simply wasn't the time to start thinking of adding someone else to the mix by getting married.

He'd jumped into that situation once before. He didn't regret it, not a minute of it. But he had to admit the timing had been lousy, the situation difficult for everyone involved. What was the point of heading back in that sort of direction when his life was still so much in flux?

Just asking for trouble, he decided.

Besides, Kate wouldn't be thinking about marriage. Would she? Of course not. She'd barely settled back into town herself. She had her school to think about. She had her freedom.

She spoke French, he thought irrelevantly. She'd *been to* France. And England and Russia. She might want to go back. Why wouldn't she want that? And he was anchored in West Virginia with a child.

Anyway, he and Connie had been stupid in love. Young and stupid, he thought with a gentle tug of sentiment. He and Kate were grown-ups. Sensible people who enjoyed each other's company.

Too sensible to get starry-eyed.

The hand that dropped on his shoulder had him jerking and nearly dropping the electric drill on his foot.

"Jeez, O'Connell, got the willies?"

Hissing out a breath, Brody got to his feet and turned to Jerry Skully. Rod's father had been a childhood pal. Even though he was over thirty Jerry maintained his cheerfully youthful looks and goofy smile. It was spread over his face now.

"I didn't hear you."

"No kidding. I called you a couple of times. You were in the zone, man."

Jerry put his hands on his hips and strutted around the room. Put a suit and tie guy in a construction area, Brody thought, and they looked like strutters. "Need a job? I got an extra hammer."

"Ha-ha." It was an old joke. Jerry was a whiz with math, great in social situations and couldn't unscrew a light bulb without step-by-step written instructions.

"You ever get those shelves up in the laundry room?" Brody asked with his tongue in his cheek.

"They're up. Beth said elves put them in." He cocked his head. "You wouldn't know anything about that, would you?"

"I don't hire elves. Their union's a killer."

"Right. Too bad, because I'm really grateful to those elves for getting Beth off my back."

It was all the acknowledgment and thanks either of them required. "Downstairs is looking real good," Jerry went on. "Carrie's driving Beth and me crazy about starting up with this ballet stuff. I guess it's going to get going next month after all."

"No reason it can't. We'll be up here awhile longer, and there's some outside work yet, but she'll have the main level ready." Brody started to set the next cabinet. "What're you doing hanging out in the middle of the afternoon? Banker's hours?"

"Banker's work a lot harder than you think, pal."

"Soft hands," Brody said, then sniffed. "Is that cologne I'm smelling?"

"Aftershave, you barbarian. Anyway, I had an outside meeting. Got done a little early, so I thought I'd come by to see what you're doing with this old place. My bank's money's getting hammered and nailed in here."

Brody tossed a grin over his shoulder. "That's why the client hired the best."

Jerry said something short and rude that symbolized the affection between two men. "So, I hear you and the ballerina are doing some pretty regular dancing."

"Small towns," Brody said. "Big noses."

"She's a looker." Jerry wandered closer, watched Brody finesse the angle of the cabinet. "You ever seen a real ballet?"

"Nope."

"I did. My little sister—you remember Tiffany? She took ballet for a few years when we were kids. Did the *Nutcracker*. My parents dragged me along. It had some moments," Jerry remembered. "Giant mice, sword fights, big-ass Christmas tree. The rest was just people jumping and twirling, if you ask me. Takes all kinds."

"Guess so."

"Anyway, Tiffany just came back home. She's been down in Kentucky the last couple of years. Finally divorced the jerk she married. Going to stay with the folks until she gets her feet back under her."

"Uh-huh." Brody laid his level across the top of the two cabinets, nodded.

"So, I was thinking maybe, since you're back in the dating swing, you could take her out sometime. Cheer her up a little. A movie, maybe dinner."

"Mmm." Brody moved the next cabinet to his mark where it would sit under the breakfast bar.

"That'd be great. She's had a tough time of it, you

know? Be nice if she could spend some time with a guy who'd treat her decent."

"Yeah."

"She had a little crush on you when we were kids. So, you'll give her a call in the next couple of days?"

"Sure. What?" Surfacing, Brody glanced back. "Give who a call?"

"Jeez, Brody, Tiff. My sister. You're going to give her a call and ask her out."

"I am?"

"O'Connell, you just said—"

"Wait a minute. Just a minute." Brody set down the drill and tried to catch up. "Look, I don't think I can do that. I'm sort of seeing Kate."

"You're not married to her or living with her or anything. What's the big deal?"

He was pretty sure there was one. Being out of the stream for a few years didn't mean he didn't remember how it was supposed to work. Moreover, he didn't *want* to ask Tiffany, or anyone else out.

But he didn't think Jerry would appreciate him saying that. "The thing is, Jerry, I'm not into the dating scene."

"You're dating the ballerina."

"No, I'm not. That is… We're just—"

Perhaps it was best all around that while he was fumbling for an excuse, he looked away from Jerry. And saw Kate in the doorway.

"Ah. Kate. Hi."

"Hello." Her voice was cool; her eyes hot. "Sorry to interrupt."

Recognizing a potentially sticky situation, Jerry flashed his smile and prepared to desert his old friend on the battlefield. "Hey there, Kate. Good to see you again. Gosh, look at the time. I have to run. I'll get back to you on that, Brody. See you later."

He made tracks.

Brody picked up his drill again, passed it from hand to hand. "That was Jerry."

"Yes, I'm aware that was Jerry."

"Setting your cabinets today. I think you made the right choice with the natural cherry. We should have the bedroom closet framed in, and the drywall set with the first coat of mud by the end of the day."

"That's just dandy."

Her temper was a live thing, a nest of vipers curling and hissing in her gut. She had no intention of beating them back to keep them from sinking their fangs into Brody.

"So, we're not dating. We're just…" She came into the room on the pause. "Would that have been sleeping together? We're just sleeping together. Or do you have a simpler term for it?"

"Jerry put me on the spot."

"Really? Is that why you told him—so decisively—that you and I are 'sort of seeing each other'? I didn't realize that defining our relationship was such a dilemma for you, or that whatever that relationship might be causes you such embarrassment with your friends."

"Just hold on." He set the drill down again with an impatient snap of metal on wood. "If you were going to eavesdrop on a conversation, you should have listened to the whole thing. Jerry wanted me to take his sister out, and I was explaining why that wasn't a good idea."

"I see." She imagined she could chew every nail in his pouch, then spit them into his eye. "First, I wasn't eavesdropping. This is my place and I have every right to come into any room in it. Whenever I like. Second, in your explanation of why going out with Jerry's sister isn't a good idea, did the word *no* ever enter your head?"

"Yes. No," he corrected. "Because I wasn't pay-ing—"

"Ah, there. You are capable of saying no. Let me tell you something, O'Connell." She punctuated the words by stabbing a finger into his chest. "I don't sleep around."

"Well, who the hell said you did?"

"When I'm with a man, I'm with *that* man. Period. If he is unable or unwilling to agree to do the same, I expect him to be honest enough to say so."

"I haven't—"

"*And,* I am not an excuse to be pulled out of the bag when you're scrambling to avoid a favor for a friend. So don't think you can *ever* use me that way, and with your pitiful, fumbling 'sort ofs.' And since it appears we aren't dating, you're perfectly free to call Jerry's sister or anyone else."

"Damn it, which is it? Are you going to be pissed off because I brush Jerry off, or pissed off because I don't?"

Her hands curled into fists. Punching him, she decided, would only give him delusions of grandeur. "Jerk." She bit the single word off, turned on her heel and, tossing something in Ukrainian over her shoulder, strode out of the room.

"Females," Brody muttered. He kicked his toolbox, and was only moderately satisfied by the clang.

An hour later, the cabinets were in place and Brody was at work on the pantry. He'd already run through the scene with Kate a half a dozen times, but with each play, he'd remembered things he should have said. Short, pithy statements that would have turned the tide in his favor. And the first chance he got, he was going to burn her ears with them.

He was not going to grovel, he told himself as he nailed in the brackets for a shelf. He had nothing to apologize for. Women, he decided, were just one of the many reasons a man was better off going through his life solo.

If he was such a jerk, why'd she bother to spend any time with him in the first place?

He backed out of the closet, turned and nearly ran right into Spencer Kimball.

"What *is* it with people?" Brody demanded.

"Sorry. I didn't think you could hear me with all the noise."

"I'm going to post signs." Brody stalked over to select one of the shelves he'd precut and sealed. "No suits, no ties, no females."

Spencer's eyebrows lifted. In all the months he'd known Brody, this was the first time he'd heard him anything but calm. "I take it I'm not the first interruption of the day."

"Not by a long shot." Brody tested the shelf. It slid smoothly into its slot. At least something was going right today, he thought. "If this is about the kitchen design for your place, once you approve it, I'll order materials. We'll be able to start in a couple of weeks."

"Actually, I'm staying out of that one. Tash has gotten very territorial over this kitchen deal. I just came by to see the progress here. The considerable progress."

"Yeah, moving right the hell along." Brody snatched

up another shelf, then stopped, let out a breath. "Sorry. Bad day."

"Must be going around." And explained, Spencer decided, why his daughter was in a prickly mood. "Kate's downstairs setting up her office."

"Oh." Brody carted his shelves into the pantry, began to set them. Very deliberately. "I didn't realize she was still here."

"Furniture she ordered just came in. I didn't get much of a welcome from her, either. So, putting the evidence together, I conclude the two of you had an argument."

"It's not an argument when somebody jumps down somebody else's throat for no good reason. It's an attack."

"Mmm-hmm. At the risk of poking my nose in, I can tell you the women in my family always have what they consider a good reason for jumping down a man's throat. Of course, whether or not it actually *is* a good reason is debatable."

"Which is why women are just too much damn trouble."

"Tough doing without them, though, isn't it?"

"I was getting along. Jack and I were doing just fine." Frustration pumped off him as he turned back to Spencer. "What is it with women anyway, that they have to complicate things, then make you feel like an idiot?"

"Son, generations of men have pondered that question. There's only one answer. Because."

With a half laugh, Brody stepped back again, automatically eyeballing the shelves for level and fit. "I guess that's as good as it gets. Doesn't matter much at this point anyway. She dumped me."

"You don't strike me as a man who typically walks away from a problem."

"Nothing typical about your daughter." As soon as it was out, Brody winced. "Sorry."

"I took that as a compliment. My impression is the two of you bruised each other's feelings, maybe each other's pride. An insider tip? Kate's usual response to bruised feelings or pride is temper, followed by ice."

Brody dug out the hooks to be used in the pantry. He should leave that job for a laborer, he thought. But he needed to do something simple with his hands. "She made herself pretty clear. She called me a jerk—then something in Russian. Ukrainian. Whatever."

"She spit at you in Ukrainian?" Spence struggled to conceal his amusement. "She'd have to have been pretty worked up for that."

Brody's eyes narrowed as he hefted his screwdriver. "I don't know what it meant, but I didn't like the sound of it."

"It might have been something about you roasting on a spit over Hell fire. Her mother likes to use that one. Brody, do you have feelings for my daughter?"

Brody's palms went instantly damp. "Mr. Kimball—"

"Spence. I know it's not a simple question, or an easy one. But I'd like an answer."

"Would you mind stepping away from the toolbox first? There are a lot of sharp implements in there."

Spencer slid his hands into his pockets. "You have my word I won't challenge you to a duel with screwdrivers."

"Okay. I have feelings for Kate. They're kind of murky and unsettled, but I have them. I didn't intend to get involved with her. I'm not in a position to."

"Can I ask why?"

"That's pretty obvious—I'm a single father. I'm putting together a decent life for my son, but it's nothing like what Kate's used to, or what she can have."

Spencer rocked back on his heels. "They gave you a bad time, didn't they?"

"Excuse me?"

"Unlike some families, ours can be nosy, interfering, protective and irritating. But you'll also find we respect and support each other's choices and feelings. Brody, it's a mistake to judge one situation by the dynamics of another." Spencer paused for a moment, then continued, "But putting that aside for the moment, since you care about Kate, let me give you some unsolicited advice. Whether you want to take it or not is up to you. Deal with the problem. Deal with her. If you didn't matter to her, she'd have ended things gently, or worse, politely."

Deciding he'd given Brody enough to think about, Spencer turned to take a survey of the total construction chaos of the kitchen. "So this is what I've got to look forward to." He shot Brody a miserable look. "And you think you have problems."

When Spencer left him alone, Brody stood, tapping the screwdriver on his palm. The man was advising him to fight with his daughter. What kind of a screwy family was that?

His own parents never fought. Of course, that was because his father set the rules, and those rules were followed. Or at least it seemed that way.

He'd never fought with Connie. Not really. They'd had some disagreements, sure, but they'd just worked through them, or talked them out. Or ignored them, Brody admitted. Ignored them, he thought, because they'd both been cut off, isolated, and they only had each other to rely on.

Temper had never gotten him anywhere but in trouble. With his father, in school, in the early days on the job. He'd learned to rein it in, to use his head instead of his gut. Most of the time, he admitted, thinking about his last altercation with his father.

Still, maybe it was a mistake to compare what had been with what was. One thing was certain, he wasn't going to get rid of this nasty sensation in his gut until he spoke his mind.

He checked his men first, ran over some minor adjustments and the basic plan for the following day. It was nearly time to knock off, so he cut them loose. He didn't want an audience.

Kate hit the nail squarely on the head and bared her teeth in satisfaction. Brody O'Connell, the pig, wasn't the only one who could use a hammer.

She'd spent the last two hours meticulously setting up her office. Everything would be perfect when she was finished. She wouldn't settle for anything less.

Her desk was precisely where she wanted it, and its drawers already organized with the brochures she'd designed and ordered, her letterhead, the application forms for students.

Her filing cabinet was the same golden oak. In time, she expected the folders inside to be full.

She'd found the rug at an antique sale, and its faded pattern of cabbage roses set off the pale green walls, picked up the tone in the fabric of the accent chairs that now faced her desk.

Just because it was an office didn't mean it couldn't have style.

She hung yet another of the framed black-and-white photos she'd chosen. Stood back and nodded with approval. Dancers at the *barre,* in rehearsal, onstage, backstage. Young students at recitals, lacing on toe shoes.

Sweating, sparkling, limp from exertion or flying. All the aspects of a dancer's world. They would remind her, on a daily basis, what she had done. And what she was doing.

She picked up another nail, set it neatly on her mark, slammed it. And what she wasn't doing, she thought, rapping it a second time, was wasting her time on Brody O'Connell.

The bastard.

Let him cozy up to Tiffany. Oh, she remembered Tiffany Skully. The busty bleached blonde had been a year ahead of her in high school. Lots of giggling. Lots of lipstick. Well, let the jerk take her out. What did she care?

She was done with him.

"If you'd told me you were going to cover the entire space with pictures," Brody commented, "I wouldn't have worked so hard on finishing the drywall. Nobody'd know the difference."

She jammed the photograph in place, picked up another nail. "One assumes you have a certain pride in your work, whether or not it can be admired. And since I paid for the wall, I'll do whatever the hell I like with it."

"Yeah, you want to riddle them with nail holes, it's your choice." The pictures looked great—not that he was going to say so. Not just the arrangement of them, which was cohesive without being rigid, but the theme.

He could see her in several of them, as a child, a

young girl, a woman. One of her sitting cross-legged on the floor, pounding shoes with a hammer, made him want to grin.

Instead he waved a finger toward it, casually. "I thought you were supposed to dance with those."

"For your information toe shoes need to be broken in. That's one method of doing so. Now, if you'll excuse me, I'd like to get my office finished. I have appointments here tomorrow afternoon."

"Then that gives you plenty of time." Particularly, he thought, since the office already looked perfect. He should have known she'd make it perfect.

"Let me put it this way." She pounded in another nail. "I'm busy, and I have no desire to talk to you. I'm not paying you to stand around and chat in any case."

"Don't pull that on me." He yanked the hammer out of her hand. "You writing checks for the job doesn't have anything to do with the rest of it. I'll be damned if you'll put it on that level."

He was right, of course, and it shamed her to have it pointed out. "True enough, but our personal business is done."

"The hell it is." He turned and shoved the pocket door closed.

"Just what do you think you're doing?"

"Getting some privacy. It doesn't seem to be in big supply around here."

"Open that door—then walk through it. And keep walking."

"Sit down and shut up."

Her eyes widened, more in shock than temper. "I beg your pardon?"

To solve the problem, he set the hammer aside—well

out of her reach—walked over and pushed her into a chair. "Now listen."

She started to leap up, was pushed down firmly again. Temper heated, but it stayed at the bubble from the sheer surprise of seeing him so furious. "So, you've proved you're big and strong," she said derisively. "You don't have to prove you're stupid."

"And you don't have to prove you're spoiled and snotty. You try to get up again before I'm done, I'm going to tie you in that chair. I was minding my own business when Jerry came in. He's a friend. He and Beth have gone out of their way for me and Jack, so I owe him."

"So naturally you need to pay him back by dating his sister."

"Be quiet, Kate. I'm not dating his sister. I don't intend to date his sister. He was running off at the mouth, and I was shimming cabinets. I wasn't listening to him, and by the time I tuned back in…"

Brody raked a hand through his hair, took a restless turn around the room. "He caught me off guard, and I was trying to backtrack without stomping all over his feelings. He and Tiff have always been tight. He's worried about her, I guess, and he trusts me. What was I supposed to say? I'm not interested in your sister?"

Kate angled her chin. "Yes. But that's not really the point."

"Then what the hell is the point?"

"The point is you indicated, and obviously feel, there's nothing between us but sex. I require more than that in a relationship. I demand more than that. Loyalty, fidelity, affection, respect. I expect a man to be able to

say—without tripping over his own clumsy tongue—
that he and I are dating. That he cares about me."

"Damn it, it's been nearly ten years since I dated anyone. You'd think you could cut me some slack."

"Then you think wrong. Are we done here?"

"Man, you're a hard case. No, we're not done." He
yanked her to her feet. "I haven't been with anyone else
since you. I don't want to be. I'll make a point of making
that crystal clear to Jerry or anyone else. I care about
you, and I don't appreciate being made to feel like an
idiot because I don't have a good handle on it."

"Fine. Now let go."

"If I could let go, I wouldn't be standing here wanting to strangle you."

"You insulted me. You insulted us. You're the one
who should be strangled."

"I'm not going to apologize again." He dragged her
toward the door.

"Apologize? I didn't hear any apology. What are you
doing?"

"Just be quiet," he ordered as he shoved the door
open, continued to pull her down the corridor.

"If you don't let go of me, this minute, I'm going
to—"

The wind was knocked out of her when he simply
hauled her up and over his shoulder. He clamped her
legs still with one arm, yanked open the front door with
his free hand.

"Have you lost your mind?" Too shocked to struggle,
she shoved her hair up out of her face as he strode with
her across the porch and down the front steps. "Have
you completely lost your mind?"

"The minute I started thinking about you." He

scanned the street, spotted a woman coming out of the apartment building. "Excuse me! Ma'am?"

She glanced over, blinked. "Ah...yes?"

"This is Kate. I'm Brody. I just wanted you to know that we're dating."

"Oh, my God," Kate whispered, and let her hair fall again.

"I see. Well..." The woman smiled, offered a little wave. "That's nice."

"Thanks." Brody shifted Kate, set her on her feet in front of him. "Would you like to keep going, or are you satisfied?"

She couldn't get the words out of her mouth. Simply couldn't shove them from where they seemed to be stuck in her throat. She solved the problem by rapping a fist against his chest and storming back into the building.

"Guess not," Brody decided, and strode in after her.

Chapter Nine

He caught her an instant before she could slam her office door in his face. Not that it would have stopped him now that he was revved up.

"Not so fast, honey."

"Don't you call me honey. Don't you speak to me." She rounded on him. "You're nothing but a bully. Manhandling me that way. Embarrassing me on the street."

"Embarrassed?" He kept his eyes, every bit as hot as hers, level as he slid the door closed behind his back. "Why is that? I simply told a neighbor, without tripping over my—what was it—clumsy tongue, that we're dating. So what's the problem?"

"The problem is…" She retreated several steps as he advanced on her. That was another shocker—not just that he was backing her into a corner, but that she was letting him. She'd *never* backed down from a confrontation, and certainly never backed down from a man. "Just what do you think you're doing?"

"Being myself." Damned if it didn't feel good. "Been a while since I cut loose like this, but it's coming back to me. We may as well find out now if you have a problem with that."

"If you think you can—" She broke off as he grabbed her arms, pulled her up to her toes. "You'd just better calm down."

"You'd just better catch up." He crushed his mouth to hers and felt her instinctive jerk of protest. Ignored it.

"You got a problem with it?" he demanded lifting his head and meeting her eyes.

"Brody—" That was all she managed to say before he took her mouth over again.

"Yes or no."

"I don't—" His teeth scraped along her neck. "Oh God." She couldn't think. This had to be wrong. There had to be a dozen, two dozen, rational reasons why this was wrong.

She'd worry about them later.

"You want me to take my hands off you?" They moved over her, rough and possessive. "Yes or no. Pick now."

"No. Damn it." She fisted her hands in his hair and dragged his mouth back to hers.

She didn't know who pulled whom to the floor. It didn't seem to matter. She couldn't tell whose hands were more impatient as they tugged at clothing. She didn't care.

All she knew was she wanted this rough, angry man every bit as much as she'd wanted the gentle, patient one. Her body was quaking for him, her heart bounding.

So much heat. She was amazed her system didn't simply implode from it. The sharp stabs of pain and pleasure fused together into one unbearable sensation.

Tangled together, they rolled over the floor. She set her teeth at his shoulder, craving that wild flavor of flesh.

He'd forgotten what it was to let himself want like this, to take like this. Without restriction or boundaries. To rush and plunder. His fingers tore at the triangle of lace that blocked her from him. And he drove her up, hard and high.

The bite of her nails on his back was a dark thrill, the blind shock in her eyes a violent triumph. Desperate for possession, he yanked up her hips and plunged.

She rose up, that agile body quivering, her fingers digging into the rug for stability as he pounded into her. An elemental mating that fed on hot blood. Even as she cried out, he dragged her up until her legs wrapped around his waist, her hands found slippery purchase on his sweat-slicked shoulders.

She held on, riding the razor-tipped edge of pleasure, clinging to it, to him. When the climax ripped through her, shredding her system to tatters, she bowed back and let him take his own.

She melted like candle wax onto the floor when he released her. Then simply lay there, weak and sated.

She'd been ravaged. She had allowed it. And she felt wonderful.

Though his vision was still a little blurry at the edges, Brody studied her, then what was left of their clothes. "I ripped your shirt." When her eyes fluttered open, he recognized the lazy gleam of a satisfied woman.

"And these things." He held up the tatters of her panties. "Well, I'm not going to apologize."

"I didn't ask for an apology."

"Good. Because if you had, I'd have been forced to haul you outside again—naked this time—to find another neighbor. Instead you can borrow my shirt. I've got a spare in the truck."

She sat up, took the offered shirt. The glow she'd felt was beginning to fade. "Are we still fighting?"

"I'm done, so I guess that's up to you."

She looked up. His eyes were clear now, and direct. This time it was she who fumbled—starting to speak, then shaking her head.

"No, go on. Say it. Let's make sure the air's completely clear."

"You hurt my feelings." It was lowering to admit it. Temper, she thought, was so much easier to handle than hurt.

"I get that." He took the shirt from her, draped it over her shoulders. "And that's something I will apologize for. If it helps any, you hurt mine right back."

"What are we doing, Brody?"

"Trying to figure each other out, I guess. I'm not embarrassed by what we've got going on, Kate. I don't want you to think that. But I don't have a handle on it yet."

"All right, that's fair enough." But it hurt a lot, she realized as she shrugged into the borrowed shirt. Hurt that she'd fallen in love, and he hadn't. Still, that didn't mean he wouldn't. She smiled a little, leaned over and up to kiss him. "You're not a jerk. I'm sorry I called you one."

He caught her chin. "You called me something worse than that, didn't you?"

Now the smile spread and was genuine. "Maybe."

"I'm going to buy a Ukrainian phrase book."

"Good luck. Besides they just don't have certain descriptive words and phrases in there."

"I'm getting one anyway." He got to his feet, drew her up to hers. "I've got to go pick up my kid."

His hair was a sexy mess, his eyes lazily satisfied. He was naked to the waist. And, she thought, he was a father who had to pick up his little boy from the school bus.

"That's part of it, isn't it? Part of your problem with getting a grip on our relationship? Trying to juggle the man and the father together."

"Maybe. Yes," he admitted. "Kate, there hasn't been anyone in…" He lifted a hand, smoothed it over his hair in some attempt to order it. "Connie was sick for a long time." He couldn't talk about that now, couldn't go back there. "Jack had a rough start. I guess we both did. All I can do is make up for it."

"You have. And you are. I know how to juggle, too, Brody. I think we can keep the balls in the air. As long as we both want to."

"I want to."

Her heart settled. "Then that's also fair enough. Go get Jack."

"Yeah." His gaze skimmed down. "Before I do, I'd just like to say you sure look good in flannel."

"Thanks."

"You want a lift home?"

"No. I really do have some things to finish up here."

"All right." He lowered his head, touched his mouth to hers. Ended up lingering. "Gotta go." But when he got to the door, he glanced back. "You want to go out Saturday night?"

Her eyebrow lifted. It was the first time he'd actually asked her out. It was, she supposed, some sort of progress. "I'd love to."

How it got to be spring break when it seemed they'd just gotten through Christmas vacation, Brody didn't know. School days had certainly not flown by when he'd been a kid.

Added to that, the Skullys had decided to take advantage of the time off to take the kids to Disney World. This had caused major problems with Jack who'd begged, pleaded and had fallen back on whining over the idea that they should go, too.

Brody had explained why it wasn't possible just now, patiently sympathized. Then had fallen back on the parental cop-out—because I said so—when the siege had shown no sign of ending.

As a result, he'd had a sulky kid on his hands for two days, and a raging case of the guilts. The combination made it very crowded in the small bathroom where he was trying to lay tile.

"You never let me go anywhere," Jack complained. He was thoroughly bored with the small pile of toys he'd been allowed to bring along.

Usually he liked coming to the job with his dad. But not when his best friend was in Disney World riding on Space Mountain. It was a gyp. A big fat gyp, he thought, relishing one of the words he'd picked up from the crew.

When his father ignored him and continued to lay tile, Jack stuck out his bottom lip. "How come I couldn't go to Grandma's?"

"I told you Grandma was busy this morning. She's

going to come by and pick you up in a couple of hours. Then you can go over to her house." Thank God.

"I don't want to stay here. It's boring. It's not fair I gotta stay here and do nothing while everybody else has fun. I never get to do *anything*."

Brody shoved his trowel into the tray of adhesive. "Look. I've got a job to do. A job that sees to it you eat regular."

Damn it, how was his father's voice suddenly coming out of his mouth?

"I'm stuck with it," he added, "and so are you. Now keep it up, Jack. Just keep it up, and you won't be going anywhere."

"Grandpa gave me five dollars," Jack said, tearing up. "So you don't have to buy me any food."

"Great. Terrific. I'll retire tomorrow."

"Grandma and Grandpa can take me to Disney World, and you can't go."

"They're not taking you anywhere," Brody snapped, cut to the bone by the childish slap. "You'll be lucky to go to Disney World by the time you're thirty. Now, cut it out."

"I want Grandma! I want to go home! I don't like you anymore."

Kate walked in on that, and the resulting angry, tired tears. She took one look at Brody's exhausted, frustrated face, the cranky little boy sprawled weeping on the floor, and stepped into the fray.

"What's all this, Handsome Jack?"

"I wanna go to Disney World."

He sobbed it out, between hiccups. Even as Brody got to his feet to deal with it, Kate crouched down between father and son. "Oh, boy, me, too. I bet we'd all like to go there more than anyplace."

"Dad doesn't."

"Sure he does. Dads like to go most of all. That's why it's harder for them, because they have to work."

"Kate, I can handle this."

"Who said you couldn't?" she muttered, but picked up the boy and got to her feet. "I bet you're tired of being cooped up, aren't you, baby? Why don't we go to my house awhile, and let Dad finish his work?"

"My mother's coming by to get him in a couple of hours. Just let me—" He reached for his son who only curled himself like a snake around Kate—and effectively cut his heart in two.

One look at the blank hurt on Brody's face made her want to sandwich Jack between them in a hard hug. But that, she thought wasn't the immediate answer. Distance was.

"I'm done for the day here, Brody. Why don't you let Jack come home with me, keep me company." *Take a nap,* she mouthed. "I'll call your mother and ask her to pick him up at my house instead."

"I want to go with Kate." Jack sobbed against her shoulder.

"Fine. Great." The miserable mix of temper and guilt had him snatching up his trowel again. Very much, Kate thought, like a cranky boy. "Thanks."

He sat down heavily on an overturned bucket as he heard Jack sniffle out, as Kate carried him off: "My daddy yelled at me."

"Yes, I know." She kissed Jack's hot, wet cheek as she walked downstairs. "You yelled at him, too. I bet he feels just as sad as you do."

"Nuh-uh." With a heavy, heavy sigh, Jack rested his head on Kate's shoulder. "He wouldn't take me to Disney World like Rod."

"I know. I guess that's my fault."

"How come?"

"Well, your dad's doing this job for me, and he promised me it would be done by a certain time. Because he promised, I made promises to other people who are depending on me now. If your dad broke his promise to me, then I broke mine to the other people, that wouldn't be right. Would it, Jack?"

"No, but, maybe just this one time."

"Does your dad break his promises to you?"

"No." Jack's head drooped.

"Don't be sad, Handsome Jack. When we get to my house, we're going to read a story about another Jack. The one with the beanstalk."

"Can I have a cookie?"

"Yes." In love, she gave him a hard squeeze.

He was asleep almost before Jack sold his cow for magic beans.

Poor little boy, she thought, tucking a light throw over him. Poor Brody.

She began to think she hadn't given the man enough credit. Parenthood wasn't all wrestling on the floor and ball games in the yard. It was also tears and tantrums, disappointments and discipline. It was saying no, having to say no, when your heart wanted to say yes.

"You're so well loved, Handsome Jack," she murmured and bent over to kiss the top of his head. "He needs you to know that."

And so is he, she thought with a sigh. "I wish the

man would buy a clue. Because I'm not waiting much longer. I want both of you."

When the phone rang, she snatched it from the cradle. "Hello. Ah." Smiling now, she walked out of the room so as not to disturb Jack. "Davidov. What have I done to deserve a call from the master?"

Later, though she admitted it was foolish, Kate freshened her makeup and tidied her hair. It was the first time she would meet Brody's parents. Since she intended for them to be her in-laws, she wanted to make a good impression.

Jack had wakened from his nap energized. This had called for some running around the backyard, a fierce battle with action figures and a race with miniature cars that had resulted in a satisfying wreck of major proportions.

They finished the entertainment off with a snack in the kitchen.

"My dad's mad at me," Jack confided over slices of apple and cheese.

"I don't think so. I think he's a little upset because he couldn't give you what you wanted. Inside, parents want to give their children everything that would make them happy. But sometimes they can't."

She remembered throwing some impressive tantrums herself—snarls followed by sulks. And ending, she thought, like this in guilty unhappiness.

"Sometimes they can't because it's not the best thing, or the right thing just then. And sometimes because they just can't. When your little boy cries and yells and stomps his feet, it makes you mad for a while. But it also hurts your heart."

Jack lifted his face, all big eyes and trembling lips. "I didn't mean to."

"I know. And I bet if you tell him you're sorry, you'll both feel better."

"Did your dad ever yell at you?"

"Yes, he did. And it made me mad or unhappy. But after a while, I usually figured out I deserved it."

"Did I deserve it?"

"Yes, I'm afraid you did. There was this one thing I always knew, even when I was mad or unhappy. I knew my dad loved me. You know that about your dad, too."

"Yeah." Jack nodded solemnly. "We're a team."

"You're a great team."

Jack turned his apple slices around, making pictures and patterns. She was pretty, he thought. And she was nice. She could play games and read stories. He even liked when she kissed him, and the way she laughed when he pretended not to like it. Dad liked to kiss her, too. He said he did, and he didn't lie.

So she could maybe marry his dad—even though Dad said she wasn't going to—and then she could be Dad's wife and Jack's mother. They'd all live together in the big house.

And maybe, sometime, they could all go to Disney World.

"What are you thinking about so hard, Handsome Jack?"

"I was wondering if—"

"Oops." She smiled, rising as she heard the doorbell. "Hold that thought, okay? That must be your grandma."

She gave Jack's hair a quick rub and hurried out to answer. With her hand on the knob, she took a quick bracing breath. Silly to be nervous, she told herself. Then opened the door to Mr. and Mrs. O'Connell.

"Hi. It's good to see you." She stepped back in invitation. "Jack's just in the kitchen, having a snack."

"It's good of you to watch him for Brody." Mary O'Connell stepped inside, tried not to make her quick scan of the entrance too obvious. She'd fussed with her makeup, too—much to her husband's disgust.

"I enjoy spending time with Jack. He's great company. Please come on back. Have some coffee."

"Don't want to put you out," Bob said. He'd been in the house plenty. When you fixed people's toilets, you weren't particularly impressed by their doodads and furniture.

"I've got a fresh pot. Please, come in—unless you're in a hurry."

"We've got to—"

Bob broke off as his wife gave him a subtle elbow nudge. "We'd love a cup of coffee. Thank you."

"Brody's going to be remodeling the kitchen for my mother," Kate began as they walked back. "My parents love the work he's done in the rest of the house."

"He always was good with his hands," Mary commented and gave her husband a quiet look when he folded his lips tight.

"He's certainly transformed the old house I bought. Hey, Jack, look who I've got."

"Hi!" Jack slurped his chocolate milk. "I've been playing with Kate."

Like father like son, Bob thought sourly, but his heart lifted as it always did at the sight of Jack's beaming face. "Where'd you get the chocolate cow, partner?"

"Oh, we keep her in the garden shed," Kate said as she got out cups and saucers. "And milk her twice a day."

"Kate's got toys. Her mom has a whole *store* of toys. She said how on my birthday we can go there and I can pick one out."

"Isn't that nice?" Mary slid her gaze toward Kate, speculated. "How is your mother, Kate?"

"She's fine, thanks."

Mary approved of the way Kate set out the cups, the cream and sugar. Classy, but not fussy. And the ease with which she handed Jack a dishrag so he could wipe up a bit of spilled milk himself.

Good potential mother material, she decided. God knew her little lamb deserved one. As for potential wife material, well, she would see what she would see.

"Everyone's talking about your ballet school," she began, flushing slightly at her husband's soft snort. "You must be excited."

"I am. I've got several students lined up, and classes begin in just a few weeks. If you know anyone who might be interested, I'd appreciate it if you'd spread the word."

"Shepherdstown's some different from New York City," Bob said as he reached for the sugar.

"It certainly is." Kate's voice was smooth and easy— though she'd heard the snort. "I enjoyed living in New York, working there. Of course it helped considerably that I had family there as well. And I liked the traveling, seeing new places, having the opportunity to dance on the great stages. But this is home, and where I want to be. Do you think ballet is out of place here, Mr. O'Connell?"

He shrugged. "Don't know anything about it."

"It happens I do. And I think a good school of dance

will do very well here. We're a small town, of course," she added, sipping her coffee. "But we're also a college town. The university brings in a variety of people from a variety of places."

"Can I have a cookie?"

"Please," Jack's grandmother added.

"Can I please have a cookie?"

Kate started to rise, then let out a gasp as she saw Brody through the glass on the back door. With a shake of her head, she walked over to open it. "You gave me such a jolt."

"Sorry." He was a little out of breath, more from excitement than the quick jog around the house. "I tried to call you," he said, nodding in greeting to his parents. "To head you off. You must've been on the road."

"Said we were coming to pick the boy up at three," Bob said. "Got here at three."

"Yeah, well. I had a little change of plans." He looked at his son who sat with his eyes on his plate and his chin nearly on his chest. "Did you have a good time with Kate, Jack?"

Jack nodded his head, slowly looked up. His eyes were teary again. "I'm sorry I was bad. I'm sorry I hurt your heart."

Brody crouched down, cupped Jack's face. "I'm sorry I can't take you to Disney World. I'm sorry I yelled at you."

"You're not mad at me anymore?"

"No, I'm not mad at you."

The tears dried up. "Kate said you weren't."

"Kate was right." He picked Jack out of the chair for a hug before setting him on his feet.

"Can I go back to work with you? I won't be bad."

"Well, you could, except I'm not going back to work today."

"Man knocks off middle of the afternoon isn't putting in a good day's work."

Brody glanced over at his father, nodded. "True enough. And a man who doesn't take a few hours now and then to be with his son isn't working hard enough at being a father."

"You always had food in your belly," Bob shot back as he shoved away from the table.

"You're right. I want Jack to be able to say more than that about me. I've got something for you," he added, cupping Jack's chin as it had begun to wobble as it always did when Brody and his father exchanged words. "It isn't Disney World, but I think you'll like it even better than a ride on Space Mountain."

"Is it a new action figure?" Thrilled he began tugging at Brody's pockets.

"Nope."

"A car? A truck?"

"You are way off, and it's not in my pocket. It's outside on the porch."

"Can I see? Can I?" He was already running for the door, tugging the knob. And when he opened it, looked down, looked up again at his father, Brody had, in that wonderful moment of stupefied delight, everything that mattered.

"A puppy! A puppy!" Jack scooped up the black ball of fur that was trying to climb up his leg. "Is it mine? Can I keep him?"

"Looks like he wants to keep you," Brody commented as the pup wriggled in ecstasy, yipping and bathing Jack's face with his tongue.

"Look, Grandma, I got a puppy, and he's mine. And his name is Mike. Just like I always wanted."

"He sure is a pretty little thing. Oh, just look at those feet. Why he'll be bigger than you before long. You have to be real good to him, Jack."

"I will. I promise. Look, Kate. Look at Mike."

"He's great." Unable to resist, she got down and was treated to some puppy kisses. "So soft. So sweet." She turned her head, met Brody's eyes. "Very, very sweet."

"It's a good thing for a boy to have a dog." Still stinging from his son's comment, Bob gestured. "But who's going to tend to it when Jack's in school all day and you're working? Problem with you is you never think things through, just do what you want at the moment you want it, and don't consider."

"Bob." Mortified, Mary reached up to pat her husband's arm.

"I have a fenced yard," Brody said carefully. "And I've worked on plenty of jobs where dogs were around. He'll come with me till he's old enough to be on his own."

"You buy that dog for the boy, or to patch up your conscience because you can't give him a holiday like his friends?"

"I don't want to go to Disney World," Jack said in a quavering voice. "I want to stay home with Dad and Mike."

"Why don't you take Mike outside, Jack?" Fixing a smile on her face, Kate walked to the door. "Puppies like to run around as much as boys do. And you need to get acquainted. Here, put on your jacket first."

Brody held it in until Kate nudged the boy out the door.

"It's none of your business if I get my son a dog, or

why. But the fact is I had this one picked out from a litter three weeks ago for him, and was waiting until he was weaned. I was going to pick him up Sunday for Easter, but Jack needed a little cheering up today."

"You're not teaching him respect by giving him presents after he's sassed you."

"All you taught me was respect, and look where that got us."

"Please." Mary all but wrung her hands. "This isn't the place."

"Don't you tell me where I can speak my mind," Bob snapped. "My mistake was in not slapping you back harder and more often. You always did run your own way, as you pleased. Nothing but trouble, causing it and finding it and giving your mother heartache. Run off to the city before you're dry behind the ears, and pissing your life away."

"I didn't run off to the city. I ran away from you."

Bob's head jerked back at that, as if he'd been slapped. He went pale. "Now you're back, aren't you? Scrambling to make do, shuffling the boy off to neighbors so you can make a living. Stirring up gossip 'cause you're fooling around with women down the hall from where that boy sleeps, and teaching him to run wild as you did, and end up the same way."

"Just one minute." If her own temper hadn't hazed her vision, Kate would have realized she was stepping between two men very near to coming to blows. "It so happens Brody isn't fooling around with women, he's fooling around with me. And though that *is* none of your business, the fooling around has never gone on when Jack's asleep down the hall.

"And if you don't know that Brody would cut his own arm off rather than do anything, *anything* to hurt that child, then you're blind as well as stupid. You should be ashamed to speak to him as you did, to not have the guts to tell him you're proud of what he's making out of his life, and of the life he's making for his son."

"You're wasting your breath," Brody began, and she rounded on him.

"You shut up. You've plenty to answer for, too. You have no right to speak to your father as you did. No right whatsoever to show him disrespect. And in front of your own child. Don't you see that it frightens and hurts Jack to watch the two of you claw at each other this way?"

She spun back, searing both of them with one hot look. "The pair of you haven't got enough sense put together to equal the brains of a monkey. I'm going outside with Jack. As far as I'm concerned the two of you can pound each other into mush and be done with it."

She wrenched open the door and sailed outside.

She was still simmering when Brody joined her a few minutes later. Saying nothing he watched Jack wrestle with the puppy and try to get Mike to chase a small red ball.

"I want to apologize for bringing that into your house."

"My house has heard family arguments before, and I expect it will hear them again."

"You were right about it being wrong for us to start on each other in front of Jack." When she said nothing, he jammed his hands into his pockets. "Kate, that's just the way it is between me and my father. The way it's always been."

"And because it's been that way, it has to continue to be? If you can change one aspect of your life, Brody, you can change others. You just have to try harder."

"We grate each other, that's all. We're better when we keep our distance. I don't want Jack to feel that way about me. Maybe I overcompensate."

"Stop it." Impatient again, she turned to him. "Is that a happy, well-adjusted, healthy boy?"

"Yeah." Brody had to smile as Jack filled the air with belly laughs as he rolled over the grass with the puppy climbing all over him.

"You know you're a good father. It's taken work, and effort, but for the most part it's easy for you. Because you love him unconditionally. It's a lot more work, a lot more effort, Brody, for you to be a good son. Because there are a lot of conditions on the love you have for your father, and his for you."

"We don't love each other."

"Oh, you're wrong. If you didn't, you couldn't hurt each other."

Brody shrugged that off. She didn't understand, he thought. How could she? "First time I've ever seen him shocked speechless. I don't believe he's ever had a woman rip into him that way. Me, I'm getting used to it."

"Good. Now if you don't want me ripping into you again anytime soon, you'll apologize to your mother at the first opportunity. You embarrassed her."

"Man, you're strict. Mind if I play with my dog first?"

She arched a brow. "Whose dog?"

"Jack's. But Jack and I, we're—"

"A team," she finished. "Yes, I know."

Chapter Ten

Kate made her plans, bided her time. And chose her moment.

She knew it was calculated. But really, what was wrong with that? Timing, approach, method—they were essential to any plan. So if she'd waited for that particular moment on a Friday night when Jack was enjoying a night over at his grandparents and Brody was relaxed after a particularly intense bout of lovemaking, it was simply rational planning.

"I've got something for you."

"Something else?" He was, as Jerry would have said, in the zone. "I get dinner, a bottle of wine and a night with a beautiful woman. I don't think there is anything else."

With a quiet laugh she slipped out of bed. "Oh, but there is."

He watched her—always he enjoyed watching the way she moved. He'd come to the conclusion there was more to this ballet business than he'd once thought.

It gave him a great deal of pleasure to see her here, in his room. The room, he thought, he'd been squeezing in hours late at night to finish. He was doing, thank you God, a lot more than sleeping there now.

The walls were finished and painted a strong, deep blue. Kate favored strong colors. The woodwork, stripped down to its natural tone and glossily sealed, was a good accent.

He hoped to get to the floors soon. Curtains and that kind of thing would be dealt with eventually.

But for now he just liked seeing her in here. The dusky skin against the smooth blue walls, and the way the shimmer of light from the low fire danced in shadows.

She'd left her earrings on his dresser once. It had given him a hell of a jolt to see them there the next morning. They'd looked so…female, he remembered.

Yet he'd been foolishly disappointed when she'd removed them.

What that had to say about him, about things, he'd just have to figure out.

She put on his shirt against the light chill of the room and walked over to her purse.

"I'm going to buy you a half dozen flannel shirts," Brody decided. "Just so I can see you walking around naked under them."

"I'll take them." She sat back on the bed, and dropped an envelope on his bare chest. "And these are for you."

"What?" Baffled, he sat up, tapped out the contents.

The two airline tickets only increased his confusion. "What's this?"

"Two tickets on the shuttle to New York. Next Friday. One for you, one for Jack."

He eyed them, then eyed her. Cautiously. "Because?"

"Because I really want both of you to come. Have you ever been to New York?"

"No, but—"

"Even better. I get to introduce it to both of you. The director of my former company called me earlier in the week," she explained. "They're putting on a special performance—one show only, next Saturday night. It's for charity. There'll be several selections from several ballets performed by different artists. He'd asked me to participate some time ago, but I passed. So much going on, and it's all but running into the opening of my school."

"But now you decided not to pass."

"The dancer who was to perform the *pas de deux* from *The Red Rose*—that's a ballet Davidov first performed with his wife when they were partners—is out with an injury. It's not career-ending, thank God, but she can't dance for at least two weeks. That's put her out. He's asked me to fill in."

Simple, she thought. It was all very simple. And she wasn't going to give Brody any wiggle room.

"I've danced this part several times. Fact is, it's what he asked me to perform originally. So when he called, I didn't want to say no. Then, of course, he talked me into doing another segment from *Don Quixote*. I should leave Monday to get in shape for it, but I couldn't shuffle everything, so I'm leaving Tuesday."

He felt a little twinge in the gut at the thought of her leaving again. "You'll be great. But listen, Kate, I appreciate the gesture, but I just can't grab Jack and take off to New York like that."

"Why not?"

"Well, work, school, for starters. A new puppy for another. Your basics."

"You can leave after school on Friday, and be in New York before dinner. We can stay at my sister's. Saturday you can see some of the city, maybe take Jack to the top of the Empire State Building. Saturday night, you come to the ballet. Sunday, we see a little more of the city, go have dinner at my grandparents, catch the late shuttle back. Everyone's at school or work Monday."

She moved her shoulders. "Oh, and as for Mike, you bring him, of course."

"Bring a dog to New York?"

"Sure, my sister's kids will love it."

He felt as though he were sitting in a box and she was slowly closing the lid. "Kate, it's just not the kind of thing people like me do. Flying off to New York for the weekend."

"It's not a flight to Mars, O'Connell." Laughing she leaned over and kissed him. "It's a little adventure. Jack'll love it—and…" She'd saved the *coup de grâce,* as any good general. "He'll be able to give his pal Rod a little back for all the bragging about Disney World. Jack'll see where King Kong fell to his tragic death."

It hit the mark and had Brody struggling not to squirm. Forget the box, he thought. Now he felt like a fish with a hook firmly lodged in his mouth. "Don't take this the wrong way, okay? But I'm really not into ballet."

"Oh." She smiled, fluttered her lashes. "Which ones have you seen?"

"I haven't seen a public hanging, either, but I don't think I'd get much of a charge out of it."

"Think of it this way. You'll be able to give Jack his first look at New York. You'll have two days to enjoy yourself and only about two hours to be bored senseless. Not a bad deal. You've never seen me dance," she added, linking her fingers with his. "I'd like you to."

He frowned at the tickets, shook his head. "Hit all the angles, didn't you?"

"I don't think I missed any. Is it a deal?"

"Wait till Jack hears he's going to take his first plane trip. He'll flip."

He did more than flip. By the time they were shuffling onto the plane on Friday afternoon, he was all but turning himself inside out.

"Dad? Can't you ask if Mike can ride up with us? He's going to be scared in that box."

"Jack, I told you it's not allowed. He'll be fine, I promise. Remember he's got his toys, and now those other two dogs are riding in the dog seats with him."

"Yeah. I guess." Jack's eyes were huge with wonder, excitement and trepidation as they stepped through the doorway and onto the plane. "Look," he said in a desperate whisper. "There's the pilot guys."

The flight attendant clued in instantly. Jack was treated to a tour of the cockpit and given a pair of plastic wings. By the time they were preparing for takeoff, he'd decided to be an airline pilot.

For the next fifty minutes, he peppered his father

with questions, often with his face pressed up to the window. Brody's ears were ringing by the time they touched down, but he had to admit, Jack was having the time of his life.

Now all he had to do was get through the next couple of days—outnumbered by Kate's family. If that wasn't enough to give a guy a headache, there was always the ballet.

What the hell are you doing here, O'Connell? he asked himself with a quick twinge of panic. A weekend in New York. The ballet. For God's sake, why aren't you home sanding drywall and thinking about making a Friday night pizza?

Because of Kate, he admitted, and the panic bumped up into his throat. Somehow she'd changed everything.

With the carry-on in one hand, and Jack's hand gripped firmly in the other, Brody came through the gate. He ordered himself to be calm—it was only a couple of days, after all—and looked for Kate. When a tall blond man waved, Brody flipped through his memory files and tried to put a name to Kate's brother-in-law.

"Nick LeBeck." Nick tugged Brody's bag free to take it himself. "You guys are bunking at our place. Kate wanted to pick you up herself, but she got hung up at rehearsal."

"We appreciate you coming out. We could've taken a cab."

"No problem. Any more luggage?"

"Just Mike."

"Right." Grinning, Nick leaned down to shake Jack's hand. "Good to see you. Max is pretty excited about you coming to visit. You met him on New Year's."

"Uh-huh, and Kate said we can have, like, a sleep-over for two nights."

"Yeah. We're having a big celebration dinner, too. You like fish-head soup?"

Jack's eyes went huge. Slowly he shook his head.

"Good, because we're not having any. Let's go spring Mike."

It wasn't as awkward as he'd expected it to be to find himself dumped in a strange city, in a strange house with people he barely knew. Jack dived right in, picking up his fledgling friendship with Max as if they'd just parted the day before. Mike was a huge hit, and in a buzz of excitement at the attention, peed on the rug.

"I'm really sorry. He's almost housebroken."

"So are my kids," Freddie told Brody, and handed him a damp rag. "We're used to spills around here—of all natures—so relax."

To Brody's surprise, he did. It was interesting, and entertaining to watch Jack interact with a family, to see how he slid into the mix with a brother and sister. It was cute the way he played with three-year-old Kelsey. Kind of like he was trying out his big brother muscles.

It wasn't always easy, Brody mused, being an only child.

"Want to escape?" Nick asked and jerked his head. As he walked out of the playroom he called out: "You break it, you buy it." Laughing moans followed them out.

He took Brody into the music room with its battered piano—one he'd kept more than a decade out of sentiment—and its wide, deep leather chairs. There were gleaming Tonys on a shelf and a clutter of sheet music on a bench.

Nick walked over to a clear-fronted minifridge. "Beer?"

"Oh," Brody said with feeling. "Yeah."

"Traveling with kids separates the men from the boys." Nick popped tops, offered a bottle. "Let's hear it for keeping them separate for ten blissful minutes."

"He never stopped talking, not from the minute I picked him up from school. I think he broke his own record."

"Wait till you try trans-Atlantic. Nine hours trapped on a plane with Max and Kelsey." He shuddered. "Do you know how many questions can be asked in nine uninterrupted hours? No, let's not think about it. It'll give us both nightmares."

At Nick's gesture, Brody sank gratefully into one of the chairs. "It's a great place you've got here. I guess when I think of New York, I think of little apartments where the windows all face a brick building, or big, sleek skyscrapers."

"We got all of that. When Freddie and I started writing together, I was living over my brother's bar. Lower East side. Great bar," Nick added, "and not a half bad apartment. But it's not the kind of place you want to try to raise a couple of kids."

He glanced up, grinned. "Ah, here's the prima now."

"Sorry I'm late." Kate rushed in, gave Nick a quick peck on the cheek, then turned, bent and gave Brody a much longer kiss. "And sorry I couldn't pick you up. Davidov's having one of his moments. The man can drive you to drink. Nick, my hero, if you get me a glass of wine, I'll be your slave."

"Sounds like a deal."

"Tell Freddie I'll be back in after I catch my breath."

"Sit," he ordered, and nudged her into the chair he vacated. "Rest those million-dollar feet."

"You bet I will." She groaned, and leaned over to slip off her shoes as Nick left the room.

Brody swore and was instantly on his knees in front of her, lifted her foot in his hand. "What the hell have you done?" Her feet were bandaged, and raw.

"I danced."

"Until your feet bleed?" he demanded.

"Why yes, when necessary. With Davidov, it's often necessary."

"He ought to be shot."

"Mmm." She leaned back, closed her eyes. "I considered it, a number of times over the last couple days. Ballet isn't for wimps, O'Connell. And aching, bleeding feet are part of the job description."

"That's ridiculous."

"That's the life." She leaned over again, kissed his forehead. "Don't worry. They heal."

"How the hell are you supposed to dance on these tomorrow night?"

"Magnificently," she told him, then let out a huge sigh of gratitude when Nick came back. "My prince. Brody thinks Davidov should be shot."

"So you've said, plenty." Nick glanced down at her feet, winced. "God, what a mess. Want some ice?"

"No, thanks. I'll baby them later."

"You're going to take care of them right now." To settle the matter, Brody got up, plucked her out of the chair and into his arms.

"Oh, really, Brody, get a grip."

"Just be quiet," he ordered and carried her out of the room.

Nick tipped back his beer. "Man, he is *toast*." He hurried off to find his wife and tell her.

"It was so romantic." Freddie's heart continued to sigh over it now, hours later, as she and Nick prepared for bed. "He just carried her right into the kitchen, with that wonderful scowl on his face, and demanded where he could find a basin and so on to soak Kate's poor feet."

"I told you." Absently Nick rapped a fist on the wall that adjoined their room with his son's. But he didn't really expect it to quiet the racket on the other side for long. "The man's a goner."

"And the way he looks at her—especially when he thinks no one, particularly Kate, is paying attention. Like he could just gobble her up in one big bite. It's great."

Nick stopped scratching his belly and frowned. "I look at you that way."

Freddie sniffed and started to turn down the bed. "Yeah, right."

"Hey." He walked over, turned her around by the shoulder. "Right here," he instructed, pointing at his own face, then attempting a smoldering look. "See?"

She snorted. "Yeah, that's it all right. I am a puddle."

"Are you insinuating that I'm not romantic? Are you saying the hammer-swinger's got me beat in that department?"

Enjoying herself, Freddie rolled her eyes. "Please," she said and wandered over to the dresser to run a brush through her hair.

The next thing she knew she was being swept off her

feet. Her surprised yelp was muffled against his very determined mouth. "You want romance, pal? Boy, are you going to get it."

At the other end of the hall, as children finally fell into reluctant and exhausted sleep, Kate belted her robe. She'd put in several long, hard days—days that wore the body to a nub and left the mind fussy with fatigue.

But now, knowing Brody was just a few steps away, she was restless. And needy. She imagined he'd consider sneaking into her room rude. But that didn't mean she couldn't sneak into his.

She slipped from her room, walked quietly down the hall to peek in on the children. Even the dog, she noted, was sprawled out limply. Satisfied, she eased out again, and made her way to Brody's door.

No light shone under it. Well, if she had to wake him up, she had to wake him up. She opened it—a little creak of sound—and stepped in just as he turned from the window.

He'd been thinking of her—nothing new there, he admitted. And stood now, wearing only his jeans loosened at the waist. His mouth went dry as he saw her reach behind and flip the lock.

"Kate. The kids."

"Out for the count." She'd bought the robe only the day before, on an hour break. A ridiculous extravagance of peach-colored silk. But seeing the way his eyes darkened, hearing the way it whispered as she crossed the room, she considered it worth every penny.

"I just checked on them," she said, and ran her hands up his chest. "And if they wake up, one of the four of us will take care of it. Taking in the view?"

"It's pretty spectacular." He took her hands. "I was just thinking I'd never be able to sleep tonight, knowing you were so close, and not being able to touch you."

"Touch me now, and neither one of us will worry about sleep tonight."

He wondered how he had ever considered resisting her. She was every fantasy, every dream, every wish. All silk and shadows. And she was real, as real as that warm yielding mouth, those long, sculpted arms.

With her, all the years of emptiness, all the lonely nights were locked away.

He slipped the silk from her shoulders, and found only Kate beneath.

Curves and muscle, sighs and trembles. He slid into the bed with her, and into that intimate world they created together. Perfumed flesh, soft, stroking hands. She was a wonder to him, a smoky-eyed seductress who could beckon with a look. A strong-minded woman who refused to back down from a fight. An openhearted friend with strong shoulders and a steady hand.

He could no longer imagine what his life would be like if she stepped back out of it.

Knowing it, finally admitting it to himself, he gathered her close, and just held.

"Brody?" Kate brushed her fingers through his hair. His arms had tightened around her so fiercely she wondered why she didn't simply snap in two. "What is it?"

"Nothing." He pressed his lips to the side of her neck and ordered himself not to think. For God's sake don't think now. "It's nothing. I want you. It's like starving the way I want you."

His mouth took hers now. Hot, ravenous, burning away all thoughts, all reason.

There was something different happening between them. Something more. But he was whipping her over the edge so fast, with a kind of quiet intensity that was kin to desperation. She could do nothing but feel, nothing but respond. Her heart, already lost to him, bounded like a deer.

City lights glanced against the dark windows. The sounds of traffic hummed on the street below. Whatever life pulsed there meant nothing in this tangle of sheets and needs.

She rose over him, slim and pale in the shadows. Her hair was a dark fall, tumbling down her back, then sliding forward to curtain them both as she leaned down to kiss him. The scent of it, of her, surrounded him. Drowned him.

Then she took him in, one fluid move that encased him in heat.

Twin moans merged. Eyes locked. He reached for her, his hands sliding, slippery, up her body, over her breasts. She covered them with her own, holding him to her. And then she began to move.

Slow. Painfully and gloriously slow so that each breath was a shudder. Pleasure slithered through the blood, and began to pulse. He watched her as she took both of them higher—that graceful arch of body, that delicate line of throat. Her eyes closed as she lost herself. Her arms lifted until her hands were buried in her own rich mass of hair.

A sound rippled in her throat of pleasure rising. She began to drive him, drive herself, her hips like lightning. It was all speed and power now. With a kind of greedy glee they dragged each other toward the edge.

Held there, held until madness had them leaping recklessly over.

When she folded herself down to him, trembling still, his arms locked around her.

Love me, she thought. Her heart was raw with loving him. Tell me. Why won't you tell me?

He shifted her so that she could curl against him, so he could hold her there. "Will you stay?"

Kate closed her eyes. "Yes."

They lay quiet in each other's arms. But neither slept for a long time.

He woke reaching for her. Confusion came first as he struggled to remember where he was. He was alone in bed, in the dark. Groggy, he glanced over at a faint sound, and saw Kate, in the faint wash of light through the window, slipping into her robe.

"What is it?"

"Oh, I didn't mean to wake you." Whispering she stepped over to the side of the bed, bent down to kiss his cheek. "I have to go. Dance class."

"Huh? You're teaching class in the middle of the night?"

"I'm taking class—and it's not the middle of the night. It's nearly six."

He tried to clear his brain, but it objected to functioning on four hour's sleep. "You're taking class? I thought you knew how to dance."

"Smart aleck."

"No, wait." He grabbed for her hand before she could move away. "Why are you taking class? And why are you taking it at six in the morning?"

"I'm taking class because I'm a dancer, and dancers

never really stop taking class—certainly not if they're performing. And I'm taking it at seven in the morning because I have a dress rehearsal at eleven. Now go back to sleep."

"Oh. Okay."

"Nick and Freddie are going to take you around later, wherever. Maybe you can drop by the theater."

She waited for a response, then leaned down. "Well," she muttered, "you didn't have any trouble taking that particular order."

She left him sleeping and went to prepare for a very long day.

"Are you sure it's okay?" Brody looked dubiously at the motley crew approaching the stage door. Three adults, three kids and a small, mixed-breed puppy.

"Absolutely," Freddie assured him. "Kate cleared it."

He still wasn't convinced, but he'd already discovered it was hard to argue with either Kimball sister.

Especially on five hour's sleep.

The kids had bounded awake by the time Kate was taking her class. And they'd created enough noise to wake the entire island of Manhattan. Anyone deaf enough to sleep through it, would have been jolted awake by Mike's high, ferociously joyful barking.

They'd had breakfast in a deli, which had delighted Jack, then had proceeded to walk their feet off. The Empire State Building, souvenir shops. Times Square, souvenir shops. Grand Central Station. God help him, souvenir shops.

Brody decided horning in on Kate's rehearsal wasn't such a bad idea after all. It was in a theater, and last time he checked a theater had chairs.

"Lips zipped," Nick warned. "Or they'll kick us out. That goes for you, too, furball," he added, scratching Mike behind the ears.

"Nothing like backstage." Freddie linked her hand with Nick as they entered.

A woman behind a high counter glanced up over wire-rim glasses, scanned, then nodded. "Nice to see you, Ms. Kimball, Mr. LeBeck. See you brought the crew."

"Kate clear the way?" Freddie asked.

"She did. Any of these kids understand Russian?"

"No."

"Good. Davidov's in rare form. You can leave the pup with me. I like dogs, and if he gets frisky out there, Davidov's liable to eat him."

"That kind of day, huh?" Nick grinned, and the woman rolled her eyes.

"You don't know the half of it. What's his name?"

"His name is Mike," Jack piped up. "He's mine." "I'll take real good care of him."

"Okay." Biting his lip, Jack passed Mike up to her. "But if he cries, you have to come get me."

"That's a deal. Go on ahead, you know the way."

If they hadn't, after a short twist through backstage, they could have followed the bellows.

"Davidov." Freddie gave a mock shudder. "We'll just detour this way and go out front—where it's safe."

"Does he really eat dogs?" Jack asked in a hissing whisper.

"No." Brody took a firm hold of his son's hand. "She was just kidding." He hoped.

He didn't eat dogs, but at the moment, Davidov would have cheerfully dined on dancers.

He cut off the music again with a dramatic slice of his hand through the air. "You, you." He pointed at the couple currently panting and dripping sweat. "Go. Off my stage. Soak your heads. Maybe you'll come back in one hour, like dancers. Kimball!" he shouted. "Blackstone! Now!"

He paced back and forth, a slim man in dull gray sweats and a dramatic mane of gold-and-silver hair. His face was carved and cold.

"He's scary," Jack decided.

"Shh." Brody hitched Jack onto his lap after they'd slipped into a row of seats behind a lone woman.

Then Kate came onstage, and his mouth simply dropped.

"It's Kate. Look, Dad, she's all dressed up."

"Yeah, I see. Quiet now."

Her hair was loose, raining down the back of a flamboyant costume, boldly red with layers of skirt flowing out from a nipped waist. It stopped just below her knees and showed off long legs that ended in toe shoes.

She sauntered, hands on hips, until she was toe to toe with Davidov. "You ordered me offstage. Don't do that again."

"I order you on, I order you off. That is what I do. What you do is dance. You." He flicked a finger at the tall, gilt haired man in white who'd come out with Kate. "Step back. Wait. *Red Rose,*" he told the orchestra. "Opening solo. Kimball. You are Carlotta," he said to Kate. "*Be* Carlotta. Lights!"

Kate sucked in a breath. Took her position. Left leg back, foot turned and straight as a ruler. Arms lifted, curved into fluid lines. Head up and defiant. When the music began, the strings, she felt the beats. The single spotlight hit her like a torch. She danced.

It was a viciously demanding solo. Fast, lightning fast and wildly flamboyant. Her muscles responded, her feet flew. She ended with a snap, in precisely the same spot and in the same position where she'd begun.

Heart pounding from the effort, she shot Davidov a defiant, and unscripted look, then pirouetted offstage as her partner leaped into his cue.

He'd never seen anything like it. Hadn't known there could be anything like it. She'd been…magic, Brody thought and was still trying to process this new aspect of her when she flew back onstage.

They danced together now, Kate and the man in white. He hadn't realized ballet could be…sexy. But this was, almost raw, certainly edgy, a kind of classic mating dance with arrogant male, defiant female.

He didn't see the small balancing steps, the sets, the releases. Didn't see how she helped her partner lift her by springing with her knees, or how the muscles in her legs trembled with the effort to keep them extended in midair.

He only saw the speed, the dazzle. The magic. And was jerked rudely out of the moment by the shout.

"Stop! Stop! Stop!" Davidov threw up his hands. "What is this, what is it? Do you have hot blood, do you have passion or are you strolling through the park on Sunday? Where is the fire?"

"I'll give you fire." Kate whirled on him.

"Good." He grabbed her at the waist. "With me. Show me." He hoisted her up even as she cursed him.

She came down like a thunderbolt, hearing the music only in her head now, soaring into a series of *jetés*. He caught her again, spun her into a triple pirouette, then lifted her, lowering her until her head nearly brushed the stage. Sharp moves, challenges, and she was back *en pointe,* her eyes firing darts into his.

"There, now. Do again. Stay angry."

"I hate you."

"Not me. Him." He flicked a hand and brought the music back.

"What the hell does he want?" Brody demanded, forgetting himself. "Blood?"

The woman in the row ahead turned, gave him a dazzling smile. "Yes. Exactly. He always has. A difficult man, Davidov."

"Daddy says he ought to be shot," Jack added, helpfully.

"Your father isn't alone in thinking that." She laughed, turning farther in her seat as the dancing, and the cursing continued onstage. "He's harder, much harder, on the dancers who are the best. I used to dance with him myself, so I know."

"Did he yell at you?"

"Yes. And I yelled right back. But I was a better dancer for it, and for him. He still made me very, very angry, though."

"What did you do?" Jack's eyes were big as saucers. "Did you punch him in the nose?"

"No. I married him." She grinned at Brody. "I'm Ruth Bannion. You must be a friend of Kate's."

"Excuse me, I'd like to get my foot out of my mouth."

"No, no." She let out a low, delighted laugh. "Davidov brings out the best, and the worst. That's what makes him what he is. He adores Kate, and is still mourning she's left the company." Ruth glanced back toward the stage. "Look at her, and you can see why."

"All right, all right. Enough." Onstage, Davidov let out a windy sigh. "Go rest. Perhaps tonight you will find me some energy."

The blood was pounding in Kate's ears. Her feet were screaming. But she had enough energy, right now, for a short tirade.

When she was done, and simply panting, Davidov lifted his eyebrow. "You think because I'm Russian I don't know when a Ukrainian calls me a man with the heart of a pig?"

Her chin shot up. "I believe I said the *face* of a pig."

She stalked offstage and left him grinning after her.

"See?" Ruth smiled. "He adores her."

Chapter Eleven

Kate was busy kissing the Russian when Brody came to her dressing room door after the evening performance. She was wearing a robe—short and red—and full stage makeup. Her hair was still pinned up in some sleek and sophisticated knot, the way it had been during her second dance—the Spanish one, in the sexy little tutu.

The audience had gone wild for her, and so, Brody thought, had he.

Now, he'd come back to tell her only to find her wrapped around the Russian she'd cursed only that afternoon.

He wondered which one of them he should kill first.

"Sorry to interrupt."

Kate merely turned her head, eyes brilliant, and beamed at him. "Brody."

She held out a hand, but Davidov merely shifted his arm around her shoulders and eyed the intruder coolly.

"This is the carpenter? The one who wants to shoot me? Now, I think, he wants to shoot me more. He doesn't like that I kiss you."

"Oh, don't be silly."

Brody cut his eyes back to hers. "I don't like that he kisses you."

"That's absurd. This is Davidov."

"I know who it is." Brody shut the door behind him. He preferred spilling blood in relative privacy. "I met your wife today."

"Yes, she likes you, and your little boy. I have a son, and two daughters." Because he rarely resisted impulses, and it was delightful to watch the man's fury heat, Davidov kissed Kate's hair. "She knows, my wife, that I've come back to kiss this one. Who was," he continued drawing back, his hands sliding down her arms to link with hers, "magnificent. Who was perfect. Who I don't forgive for leaving me."

"I felt magnificent. I felt perfect." Still so perfect none of the aches could push through. "And I'm happy."

"Happy." He rolled his eyes to the ceiling. "As your director, what do I care if you're happy as long as you dance? As your friend." He heaved a sigh and kissed her hands. "I'm glad you have what you want."

"We'll all end up a lot happier if you step back," Brody commented.

Kate frowned. "Jealousy isn't attractive—and in this case certainly misplaced."

"Murder isn't attractive. But it really seems to fit."

"One minute," Davidov said, dismissively, to both of them. "You want to snarl at each other, wait until I finish. I wrote *The Red Rose* for my Ruth," he said to Kate.

"My heart. There's no one but you who has been Carlotta as she was Carlotta."

"Oh." Tears swirled into her eyes, spilled out. "Damn it."

"You are missed. So I insist you be very, very happy, or I will come to your West Virginia and drag you back." Now he cupped her face, spoke quietly in Russian. "You want this man?"

She nodded. *"Da."*

"Well, then." He pressed his lips to her forehead, then turned to study Brody. "Me, I'm a man who loves his wife. You met her, so you should see that she is all I treasure. I kiss this one because she is also a treasure. If you had eyes in your head to watch her tonight, this you should also know."

His eyes gleamed now in amused challenge. "Still, if I find another man kissing what's mine, I break his legs. But I'm Russian."

"I usually start with the arms. I'm Irish."

Davidov's laugh was rich, and his face went brilliant. "I like him. Good." Satisfied, he slapped Brody on the shoulder on his way out the door.

"Isn't he wonderful?"

"A few hours ago, you hated him."

"Oh." She waved a hand and sat down to cream off her makeup. "That was rehearsal. I always hate him during rehearsals."

"Do you always kiss him after a performance?"

"If it goes particularly well. He's a bully, a genius. He's Davidov," she said simply. "I wouldn't be the dancer I am, maybe not even the woman I am without having worked with him. We're intimate, Brody, but not sexually. Not ever. He adores his wife. All right?"

"You're saying it's an art thing."

"In a nutshell. Not that removed from ballplayers hugging each other and patting each other's butts after a really good game."

"I don't remember ever seeing your brother kiss his shortstop after a double play, but okay. I get it."

"Good. It went beautifully, didn't it?" She spun around on her stool. "Did you like it?"

"You were incredible. I've never seen anything like it. Never seen anything like you."

"Oh." She leaped off the stool, threw her arms around him. "I'm so glad! Oh." She laughed and rubbed at the smear she'd transferred to his cheek. "Sorry. I wanted it to be incredible. I got so nervous when I realized the family was here. Mama and Dad sneaking up from home, and Grandma and Grandpa. All the aunts and uncles and cousins. And Brandon sent flowers."

She grabbed more tissue, sniffling as she sat again. "I thought I might be sick, my stomach was churning so." She pressed a hand to it now. "But then all I felt was the music. When that happens you know. You just know."

He glanced around the room. It was crowded with flowers, literally hundreds of roses. Bottles of champagne, her exotic costumes. All of those glamorous things filled it, and were pale next to her excitement.

How could she leave all this? he wondered. Why should she?

He started to ask, then her door burst open. Her family poured in and the moment was lost.

She seemed to be just as much in her element the next day in the house in Brooklyn where her grandparents lived. The exotic siren who'd flamed across the stage the night before had been replaced by a lovely woman comfortable in jeans and bare feet.

It was a puzzle, Brody decided, trying to fit the two of them together into a whole. He intended to take the time to do so.

But for now, the best he could do was experience. The house was crammed with people—so many of them, he wondered if there was enough oxygen to go around. The noise level was a wonder.

A piano stood against one wall and was played by various fingers at various times. Everything from rock to Bach. The scents of cooking wafted through the air. Wine was poured with generous hands, and nobody seemed to stay still for more than five minutes.

His son was wallowing in it. He could see him, if he angled his head through other bodies, sprawled on the worn rug with Max, bashing cars together. The last time he'd been able to spot Jack he'd been sitting on Yuri's lap having what appeared to have been a serious conversation that had involved a number of gumdrops.

And before that, he'd raced down the stairs in the wake of a couple of young teenagers. Since Brody hadn't seen him go up the stairs in the first place, he was trying to keep a closer eye on his son.

"He's fine." A woman with the trademark Stanislaski looks—wild, bold, beautiful—dropped onto the couch beside him. "Rachel," she said with a quick grin. "Kate's aunt. Hard to keep us straight, isn't it?"

"There are a lot of you." Rachel, he thought, trying desperately to remember the details. Kate's mother's sister. A judge. That's right. Married to…the guy who owned the bar. And the guy who owned the bar was Nick's stepbrother.

Was it any wonder a man couldn't keep them lined up?

"You'll get the hang of it. That's my guy there." She gestured toward a tall man who had his arm hooked around the throat of a gangly boy with dark hair. "Currently choking our son Gideon while he talks to Sydney—the exceptional redhead who's married to my brother Mik—and Laurel, Mik and Sydney's youngest. Mik's over there, arguing with my other brother Alex, while Alex's wife, Bess—the other exceptional redhead—appears to be discussing something of great importance with her daughter, Carmen, and Nick and Freddie's Kelsey. The tall, handsome young man just coming out of the kitchen is Mik's oldest, Griff, who seems to have charmed some food out of my mother, Nadia. Got that?"

"Ah…"

"You absorb that awhile." She laughed and patted his knee. "Because there are so many more of us. Meanwhile, your son's fine—and you don't have a drink. Wine?"

"Sure, why not?"

"No, I'll get it." She patted him again and dashed off. Almost immediately, Griff plopped down and began to talk carpentry.

That, at least, Brody had a handle on.

Kate wound her way through the bodies, sat on the arm of the couch and offered him one of two glasses of wine. "Okay over here?"

"Yeah, fine. I figure it's kind of like the Boy Scout rule—when you're lost sit down in one spot, and they'll find you. People drop down here, talk for a couple minutes, then move off. I'm starting to be able to keep them straight working it that way."

Even as he spoke, Alex settled on the couch, propped his feet on the coffee table. "So, Bess and I are thinking about adding a couple of rooms onto our weekend place."

"See," Brody said to Kate, then shifted. "What did you have in mind?"

Kate left him to it and wandered into the kitchen. Her mother was at the table, putting the finishing touches on an enormous salad. Nadia was at the stove, supervising as Mik's youngest son, Adam, stirred something in a pot. "Need some more hands?"

"Always too many hands in my kitchen," Nadia said. Her hair was snow-white now—a soft wave around a strong face lined with years. But her eyes danced with amusement as she patted Adam. "There, you have done well. Go."

"But we're going to eat soon, right? We're starving."

"Very soon. Tell your brothers and sisters, your cousins, my table must be set."

"All right!" He shot out of the room, shouting orders.

"He wants to be in charge, that one."

Natasha laughed. "Mama, they *all* want to be in charge. How's Brody holding up, Katie?"

"He's talking with Uncle Alex." Kate snitched a crouton then wandered to the stove to sniff at pots. "Isn't he adorable?"

"He has good eyes," Nadia said. "Strong, kind. And he raises his son well. You show good taste."

"I learned from the best." She leaned over to kiss Nadia's cheek. "Thank you for welcoming him."

Nadia felt her heart sigh. "Go, help set the table. Your young man and his little boy will think no one eats in this house."

"They'll soon find out differently." She snatched another crouton and kissed the top of her mother's head on the way out.

"Well." Nadia stared hard into a pot. "We'll be dancing at her wedding. You're pleased with him."

"Of course." Natasha could barely see as she prepared to dress the salad. "He's a good man. He makes her happy. And to be honest, I think if I could have chosen for her myself, it would have been Brody. Oh, Mama." Eyes drenched, Natasha looked over at the stove. "She's my baby."

"I know. I know." Nadia hurried over for the hug, then offered Natasha one corner of her apron while she used the other to dry her eyes.

By midweek, Kate was hard at work and anxious to open her doors for the first students. The studio itself was complete. The floors were smooth and gleaming, the walls glistening with mirrors. Her office was organized, the dressing areas outfitted.

And now the front window was finished.

Kimball School Of Dance

She stood out on the sidewalk, her palms together and pressed to her lips, reading it over and over again.

Dreams, she thought, came true. All you had to do was believe hard enough, and work long enough.

"Oh, miss?"

"Hmm?" Lost in her own joy, she turned, then blinked at the woman crossing the street. The woman, Kate remembered with a sinking stomach, who'd seen Brody cart her outside over his shoulder. "Oh. Yes. Hello."

"Hello. We didn't really meet before." The woman looked as uneasy as Kate and fiddled with the strap of her shoulder bag. "I'm Marjorie Rowan."

"Kate Kimball."

"Yes, I know. Actually, I sort of know your boyfriend, too. The landlord's hired him a couple of times to see to things in my building."

"Ah," Kate said. "Hmm."

"Anyway, I picked up one of your brochures the other day, from your mother's store. My little girl, she's eight, she's just been nagging me half to death about taking ballet classes."

Relief came first. It was not to be a conversation about creating public scenes on quiet streets. Then came the pleasure at the possibility of another student.

"I'd be happy to talk to you about it, and to her if you'd like. First classes start next week. Would you like to come in, see the school?"

"Truth is, we've peeked in the window a few times. I hope you don't mind."

"Of course not."

"I've been telling Audrey—that's my girl—that I'd think about it. I guess I have. I'd like her to be able to try it."

"Why don't you come inside, and tell me about Audrey."

"Thanks. She'll be home from school soon. This'll be a nice surprise." She started up the stairs, relaxing now. "You know I always wanted ballet lessons when I was a girl. We couldn't swing it."

"Why don't you take them now?"

"Now?" Marjorie laughed and stepped inside. "Oh, I'm too old for ballet lessons."

"They're wonderful exercise. It increases flexibility. And they're fun. No one's too old for that. You look to be in very good shape."

"I do what I can." Marjorie looked around, smiling a little dreamily at the *barres,* the mirrors, the framed posters. "I guess it would be fun. But I couldn't afford classes for both of us."

"We'll talk about that, too. Come on back to my office."

An hour later, Kate rushed upstairs. She wanted to share with someone, and Brody was elected. She had two new students—her first mother and daughter team. And the accomplishment had given her yet one more angle for her school.

Family plans.

She started to dash across the little living room and stopped in her tracks. Slowly she turned a circle. It was done. She hadn't been paying enough attention, she decided, and the progress had zipped right by her.

The floors and walls were finished. The woodwork glowed like silk.

Dazzled, she walked into her kitchen where everything gleamed. Cabinets waited only to be filled. The windowsill cried out for flowerpots.

She ran a fingertip along the countertop. Brody had been right about the breakfast bar, she thought. He had been right—no, *they* had been right, she corrected, about everything.

The apartment, just like the rest of the building, had been a team effort. And it was perfect.

She hurried into the bedroom where Brody was kneeling on the floor installing the lock sets on her closet doors. Jack sat crossed-legged, tongue caught in his teeth as he carefully tightened a screw in a brass plate on a wall plug.

Mike snored contentedly between them.

"There's nothing quite like watching men at work." They glanced up, and made her heart sing. "Hello, Handsome Jack."

"We're punching out," he told her. "I got to come help because Rod and Carrie had to go to the dentist. I went already and no cavities."

"Good for you. Brody, I've been so involved downstairs that I haven't taken in what you've done up here. It looks wonderful. It's exactly right."

"Still got a few details. Some outside work, too. But you're pretty much good to go." But he didn't have that lift of satisfaction he usually experienced toward the end of a job. He'd been depressed for days.

"I love it." She crouched down as Mike woke and gamboled over to greet her. "And I just signed two more students. Now, if I could just find a couple of handsome men who'd like to go out and celebrate, it would really round things off."

"We'll go!"

"Jack. It's a school night."

"I was thinking about an early dinner," Kate improvised as Jack's face fell. "Burgers and fries at Chez McDee."

"She means McDonald's," Jack explained, then fell on his father's back, hugging fiercely. "Please, can we?"

Cornered again, Brody thought. "Pretty tough for a guy to turn down a fancy meal like that."

"He means yes." Jack swung over to Kate and hugged her legs. "Can we go now?"

"I got some things to finish up here." Brody pushed his hair back. And just looked at her.

He'd been doing that quite a bit, Kate thought, since they'd come back from New York. Looking at her— and looking at her differently somehow.

Differently enough to have frogs leaping in her belly again.

"An hour okay with you?" he asked.

"Perfect. Do you mind if I steal your helper here? I want to go tell my mother. We can give Mike a little exercise on the way."

"Yeah, sure. Jack? No wheedling."

"He means I can't ask for toys. I'll get Mike's leash. Dad, can I—" He broke off then ran over to whisper in Brody's ear.

"Yeah, go ahead."

"We'll be back in an hour."

"Great." Brody waited until they'd chased Mike downstairs, then sat back on his heels.

He was going to have to make some decisions. And soon. It was bad enough he was stuck on Kate, but Jack was crazy about her.

A man could risk a few bumps and bruises on his own heart, but he couldn't risk his child's. The only thing to do was to sit down and have a talk with Kate. It was time they spelled out what was going on between them.

More, he was going to have to have a talk with Jack. He had to know what the boy was thinking, what he was feeling.

Jack first, Brody decided. Could be, could very well be, his son looked at Kate as nothing more than a friend and would be upset at the idea of her being a more permanent, more important part of their lives. It had been the two of them as long as Jack could remember.

He looked over with a little jolt as a movement caught the corner of his eye.

"You turn that noise down," Bob O'Connell said, "you wouldn't get taken by surprise."

"I like music on the job." But Brody rose, shut off the radio. "Something you need?"

They hadn't spoken since the scene in the Kimball kitchen. Both men eyed each other warily.

"I got something to say," Bob stated.

"Then say it."

"I did my best by you. It ain't right for you to say different, when I did my best by you. Maybe I was hard on you, but you had a wild streak and you needed hard. I had a family to support, and I did it the only way I knew how. Maybe you think I didn't spend enough time with you—" Bob broke off, jammed his hands into his pockets. "Maybe I didn't. I don't have the knack for it, not the way you do with your boy. Fact is, you weren't the same pleasure to be around Jack is. He's a credit to you. Maybe I should've said so before, but I'm saying so now."

Brody said nothing for a long moment, adjusting to the shock even as his father glared at him. "You know, I'm pretty sure that's about the longest speech you ever aimed in my direction."

Bob's face hardened. "I'm done with it," he said and turned.

"Dad." Brody set his drill aside. "I appreciate it."

Bob let out a breath, the way a man might as the trapdoor opened under his feet. "Well." He turned back, fought with the words in his head. "Might as well finish it off then. Probably I shouldn't have jumped on you the other day, not in front of your boy and your...the Kimball girl. Your mother lit into me over it."

Brody could only stare. "Mom?"

"Yeah." With a look of frustrated disgust, Bob kicked lightly at the doorjamb. "She don't do it often, but when she does, she can peel the skin off your ass. Hardly speaking to me yet. Says I embarrassed her."

"I got the same line from Kate—she did some peeling of her own."

"Didn't much care having her claw at me the way she did. But I gotta say, she's got spine. Keep you straight."

"It's my job to keep myself straight."

Bob nodded. The weight that had been pressing on his chest for days eased. "Guess I figure you've been doing your job there. You do good work. For a carpenter."

For the first time in a long while, Brody was able to smile at his father and mean it. "You do good work. For a plumber."

"Didn't have any problem firing me."

"You pissed me off."

"Hell, boy, you fire every man who pisses you off, how are you going to put a crew together? How's the hand?"

Brody lifted it, flexed his fingers. "Good enough."

"Since you've got no permanent damage, maybe you can use that hand to dial the phone. Call your ma and let her know we cleared the air some. She might not take my word on it, given her current state of mind."

"I'll do that. I know I was a disappointment to you."

"Now, hold on—"

"I was," Brody continued. "Maybe I was a disappointment to myself, too. But I think I made up for it. I did it for Connie, and for Jack. For myself, too. And I did it, partly anyway, for you. So I could show you I was worth something."

"You showed me." Bob wasn't good at taking first steps, but he took this one. He crossed the room, held out his hand. "I guess I'm proud of how you turned out."

"Thanks." He took his father's hand in a firm grip. "I've a kitchen remodel coming up. Needs some plumbing work. Interested?"

Bob's lips twitched. "Could be."

Chapter Twelve

While father and son were closing a gap, Kate strolled with the third generation of O'Connell male.

"I didn't wheedle, right?"

"Wheedle?" She sent him a shocked stare. "Why Handsome Jack, Mama and I had to practically force that plane on you. We had to *beg* you to accept it."

Jack grinned up at her. "You'll tell Dad?"

"Of course. He's going to want to play with it, you know. It's a very cool plane."

Jack swirled it through the air. "It's like the one I got to fly on, all the way to New York and back again. It was fun. I told everybody thanks in the cards I sent. Did you like your card? I did it almost all by myself."

"I loved my card." Kate patted her pocket where the thank-you note, painstakingly printed, resided. "It was very polite and gentlemanly of you to write one to me, and to Freddie and Nick and to my grandparents."

"They said I could come back. Papa Yuri said I could sometime spend the night at his house."

"You'd like that?"

"Yeah. He can wiggle his ears."

"I know."

"Kate?"

"Hmm." She bent to untangle Mike from his leash, then glanced up to see Jack studying her. So serious, she thought, so intent. Just like his father. "What is it, Handsome Jack?"

"Can we…can we sit on the wall so we can talk about stuff?"

"Sure." Very serious, Kate realized as she boosted him up on the wall in front of the college. She passed Mike up to him, then hopped up beside them. "What kind of stuff?"

"I was wondering…" He trailed off again while Mike scrambled off to sniff at the grass behind them.

He'd talked it all over with his best friends. Max in New York, and then Rod at school. It was a secret. They'd spit on their palms to seal it. "You like my dad, don't you?"

"Of course I do. I like him very much."

"And you like kids. Like me?"

"I like kids. I especially like you." She draped an arm around him, rubbed his shoulder. "We're friends."

"Dad and I like you, too. A whole lot. So I was wondering…" He looked up at her, his eyes so young, so earnest. "Will you marry us?"

"Oh." Her heart stumbled, then fell with a splat. "Oh, Jack."

"If you did, you could come live in our house. Dad's fixing it up good. And we have a yard and everything, and we're going to plant a garden soon. In the mornings you could have breakfast with us, then drive to your school and teach people how to dance. Then you could drive home. It's not real far."

Staggered, she laid her cheek on the top of his head. "Oh, boy."

"Dad's really nice," Jack rushed on. "He hardly ever yells. He doesn't have a wife anymore, because she had to go to heaven. I wish she didn't, but she did."

"I know. Oh, baby."

"Maybe Dad's afraid to ask you in case you go to heaven, too. That's what Rod thinks. Maybe. But you won't, will you?"

"Jack." She fought back tears and cupped his face. "I plan to stay here for a very long time. Have you talked to your father about this?"

"Nuh-uh, 'cause you're supposed to ask the girl. That's what Max said. The boy has to ask the girl. Me and Dad'll buy you a ring, 'cause girls need to have one. I won't mind if you kiss me, and I'll be really good. You and Dad can make babies like people do when they get married. I'd rather have a brother, but if it's a sister, that's okay. We'll love each other and everything. So will you please marry us?"

In all her dreams and fantasies, she'd never imagined being proposed to by a six-year-old boy, while sitting on a wall on an afternoon in early spring. Nothing could have been more touching, she thought. More lovely.

"Jack, I'm going to tell you a secret. I already love you."

"You do?"

"Yes, I do. I already love your dad, too. I'm going to think really hard about everything you said. Really hard. That way, if I say yes, you're going to know, absolutely, that it's what I want more than anything else in the whole world. If I say yes you wouldn't just be your dad's little boy anymore. You'd be mine, too. Do you understand that?"

He nodded, all eyes. "You'd be my mom, right?"

"Yes, I'd be your mom."

"Okay. Would you?"

"I'm going to think about it." She pressed her lips to his forehead, then hopped down.

"Will it take a long time to think?"

She reached up for him. "Not this time." She held him close before she set him on his feet. "But let's keep this a secret, a little while longer, while I do."

She gave it almost twenty-four hours. After all she was a woman who knew her own mind. Maybe the timing wasn't quite perfect, but it couldn't be helped.

Certainly the way things were tumbling weren't in the nice, neat logical row she'd have preferred. But she could be flexible. When she wanted something badly enough, she could be very flexible.

She considered asking Brody out for a romantic dinner for two. Rejected it. A proposal in a public restaurant would make it too difficult to pin him down, should it become necessary.

She toyed with the idea of waiting for the weekend, planning that romantic dinner for two at Brody's house. Candlelight, wine, seductive music.

That was her next rejection. If Jack hadn't spilled the beans by then, she very likely would herself.

It wouldn't be exactly the way she'd pictured it. There wouldn't be moonlight and music, with Brody looking deep into her eyes as he told her he loved her, asked her to spend her life loving him.

Maybe it wouldn't be perfect, but it would be right. Atmosphere didn't matter at this point, she told herself. Results did. So why wait?

She started upstairs. It was good timing after all, she realized. He was just finishing the job that had brought them together. Why not propose marriage in the space they had, in a very real way, made together? It was perfect.

Convinced of it, Kate was very displeased to find the rooms over the school empty.

"Well, where the hell did you go?" She fisted her hands on her hips and paced.

School bus, she remembered, spinning for the door. It was one of his days to pick up Jack. She glanced at her watch as she sprinted down the stairs. He couldn't have been gone more than a few minutes.

"Hey! Where's the fire." Spence caught her as she leaped down the last steps.

"Dad. Sorry. Gotta run. I need to catch Brody."

"Something wrong?"

"No, no." She gave him a quick kiss on the cheek and wiggled free. "I need to ask him to marry me."

"Oh, well…whoa." She was younger, faster, but parental shock shot him to the door in time to snag her. "What did you say?"

"I'm going to ask Brody to marry me. I've got it all worked out."

"Katie."

"I love him. I love Jack. Dad, I don't have time to explain it all, but I've thought it through. Trust me."

"Just catch your breath and let me…" But he looked

at her face, into her eyes. Stars, he thought. His little girl had stars in her eyes. "He hasn't got a prayer."

"Thanks." She threw her arms around her father's neck. "Wish me luck anyway."

"Good luck." He let her go, then watched her run. "Bye, baby," he murmured.

Brody made a stop for milk, bread and eggs. Jack had developed an obsession with French Toast. As he turned into his lane, he checked his watch. A good ten minutes before the bus, he noted. He'd mistimed it a bit.

Resigned to the wait, he climbed out, let Mike race up the hill and back. Spring was coming on fine, he thought. Greening the leaves, teasing the early flowers into tight buds. It brought something into the air, he mused.

Maybe it was hope.

The house, the ramble of it, was looking like a home. Soon he'd stick a hammock in the yard, maybe a rocker on the porch. Maybe a porch swing. He'd get Jack a little splash pool.

Jack and Mike could play in the yard, roll around on the grass on those long, hot summer evenings. He'd sit on the porch swing and watch. Sit on the swing with Kate.

Funny, he couldn't put a real picture into his head anymore, unless Kate was in it.

And didn't want to.

He'd have to take his time, Brody mused. Get a sense of where Jack stood in all of it. After that, it would be a matter of seeing if Kate was willing to take everything to the next level.

Maybe it was time to give her a little nudge in that

direction. Nothing was ever perfect, was it? Everything in life was a work in progress.

It was like building a house. He figured they had a good, solid foundation. He had the design in his head—him, Kate, Jack and the kids who came along after. A house needed kids. So it was time to start putting up the frame, making it solid.

Maybe she wouldn't be ready for marriage yet—with her school just getting off the ground. She might need some time to adjust to the idea of being a mother to a six-year-old. He could give her some time.

He stood, looking over his land, studying the house on the hill that just seemed to be waiting.

Not a lot of time, he decided. Once he started building, he liked to keep right on building. And he wanted Kate working on this, the most important project of his life, with him.

The first thing to do, he decided as he walked to the mailbox, was to talk to Jack about it. His son had to feel secure, comfortable and happy. Jack was crazy about Kate. Maybe Jack would be a little worried about the changes marrying her would bring, but Brody could reassure his son.

They'd talk about it tonight, he decided, after dinner.

He just couldn't wait any longer than that to start things moving.

When he and Jack were square, he'd figure out what to say to Kate, what to do, to move everybody along to the next stage of the floor plan.

He got the mail out of the box, and was sifting through it on the way back to the truck when Kate pulled in beside him.

"Hey." Surprised, he tossed the mail into the cab of his truck. "Didn't expect to see you out this way today."

After she got out of the car, she picked up the mangled hunk of rope Mike spit at her feet, engaged him in a brief bout of tug-of-war, then threw it—she had a damn good arm—far enough to keep him busy awhile.

Watching her playing with the dog, all Brody could think about was that he couldn't wait very long.

"I just missed you at the school," she told him.

"Problem there?"

"No, not at all. No problem anywhere." She walked to him and slid her hands up his chest, a habit that never failed to pump up his heart rate. "You didn't kiss me goodbye."

"Your office door was closed. I figured you were busy."

"Kiss me goodbye now." She brushed her lips over his, arched a brow when he kept it light and started to ease back. "Do better."

"Kate, the bus is going to come along in a couple minutes."

"Do better," she murmured, and melting against him shifted the mood.

He fisted a hand in the back of her shirt, another in her hair. And indulged both of them.

"Mmmm. That's more like it. It's spring," she added, tipping back so that she could see his face. "Do you know what a young man's fancy turns to in spring? Besides baseball."

He grinned at her. "Plowing?"

She laughed, linking her fingers behind his neck. Yeah, the frogs were still jumping. But she liked it. "All right, do you know what a young woman's fancy turns to? What this young woman's fancy turns to?"

"Is that what you came out here to tell me?"

"Yes. More or less. Brody…" She nibbled her bottom lip, then just blurted it out, "I want you to marry me."

He jerked, froze. There was a buzzing in his ears— a hive of wild bees. He had to be hearing things, he decided. Had to. She couldn't have just asked him to marry her when he'd spent the last five minutes trying to figure out how and when to ask her.

To get his bearings, he retreated a step.

"It's not very flattering for you to gape at me as though I'd just hit you over the head with a two-by-four."

"Where did this come from?" Maybe he was just dreaming. But she looked real. She'd tasted real. And the thundering of his own heart wasn't the least bit dreamlike. Besides, in his dreams, he asked her. Damn it. "A woman doesn't just walk up to a man in the middle of the day and ask him to marry her."

"Why not?"

"Because…" How was he supposed to think of reasons with all those bees in his head? "Because she doesn't."

"Well, I just did." She felt her temper sizzle into her throat and managed to swallow it. Her fingers shook slightly as she lifted them to begin ticking off points. "We've been seeing each other exclusively for months. We're not children. We enjoy each other, we respect each other. It's a natural and perfectly logical progression to consider marriage."

He needed to take control back, he realized. Right here, right now. "You didn't say let's consider marriage, did you? You didn't say let's discuss it." Which had been his plan if she'd given him the chance. "There are a lot of factors here besides two people who enjoy and respect each other."

And love each other, he thought. God, he loved her. But he needed to know what they wanted for the future—separately, together, as a family. There were things they were just going to have to set straight, once and for all.

"Of course there are," she began. "But—"

"Let's start with you. Right now, you're free to pick up your dance career anytime you want. There's nothing stopping you from going back to New York, back on stage."

"My school is stopping me. I made that decision before I met you."

"Kate, I saw you. I watched you up there, and you were a miracle. Teaching's never going to give you what that gave you."

"No, it's not. It's going to give me something else, the something else I want now. I'm not a person who makes decisions lightly, Brody. When I left the company to come back here, I knew what I was doing. What I was leaving behind, what I was moving toward. If you don't trust me to make a commitment, then stand by it, you don't know me."

"It's not a matter of trust. But I wanted to hear you say it, to me, just like that. You say you mean to stay, you mean to stay. I've never known anybody as focused on a goal as you."

He'd thought, moments before, he'd known how he would handle this. The steps he'd take toward asking her to share his life. Building on that foundation. Now the woman had finished nailing on the trim and wanted a wreath for the door.

She was going to have to back up a few steps, because he built to last. "I've got something more than a career decision to consider. I've got Jack. Everything I do or don't do involves Jack."

"Brody, I'm perfectly aware of that. You know I am."

"I know he likes you, but he's secure the way things are, and he needs to be sure of me. Kate…God, he's only ever had me. Connie, she got sick when he was only a few months old. Between doctors and the treatments and the hospitals…"

"Oh, Brody." She could imagine it too well. The panic, the upheaval. The grief.

"She couldn't really be there for him, and I was just trying to hold it all together. The world was falling apart on us, and I had nothing extra to give Jack. The first two years of his life were a nightmare."

"And you've done everything you can to give him a happy and normal life. Don't you see how much I admire that? How much I respect it?"

Flustered, he stared at her. He'd never thought of parenting as admirable. "It's what I'm supposed to do. Thinking of him first, that's how it has to be. It's not just you and me, Kate. If it were…but it's not. A change like this—a life-altering one—he has to be in on it."

"And who's saying differently?" she demanded.

"Well, damn it. I can't just go tell him I'm getting married, just like that. I need to talk to him about it, prepare him. So do you. That's the kind of thing you'd be taking on. He needs to be as sure of you as he is of me."

"For heaven's sake, O'Connell, don't you think I've

taken all of that into account? You've known me for months now. You ought to be able to give me more credit."

"It's not a matter of—"

"It was Jack who asked me to marry you in the first place."

Brody stared into her flushed and furious face, then held up his hands. "I have to sit down." He backed up, dropped down on a flattened stump. Because the dog was shoving the rope into his lap, Brody tossed it. "What did you just say?"

"Am I speaking English?" she demanded. "Jack proposed to me yesterday. Apparently he doesn't have as much trouble making up his mind as his father. He asked me to marry you, both of you. And I've never had a lovelier offer. Obviously, I'm not going to get one from you."

"You would have if you'd waited a couple of days," he muttered under his breath. "So are you doing this to make Jack happy?"

"Listen up. However much I love that child, I wouldn't marry his bone-headed father unless I wanted to. He happens to think we'd all be good for each other. I happen to agree with him. But you can just sit there like a—like a bump on that log."

Not only had Kate beat him to the punch, Brody thought, his six-year-old son had crossed the finish line ahead of him. He wasn't sure if he was annoyed or delighted. "Maybe I wouldn't be if you hadn't snuck up on me with this."

"Snuck up on you? How could you not *see?* I've done everything but paint a heart on my sleeve. Why haven't I moved my things out of storage and into that apartment, Brody? An organized, practical woman like me doesn't ignore something like that unless she has no intention of ever living there."

He got to his feet. "I figured you just wanted…I don't know."

"Why have I squeezed every minute I could manage out of the last few months to spend with you, or with you and Jack? Why would I come here like this, toss away my pride and ask you to marry me? Why would I do any of those things unless I loved you? You idiot."

She whipped around and stomped off toward her car while tears of hurt and fury sparkled in her eyes.

There was a fist squeezing his heart. Brutally. "Kate, if you get in that car, I'm just going to have to drag you out again. We're not finished."

She stopped with her hand on the door. "I'm too angry to talk to you now."

"You won't have to do that much talking. Sit," he said, and gestured to the stump.

"I don't want to sit."

"Kate."

She threw up her hands, stalked over and sat. "There. Happy?"

"First, I don't intend to marry anyone just to give Jack a mother. And I don't intend to marry anyone who can't be a mother to him. Now let's put that aside and deal with you and me. I know you're mad, but don't cry."

"I wouldn't waste a single tear over you."

He pulled out his bandanna and dropped it in her lap. "Get rid of them, okay? I'm having a hard enough time."

She left his bandanna where it was and dashed tears away with her fingers.

"Okay, this is a box." He pointed at the ground. "Everything we've just said is going into this box, and I'm closing the lid. We can open it later on, but we start fresh right here and right now."

"As far as I'm concerned you can nail the lid on it and throw the entire thing into a pit."

"I was going to talk to Jack tonight," he began. "See how he felt about some changes. I figured he'd have liked the idea. I know my kid pretty well. Not as well as I assumed since he's going around proposing to my woman behind my back."

"Your woman?"

"Quiet," he said mildly. "If you'd been quiet a little while longer, we'd have started out this particular area of discussion more like this."

He moved closer, took her lifted chin in his hand. "Kate, I'm in love with you. No, you just sit there," he told her as she started to rise. "I was trying to work out how I'd do this right before you drove up."

"Before I…" She let out a long breath. "Oh." As her heart began to thud she shifted her gaze to the ground. "Is the lid on that box really tight?"

"Yeah, it's really tight."

"Okay." She had to close her eyes a moment, try to clear her head. But the thrill racing through her refused to let her think straight. And that, she decided, was perfect. Just perfect.

"Would you mind starting again?" she asked him. "With the I love you part?"

"Sure. I love you. I started sliding the first minute I saw you. Kept thinking I'd get my balance back, that you couldn't be for me. Every once in a while I'd start sliding fast, I had to pull myself back. I had lots of reasons to. I can't think of a single one of them right now, but I had them."

"I was for you, Brody. Just like you were for me."

"That night in your sister's house, I couldn't pull myself back anymore. I just dropped off the edge in love with you, I'm still staggering the next day when I see you dance. Not like I saw you that day in your school where it was pretty, and like a dream. But strong and powerful. That messed me up some again."

He crouched down in front of her. "Kate, a few minutes ago I was standing here, putting a picture in my mind. I do that sometimes. You and me, sitting on a porch swing I still have to buy."

Tears wanted to come again, but she held them back. "I like that picture."

"Me, too. See, I was figuring we were building a house—not the kind up the hill there. A kind of relationship house. I take my time building things because it's important to build them right—to build them to last."

"And I rushed you."

"Yeah, you rushed me. Something else I figured out. Two people don't always have to move at the same pace for them to end up at the same place. The right place."

A tear escaped. "This is the right place for me." She framed his face with her hands. "I love you, Brody. I want—"

"No, you don't. I'm making the moves here." He drew her to her feet. "See that house up there on the hill?"

"Yes."

"Needs work, but it's got potential. That dog chasing his tail in the yard's just about housebroken. I've got a son who's coming home from school on a bus that's running late. He's a good boy. I want to share all that

with you. And I want to come to your school sometimes, just to watch you dance. I want to make babies
with you. I think I'm good with them."

"Oh, Brody."

"Quiet. I'm not finished. Come summer, I want to sit
out in the garden we'll plant together. You're the only
one I want to have all that with."

"Oh, God, just ask me before I fall apart and can't
even answer you."

"You're pushy. I like that about you. Marry me,
Kate." He touched his lips to hers. "Marry me."

She couldn't answer, could only lock her arms
around him. Her heart poured into the kiss and gave
him more than words. The dog began to yip and race
in desperate circles around them. Clinging to Brody,
Kate began to laugh.

"I'm so happy."

"I still wouldn't mind hearing you say yes."

She tipped her head back, started to speak. And the
rude blast of the school bus's air brakes drowned out
her words.

She turned, sliding her arm around Brody's waist
and watched Jack burst out the door. The pup took a
running leap into Jack's arms.

"Let me," Kate murmured. "Please. Hey, handsome."

"Hi." He looked at the tears on her cheeks and sent a
worried look at his father. "Did you get hurt?"

"No, I didn't. Sometimes people cry when they're
so happy everything bursts inside them. That's what I
am right now. Remember what you asked me yesterday, Jack?"

He bit his lip, glanced warily at his father again.
"Uh-huh."

"Well, here's the answer for both of you." With one hand still caught in Brody's, she touched Jack's cheek. "Yes."

His eyes went huge. "Really?"

"Really."

"Dad! Guess what?"

"What?"

"Kate's going to marry us. That's okay, right?"

"That's absolutely okay. Let's go home."

They left the truck and car parked where they were, and started walking toward the house together. Jack raced ahead, the dog at his heels. At the edge of the lawn, Brody stopped, turned, kissed her.

No, it wasn't okay, Kate thought.

It was perfect.

Epilogue

"Dad? How much longer?"

"Just a few minutes. Here, let me fix this thing." He hauled Jack up on a chair and straightened his fancy black tie. Fiddled with the red rosebud on his lapel. "My hands are sweaty," Brody said with a little laugh.

"Do you got cold feet? Grandpa said how sometimes guys get cold feet on their wedding day."

"No, I don't have cold feet. I love Kate. I want to marry her."

"Me, too. You get to be the groom, and I get to be the best man."

"That's it." He stepped back, surveyed his son. A six-year-old in a tux, he thought. "You sure look slick, Jacks."

"We look handsome. Grandma said so. And she cried. Girls cry at weddings, that's what Max said. How come?"

"I don't know. Afterward, we'll find a girl and you can ask her."

He turned Jack so they could look in the mirror together. "It's a big day. Today, the three of us become a family."

"I get a mom and more grandparents and aunts and uncles and cousins and *everything*. After you kiss the bride, we get to go have a party and lots of cake. Nana said so." Kate's mother had said he could call her Nana. Jack liked saying it.

"That's right."

"Then you go on your honeymoon so you can do lots more kissing."

"That's the plan. We're going to call, Jack, and send you postcards," he added, trying not to fret about going away without his boy.

"Uh-huh, and when you come back, we'll all live together. Rod said you and Kate are going to make a baby on your honeymoon. Are you?"

Oh, boy. "Kate and I will have to talk about that."

"I can call her Mom now, can't I?"

Brody shifted his gaze back to Jack's in the mirror. "Yeah. She loves you, Jack."

"I know." Jack rolled his eyes. "That's why she's marrying us."

Brandon opened the door to see the groom and his best man grinning at each other. "You guys ready?"

"Yeah! Come on, Dad. Come on. Let's get married."

Kate stepped out of the bride's room, held out a hand to her father.

"You're so beautiful." He lifted her hand to his lips. "My baby."

"Don't make me cry again. I've just put myself back together from Mom." She brushed fussily at his lapel. "I'm so happy, Daddy. But I am *not* going to walk down the aisle with wet cheeks and red eyes."

"Frogs in your stomach?"

"I think they're doing the polka. I love you."

"I love you, Katie."

"Okay. We're okay." She heard the music, nodded. "That's our cue."

She waited, her arm tucked in her father's while her sister and her cousins who were her attendants walked down the aisle. While her little niece sprinkled rose petals on the long white runner.

Then she stepped into the doorway, in the billowing white dress and sparkling veil. All the nerves faded into sheer joy.

"Look at them, Daddy. Aren't they wonderful?"

She walked to them, feeling the music. And when her father put her hand in Brody's, it was steady and sure.

"Kate." As her father had, Brody lifted her hand to his lips. "I'll make her happy," he said to Spence, then looked into Kate's eyes. "You make me happy."

"You look pretty." Forgetting himself Jack bounced in his new shoes. His voice carried through the church. "You look really pretty. Mom."

Her heart, already full, overflowed. She bent to him, kissed his cheek. "I love you, Jack. You're mine now," she told him, then straightened, met Brody's eyes. "And so are you."

She passed her bouquet to her sister, took Jack's hand in her free one.

And married them both.

* * * * *

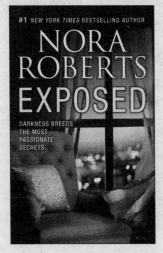

Meet the Carsons of Mustang Creek: three men who embody the West and define what it means to be a rancher, a cowboy and a hero in this brand-new series from *New York Times* bestselling author

LINDA LAEL MILLER

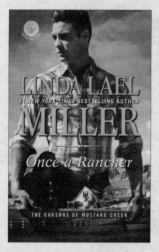

Slater Carson might be a filmmaker by trade, but he's still a cowboy at heart—and he knows the value of a hard day's work under the hot Wyoming sun. So when he sees troubled teen Ryder heading down a dangerous path, he offers the boy a job on the ranch he shares with his two younger brothers. And since Ryder's guardian is the gorgeous new Mustang Creek resort manager, Grace Emery, Slater figures it can't hurt to keep a closer eye on her, as well…

Grace Emery doesn't have time for romance. Between settling into her new job and caring for her ex-husband's rebellious son, her attraction to larger-than-life Slater is a distraction she can't afford. But when an unexpected threat emerges, she'll discover just how far Slater will go to protect what matters most—and that love is always worth fighting for.

Pick up your copy today!

Be sure to connect with us at:

Harlequin.com/Newsletters
Facebook.com/HarlequinBooks
Twitter.com/HQNBooks

HQN™

www.HQNBooks.com

PHLLM968

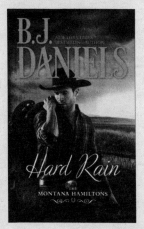

REQUEST YOUR FREE BOOKS!

2 FREE NOVELS
FROM THE ROMANCE COLLECTION
PLUS 2 FREE GIFTS!

YES! Please send me 2 FREE novels from the Romance Collection and my 2 FREE gifts (gifts are worth about $10). After receiving them, if I don't wish to receive any more books, I can return the shipping statement marked "cancel." If I don't cancel, I will receive 4 brand-new novels every month and be billed just $6.49 per book in the U.S. or $6.99 per book in Canada. That's a savings of at least 19% off the cover price. It's quite a bargain! Shipping and handling is just 50¢ per book in the U.S. and 75¢ per book in Canada.* I understand that accepting the 2 free books and gifts places me under no obligation to buy anything. I can always return a shipment and cancel at any time. Even if I never buy another book, the two free books and gifts are mine to keep forever.

194/394 MDN GH4D

Name	(PLEASE PRINT)	

Address		Apt. #

City	State/Prov.	Zip/Postal Code

Signature (if under 18, a parent or guardian must sign)

Mail to the **Reader Service:**
IN U.S.A.: P.O. Box 1867, Buffalo, NY 14240-1867
IN CANADA: P.O. Box 609, Fort Erie, Ontario L2A 5X3

Want to try two free books from another line?
Call 1-800-873-8635 or visit www.ReaderService.com.

* Terms and prices subject to change without notice. Prices do not include applicable taxes. Sales tax applicable in N.Y. Canadian residents will be charged applicable taxes. Offer not valid in Quebec. This offer is limited to one order per household. Not valid for current subscribers to the Romance Collection or the Romance/Suspense Collection. All orders subject to credit approval. Credit or debit balances in a customer's account(s) may be offset by any other outstanding balance owed by or to the customer. Please allow 4 to 6 weeks for delivery. Offer available while quantities last.

Your Privacy—The Reader Service is committed to protecting your privacy. Our Privacy Policy is available online at www.ReaderService.com or upon request from the Reader Service.

We make a portion of our mailing list available to reputable third parties that offer products we believe may interest you. If you prefer that we not exchange your name with third parties, or if you wish to clarify or modify your communication preferences, please visit us at www.ReaderService.com/consumerschoice or write to us at Reader Service Preference Service, P.O. Box 9062, Buffalo, NY 14240-9062. Include your complete name and address.

Turn your love of reading into rewards you'll love with
Harlequin My Rewards

**Join for FREE today at
www.HarlequinMyRewards.com**

Earn **FREE BOOKS** of your choice.

Experience **EXCLUSIVE OFFERS** and contests.

Enjoy **BOOK RECOMMENDATIONS** selected just for you.

PLUS! Sign up now and get **500** points right away!

Earn
FREE
REWARDS
HarlequinMyRewards.com
Join
Today!

NORA ROBERTS

28590	SWEET RAINS	__ $7.99 U.S.	__ $9.99 CAN.
28194	STARLIGHT	__ $7.99 U.S.	__ $9.99 CAN.
28193	CHRISTMAS WITH YOU	__ $7.99 U.S.	__ $9.99 CAN.
28187	THE CALHOUN WOMEN:	__ $7.99 U.S.	__ $8.99 CAN.
	AMANDA & LILAH		
28177	WILD AT HEART	__ $7.99 U.S.	__ $8.99 CAN.
28165	CAPTIVATED & ENTRANCED	__ $7.99 U.S.	__ $9.99 CAN.
28160	THE MacGREGOR GROOMS	__ $7.99 U.S.	__ $9.99 CAN.
28156	DANIEL & IAN	__ $7.99 U.S.	__ $9.99 CAN.

(limited quantities available)

TOTAL AMOUNT	$ _____
POSTAGE & HANDLING	$ _____
($1.00 FOR 1 BOOK, 50¢ for each additional)	
APPLICABLE TAXES*	$ _____
TOTAL PAYABLE	$ _____

(check or money order—please do not send cash)

To order, complete this form and send it, along with a check or money order for the total above, payable to Harlequin Books, to: **In the U.S.:** 3010 Walden Avenue, P.O. Box 9077, Buffalo, NY 14269-9077; **In Canada:** P.O. Box 636, Fort Erie, Ontario, L2A 5X3.

Name: _____

Address: _____ City: _____

State/Prov.: _____ Zip/Postal Code: _____

Account Number (if applicable): _____

075 CSAS

*New York residents remit applicable sales taxes.
*Canadian residents remit applicable GST and provincial taxes.

Visit Silhouette Books at www.Harlequin.com

PSNR0316BL